MOVING ON

P.F. Dinnage

Book design by PublishingPush

ISBN:
Paperback: 978-1-80227-103-4
eBook: 978-1-80227-104-1

Disclaimer

This is a work of fiction. Any resemblance to actual events or persons, living or dead, is entirely coincidental.

ACKNOWLEDGEMENTS

There are a few people that I wish to thank who made this, my first novel, a reality and made it possible for me to bring it to you.

The support and encouragement given to me by Jack, Melanie, Lucy and Amy, and their immense desire for me to finish what I started in 2016, inspired me to complete this story, even through the tough and lonely times brought about by the 2020 pandemic. They continue to be my motivation and I cannot thank them enough.

I would also like to thank Charlotte (Charlie) and Sophie, who are the inspiration behind the two little girls in this story. Their character, honesty, and innocence, which I have observed from the day they were born, has made it almost effortless for me to write about life from a young person's perspective and I can only hope that I have done them justice.

My thanks also go to Kim and the team at Publishing Push for their dedication and support in helping me bring this story to you.

And finally, I would like to thank you, the reader, for purchasing this book. I hope you enjoy it and will look forward to reading more of my works in the future.

1

It was a bright morning when I awoke to the sound of a car honking outside our four-bedroom semi-detached in north-west London. The sun shone through a slight crack in the blackout blinds causing me to open one eye, and then try to decipher the noise emanating from the street below. It didn't take too long for me to realise that the noise was indeed coming from my wife's car: a three-year-old Ford Focus RS, more orange than a flaming sun and just as hot! As I rushed to the window, peeled back the blind and stared in confusion at her car below, her perfectly formed head, followed by her gorgeous blonde locks appeared from the driver's window, swiftly followed by a flawlessly extended middle finger on her right hand. Bastard! I think that was the word that was mouthed in my direction before the accelerator pedal was pushed firmly to the floor and the vehicle was released from its previously motionless stance.

Although shocked, my first reaction was to quickly look up and down the street at the neighbours' windows to see if anybody had also been a witness to my wife's performance. I thought I had got away with it until I noticed old Mrs Mathews holding back her living room net curtain with her left hand while watching the orange fire-ball speed off down the road before turning and looking upwards to my bedroom window and slowly shaking her head. Not quite knowing how to react, I gave her a smile and a wave before swiftly releasing the blind! I stood there naked in semi darkness; trying to figure out what had just happened and more importantly - why! Then it slowly started coming back to me.

It was 9:30 a.m. on Saturday morning with no work, and luckily for me, no kids as my wife, Cheryl had taken our kids to her parents the afternoon before so that we could enjoy an evening out with our friends, Luke, and Sally. I assumed that Cheryl had gone to collect them and when she returned the inquest into last evenings' fiasco would begin. I estimated that as it would take Cheryl about twenty-five minutes to drive to her parents - and following the usual routine of coffee and a chat with her mum- she should be back with the kids around 11:30 a.m. I decided that I would make a stunning brunch for when they all arrived to soften the impending slaughter that I was about to encounter. Firstly, I headed for the shower! After getting dressed and brushing my teeth, I went downstairs to the kitchen to put the 'save my arse' plan into action.

Once in the kitchen, I started hunting around for ingredients to make a delicious brunch for my beautiful wife and two adorable daughters – Emily, seven and Amy, five. For the adults- something special and for the two wonderful, little ladies - something sweet and chocolatey! The ingredients looked up at me from the kitchen work surface where a bowl containing three oranges, four bananas, one peach....and two avocadoes were waiting. Now, any flatbread in the cupboard and maybe eggs in the fridge? Yes, all present and ready for my culinary expertise to commence. But first, whip up the dough for the children's waffles, laced with melted chocolate, and maybe a couple of those bananas. Perfect! Once the dough had been mixed and poured into the waffle machine, I set about peeling the avocados, dicing them, and then adding a chopped red chilli, the zest and juice of a lemon, mixed herbs, and seasoning.

Although I was concentrating on what I was doing, my mind slipped back to the events of last evening and the reason why my Saturday morning had not begun in the way that I had wanted it to. You know, waking up peacefully and looking over at the woman I love, who slowly opens her eyes and mouths very gently 'Good morning my love' and then very softly lays her head on my chest, kissing my collar bone as she shifts across the bed and places her hand between my legs!

"Excited my love?"

"Erm - yep!", would be my thrilled response; before we would embark on a passionate, almost primal engagement of love making. Well, you should make the most of these opportunities when you have two children. It is not easy to find the time for each other these days. Although the mind does not want to give up on how things used to be before the rigours of family life; the reality is that routines and familiarities creep into relationships and before you know it - sex is a thing of the past!

So why was my wife so upset with me this morning? What had I done (or not done, which is sometimes more to the point) that had caused such a fierce and angry reaction this morning? Yes, it was all coming back to me now.

The evening before, we had been out for dinner with our friends Luke and Sally. We had been friends with these guys since our university days from the late nineties, in Portsmouth. Cheryl was studying English and had met Sally during our first year there. It took a few months for them to bond - probably through their love of Take That, the iconic British boyband. They discovered that they had both cried their eyes out when it was announced that the band would split up when they were sixteen and seventeen, respectively. However, it was not all doom and gloom as they eventually reformed and performed a sell-out reunion tour ten years later! Obviously, the girls wanted tickets for the event, and I remember Cheryl was at her happiest, when I told her that I had bought two tickets for her and Sally. There were only two tickets as it was not really mine and Luke's thing. The girls danced the night away that night at the Wembley Arena paying homage to their idols!

As for Luke - well, I met Luke at school in the fifth grade and we became firm friends. He had just moved to our school from a rather rough inner-city school in Birmingham. Being black and talking with a heavy 'Brummie' accent made him a target for most of the other kids. Not me though. I thought he was cool, and our relationship was cemented when not long after he arrived at the school, I was cornered by 'The Wesley Gang' and facing a certain, severe beating.

"Right, George Hart, you're gonna get your face smashed in!" came the words out of Ben Wesley's mouth in my direction. He was the leader of 'The Wesley Gang' and head thug of our year. Ben had it in for me, and all because I had kissed Jennifer Parks, whom Ben thought was his girlfriend. The only problem was that Jennifer was not aware of this and she liked me instead!

"Come on Ben, it was only a kiss!" I said, trying to delay the inevitable by somehow engaging him in conversation.

"She's mine!" was the instant response from Ben, as he and his three henchmen - Will Barns, Frank Zarelli and Owen Mills (The Wesley Gang) - took slow steps towards me.

"Leave him alone or I'll kick your teeth in!" came an unexpected, but most welcome distraction in a heavy Brummie accent. Before I knew it, Luke had pushed Will, Frank and Owen onto the ground and was nose-to-nose with Ben. Feeling a lot braver now, I also took a step closer to Ben to join in the stand-off. Ben never bothered me, or indeed, Luke again after that incident.

It was like a turning-point in my school career. Instead of previously dreading going to school because of the boredom of the lessons - and the probability that Ben Wesley and his associates would try to inflict some form of terror and pain - I really enjoyed school and indeed looked forward to it! There was no doubt that Luke and I would be the best of friends from that day onwards and our school life was filled with days of fun, laughter and surprisingly - achievement. Luke's dad really drilled it into Luke that he needed to work hard at school to achieve something in his life.

Being black means that you need to work twice as hard as the white kids to secure a decent future for yourself, was the kind of thing that Luke was told by his dad. It really helped Luke to become a model student. It helped me too!

My dad died of testicular cancer when I was ten just prior to Luke coming to my school. It was an awfully hard time for me as I had the best dad in the world. He was caring, loving, funny and always made time to play with me. He was a big Manchester United fan as his father had been to the 1968 European Cup Final at Wembley Stadium and witnessed the great George Best secure Manchester United's first victory in the competition. The resulting merchandise purchased at that game ensured my dad was a Red Devil supporter and in turn, that I was too.

I missed him terribly when he died and that feeling has never really left me. Mum took it badly too. She was never quite the same after he had passed, which was the main contributing factor in the deterioration of her mental health - and subsequent suicide from an overdose of Anadin and a cocktail of white rum and brandy - some eight years later. Although, it is less painful for me today; I still have times when I think it would be so great to have them both around, to talk about their grandchildren, the events of the world, football and, of course, take their advice on any issues of the day. So, I took my fatherly advice from Mr Samprass, Luke's dad. That is why we both ended up at Portsmouth University- Luke studying Economics while I opted for a Business degree.

We met the girls at a University Bar called 'Gees'. The owner did try once to explain to me why it was called Gees, something to do with a degree, but I never really got it! There was an instant attraction between Luke and Sally, so much so that they were kissing before the night was out on that first meeting. With Cheryl and I, it took a little bit longer. But we got there in the end and our love for each other took hold of us, materialising in unbridled love-making that I could never have imagined possible.

After University we all got good jobs, Sally became a Human Resource Director at a large department store; and Cheryl got a job teaching primary school kids. Luke went into investment banking, and I became a Sales and Marketing Director with the largest global In-Flight Catering company. I love my job, although it does mean that I have to be away from home a fair amount of time.

Luke and I were Best Man for each other, and all four of us have remained very close friends. Luke and Sally are Godparents to Emily and Amy. Cheryl and I are Godparents to Luke and Sally's little boy, Ben who is two. Yes Ben! Pretty ironic when you think back to Ben Wesley and his gang.

So back to last evening and what was the cause of me having to prepare a superb brunch so as to gain my wife's forgiveness? Well, we had been to dinner at a little French restaurant close to Covent Garden. The evening had gone very well and the cocktails prior to, combined with the vino during dinner, resulted in us all being very relaxed and in a jovial mood. After dinner, it was suggested that we go back to our place to continue the drinking - either coffee or more alcohol, we would see when we got there! We walked down Shaftesbury Avenue and jumped on a tube at Piccadilly Circus on the Baker Line, changed at Baker Street to the Jubilee Line and approximately thirteen minutes later, got out at Dollis Hill station. Then, a short walk to Dewsbury Road and we were home. We had taken this journey many, many times before as our nights out together had become a regular event in the diary. Usually, and it was no different last night, on the way home Luke and I tended to talk about football and the girls huddled together and talked about - well, whatever girls talk about!

We arrived home and I think it was me that suggested opening a bottle of brandy that I had picked up at Orlando Airport a couple of months ago, while I was visiting one of my catering facilities in readiness for a customer visit. It was a Hennessey VS that I had paid about $45 for and thought it would be a good night cap to finish the evening with. As Luke and Sally only lived a short walk from us, everyone decided to have a glass. It only now dawns on me that this was the first mistake in a series that led to this mornings' performance from Cheryl.

The brandy was warm, smooth, and slipped down the throat very easily, so much so, that one glass was never going to be enough. After the second glass, the topic of conversation went on to reminiscing about our University days and how we all met. This was my second mistake as I should have changed the subject straight away. You see, when we were at University, I had a brief fling with a girl before meeting Cheryl. Her name was Jenifer Parks. Yes, the same Jenifer Parks that had caused me all the bother with Ben Wesley, the same Jenifer Parks that I had kissed at the age of ten and the same Jenifer Parks that had led to my close friendship with Luke. I told Cheryl all about Jenifer soon after we got together and told her the whole story of how Luke and I became friends, all the way through to my fling with her. Cheryl made me promise her that I would never see, speak, or have any other communication with Jenifer ever again! That would obviously be difficult as we were all at the same University; but we managed it quite well and got through the remaining two and a half years in Portsmouth without any hiccups.

Over time, from finishing University, then going on to our individual careers and living our lives, I never thought of Jenifer again. However, three weeks ago, I was in a small coffee shop in Chelsea minding my own business, catching up with the football reports from the previous evenings' matches, when I got a little tap on my right shoulder from behind. Lo and behold, it was Jennifer Parks!

"Hey handsome, fancy seeing you here," Jennifer said looking over the top of her dark rimmed Gucci spectacles, with her big hazel eyes, luscious black hair, pearly white teeth surrounded by plump, red lips and the unmistakeable aroma of Coco Mademoiselle filling the air! Yeah, I always had a little bit of something left inside my heart for Jennifer!

"Hey Jen, what a lovely surprise!" was my instant response in a very cool, laid-back tone that suggested that I was relaxed and perfectly at ease with seeing an old flame that had extinguished many a year back. How deceptive my outer posture was, compared to the racing of my heart and instant flashback in my head of the highly energetic sex sessions we had once enjoyed together in the University dorms.

"Do you want a refill?"

"Erm, yes, why not?" I agreed in a nonchalant way, as if to say I could take it or leave it really. However, I was delighted to see her, and she looked absolutely stunning in her tight, low-cut pale green sweater which clung effortlessly to her beautifully formed 36B breasts. Yes, I did remember those sort of things! To complete the look, Jennifer was wearing a pair of skinny black jeans which just accentuated the curve of her firm buttocks. Again, my mind drifted back to those heady times in the University dorms.

"Be right back," she said and headed off to the serving counter to procure two coffees. Why was I acting like a school kid in this woman's presence? I had an equally beautiful wife, whom I loved unconditionally, who had given us two adorable girls of our own. My life was pretty much perfect.

"Stop it!" I whispered to myself and, somehow, managed to regain control before Jennifer headed back to my table with our refreshments.

"Budge up," said Jennifer and as I moved across to the next seat, she slid into my vacated one and placed the coffees down on the table.

"Cappuccino okay for you? I remember you used to love that back in the day, no sugar but must have the chocolate powder topping," she said giving a little smile.

"Great, thanks. So great to see you. How are you?"

"Yeah, really good. I have just landed a job in Johannesburg filming the real people of the city. You know, the deprivation, poverty, and sadness of the locals; and how things have not really improved a lot for the majority - even though the Black Economic Empowerment programme has been in effect there for over a decade. I'm really looking forward to it and the agency has set me up with a local guide, who will take me into the townships to meet with the people. It's a bit scary, but I've been told that the guide will make sure I'm kept safe."

"Wow! I've been there too!" I replied. "You definitely need the guide because it can get pretty hairy down there."

Jennifer was a freelance photographer and had earned a photography degree in Portsmouth. She always had an eye for the odd angle to get a great picture or for filming things upside down to create confusion and contrasting light schemes. She was incredibly good at what she did, and although I had known that she had made a career in photography, I did not realise that she was doing shoots with political connotations.

For the next thirty minutes, we talked about our work, family life and generally filling in some gaps since we last saw each other. Jen even asked after Cheryl. We did not talk about our prior intimacy; and after swapping numbers, we departed the coffee shop, going our separate ways after a big hug and a kiss on the cheek. Although, I had her number it was firmly put to the back of my mind, and the original rush of excitement that I had felt when we first met, faded instantly.

The problem was that I had inadvertently mentioned this meeting to Luke a few days later; and told him how great it was to see

Jen and how we had talked and had coffee together. What I did not tell Luke was that under no circumstances should he mention this to Cheryl or Sally. Unfortunately, after two glasses of Hennessey VS, Luke uttered the devastating words:

"Talking of University, George ran into Jennifer Parks the other week, didn't you George?"

"Erm, yeah, sort of."

"What! What does 'sort of' mean George?" accused Cheryl; interrupting my failing attempt to cover over the story and telling Luke with my eyes and facial expression that he had just lit a very big fuse!

"Well yeah - I was in that coffee shop along the Fulham Road a few weeks ago, and was just reading the paper when erm, Jen, erm, Jennifer walked in and we…"

"We what?" again came the interruption from Cheryl.

"Had a coffee and a chat!" I said defiantly as I had done nothing wrong and started to feel a bit aggrieved about the way Cheryl was reacting to this revelation that Luke had made. Of course, this just infuriated Cheryl even more and before long, Luke and Sally had left, amid profound apologies from Luke. Cheryl and I were arguing, and suddenly I was left in silence in the living room clutching an empty brandy glass as Cheryl had stormed off to bed. I quickly set about refilling my glass, grabbed the television remote control, and slumped onto the sofa. I then watched a crappy programme with a woman in the bottom corner of the screen repeating the spoken words through sign language for the hard of hearing, about the life cycle and sexual habits of an amoeba!

I opened my eyes, looked at my watch and found that the time was 3:45 a.m. Time for bed I thought. I crept up the stairs and opened our bedroom door ever so slowly, peeping around to see if Cheryl was asleep. She was! I got undressed and slid into bed as quietly as possible.

So, there you have it. That is why when I awoke this morning, Cheryl was already up, dressed, and in the car on the way to picking up the kids from her parents. And that is why, I had to get cracking, making this superb brunch for my girls; all three of them. Now for those waffles...

2

When the doorbell sounded, it took me a little bit by surprise and my immediate thought was that it was probably some inconsiderate arsehole wanting to sell me something that I did not want, and basically delaying my fantastic brunch surprise for my three lovely ladies. Therefore, I was not in the friendliest of moods walking down the hallway from the kitchen to the front door.

"Yes," I said abruptly before even realising that standing in my doorway were two police officers, one male, tall and thick-set with a bushy beard. The other, female, shorter, blond hair tied up on her head in a bun, and a warm, friendly face. Both were holding their ID badges for me to see.

"Mr Hart, Mr George Hart?"

"Erm - yes. Sorry about that I thought you were a couple of salesmen trying your luck on a Saturday morning, catching people unaware, and making them purchase some timeshare or whatever. Again sorry, waffling on a bit now; what's this about? Why are you looking for me?" came my embarrassed response. You do not very often, and in my case never, get two police officers standing on your doorstep on a Saturday morning!

"May we come in?" said the female officer in a very calm and gentle voice.

"Yes, certainly," I said showing them into the hallway and leading them into the lounge.

"Please, take a seat, excuse the mess but the wife and I had a couple of friends round last night and we haven't had a chance to clean up yet."

"Thank you, Mr Hart. In fact, it is your wife that we are here to talk to you about," continued the female officer.

"Oh God, what's she done? Has she run a light this morning? Been caught speeding? Not bumped into the back of someone has she?" Because there was no response from either of the two police officers and given the speed Cheryl had driven off at, and mood she was obviously in, my inner fear started to grow, and I felt a sharp, prickly sensation moving down my arms and legs.

"Please sit down, Mr Hart. I have something very serious to inform you about," came the words from the female officer. The male officer with the bushy beard never said a word. "At approximately 9:45 a.m. this morning, a vehicle with the registration number BG12 NVA, an orange Ford Focus registered to a Mrs Cheryl Hart, was involved in a fatal road collision on the northbound carriageway of the A1. A vehicle travelling along the southbound carriageway somehow careered through the central reservation and struck your wife's vehicle head-on, causing fatal injuries to both drivers. It is with regret and my deepest sympathy that I must inform you that we believe your wife was driving at the time and was pronounced dead at the scene at approximately 9:57 a.m. We will, of course, need to ask you to formally identify the deceased's body... Mr Hart, Mr Hart are you okay?"

"I-, I just have to turn the waffle machine off and...," was my shocked response as I got up from the sofa, turned and walked slowly from the lounge to the kitchen. I came to a stop by the kitchen work surface where the waffle machine was and without looking, lifted its lid and pulled two freshly made waffles from the hot plates, somehow managing to touch the plates, and slightly burning my fingertips in the process. I did not feel a thing. I stared out of the kitchen window, completely lost in my thoughts. The problem was that my thoughts were kind of weird for someone who had just been told his wife, the mother of his two children and the love of his life, had just been killed in a senseless car crash.

"Breakfast is ruined, and I need to clear up all this mess before Cheryl gets back with the kids," was my first thought. Then an, ever so slight, realisation of the situation hit me as I started to bite the nail on my little finger of my right hand and my thoughts turned to the fact that Cheryl might not be coming back, ever again.

"No, come on George, there are plenty of Orange Ford Focus cars on the streets around here and the Police must have got it wrong. A simple case of mistaken identity, surely that's all this is," I said to myself in a quiet voice so as not alarm the two police officers that were standing in my lounge. As I turned to go back to the lounge to plead my case that they had got it wrong, and Cheryl would be home soon with the kids, I noticed the female officer was standing in the doorway of the kitchen, having followed me out there.

"Mr Hart? Are you okay Mr Hart?" came this sweet, gentle voice. "Can I call someone for you, a relative, friend or even a neighbour?" continued the female officer.

"I know this sounds really silly, but are you sure about all of this? Cheryl's a fantastic driver and never had an accident in her life, always really careful, and I've never seen her with road rage," I replied (while thinking except for this morning, of course!) "And she wouldn't have been driving on the A1 this morning anyway," I continued, completing my increasingly desperate response. But of course, she would have been driving that way this morning to her parents' house to pick up the kids. Once you get onto the North Circular Road, it is only a matter of twenty minutes until you get onto the A1. But you are not on the A1 for long, before you have to turn off at Holmshill Lane and then you are nearly at Crossoaks Lane, where Cheryl's parents lived in a fantastic five-bedroom mansion, complete with swimming pool and marvellous country views. You would hardly think you were so close to London really, and it was always a real pleasure to visit them, not just because of their house, but also because they were genuinely wonderful people. They were always nice to me from the first moment I met them. So, I knew the route well, and subsequently, also knew that my vain attempt to push away and deny what was happening was, indeed, futile.

"Mr Hart, I know this is all very difficult for you to take in right now. Is there someone we can contact for you? Would you like to come and sit down?" was once again the gentle, kind response from the female police officer. Saturday, the 13th of August 2016 was a date I would never forget for the rest of my life.

To be honest with you, the rest of that morning, day and probably the whole period leading up to Cheryl's funeral was a bit of a blur. Cheryl's parents, Derek and Barbara were naturally devastated, but were brilliant. They arranged everything, and even kept the girls with them so that I could concentrate on sorting out the more practical things that needed doing. All the different organisations that needed notifying seemed to take an age, but it kept me busy and focussed enough to suppress any grieving that I probably should have been doing. And they all started with the same sympathetic rhetoric when I called them and uttered those words "I wanted to inform you that my wife passed away-"

"Oh! I am so sorry for your loss Mr Hart, please accept our deepest sympathy. Now, do you have you account number handy?" was the tried and tested formula - I think!

Luke and Sally were also a terrific help and support for me. They were as shocked as I was but were very much more open about their grief. I had never seen Luke cry before, not even as kids. But as soon as I saw him after it had happened, he gave me a big hug and the tears started streaming down his face. Sally was worse, of course, but after the three of us had finished that emotional embrace, they both somehow managed to hold themselves together, well, up to the funeral anyway…

The hardest part for me was when I had to tell Emily and Amy that their mum had died. After talking to Derek and Barbara on the day of the crash, we decided that I should be the one to tell the girls, so I drove up to their place the next day, after their grandparents had informed them that they were now having an extended one-night stay. How they managed to keep a happy demeanour whilst also grieving for their daughter, I will never know. I arrived on the Sunday morning, after taking the same route that the crash had occurred on the previous day -only a missing piece of central reservation on the A1 was evidence that anything had happened there just twenty-four hours earlier. I promptly greeted the girls, as I always did when I had not seen them for a while - either due to working away, or an evening with friends as was the case this time.

"Hey Emster, hey Amster, how are my big, beautiful sweethearts?" Emily and Amy always laughed when I called them Emster and Amster, and always seemed genuinely pleased to see me whenever I had been away. We decided to take a walk in the nearby field, and it is there that I asked them to sit on a large fallen tree trunk because 'daddy had something very important to tell them'. Emily managed to climb up straight away and quickly positioned herself on the flattest part of the fallen tree trunk, with her legs dangling down each side. I helped Amy up and promptly sat her next to her big sister.

"I have something incredibly sad to tell you about Mummy. You asked this morning when I arrived where she was, I said that I would explain later. Well, yesterday Mummy was driving her car when she had an accident and another car crashed into Mummy's car."

"Gosh, I hope Mummy is okay," said Emily, "and the car!"

"Mummy was very brave but unfortunately, the impact of the crash was too much for her body and although she tried to stay awake, she couldn't, and fell asleep. But before she fell asleep, she said that she loved you both so very much and knew what brave girls you were and that she was enormously proud of you both."

"Is Mummy going to wake up again?" asked Amy.

"Of course, she is, isn't she Daddy, isn't she?" said Emily.

"No. I'm afraid Mummy didn't have any strength left and couldn't wake up. We can't see Mummy any more with our eyes. But we can feel her in our hearts and remember her in our thoughts and she will always be with us. I'm so sorry girls. You will not be alone though, and I will always be here for you and so will Nanny and Grandad. We all love you so much and although we will all greatly miss Mummy, we will never forget her, and she will never forget us."

"How did the car crash, Daddy?" asked Amy, but before I could reply, Emily had jumped down from the trunk and started running as fast as she could across the field in the direction of her grandparents' house. I gathered up Amy in my arms and we headed back across the field just keeping Emily in our sights. When we arrived at Cheryl's parents place, Emily was sitting on Barbara's lap, with her head nuzzled into her bosom, crying uncontrollably. Barbara, although motionless and soundless, also had tears rolling down her cheeks. It was an incredibly sad and emotional image. I was still standing with Amy in my arms and could feel my eyes becoming damp, when Derek, tapped me on the shoulder and proceeded to take Amy from me. I think Derek could see the raw emotion of the situation and offered me the chance of just stepping outside to gather my thoughts. I gladly took him up on this, and exited the room to the garden, where I continued to the very end. But no tears came, and I was comfortable enough to go back inside within a short time.

As I have mentioned, I was glad of Derek and Barbara's support during this period. However, it disturbed me that I had only really seen the girls the day after the crash. It disturbed me greatly. I did not want them to think that they had lost both of their parents, which is exactly the way I felt when my dad passed, due to the inadequacy of my mum to deal with the situation. Not blaming Mum, but I do not think there was much thought given to me. Although I did my best in trying to explain to the girls what had happened, I am sure they had some questions. Particularly Amy. Amy was very much a thinker and for a five year-old, she had an uncanny way of computing information in her little mind; she would realise that there were pieces of information missing that she would need to make sense of things. I had not answered her question about how the car had crashed, and I am sure that would still be playing on her mind. She would need this information to reconcile what had happened to her mum. As for Emily, she was a young intellectual. Someone that was very expressive, had a wide range of vocabulary, learnt very quickly how to read music, could solve puzzles beyond her seven years, and was generally never phased in anyone's company. Emily was slightly more loving than Amy, and definitely freer with her emotions. I, therefore, decided that once the funeral was over, I would take the girls away on vacation and try to start the process of mending all our fractured hearts. The girls' school were very accommodating in allowing them time off during school term to take them away; especially as the new school term had only just started. My employers were also very sympathetic and allowed me paid compassionate leave as well. I booked a small villa in Majorca, not far from the beach, but still quite secluded and quiet. Perfect for us three to start building up a new kind of relationship with each other.

I was dreading the day of the funeral and when it came, I just hoped that I could remain as collected and calm as I had done during the preceding twelve days since the crash. Everyone during that time had remarked on how brave and together I had been, even though I knew that secretly, they were all whispering that I was going to break soon.

Although I did not really want Emily and Amy to attend the funeral - as I thought it would be too upsetting for them - it was decided with Derek and Barbara that it was probably best that they did. After all, it was their mum, not a distant relative like an uncle or aunt. They probably needed to say goodbye as much as I did. So, they were either side of me, Emily holding my left hand and Amy holding my right hand, sitting in the back of the large, black funeral limousine. The two seats directly in front of us were occupied by Derek and Barbara, Derek just obscuring the chauffer's cap.

Cheryl and I were both only children and, therefore, blood relatives attending the funeral were few and far between. However, Cheryl was very popular and a long line of vehicles carrying friends, work colleagues and neighbours followed us on the way to the church for the funeral service. It was a pleasant, sunny morning, and we were all grateful for the air conditioning being on in the car, as we were wearing full mourning suits. The girls wore white dresses with black belts and pink hair ribbons. Cheryl used to love doing the girls' hair, making plaits and ponytails and buns using some sort of doughnut shaped sponge. And as pink was Emily and Amy's favourite colour, the ribbons and hair clips were always that colour. Barbara had done their hair today, and I must say she had done a particularly good job of it. Almost to the same standard as Cheryl. How was I going to cope doing it myself? I was rubbish at doing their hair! Probably the least of my problems though.

During the service, the girls sat quietly either side of me. As I looked around behind me, all the pews were full. I saw Luke and Sally and gave a quick wave. Sally was already in floods of tears and, unfortunately, Luke was not that far behind. The vicar started the ceremony with a prayer and then proceeded to talk about Cheryl, who he had known since she was a girl. Although Cheryl was not particularly religious, her parents were, and she did attend church regularly as a child. Various people walked to the altar and gave sterling performances in describing their experiences and thoughts about Cheryl, which was met with a mixture of laughter, happiness, and the inevitable sadness. All this time, Cheryl's coffin was in full view of everyone, and it was becoming increasingly difficult for me to think that she was lying there, listening to all these wonderful things being said about her and knowing I would never see her or talk to her again. My eyes started to dampen, and I thought I would start blubbering uncontrollably. But then it was my turn to speak, so I gathered myself together and with a quick word of encouragement under my breath, "Come on George, you can do this," I waited for Barbara to come and take my place in between Emily and Amy. I rose from the front pew and made my way to the altar, turned, stood behind the podium, and reached into my pocket for the notes I had made about what I wanted to say. I placed them on the podium and looked up at my audience. There was silence.

"I would firstly like to thank you all for coming here today and for sharing your warmth, kind words, and love for Cheryl. I know that she would be deeply moved and somewhat embarrassed by the wonderful things that have been said about her today, all of which are true. Cheryl was a lovely, kind-hearted soul, a brilliant mother, daughter, friend, colleague and of course, wife. My wife." After uttering these last two words, I thought that this was all wrong. Too scripted and not really what I wanted to say at all. I think everyone was expecting me to break down and here I was delivering a speech that was controlled, predictable and not demonstrative of how I was feeling at all.

"I'm sorry everyone," I said as I picked up my notes and placed them back in my inside jacket pocket. "This speech just isn't working for me. So, I'm going to put it away and start again - if that's okay with all of you?" This was met, to my surprise, with a spontaneous round of applause and cheering from everyone.

"Cheryl was my life; the mother of our beautiful girls Emily and Amy and we will miss her terribly. It's not fair that she has been taken from us so early in our lives together and through no fault of her own. She was just in the wrong place at the wrong time. And that hurts so much. But she was in the right place at the right time when we met and I will always remember her long blonde hair, tied up in a ponytail with what looked like an old man's dirty handkerchief! She wore ripped jeans, tight crop tops and was an instant attraction to all the guys at Portsmouth University. She had wonderful, gleaming, pure white teeth that could literally dazzle you when she smiled. And because my best friend Luke had the courage to talk to her best friend Sally, I got the opportunity to meet this beautiful, funny, intelligent, caring, loving young woman. And she chose me! Out of all the good-looking guys around at that time, she chose me. She said I was the one. The one to comfort her, love her, care for her and be the father of her two children."

I looked around the church at the congregation before pausing and looking at Emily and Amy. I continued. "You see, what you don't know about Cheryl, is that she already knew she would have two children and had a plan mapped out for-well the rest of her life. We would talk endlessly about the future, our future together and where we would be once the children had grown up and delivered us our very own grandchildren. That we would one day end up in a beachside villa in southern Spain, sitting on our Hollywood swing, holding hands, looking out to sea and more in love than ever. Me, with a balding head and her, although now greyer, still holding her natural beauty through the passage of time. Anyone who met Cheryl knew of her passion for life and making the most of each and every day, and we tried to do that no matter what came our way. Only now, what has come our way has fractured the future we had dreamed about. It is no longer a future with Cheryl firmly rooted in the middle of it. But together, Emily, Amy and I will not give up on her dreams and we will stay strong for each other and never forget the joy and laughter that we have had as a family. Their mum will not be forgotten," and I once again turned to the girls who by now where staring at me, tears rolling down their crimson cheeks. "I promise you both, Mummy will not be forgotten."

It was time for me to stop talking now. This was a scary moment for I knew that when my speech had finished, it would be time for the pall bearers to take Cheryl to her final resting place. So, I looked up from the podium and with a lump in my throat, and fiercely trying to fight back my tears, I said, "Having discussed this with a few of Cheryl's closest friends, we felt it would be only fitting for Cheryl to, to erm, leave us today with the sound of her favourite record, sung by her favourite boy band." With that, I returned to my seat in between Emily and Amy and as I did so, Luke and five of our closest male friends stepped up to the altar and guided by the funeral director, slowly and carefully, lifted Cheryl's coffin

The song? Well, it had to be 'Never Forget' by Take That, of course.

3

The long days and nights that followed our return from vacation after Cheryl's funeral were hard, extremely hard for all of us. While we were in Spain, in different surroundings, with different smells and unfamiliar noises, it appeared to mask the realisation that Emily and Amy had lost their mum and I had lost my wife and soul mate. We did all the usual vacation type things, you know the sort of stuff, visiting the beach, eating out, playing games in the pool, visiting the local shops and attractions. It did feel a little strange for us and when we went for dinner one night at a local restaurant, I asked the girls if they wanted to talk about anything, anything about their mum or how they were feeling. Emily looked at me and as soon as our eyes met, she turned her head away. Amy thought for a moment.

"If we're not going to see Mummy anymore, does that mean we can't see Nanny and Grandad as well?"

"No, silly. It's just Mummy we can't see anymore," snapped Emily. It was the first indication of anger that I had noticed about how Emily was feeling.

"Emily's right," I said in a calming voice to Amy, "Nanny and Grandad will be waiting for us when we get back home and they're probably missing you like crazy at the moment," I said gently, trying to give as much comfort as I could to Amy.

"You see, sometimes you are just so stupid," again snarled Emily.

"Emily. Please do not talk to your sister like that. I want you both to feel that you can ask any questions that you want to. Anything that is puzzling you or troubling you, anything that you want to know about Mummy, absolutely anything. And please remember, there are no 'silly' questions." With that Emily looked soulfully at Amy and whispered, 'I'm sorry'.

That evening in our villa, the flood gates opened and the girls had so many questions about their mum, me, them and just about anything in between. Ranging from how Cheryl and I met, to more difficult questions about where Mummy was now and was she alright? I did my best to answer them all, and even Emily opened up to me about how she was feeling. After a good cry, the girls cuddled up to me, one on each of my arms and fell asleep.

I was left in the darkness, holding my two precious darlings and alone with my thoughts. It was only then that something that had been troubling me about the events of the last few weeks came to light. All I had been thinking about since the crash was about the girls, how they were feeling, about how they were going to cope and getting the practical things done, funeral arrangements, insurances, mortgage and all those mundane things. And I cannot lie, I had also thought about how I was feeling, and my love for Cheryl and how great she was, how I missed her so much and how my life was never going to be the same again. But now an avalanche of guilt raced through my thoughts! The last word that Cheryl had said to me was 'Bastard' due to the row we had had the night before about Jennifer Parks.

My God! What must have been going through Cheryl's mind when the crash happened? What must have been her thoughts about me? Was she thinking about Jennifer and me at the actual time of the crash? Had that contributed to the crash? Maybe she could have avoided it altogether if she were more concentrated on driving, rather than thinking about me. But wait a minute, she left around 9:30 a.m.

on that fateful Saturday morning to retrieve the kids from their grandparents. Normally when we had friends over and the kids stayed away for the night, either one of us would drive to get the kids, but it would be around 10:30 a.m. Yes, Cheryl had gone earlier that morning because of our row the night before. My heart sank, my brow started to sweat, and I could feel my legs starting to twitch beneath the bed sheets.

I carefully unloaded Emily and Amy from my arms and laid them down, side by side, each of them sharing the big pillow on the bed. I slipped out of the room and walked into the lounge area and sat down on the sofa, staring out into the dark night. All that could be heard was the gentle rush of the waves not fifty metres from the villa. My head fell into my hands and I started to cry. All of this, this sadness and excruciating pain that had been caused by the crash resulting in Cheryl's death, had been preventable. The fact that Emily and Amy would now grow up without their mum to share in their experiences of happiness, triumphs, disasters, spots, exams, boyfriends, girlfriends, teenage moods, driving tests, marriage, children and just about anything that we all go through in life, was down to me. If only I had not gone to the café in Chelsea that day. That day when I was just minding my own business and who should walk into my life but Jennifer 'bloody' Parks! And if only I had not mentioned the meeting with Jennifer to Luke, who immediately asked me if something had gone on that day but did eventually believe me when I said, of course not.

If only I had not suggested opening that bloody bottle of Hennessey the night before the crash, Luke might not have blurted out that I had met Jennifer and we would not have had the row. I would have awoken the next morning in the arms of the woman I love, made passionate love together, had a leisurely breakfast, picked the kids up together from her parents and… and Cheryl would still be alive today. I lost control and sobbed into the early hours of the morning. Luckily, the girls were exhausted, and their sleep was not interrupted.

They slept through until 10:45 a.m. by which time my sobbing had stopped and I had already decided not to tell them of the circumstances of the night before their mother's death. However, I knew that the guilt I felt now would always be with me and it would be a burden I would deservedly have for the rest of my life for being responsible for my wife's death. For making her feel so bad that morning; it was probably what she was thinking about instead of the road ahead. She could possibly have avoided the oncoming vehicle had she been her usual alert, cheery self.

The rest of the holiday passed quickly and the girls, although understandably much quieter than usual, appeared to be coping quite well. But our return took its toll on all of us. Before Cheryl died, we were a well-oiled machine and our daily routines were well rehearsed and unflinching in their military like precision.

On weekdays, Cheryl and I would awake at 6:45 a.m. Cheryl would go downstairs to start breakfast, while I headed for the shower. Cheryl would then wake the girls and start to get them dressed. I would take over once I had finished my shower and got dressed and Cheryl would head for the bathroom for hers. We would all meet downstairs an hour later at the breakfast table and begin to eat as a family. Cheryl would then do the girls hair. Although Cheryl was not a hairdresser, she was excellent at doing the girls' hair. There was nothing that she could not do - plaits, crowns, single braids, or a doughnut bun or just about anything they wanted. With Amy, who had a little bit shorter hair and natural tight curls, it was braids, or all done up fancy on top, or left natural but kept tidy with the characters from her favourite Disney movie emblazoned on multi coloured hair clips. Just stunning every time. We would then clear the table, I would kiss the girls and wish them a good day, give Cheryl a long tender kiss on the lips, tell her to 'go careful' before I jumped in the car and went to work. Cheryl would then take the kids to school and then go to school herself. She was still teaching primary school kids.

All of that had gone out of the window. Our well-oiled

machine had lost its biggest and strongest cog.

I got up earlier now to try and get everything done. And I did manage to get a routine going. The girls helped enormously as they could tell I was struggling a bit. They would dress themselves, even getting their school uniforms out and neatly piled up at the end of their beds the night before in readiness for the morning. One of the things I struggled with the most was, of course, their hair. I was just not particularly good at this at all! But I tried and as the days and weeks rolled by, I got better and better. However, if you were to compare my hair dressing skill to Cheryl's, it would be like comparing a Premier League footballer with a part-time semi-pro for Dagenham, working as a car mechanic! No comparison really.

Another thing I struggled with was taking the kids to school. Walking them to the gate was a nightmare for me. The other kids' mums would always be whispering to each other about me. "Ah, poor soul, struggling to bring up those two beautiful girls," and "He looks pale, I wonder if he's eating okay," were the usual sort of comments I could hear. But it was even worse when they did actually talk to me. One of the mums, a young girl, quite pretty actually with rather a large chest squeezed into a tight low-cut top, nipples sticking out like fighter pilot's thumbs, approached me one day and just came out with it.

"I know it's only been a few months since your wife died, but if you are feeling lonely in the 'downstairs' department, I am offering my services to relieve you. I can use it all, my hand, mouth, arse or just straight sex, whatever you want" and she gave a little smile and winked her left eye! Luckily, I had already dropped off Emily and Amy, so they did not have to hear it. I just thanked her for her support and walked off, rather red-faced, I think! Still, it was nice to know that someone found me attractive enough to offer me sex, or was it just sympathy? Either way, I felt flattered, scared and a little embarrassed all at the same time!

During the first six months, following Cheryl's death, Emily and I had some 'falling outs' about her behaviour and although I completely understood why, I still thought it was right to talk to her about it. She just thought I was picking on her and that Amy being the youngest, was my favourite, and she thought that I cared more for Amy than I did about her. It broke my heart, but again, I understood why and just hoped that I could help her through this difficult time.

Shortly after Cheryl died, I was offered counselling for the children by the local Health Authorities but decided against it. I thought I could deal with all of this: their feelings and my feelings all by myself. But I was beginning to have second thoughts. Amy appeared to be fine. But what if she were really suffering inside and I could not reach her, to let her know that everything was okay? Emily was obviously not taking the situation well at all and it came to a head one day when I caught her screaming at Amy, holding a broken, china money box in her hand.

"Mummy bought this for me and now you have broken it. I hate you; I wish you were dead instead of Mummy!" Emily raged at poor little Amy. Both girls were crying. It was a devastating scene to witness and, in a flash, I picked up both girls, put them in the car and drove to Cheryl's parents' place. When I got there, I explained the situation and asked if Derek and Barbara could take Emily for a few days to give us all some space. Of course, they readily agreed and told me not to worry.

I went back with Amy and we spent the next three days together doing all sorts of father and daughter things, like baking cakes, painting pictures, doing jigsaw puzzles, playing 'Pop up Pirates', hoovering, making dinner, reading books, watching Frozen and lots more besides. Every night when I had put Amy to bed, I would call Derek and Barbara to check on Emily, desperate to find out if she were okay, and if she had been asking after me or Amy? The third night, Barbara called me before I had a chance to ring her and told me of a breakthrough.

"She finally opened up to me George. She finally told me how much she misses Cheryl and how unfair life is that she can never see her mummy again."

"Poor little sod. Did she mention anything about Amy?"

"Yes. She was terribly upset about how she has been behaving towards Amy. But not just Amy, you as well. She said she loved you both very much and did not want to be without you ever again. She was so sorry and now realises that it has been just as tough for Amy as it has been for her. She was sorry for you too. She knows you are trying your best and wants to apologise for making it so hard for you."

"Tell her we love her too and we are coming to bring her home. We will leave first thing in the morning and Barbara, thanks for all your help and support, and Derek's. It really means a lot to me to have you in our lives. The girls adore you both and I don't know how I would have coped without you."

"George, you don't have to thank us. Cheryl was our daughter. We know the pain that you and Emily and Amy are going through and if we can help in any way, we gladly will. You are like a son to us; and the girls - well we see a lot of Cheryl in both of them. We love them dearly. Get some rest and we will see you in the morning". With that, I managed to get a good night's sleep for the first time in months and was relieved that tomorrow I was going to get my family back together.

When Amy and I arrived at Derek and Barbara's house, Emily was already waiting by the big, oak, front door with a huge smile on her face. Barbara and Derek were standing either side of her, Barbara's hands resting on Emily's shoulders. Emily waved excitedly and as I turned the key to stop the engine, and opened my door, Emily ran towards me like a greyhound being released from its trap. She jumped into my arms and gave me a noticeably big hug before whispering very gently in my ear "I'm sorry Daddy, I really am," which immediately brought a swelling to my throat and a tear to my eye. As I looked around, Barbara was already in the back of the car, releasing Amy from her child seat and giving her a big cuddle.

"Do you have anything to say to Amy?" I asked hoping that Emily would positively respond.

"Yes Daddy, I do. Can you put me down?" I gently lowered Emily to the ground, and she walked around the front of the car to where Barbara and Amy were standing.

"I am so sorry Amy for being horrible to you. You are my sister and sisters should always stick together, look out for each other and never be nasty to each other. Mummy would be very cross with me for my behaviour towards you and Daddy. Can I have a hug?" With that Amy flew towards Emily and they embraced in a warm hug, both had their eyes closed, with big smiles on their faces. It was a really touching moment, and I thought that this would be a moment that they would never forget. A moment that they would talk about when they were very old ladies, with children, grandchildren, and even great grandchildren of their own.

The girls went off to play and I followed Barbara and Derek into the hallway and through to the kitchen.

"Coffee?" asked Barbara.

"Yes please, although after witnessing that I think a glass of champagne might be in order," I replied with a rueful smile on my face. Barbara smiled back at me and began pouring the water into the kettle from the tap.

"Don't worry George, everything will be alright. We think that Emily will only get stronger now," said Derek.

"I hope so and once again, I can't thank you both enough for what you have done for the girls and me. I know I would not have coped without you both. Your support has been incredible, and I just wish I could do something for you, to show you how much I love you both. You have been more like parents to me than my own when they were alive," and with that, the buried guilt came over me, regarding the circumstances of Cheryl's death. The guilt I had desperately been trying to suppress. For it just dawned on me that for Cheryl to have gone to pick up the kids earlier than usual on that terrible day, she must have telephoned her parents ahead of time. She most likely would have talked to Barbara as Derek hardly ever answered the telephone, and she must have told Barbara about our row relating to Jennifer Parks and my impromptu meeting with her. My God, Derek and Barbara must have known all along that it was my fault! They must have known that I was probably responsible for Cheryl's distressed state of mind that morning, which probably contributed to the accident. And yet, they had been so good to me. To me and the girls.

"Hey George, we know, don't worry, you don't have to do anything for us, we know," came the empathetic response from Barbara, who was now busy pouring the coffees. I had to say something. I was compelled to let them both know that I knew they knew, and that I accepted the responsibility that would live with me for the rest of my life.

"Derek, Barbara, I have something to tell you both," I said staring down at the kitchen table. Barbara looked up from pouring the coffees and Derek moved closer to the opposite side of the kitchen table. Although I was staring down, I could feel Derek's eyes transfixed on my face.

"There's something I need to tell you both about the morning that Cheryl died. Something that I am fairly sure you already know about, but I need to tell you anyway, and to try to explain as best as I can how sorry I am. You see the night before, we had our friends, Luke, and Sally back to the house for drinks following our night out together and Luke happened to mention that I had seen a girl a few weeks earlier in a café, purely by chance mind you, who had been my girlfriend before Cheryl and I had got together. We had a coffee and talked for a bit before going our separate ways. That was it, I swear. Nothing else happened. But Cheryl had made me swear to her back when we were at University never to see or talk to this girl ever again. Luke and Sally left, we had a row, Cheryl went to bed and the last time I saw Cheryl alive, was when I looked out of our bedroom window as she was driving away to pick up the kids from you. If we had not had the row, Cheryl would have been in a better state of mind and maybe could have avoided the collision with the other car." I looked up and both Barbara and Derek were standing opposite me at the other end of the table.

"Oh George, you poor boy," said Barbara. "Yes, we do know about the row. Cheryl called me early that morning and told me everything. I told her to stop being so bloody paranoid and stupid. I told her that you would never cheat on her and so what if you had had a chance meeting with an old flame? Do you know what she said to me George?" I slowly shook my head.

"You are right Mum. I am being stupid. George would never do anything to hurt me or the girls," continued Barbara. "What have I done! I feel terrible about taking this out on George. I'll collect the girls from you and then I'll come back home and make it up to him."

"You mean, she was not in an angry, upset state of mind when she left me that morning?"

"No George. She was happy. Happy to have you as her husband and the father of her two beautiful girls. She could not wait to get back to you, to make it up with you. Cheryl knew she had completely overreacted and thanked me for helping her see sense."

Barbara moved around the table towards me and when she was close enough, she hugged me tightly.

"You poor boy. Have you been carrying this around with you since it happened?"

"Yes," I said, and the weight of my guilt started to lighten causing me to lose control and cry.

"If anyone should feel guilty, it is me, George. I should have told her to stay with you that morning. I should have told her that we would keep the girls until the afternoon to give you two some time alone together. But I did not," and with that Barbara also started to cry. Derek came over to comfort both of us and the next few minutes were filled with genuine raw emotion. Me, feeling my guilt slightly ease and Barbara saddled with the stuff, weighing her down like the satchels carried by a mountain donkey. When the moment passed, we sat at the table drinking our coffee. We all agreed that it made no sense at all to blame anyone for Cheryl's death (well, perhaps other than the second driver) but certainly not us. We could not have foretold what would happen that day and were by no means responsible for Cheryl's death. We then chatted about the girls and a sense of normality returned.

The girls and I did not leave Derek and Barbara's until 8 p.m. that day. On the way home, the girls fell asleep in the back of the car. It is only a short journey from their grandparents' house, so it was somewhat surprising. Nevertheless, it had been a long day, and this had obviously contributed to the girls' exhaustion. I carefully put them to bed when we arrived home and then poured myself a large scotch and sat on the sofa in the lounge.

So, what had I really seen that morning when I looked out of the bedroom window? Cheryl put her head out of the driver's door window, gave me the middle finger and mouthed the word 'Bastard' is what I had thought had happened. But if she was in a happy mood when she left after talking to her mum, what really happened?

Admittedly, I was a little bit dazed having just woken up after a skinful of brandy the night before; but I was sure that is what I saw. I thought again and again, replaying that moment repeatedly in my mind until, I figured out exactly what she was doing. The middle finger on her right hand, was not the middle finger at all! It was her index finger, and she was pointing it upwards denoting that I was the one. She had often done that during our university days, across crowded lecture halls, or the noisy, busy, student bar. 'You're the one,' she would say and point that sensual finger upwards! And as for Bastard? Well it was not bastard at all. It was Big Boy alluding to well, my penis. Although I had never thought I was that well-endowed down there, Cheryl had always said that I was bigger than most men, and that I would not have anything to worry about in the blokes' showers! That was good enough for me!

It had been ten months since Cheryl's death and although work had been incredibly good to me and very understanding of my situation, they had started to quiz me about when I would be back to full speed and full attendance. There were some big things happening; expansion in the African market, including mergers and acquisitions of some locally run catering companies. All extremely exciting stuff to any normal person, but to me; my girls came first. I could not be jetting off to these places, representing the company and staying abroad for days on end. Who would look after the girls? My first mistake was mentioning this to Barbara. She immediately hit on the idea of a live-in nanny. She said it would be good for the girls to have a permanent female around the house and it would take a lot of pressure and stress off me. My second mistake was to ask Sally if she could help me with the interview process, being in HR and all that. Between the two of them, they practically took over the whole thing! Within two days of Barbara and Sally knowing, advertisements had been placed in several nanny agencies and, of course, Gumtree! It did not matter to them that I was not sure about the whole thing. They just kept giving me reasons why it made perfect sense.

"You have plenty of space in the house and she, or he, can have her, or his, own bathroom. You need someone who can take the pressure off you. You need to get back to work, they won't be sympathetic forever you know," were the main reasons that kept being held up in front of me by the two female enforcers.

I reluctantly agreed, and after a week of the advertisements being placed, on one sunny Friday afternoon, I had seven interviews lined up. Now, interviewing people for roles such as sales managers, analysts, purchasers, or any number of positions within a normal company framework had never held any fear for me whatsoever. However, the thought of interviewing people for the job of my nanny, a nanny for my gorgeous girls, filled me with dread and abject horror! Luckily, both Sally and Barbara were available for the interviews. Well, when I say available, they absolutely insisted on being present actually!

The first lady to be interviewed was Polish. Martyna Kowalski was her name. I was guessing she was in her mid to late twenties. She had five years of live-in nanny experience, came with two fantastic written references, having worked with two families looking after children aged between four and nine years old. She spoke perfect English, as well as German and French, had a clean driving license, and looked absolutely stunning! Not in a tasteless sort of way, but more of a comfortable, look good in anything type thing. You could have put her in ripped jeans, converse shoes and a vest top and she would have looked just as stylish had she been wearing high heels and an evening dress made by Giorgio Armani himself! Of course, her figure was extremely pleasing too. Probably 5'8, slim, brunette, green eyes and naturally deep, pink lips - I wasn't really looking that closely!

"Her eyes were a bit too close together and she appeared a little shifty and fidgety," said Barbara after Miss Kowalski had left.

"Couldn't take her eyes off of you," commented Sally. "No, no she won't do!"

"I thought she was quite nice, well qualified and I think the girls would have benefited hugely from maybe learning a foreign language," I said hoping to generate some interest with Barbara and Sally. They both just looked at me with that sort of stern teacher look and although they did not say it, you could almost hear the words "You were just looking at her boobs!" So, I had to reluctantly strike her from the list.

The next lady was a local woman, born and bred in London, late fifties and looked like she probably had grandchildren of her own. Very kindly demeanour, warm personality, a bit plump (probably knew her way to the biscuit barrel if you know what I mean!) and very presentable.

"So, Mrs Hansen," I said looking down at my notes and then returning to eye contact. "Did you have far to come today?"

"Not really, but the bloody buses are always running late, aren't they? So you don't know what time they'll turn up, then the sodding wind gets up while you are waiting at the bus stop, wafting your skirt up, showing all your arse off and causing your frigging hair to get messed up - I must look a right mess! And then when you do get on the bus there's always some filthy foreigner sitting next to you, you know the sort, makes you feel like having a fucking bath as soon as you get indoors in case you've caught something nasty," and she gave out a witch-like cackle to emphasise the point!

"So not far then?" I said trying to contain my laughter, as a little smile came across my lips. I looked at Barbara and Sally, both appeared in shock, slightly opened mouthed and deadly silent. "Do you have family of your own?" I continued.

"No, all my kids fucked off some years back and my old man, the bastard, he left me for some fancy woman with red nails, pink lips and tits the size of a small Pacific island."

"So competent in Geography then?" I muttered, trying not to laugh before Mrs Hansen continued.

"Good riddance to all of them. I'm sort of in between living accommodation now so that's why I thought about being a live-in nanny. Roof over my head, decent pay, play with the kids a bit and nights off! Bloody brilliant!"

"So, no chance of a reconciliation with Mr Hansen then?" I enquired, still trying to keep a straight face.

"Fuck no," came the instant reply. At this point, Sally leaned over to me and pointed to my notes. What she actually pointed to was the word Gumtree!

"Ahhhh-," I said to Sally, but could not help continuing my line of questioning. I was having fun! "So, have you brought any references with you and I do wonder what qualifications a woman of your integrity and blessed oral fortitude has?"

"Well, no I haven't got any references. I haven't done this bloody job before. I told you, I'm looking for somewhere to sodding live, first and foremost. I just saw it on Gumtree and thought I'd give it a go. These fucking, little phones these days are great for looking at jobs and horoscopes, and my Facebook and Twitter. I like to 'twit' with people or is it 'twat'? No - that's a bloody swear word isn't it? Anyway, you know, I like to let people know what I'm doing and what I've been up to." she said while pulling her I-phone from her pocket.

"Right," I said. And that was the end of that! Sally and Barbara quickly ushered Mrs Hansen out of the house, with the fatal words 'we'll let you know' and when they returned to the lounge where I was still sitting, I could not resist it.

"I quite liked her," I said and all three of us burst out laughing! The remaining five interviews all sort of merged into one in my mind as all the potential candidates were of similar age (about fifty), similar experience, similar references, and similar outlooks on life. Don't get me wrong, there was nothing wrong with any of them, but I just could not see them living in my house and looking after my kids. The good thing is that both Sally and Barbara agreed!

We only interviewed people that had been sent via a reputable agency after the 'Mrs Hansen' experience. However, two months and nine interviews later, no one really stood out as 'the one' who would become Emily and Amy's new nanny. Barbara, Sally, and I sat together in my kitchen one morning after a week or so had passed from the last interview, to see if we could finally decide on who to appoint.

"Well, I liked Mrs Daniels, she had a lovely warm feel about her, and I think that Emily and Amy would really take to her. She has great references and…"

"But she can't drive Barbara," I said interrupting Barbara mid-speech. "Which does make it a bit difficult. I know it is not the end of the world, but if I get a nanny that can't drive, it sort of limits my flexibility a bit. Not ideal if you know what I mean?"

"Yes, I suppose you are right George. Still, it is a shame, she was nice."

"I like Miss James. Although she came across as a bit of a Head Mistress. I think she would not only be good for the girls George, but for you too! You know, keep you in your place."

"Thanks for your vote of confidence Sal." I said in a sarcastic way which immediately brought a smile to Barbara's face.

"Alright then how about Mrs Benjamin, the West Indian lady. She was really nice, and I think the girls would have such a fun time with her. Again, good references and…"

"And again, no driving licence Barbara!" It was beginning to look and sound like 'Groundhog Day' where everything was the same, day after day! I thought to myself for a moment and decided now was the time to throw my suggestion into the ring.

"What about Miss Kowalski?"

"Who?" said Barbara.

"Oh, I know, the young Polish girl who we saw first of all."

"Yes Sal. I think she was great and not because of the way she looked, or should I say not 'just' because of the way she looked. She has great references, great qualifications, speaks multiple languages, has the experience and of course, can drive!"

"Let me see her application again," said Sally and I handed it to her from the stack of application forms lying on the kitchen table. It was not hard to find as it had been the one on the top of the pile from day one of the whole process!

"Hmmm, good, yes, maybe," were the noises coming from Sally and then she passed it onto Barbara and as she did so, pointed to something on the application form.

"Oh, right," said Barbara acknowledging whatever Sally had pointed out. Then the same noises started coming from Barbara!

"Well? The noises all appear good, but what was all the pointing business on the form?" I asked.

"Holland Park," said Barbara. "Sally was just pointing out that Miss Kowalski's last job was for a family in Holland Park."

"What does that mean?"

"Nothing really, it's just she has been used to living in very fine surroundings, Holland Park you know, awfully expensive area. I'm just not sure she is going to want to work for you here in North West London!"

"Well, there's only one way to find out isn't there?" I said and pulled out my phone. I called the agency and asked if Miss Kowalski is still available for the position and if so, could the agency arrange a second interview at my house so that she could meet the children. As luck would have it, Miss Kowalski was still available. Within two hours, I had received a call back from the agency confirming the second interview with Miss Kowalski for the following Wednesday at 4:30 p.m. thus allowing time for the girls to get home from school. For some reason, I decided not to tell Sally and Barbara about the second interview. Obviously, I knew they always had my best interests, as well as those of the girls at heart, but I just thought on this occasion,

I did not need their advice or support. Only time would tell if I had been too hasty in my decision.

Although Emily and Amy were aware that I was in the process of choosing a live-in nanny for them, I wanted to give them an opportunity to let me know exactly what they thought about the idea, and to see if either of them had any ideas as to what they would like the person to be like. So, on the Monday before the second interview, I picked the girls up from school and instead of taking them straight home, I decided to take them for a treat.

"Okay girls, we're not going home just yet," I informed them as I got into the driver's seat having strapped them safely into their car seats in the back.

"Why? Are we going somewhere?" asked Emily with a slightly worried tone in her voice like that used when she knew we were going to the dentist.

"Don't worry girls, it's just I want to take you to London Zoo! I know it's a bit late, but it will only take twenty minutes to get there and we haven't been for such a long time."

"I love London Zoo!" said a thrilled Amy. "Are we going right now?"

"Yes, and maybe we can grab a McDonalds on the way back? What do you think?" This was met with a shriek of excitement and the consensus from the girls was most definitely yes!

We travelled to the zoo talking about what the girls had been up to at school that day. It ranged from a painting of Emily and Amy skipping in our back garden, painted by Amy, to maths comprising of multiplication and long division! All pretty tricky stuff for an eight and six year-old. Yes, since Cheryl's passing, both the girls had had their birthdays. Emily first and then Amy. I thought it would have been a very emotional occasion being the first time in their lives that their mum had not awoken them on their 'special day' and, in between the presents and cards elegantly presented on the kitchen table, a homemade birthday cake, candles lit as they came downstairs to a chorus of 'Happy Birthday to You.' The presents, cards and, unfortunately, shop bought birthday cake were all there. But I could not replicate the presence and voice of their mum waking them up. However, to the girls' credit, they understood that Mummy could not be there for their birthday and that she could never again be there not just on their birthdays, but any day for the rest of their lives.

We did start a new tradition though on our birthdays, of going to the cemetery on those days, laying flowers and whoever's birthday it was, had their own special time with Cheryl to talk to her about whatever they wanted to. It was a small way of making it special for the birthday person, a sort of one to one with Cheryl. Of course, we would visit the cemetery regularly as a family and I found myself there many times on my own, just telling Cheryl about my day, what the girls had been doing at school, the funny things they come out with and, of course, how much I loved and missed her.

It is one of those things that you read about, or see in a film, or someone tells you that they have a friend, who lost their other half and when visiting their grave, they would openly talk out loud and shed a few tears. And when you do read it, see it in a film or someone tells you about it, you always think "No, not me, if anything like that ever happened to me, I would never be like that, I am too strong to be talking out loud like some sort of nutter, shedding a tear? No not me." But the thing is, you do. And what is more, you do it again without fear, or hesitation because that is what real love is. It is not about looking or sounding foolish in front of anyone else. It is about sharing your feelings with that one person, hoping that they share theirs with you. And when they are no longer able to share their feelings, that is when it hurts the most. The pain never goes away, only the acceptance of the situation increases with time.

We parked the car in Gloucester Slips Car Park and walked to the Zoo entrance. Once inside, we headed straight for the gorilla enclosure as they were the girls favourite animals. Especially, since the new main attraction, a baby boy silverback named Gernot, was born. We had visited the zoo a few months before Cheryl died, to see Gernot a tiny little gorilla, safe in his mother's arms and his delighted dad, Kumbuka, strutting around like a proud, overprotective father. As we sat watching the gorillas, it seemed as though the girls were lost in their thoughts, remembering that day.

"Mummy would have liked to have seen Gernot and Alika today, wouldn't she Daddy," said Emily with a very heavy heart.

"Yes, she would have loved it Emily. Mummy loved the gorillas as much as you two do, but don't forget, she loved you and Amy much, much more," I said putting my arm around Emily's shoulders, trying to comfort her as best I could.

"But Mummy can still see the gorillas from up there, can't she," was the typically thoughtful response from Amy, as she lifted her finger and pointed to the sky.

"I'm sure she can Poppet, I'm sure she can," and we all looked up at the sky. After a poignant moment or two of silence, where we all appeared to be lost in our own thoughts, I thought I should tell the girls about Miss Kowalski.

"Girls, you know Nanny Barbara, Sally and I have been looking to see if there was a suitable nanny available to look after you while I try to get back to work. Well, I think I have found a person who might just be perfect for us." Both girls looked at me and I knew it would be Emily to speak first.

"But we had made a list of what things we would like the nanny to be like, Daddy," she said.

"Great," I replied. "Do you remember what is on your list because if you do, you can tell me now and I'll make sure that whoever we get, is just like the person you want." I said, trying to avoid the fact that Mrs Kowalski would be with us in two days' time to meet the girls.

"Well, she's got to be kind."

"And she has to be pretty," chipped in Amy.

"Yes, that's important too," a supportive Emily said to her little sister. "But also, she needs to be fun, enjoy going out to the play park, riding a bike, making stuff out of, well, just about anything, likes ponies, good at colouring-in, can play an instrument, can read a good story, must never be cross with us, can play football and like Manchester United like Grandad used to before he died." The last bit about Grandad brought a broad smile across my face. I had told the girls from an early age all about their other grandad, my dad. I thought it was important that they knew that they did have another set of grandparents but unfortunately, they had died before they were born. The fact that Emily had now brought my dad into the list of their requirements for a nanny made me both smile and feel immensely proud of my little girls.

"Well, that's a big list! But I'm sure there is someone out there who will meet all your requirements. In fact, I have a lady coming to the house on Wednesday who has applied for the position. I would like you girls to meet her to see if she comes up to scratch, and if you don't like her for any reason, we'll keep looking until we find the right person. What do you think?"

"Can we ask her some questions?" asked Amy.

"Of course, you can sweetheart, as many questions as you like. In fact, I think you should bring your list along with you, so you don't forget anything!"

"Thanks Daddy. I hope she is pretty," said Amy. With that, the conversation stopped about the nanny and we moved on around the rest of the zoo, visiting the penguins, butterfly enclosure, lions, llamas, tigers, and the reptile house before ending up back at the gorillas and saying a final goodbye to Kumbuka and his family. Home via McDonalds, two chicken nugget meals with plastic toys representing the latest children's film craze and a large, Big Mac meal for me!

Once again, the girls were exhausted by the time we got home. After a quick bath, brushing of the teeth, and a bedtime story; they were asleep inside an hour of our arrival. I sat in the lounge, switched on the television, and thought to myself what wonderful girls I have. An absolute credit to Cheryl. She would be so proud of them. The way they have coped with everything that has happened has been nothing short of incredible. I love them dearly and they are a constant reminder of my love for Cheryl too.

5

I picked the girls up from school on the day of the second interview at 3 p.m. as usual, and we walked back to the house. The girls appeared slightly agitated at the prospect of meeting Miss Kowalski so once we arrived at home, I sat them on the sofa in the lounge and went to the kitchen to pour some juice for them. When I returned, I put the glasses of juice on the coffee table, sat down on the sofa between Emily and Amy and put an arm around each of them.

"So, ladies, what are we going to ask Miss Kowalski then?"

"Daddy, do we really need a live-in nanny? I wish Mummy were here to look after us again," asked Emily.

"I know Emily, I know. I wish Mummy were here too. But we know that she can't be and although it is incredibly sad, we have to still remember all the times that Mummy was here."

"Yes Daddy, and I'm sure Mummy will make sure that whoever looks after us, will be just like the things on our list," said Amy as she took out a piece of neatly folded paper from her pocket and started to unfold it. This brought a big smile to my face, which in turn brought smiles to both Emily and Amy's faces.

"I'm glad you remembered your list!", I said. The next hour or so went quite quickly and, before long, the doorbell rang.

"Stay there, girls, I'll answer the door," and with that I got up and walked to the front door. As funny as it seems, I stopped halfway down the hall to glimpse in the mirror to examine my hair, clothes, and practise my smile! It was as if I was meeting a new girlfriend and had to create a good impression! Slightly embarrassed, I muttered 'silly sod' as I continued to the front door.

"Hello Miss Kowalski, good to see you again," I said, opening the door and extending my hand in readiness to receive hers for the obligatory, if not slightly awkward, handshake.

"Hello Mr Hart," came her reply and she also extended her hand.

"Please come in. Can I take your coat?"

"Yes, thank you." She removed her coat and handed it to me. I hung it in the closet and turned back to look at her. She was wearing a stylish, black, jacket and trousers, with a white blouse. She looked very 'business like' and a little nervous.

"Come through to the kitchen, would you like a cup of tea or coffee?"

"Tea would be very nice, thank you Mr Hart."

"Look, I know that we haven't decided anything yet and you haven't even met the girls. And you probably won't like your room and we haven't even talked about money or anything really; but, please call me George. I hate this Mr Hart business, it just doesn't feel right, okay?"

"Thank you, Mr - sorry, George, and please, you must call me Martyna." We smiled at each other, which appeared to lighten the atmosphere.

"Now I hope you have come prepared Martyna? The girls have drawn up a list of questions for you. Some are very tough! And I hope you like Manchester United!" I said preparing the tea.

"You are making me more nervous now," Martyna said, with a confident smile. "However, I do know about Manchester United."

"Great, that's one tick on the list. Seriously, I hope you don't mind, but the girls made a list of things that they wanted from their new nanny, and I said it would be okay to ask you some questions."

"No problem. I can't wait to meet them. Are they here already?"

"Yes, they are in the lounge. I told them to wait there, and I would come through with you when we were ready." I made the tea and then sat down at the kitchen table with Martyna. We chatted very easily for a few minutes and I got an instant warmth from her, and a feeling that she would be perfect for the girls. I then left Martyna in the kitchen and went into the lounge.

"Ok girls, Miss Kowalski is here, and I've made her a cup of tea. She is waiting in the kitchen and I thought I would bring her through to the lounge now, so that she can meet you guys and you can ask her your questions, is that okay?"

"Yes Daddy, I'm really looking forward to meeting her, really!" said Emily in a very grown-up manner.

"Is she as nervous as I am Daddy?" asked Amy. I moved closer to both of them and whispered to them so that Martyna couldn't hear me.

"I think she is. Probably more nervous, actually. But I'm sure you two will make her feel welcome."

"Of course, Daddy," said Emily. With that I went back to the kitchen to collect Martyna. I escorted Martyna into the lounge and offered her the armchair close to the front window. I sat down on the sofa in between the girls and did the introductions.

"Ok girls, this is Miss Kowalski, but she has told me I can call her Martyna. Martyna, this is Emily, who is eight and Amy, who is six."

"Hello Emily. Hello Amy. And please, you can also call me Martyna."

"Hello Martyna," came the soft and perfectly harmonious, yet slightly anxious response from the girls.

"Your dad told me so much about you both when I had my first interview, so I'm thrilled to actually meet you now. But it's all a bit daunting isn't it? I know I feel a bit scared, do you?"

"Well…, not really," came a confident response from Emily. "I thought I might be a bit scared, but you look really nice and…"

"Are you kind? Can you read nice stories?" interrupted Amy before Emily could finish her sentence.

"I always try to be kind and yes, I think I can read good stories. What kind of stories do you like Amy?"

"Normally, I like stories about Princesses and magic castles; and pirates, and dogs."

"We both do," said Emily interrupting Amy this time. "Do you like to make things out of cardboard or paper?"

"Oh yes. And I love drawing and painting and colouring in and playing with dollies and doing puzzles, riding ponies, playing the piano, singing, oh and of course Manchester United." Emily and Amy looked at each other, smiled and then looked back at Martyna.

"Will you ever get cross with us?" Amy asked in a quiet, inquisitive way. Both Emily and Amy appeared to wait with bated breath as to what Martyna would answer to this question.

"Well, your dad tells me you are both incredibly good girls, and you always try to behave and do the right things. So, I don't think I will ever need to get cross with you. But we all do things sometimes that we shouldn't, even me. So, when we do, it is up to the people around us to tell us. Not to be cross, but to explain why it was not right, so that we don't do those same things again. Shall we have a 'pinkie' promise between us, that we will never be cross with each other, but we will explain when we should maybe have done or said things differently, is that okay?" Martyna got out of her chair, walked over to the girls, knelt down, and held up the little finger on each of her hands. The girls, in turn, held up the little finger on their left and right hand respectively and linked with Martyna's. It sounds a bit silly, but it felt like a connection had been made between the three of them, and it made me feel incredibly happy and content.

I told the girls and Martyna that I needed to do something in the garden and left the room so that they could continue their conversation and really get to know one another. After twenty minutes of pottering around, I returned to the house to find the lounge empty. I could hear the girls' voices upstairs. I proceeded up the stairs to their bedroom and found all three of them on the floor, playing with the girls' gigantic floor puzzles. Martyna noticed me approaching, looked up and smiled at me.

"We're doing just fine," she whispered to me and continued to play with the girls. I smiled back and made a hasty retreat down the stairs, into the kitchen and made a fresh cup of coffee. Martyna seemed at perfect ease with my girls and, in turn, Emily and Amy appeared to be extremely content in Martyna's company. Maybe things would start to get better for all of us now. I just hoped that Martyna would agree to my offer and would like to come and live with us.

After about an hour, Emily, Amy and Martyna came down the stairs, still deep in conversation, this time about some boy band, and whether or not they would ever get back together again? When they arrived in the kitchen, I asked Martyna if she minded waiting in the kitchen whilst I had a quick 'chat' with Emily and Amy in the lounge. Of course, she said, she did not mind at all, so I led the girls into the lounge, closing the door behind me.

"Well, you two, what do you think of Martyna?"

"She's brilliant," said Amy. "Can she stay for tea?"

"Yes Daddy, Martyna is really nice. I think she would make a wonderful nanny for us. I do hope she says yes and agrees to come and live with us," said Emily.

"Are you sure girls? Do you want some time to think about it? We don't have to make a decision today," I replied.

"Do you like her Daddy?" asked Amy, which in a strange way knocked me back a bit. Was Amy asking me if I liked Martyna as an employee, a nanny to the children? Or was she asking me if I liked Martyna as a person, a friend, a woman, a girlfriend perhaps?

"I like Martyna very much," I said, and it was true, I liked her for all those reasons. But first and foremost, as a nanny to the children!

"Then please go and ask her to stay Daddy, please," said Amy, but before I could respond, Emily looked at me with a concerned expression on her face.

"What is it Emily? What's wrong?"

"Martyna is lovely and I would like her to be our nanny. Only, she will not be replacing Mummy, will she?" To be honest, I would have expected this question to come from Amy, not Emily.

"Emily, Amy," I said holding each girl's hand. "Nobody will ever replace Mummy, okay? If Martyna agrees to be our new nanny and I hope she does, she will not become your mummy. She will look after you, care for you and help you with lots of things. Martyna will collect you from school, take you places, help you with your homework, your reading, and maybe teach you the piano, or even Polish. She will not become your mummy. Mummy, will always be mummy."

"Thank you, Daddy," said Emily which was promptly followed by a big three-way hug.

"Now, shall I go and talk to Martyna? You stay in here for a bit, while I try to convince her to be our new nanny, okay?" With that, I left the lounge and went back into the kitchen. Martyna was sitting at the kitchen table, legs crossed and hands resting on her upper knee. She gave me a lovely broad smile, and her green eyes appeared to shimmer, as I sat down on the opposite side of the table.

"Well, you've made quite an impression on Emily and Amy," I said as I picked up my coffee cup.

"They have made quite an impression on me too."

"That's genuinely nice of you to say so Martyna. Look, I am not going to beat around the bush with this. If you would like the position, it is yours. I will call the agency and we can get things moving. I hope you had a look around upstairs. I am sure the girls showed you what would be your room. I know it's not much, and probably not what you are used to having previously worked for that family in Holland Park, and probably the benefits you got from there were terrific too. Plus, you would need to do a bit of cooking and cleaning - I'm sure the Holland Park family had specific cleaners and cooks to do all that stuff, and…"

"George. I accept the offer," interrupted Martyna. "So long as I get to drive the Ferrari at weekends!" she said, again with that dazzling smile of hers. I smiled back.

"Thank you Martyna."

"No, thank you George. Your girls are wonderful and that is what attracts me to the job. Not the house, my room, the car I drive, what my duties are or any benefits," she said. "Not that there is anything wrong with your house or anything else." Which was very comforting to hear, however, it wasn't because of me either, which somehow in a silly way deflated me a little bit. "And of course, you George, I like you," she added. Phew! She does like me a bit. Now this was probably just a reference to liking me as a person or an employer, but you know what men are like. Now, don't get me wrong, I was not about to fall deeply in love with this woman, however it gave the old self-confidence a bit of a boost to hear a young, extremely attractive woman tell you that she likes you!

After going through the details of my offer with Martyna, and some additional small talk, Martyna said goodbye to us and left. I offered to drive her back, but she insisted on taking the tube, stating that she did not want me to drag the girls out of the house at that time of night. I telephoned the agency the next morning and everything was arranged. The starting date would be in two weeks' time.

Once this had all been agreed, I thought I should inform Barbara and Derek, and of course, Sally. So, on the weekend before Martyna started, I took the kids to see their grandparents. It was the usual warm welcome when we arrived, with both Barbara and Derek making a fuss of the girls, and me! Once inside their house, the girls went upstairs to play in 'Nanny Barbara's Magic Room', just a normal bedroom to me and you, but to the girls, a magic room filled with strange and wonderful objects that Nanny Barbara had collected over the years.

"Coffee, George?" said Barbara as we walked into the kitchen. Derek and I sat at the kitchen table.

"Yes please, Barbara. That would be great."

"Me too, Babs," said Derek.

"Yes, I know you want one. You always do!" came a snappy response from Barbara. "You drink far too much coffee you do," she continued. It felt a bit frosty between them so I was wondering whether, it would be a good idea to tell them about Martyna. However, that was the reason I was there, so I thought I might as well push on with it.

"Barbara, obviously you know that I have been looking for a nanny to help me out with the girls, and indeed you and Sally have been really helpful in the process, and I want to say thank you for all that help and support."

"That's okay, George. It was my pleasure. And besides, someone had to keep you on the right track and stop you from hiring that dreadful Polish girl," came the swift response from Barbara. However, it did not stop there as she continued. "Her eyes were too close together and I thought I detected a slight body odour problem. Probably only washes once a week. You know, I think she must have been fired from her previous position - stealing or flirting too much with the children's father. You can never trust these foreign girls you know!"

"Right… Erm, well the thing is, I have hired someone."

"Really George, well who is it? What's her name? I'm assuming that it is a 'she' of course, you never know what to expect these days, do you! I hope it is a nice English girl, good teeth and strongly built to take on the rigours of looking after my grandchildren. Well? Go on?"

"Well, actually, I have hired Miss Kowalski, Martyna erm - the Polish girl," I somehow managed to stutter out of my mouth, anticipating the tirade of anger, disappointment and resentment, wrapped up in an old 'head mistress' tone of voice that I believed was about to erupt! Instead, Barbara burst into uncontrollable laughter; swiftly followed by Derek!

"Am I missing something?" I gingerly enquired between the shrieks of laughter. "Barbara, what's so funny?"

"George, my dear boy. I am so sorry. I talked to Sally last week and she told me that a couple of weeks ago she was on her way round to see you when she saw your Miss Kowalski enter the house. She had some calls to make, so waited in her car near to your house and, after a while, she saw her leave. She thought you were, you know, having some fun shall we say, until she also saw the girls waving goodbye to Miss Kowalski when she left. She put two and two together and thought you must have hired her. So, I thought, right you little bugger, I'll give you a hard time about her, when you come to tell us about it, as payback for not telling us in advance."

"That's cheeky of you," I said smiling with relief.

"But seriously George, she is exceptionally good and probably very right for both the girls and you. She, of course, will never be Cheryl. She will never be the girls' mother. But I have a feeling, she will be great for all of you. So really, I'm rather pleased. However, I am sorry for playing my little trick on you. Derek told me not to, and that is why we were arguing prior to you getting here. And he was probably right," she said, turning to Derek. "Sorry Derek," she continued and gave him a smile and big kiss.

"Thank you, Barbara. I know Martyna is the right choice. But it wouldn't have felt quite right without your blessing."

"Oh, come here George," and with that Barbara leant forward and cuddled me. The rest of the day was spent playing board games and watching Frozen (for the thirty-seventh time, I think!) with the girls and Barbara. Derek went for a nap as he just could not keep his eyes open during the film, and I must admit to having sympathy for him as I too, fell asleep!

After the film came the hearty Sunday Tea spread! This was a Barbara speciality -whereby the dining room table would be filled with a finger buffet, including a variety of meats, salad, buttered bread triangles, a tin of salmon, pickles, cheeses of all varieties, tomatoes, cucumber slices, dressings, sausage rolls and just about anything else you could think of! On top of that, there was always the desserts, always cake and then something else like trifle, or ice cream, or fresh fruit salad and pouring cream. The girls absolutely loved Barbara's Sunday spread and always tucked in vigorously; so much so, that I often thought they would feel ill on the way home. They never did, of course, and as usual, fell asleep the moment I pulled the car off their grandparent's drive.

When we arrived home, it was a case of a quick shower for the girls, teeth brushed, a bedtime story and a five minute cuddle on my bed. Then straight to sleep in their own beds. The girls had always been great at going to bed without any fuss. I had often heard stories from work colleagues about how their children were a 'nightmare' at going to bed. Crying, kicking, screaming, wanting to stay up and deliberately wetting their beds -were some of the things that frequently got mentioned. I used to listen to them in amazement, and although I should have felt some sympathy for my colleagues, I did not. To my mind, it was their own fault. Allowing their children to dictate to them how things were going to be, instead of the other way round! So, no! No sympathy from me. My girls were brought up to respect their parents and if they were asked to do something by them, then that is what they did. Obviously, there were occasions when the whingeing and moaning would start, but if you were consistent, they soon realised that there was no point in trying to get their own way, they would not win. It is hard work for the parent, but worthwhile in the end. I am afraid to say that this is why so many children today are not well behaved. It is because consistency takes time, effort, and hard work. It is not easy to keep repeating yourself with small children, but it is how they learn. Most parents today want to be their child's best friend at all costs. That means giving in to them, which allows the child to start to manipulate the parent. Sorry, I digress! Enough of the parenting lesson, I think!

6

It was 9 a.m. on Monday morning, and I had just arrived back home after dropping the girls off for school. Just enough time to get the coffee going, before Martyna arrived on her first day. I had previously asked her if it would be okay if she arrived after the girls had gone to school, so she could have time to settle in during the day, before collecting them at home time. She agreed and thought it was a good idea. Martyna had already started moving in some of her personal possessions during the previous couple of weeks, which also helped in cementing her relationship with the girls. Every time she popped in with something, she ended up spending an hour or so playing, and talking with the girls.

The doorbell rang at 9:20 a.m. and I made my way to the front door to greet Martyna. Once again, I checked my appearance in the hallway mirror before answering the door to her. The difference today being that as I was about to go to work, my first full day really since Cheryl's passing, and was wearing a suit and tie, something Martyna had never seen me in before.

"Hi Martyna," I said as I opened the door, but to my surprise, I was greeted with a huge cardboard box!

"Hi George," came the muffled reply from behind the box. "A little help please?"

"Here, let me take that from you," I said in my most gallant voice. Although I was expecting the box not to be too substantial, you know heavy for a girl, but not a strapping bloke like myself, I almost dropped it as I took it from her. It was bloody heavy!

"Please don't drop it George, it is very valuable to me," Martyna said, and I think she sensed that I was shocked at its weightiness!

"No worries Martyna. But all the same, what is in here? It's monstrous!"

"Ah, now George, in that box is my history, my soul, my pleasure, my sadness, my pain and my happiness. It grows each year of my passing life and it never ceases to amaze me how often I turn to it in times of comfort, anger, love, hate-"

"I get it! It's your cd collection, right?"

"Of course," came the soft response, immediately followed by a broad smile. "Very clever George." Martyna then proceeded to look me up and down before commenting "And very smart George. You look every bit the sharp businessman, very smart indeed," again ending with a big, broad smile.

"Thank you Martyna, I try to make the most of what I have," I said modestly. "But if you don't mind, I'm going to run this 'slightly' heavy box straight up to your room."

"Thank you, George, I'll unpack it during the day."

When I returned from Martyna's room, I entered the kitchen to find Martyna pouring the coffee.

"Hope you don't mind George, I saw that the filter coffee was ready, so thought I would pour some for you, okay?"

"Excellent Martyna, just what I need after lifting that box! Tell me, how did you struggle over here on your own with it?"

"I got a taxi. The driver was most unhelpful! He said he couldn't help me with the box because of some sort of Health & Safety issue and that if he dropped it, I would probably sue him. Therefore, I had to put the box in the car myself and struggle getting it out again this end."

"Yes, I'm afraid some people are not the most helpful," I said. "But never mind, you got it, and yourself here in the end."

We started to drink our coffee and then Martyna looked at me quizzically.

"Anything wrong?" I asked.

"George, I know that this is my first day and I will definitely be picking the children up from school, but I do have a few more things to pick up from my old place and I was wondering if you had managed to - goodness this sounds really awful and you must think really badly of me; but did you manage to sort out a car for me? I'm really sorry, don't worry about it, I'll just take a few taxis, shouldn't take long, definitely be back in time to pick up the children."

How do I play this I thought to myself? Do I become all apologetic and tell her I am really sorry, but I haven't had time to sort out the car yet and make her feel even more upset about having to bring the subject up? Or do I just tell her the truth and hand over the keys to the brand, new Ford Fiesta parked out the front!

"Martyna please do not feel guilty about asking me for something that we have already agreed upon in our contract. In fact, please don't feel reluctant or apprehensive about asking me anything. I don't think badly of you at all for bringing this up. You need to have a car to get around and for the girls as well, so please, you must always talk to me if there is anything bothering you, okay?"

"Sorry George, it's just I know how much you have to do, and how much is on your mind all the time, I just don't like to bother you, especially on my first day, within my first ten minutes! Wow, I'm really sorry George."

"If you apologise one more time then I will start to get upset with you! Please remember, although I have employed you as a nanny to my girls, I already see you as part of this family, not an employee. You can talk to me about anything, do you hear, anything! And as for the subject matter at hand, yes, I did manage to get you a car. Might not be what you are used to, but it's parked outside, the white fiesta, four doors, brand new and awaiting its new driver, one Miss Martyna Kowalski! Here are the keys," I said handing over two sets to Martyna. She took them slowly from my hand and looked up at me with her big, green eyes.

"I was going to say sorry again. But I'm just going to say thank you George. Thank you for everything." And with that she put her arms around my neck and gave me a big hug. "Now look George, I don't want you to be late for your first full day back at work. You can leave me now; I will be fine. As I said, I just need to collect a few more things and I will be done. I'll collect the children from school, and we can start making dinner. What time do you think you will be in tonight?"

"Not really sure Martyna. Probably best if you don't make dinner for me, I'll sort myself out today. Just tell the girls that if I am a bit late, I will definitely come and say goodnight to them. And by the way, here are a set of keys for the house. You won't get very far today without them!"

"Thanks again George and no worries about dinner. You get off and I'll see you later."

"Thanks, Martyna. Just one more thing. I think you will either get a visit or at least a phone call from Barbara today. Just to see how you are settling in, you know. Don't take it personally, she absolutely adores her grandchildren and just wants to make sure everything is okay."

"No problem George. I would do the same thing if they were my grandchildren too! Have a great day and please don't worry about anything."

"You do have my contact number in case of an emergency, right?"

"Yes, of course I do. But please don't worry, everything will be fine, and I will see you later tonight. Take care." I left the house, got into my car, and started the thirty minute drive to my office.

Once I had arrived at the office, parked my car, and entered the building, a strange feeling came over me. This was my first full day back at work for more than a year. I had done the odd days and quite a lot of 'home office' work to keep up to speed. I had kept in regular contact with my boss, a German lady based in our headquarters in Frankfurt, Germany. Her name was Tanja Weber, a kind woman in her early fifties, who spoke exceptionally good English, having spent many years living in Washington DC. However, her accent had a definite English tint, rather than that of an American native. She was the Vice President of EMEA (Europe, Middle East & Africa) responsible for sales and mergers and acquisitions for the region.

I had impressed Tanja some years earlier, when I was working for the UK region on a joint European Catering tender for an American airline, involving multiple European cities, including Frankfurt. As Project Manager for the tender, she witnessed 'first-hand' my organisation, people management, creativity and negotiating skills which she immediately identified with, being of a similar ilk. In those days, prior to having children, work kept me apart from Cheryl for long days at a time. When tenders were happening, it would not be uncommon for me to get to the office early, stay extremely late, go home, creep into bed without disturbing Cheryl and not actually see the person I loved and was living with, for days on end. If the tender were happening overseas, I could be away for a week at a time.

Cheryl obviously understood this and was always incredibly supportive. That was one of her strengths that I always admired her for. She knew that I had a passion for my job and was good at it. She also knew that the financial rewards were there for both of us, and therefore, it came as second nature to her to be sympathetic to my somewhat disruptive lifestyle. I obviously reciprocated this support for

Cheryl's work as a teacher. We both took an interest in each other's career and would often talk into the night about what we had done that day, seeking advice from one another. Obviously, things changed when first Emily, and then Amy arrived. Cheryl took a step back from her career to concentrate on the girls, but never forgot to be supportive of me.

I also tried hard to reduce the number of hours I was doing, and so we somehow adjusted our lives and lifestyle accordingly. I have to say, having the girls gave me the best excuse in the world to reduce my workload. My boss, Tanja, could never have children but was so pleased for us and totally understood my situation. She became so close to us a family that she is Godmother to both Emily and Amy!

As the lift finally stopped at the third floor, I felt my stomach start to churn. On exiting the lift - directly in front - there was a long walkway, flanked either side by row upon row of desks, where the customer service managers sat. At the end of the walkway, sat Sarah Castle - the twenty-five year old, sex-bomb secretary to the UK Vice President. Behind her were three individual offices belonging to Frank Stanley, the UK Vice President (naturally, he had the biggest office), Hilary Smith, HR Vice President (second biggest office), and my office (smallest, but a corner office that had views out to Heathrow airport).

Because I did not report to anyone in the UK, I was perceived as a bit of a threat to the UK leadership team (a sort of spy for our German headquarters if you like). Therefore, I got the smallest office as a sort of punishment!

Now normally, you would only be able to hold your hand up and mouth 'Morning' to everybody that you passed, heading towards Sarah because they would inevitably be on the telephone talking to customers. A real buzz of noise and activity, with the reciprocal hand in the air and nod of 'Morning' coming back in your direction. Today, however, was different. It just had to be different didn't it! As the lift doors opened, there were no phones ringing, no one talking to customers, and an almost deafening silence!

I started to walk slowly out of the lift and along the corridor, hoping to get to my office before anyone would actually see me.

"Hey George, good to see you," came the words from Gavin Preston, a customer Service Manager looking after UK 'Low Cost' airlines. Gavin was a nice guy, someone you could have a laugh with, but took his job seriously. He was one to watch for future progression within the company.

"Hi Gavin. Still hard at it I see?"

"You know it's true," came Gavin's response and in that one instant, all my concerns and fears about people being overly sad for me about Cheryl, evaporated. I even managed to speak to practically everyone up the corridor and thought I had made it without any depressing comments about my tragic loss. That is until I came upon Sarah Castle. The instant she saw me, she backed her chair away from her desk, swung round her lovely, long legs on her swivel seat, stood and slowly walked around her desk, revealing she was wearing a tiny, short skirt; a white, sheer blouse and what appeared to be a pink, balconette bra. She strolled up to me, pressed her body against mine, and put her arms around my neck whilst cupping the back of my head with her left hand!

"Oh George, I'm so sorry about Cheryl," she said. "You must be devastated and those poor little girls you have, alone without a mother. You must be so sad, and depressed. If there is anything you need, and I mean anything, you just let me know, you hear. I think you must be the bravest man in the world. I know I just could not carry on if something like this happened to me. Remember George, anything at all."

"Thanks Sarah," came my somewhat embarrassed response. "But really, I'm fine. I just need to get back to some sort of normality and you can help me with that by just being normal yourself, okay? But thanks again for your caring words and compassion, I really appreciate it." With that, Sarah relinquished her hold on me, smiled, wiped a tear from her eye and went back to her swivel chair.

"Oh, and a cup of coffee would be great," I said as I entered the sanctity of my office, closing the door behind me. As I sat down in my chair, I swivelled around and took in the view of London Heathrow Airport. I must have just sat there for a good ten minutes just watching the planes take off, before my trance was broken by the sound of knocking on my door.

"Come in."

"White no sugar, that's right George isn't it?" Sarah said placing a cup of coffee on my desk. "And remember George, anything!" she continued, as she turned and walked like a model on the catwalk back to the door, looking round at me and winking, before finally making her exit and closing the door behind her. Now I am only human, and a man at that! Weak, easily-lead, and all too easily transformed into a teenage boy when pretty girls take an interest. Now before, I was a happily married man, having regular sex, enjoying the passion and animalistic pleasures of intimacy with the woman I loved, and the mother of my two beautiful daughters. But I have to say that my eyes did not leave Sarah's backside as she walked away from me to the door. So pert were her buttocks; beautifully formed (without the need for conventional knickers as there was no vpl!) under that skin-tight short skirt, that I found myself for a split second imagining what it would be like to have sex with this young woman. Luckily, the moment she turned to look at me, my eyes immediately met hers - I think I got away with it.

Although Sarah was 'hot' and quite flirty, she was also particularly good at her job, and I had in the past asked Frank why he had not developed her career more and given her more responsibility. Frank always said, he was not sure if that is what she wanted, so he did not push her. It was a shame, I thought she had potential.

I had taken just one sip of my coffee when the office phone rang. It was Frank.

"Hey George, good to see you back. I'm sorry about what happened, you know, with Cheryl."

"Hey Frank, thanks. Things have been tough, but we are trying hard to get back to some sort of normality, hence I am back to work and looking forward to the challenges ahead. What can I do for you?"

"Do you have a minute? Come over to my office, there's some things I need to talk to you about."

"Sure Frank, but you do know that Tanja will be here soon. She has some news for me and wants to discuss what I will be working on."

"I know, that's what I want to talk to you about. Come over in five minutes, I just have to make a quick phone call, okay?"

"Okay, Frank," I said, hanging up.

Frank was a good guy deep down. As I have mentioned, the UK team were always a bit suspicious of me since I reported into Frankfurt. However, Frank did trust me and respected the work I did for the company, often for the good and financial benefit of the UK region. So, I was intrigued as to what he was going to tell me. I finished my coffee and walked over to Frank's office, passing Sarah's desk. As I passed, Sarah looked up and just gave me a big smile, said nothing, and returned to typing on her laptop. I knocked on Frank's door and was called in.

"George, sit down my friend. Look before we start, I just wanted to say that I genuinely can sympathise with you as you know. Marie has been dead for five years now, and not a day goes by when I don't think about her. Obviously, my kids are now grown up and can look after themselves, although I still get the 'Dad can you...' phone call every now and then. I suppose they will always be your kids right? But what I am saying is, if you need to talk to someone, I'm your man, okay, George?"

"Thanks Frank, I really appreciate it," I said, genuinely touched, as I knew that Frank had sincerely just made that offer. You see, Frank lost his wife to breast cancer five years ago, and although his two children were fifteen and seventeen at the time, he went through a difficult time of adjustment with his family. Even though they had time to come to terms with the inevitability of the breast cancer prior to Marie's passing, it seemed to make it more difficult for them as a family. It was as if each day they thought a cure would be found, right up to the day Marie died. Frank was probably the one person who really understood what I was going through. Knowing how badly he had suffered; it was quite a task for him to talk to me in that way. It must have brought back so many traumatic feelings and tangible pain for him.

"Now, I'm not sure how much you know, or if Tanja has mentioned anything to you yet, but the company is looking to expand. We are looking at opening new catering facilities in Sub Sahara Africa. There is a market out there, and it is ripe for a global company like ours to invest in. Sure, they currently have catering units at the big African airports: Johannesburg, Nairobi, Accra, Addis Ababa, etc., but those catering facilities are run by local companies who have no idea about hygiene, HACCP, procedures, operations and most importantly International Airlines. Nigel told me last week that if things go ahead and I was willing, I could head up the Sub Sahara Region. What do you think of that?"

Nigel Colnbrooke was the Senior Vice President of Global Operations based in Frankfurt. He was the sort of guy who was always looking for his next career move and knew how to use others to get it. If Frank did a good job in the new region and being chosen by Nigel, then it could open up his path to becoming a board member.

"Well, I was aware of some movement in that area, but I have not heard anything official yet. Maybe that is what Tanja is here to see me about today. But if there is any truth in it, it looks like Nigel has found his man," I said trying to sound enthusiastic for Frank. The thing is, I knew how Nigel operated. He would have probably said the same thing to half a dozen country Vice Presidents, trying to get them all worked up and on his side. He was great at doing that when promotions were in the air, or new positions opened up. Then, when someone was eventually chosen, he would carefully point out to the unsuccessful applicants that the decision was 'taken out of his hands,' and no matter how hard he fought for that individual, the Board overruled him. I had never really trusted Nigel and I think he knew that I had worked him out. I did not have many dealings with him, but when I did, it was strictly professional, and I never gave him the opportunity to manipulate me.

"If I become the Sub Sahara Regional Vice President, I would need someone I trusted to look after the Sales and Services," continued Frank. "And I can't think of a better person than you George. Would you be interested in that?"

"I think we're getting a bit ahead of ourselves Frank. Let us just see what develops," I responded trying to dampen the situation. I knew that Frank would be devastated if all this went ahead, and he was not chosen for the position. So, I continued playing down the scenario for the next five minutes and eventually Frank understood that maybe he was getting a bit carried away with the whole thing. I left Frank's office and returned to my own, again swivelling in my chair to watch the morning's flight activity at Heathrow airport.

Thirty minutes later, there was a slight tap on my door, and then it slowly opened. I looked up from the emails I was catching up with on my laptop and knew instantly that Tanja was about to come through the door. She always knocked softly, before slowly coming into my office. Normally, my office door was always open, and I would usually see her before she entered, but today, I just wanted a little privacy.

"Hey Tanja, how are you?"

"Oh George, I'm just fine but more importantly, how are you?" came the concerned reply from Tanja. She crossed my office floor, I got up from behind my desk and we embraced. Tanja gave me a good, warm, tight hug and whispered in my ear "No tears, I promised myself no tears!" After releasing from our embrace, we sat opposite each other across my desk.

"And how are my beautiful girls, George? Are they coping okay?" It was a moment that caught me by surprise. Knowing how much Tanja cared for Emily and Amy, and how painful the whole experience was to her personally, brought a lump to my throat and I felt a slight dampness in my eyes.

"They're coping well. As well as can be expected." Tanja obviously sensed the sadness from my reply and could see the sorrow in my eyes.

"I'm sorry George. You know, with a father like you and the support of Cheryl's parents and of course, you can always count on me to help in any way I can, your little girls will not be sad. They will know only love and will always carry their mother with them in their hearts. They will remember her with happiness and will grow up into adorable, intelligent, beautiful young ladies of whom you will be so proud. Don't be sad George."

"Thank you, Tanja. No tears, right?"

"No tears," and with that, a sigh of relief, was let out by both of us, and we knew that we could now start to continue our professional relationship once again.

7

The meeting with Tanja lasted for about an hour and a half. When we had finished, Tanja said that she had ordered a cab to take her to the airport because she felt I needed some time to think, and to go home early to see my 'lovely children' as she put it! Ordinarily, I would have taken Tanja back to the airport myself, but she was insistent that it was not necessary on this occasion. As soon as she had left the building, the anticipated call on my office phone line that I was expecting, arrived.

"Has she gone?"

"Yes Frank, you know she has gone, I saw you peeping through your office door as I was seeing Tanja out of the building."

"Can I come and have a chat?"

"Yes mate, come over," I said and hung up. Within a matter of five seconds, Frank was standing in my doorway. I beckoned him in, and he entered, closing the door behind him.

"So, what did she have to say? Any news?" I smiled at Frank and took a brief, but thoughtful pause before responding to this man sitting in front of me, who at this moment in time, resembled a small child eager to find out from his brother if their mum had let on what he was getting for his birthday!

"Well mate, there is some truth in the rumours about expansion within Sub Sahara Africa. I have to attend a meeting next week in Frankfurt with Tanja, Nigel and a few others to discuss the next steps and possible fact-finding visits to several African cities."

"Nigel, eh! But what others? Not Country Vice Presidents?" said Frank, with trepidation.

"No, I don't think so. Probably corporate finance and the M&A department, you know those guys always like to be involved."

"Yeah, good, I'm sure that's who it will be. Too early for anybody else, at the moment. No decisions to be made yet. Yes, that's what it will be," said Frank, processing this information in his mind.

"Probably Frank. I will know more after next week's meeting. Until then, we just have to wait and see."

"Yes, that's right. Play it cool. You are a good man George, and I think we work well together. It would be great to work with you down there. I think we would make the ideal team."

"Whoa Frank! Let's just wait, and see," I said and gave Frank a look which told him the conversation was now closed. Frank thanked me and left my office. I'm not sure if he was pleased and positive, or angry and annoyed, but either way, I was grateful he had left.

Now it was my turn to think. It was my turn to go over in my mind what Tanja had discussed with me. I looked at my scribbled notes from the meeting, desperately hoping that they made enough sense for me to remember everything that had been said. I was always particularly good at making notes during any meeting I had. You never know when someone might try to deny they had said something, or try to back track on an agreement. Therefore, I always made sure that my notes were clear and concise. As I looked at my notes from my meeting with Tanja, all I could see were cuboids and crosses, funny shapes, and squiggly lines! There were the odd words and sentences that made sense, of course. I knew my concentration had drifted a couple of times during our conversation and I knew that it was because my thoughts had turned to Emily, Amy, Cheryl and oddly enough, Martyna. I hoped there was enough legible notes for me to prepare myself for next week's meeting in Frankfurt!

After finishing up some paperwork and making a few calls to colleagues and customers, I decided to call it a day. The first part of each of the calls had all been similar; the person on the other end asking concerned, but ultimately predictable questions about how I was, and how were the girls coping. My reply became somewhat polished, so much so that by the third call, I was almost answering the other person's questions before they had even asked them! The day passed steadily, and although it was only 4:45p.m. I thought it wouldn't be inappropriate for me to leave the office, bearing in mind it was my first official day back. I said my goodbyes as I walked through the open office to the lift and felt relieved to be inside it. The doors closed, and I was on my way down to the ground floor. I thought I would let Martyna, and the girls know that I would be home soon, and that we could all have dinner together. However, just as I was about to dial her number, my phone rang. It as Luke.

"Hey Luke," I said, genuinely pleased to hear from him.

"Hi George. Am I disturbing you?"

"No, Not at all. In fact, I've just finished for the day, I'm in the car and about to drive home to have dinner with the girls and Martyna."

"Great mate. But I was wondering do you fancy a quick drink somewhere? I've just finished too and knowing it was your first day back and all that, I wondered if you needed a friendly face to let all the frustration out on from all the constant sympathising that I'm sure you've had today. Well?"

"Do you know what Luke; you are spot on as usual. I could do with seeing you and I did tell Martyna I might be late tonight. Sounds like a great idea," I said with a smile on my face.

"The usual place?" said Luke, knowing that although the 'usual place' had many memories of Cheryl for me, I would also be comforted by going there.

"Yes, the usual place. See you in forty minutes?"

"Great, see you then mate," Luke replied.

"And drive carefully Luke." The 'drive carefully' was just something I had got used to saying to people since Cheryl's accident.

I called Martyna, and said I was on my way home but would be just parking the car before meeting a friend for a drink, so not to be surprised if she saw my car outside. Martyna was cool about this and told me to enjoy myself. She was already having fun with the girls anyway, and Dad would probably ruin that! The pub I was meeting Luke in, was a ten minute walk from my house called Mulligans. Cheryl and I often met Luke and Sally there for drinks after work in our early days before the children came along. We always felt a sense of loyalty to the place, even when our visits started to dwindle.

It was a traditional pub, cosy, great clientele, and we were well known to the landlord and the staff. In fact, Luke and I used to go to school with the pretty looking, strawberry blonde girl now working behind the bar. Her name was Samantha Williamson; I always had a soft spot for her, and I think she knew it. We used to sit next to each other in English classes. It was not by choice though! The class had become so disruptive that one day the teacher, Miss Bewley, decided that she would create a seating plan herself and if the students didn't like it, they could sit outside the classroom in the hallway, on their own! Needless to say, half of the class sat in the hallway for the first few lessons; but to Miss Bewley's credit, she persevered with her plan and eventually everyone came back to the classroom and sat with their designated partner.

I felt rather fortunate that I had been given the opportunity to sit with Samantha! Although not the prettiest girl in the school at that time, she had a charm and calmness about her that immediately drew all the boys' attention. Mine included. And because she was neither 'Miss Popular' and, therefore, in the cool girls' camp, nor 'Miss Geeky' and therefore, pigeon-holed into the freaky, geeky group, she didn't seem to have too many friends! From the moment we looked at each other and commented on 'making the most of the situation' we became good friends, which lasted until I left to go to University. We sort of lost touch after that, but soon found each other again when she turned up in Mulligans behind the bar. She is still very much the same today, quiet, calm, charming, and even more beautiful today than she was back in school. Striking, natural, strawberry blonde hair, extremely fit, but always lacking a little in confidence. She had some problems with two previous marriages that really didn't last long at all, and that seemed to add to her confidence issues.

As I approached the pub, I saw Luke walking towards me from the opposite direction.

"Hello mate," I said with the usual smile on my face that always seemed to appear when I met Luke.

"Hello George," came his instant reply, with the same smile, reflecting back at me. We embraced as full bloodied, manly, heterosexual males do (a big hug and slap on each other's back) and promptly entered Mulligans!

"So, my old mate, how was the first day back?" said Luke as we waited at the bar. Whilst awaiting my response, Luke caught the attention of Samantha and beckoned her over so he could order the drinks.

"Well after the initial slow walk through the office, waiting for the sympathetic comments, which incidentally didn't happen until I got to my office door, when Sarah Castle decided it was the right time to let me know how desperately sorry, she was and 'to let her know' if she could do anything for me; it wasn't too bad!" I replied with a wry smile on my face.

"You poor bastard!" was Luke's forthright response. "Hi Samantha," he continued as she stood in front of us.

"Hi guys. The usual?" Luke looked at me and with a quick nod I confirmed that 'the usual' would be fine by me.

"Yeah, thanks Samantha," confirmed Luke and he handed her a £10 note.

"Go and sit down, guys and I will bring it over to you. We're not that busy yet, and I could do with stretching my legs a bit," came Samantha's reply; and with that we turned away from the bar and found our usual table in the corner of the pub, by a window facing the street outside.

"So, mate. Tell me, how are you really, how are those lovely girls, how is Martyna? You know Sally has already told me a lot about her; and well, is there anything I can do for you?"

"Mate, both you and Sally have been great, and I really couldn't ask for any more support than what you two have given me. The girls and I really appreciate it and I know that somehow, somewhere, Cheryl is really thankful that you guys have been around to help us all get through this," I said, as the mere mention of Cheryl's name brought a moistness to Luke's eyes.

"Sorry mate," Luke said, wiping his eyes as he realised that I had noticed. "But I still feel so upset about it all. God knows how you feel or how you cope with all of this. All because of some stupid, fucked-up driver your life will never be the same."

"No one can prepare you for something like this. And yes, it's been very tough, emotional, and draining. And I've needed your support and Derek and Barbara's too, to help me cope with the situation. But in the end, there is nothing that anyone can do to bring Cheryl back. To bring back Emily and Amy's mum. So, we have to get on with things, and try to live life how Cheryl would have wanted us to. And that's exactly what I intend to do. Be a good dad, be a good friend and you never know, maybe someday be a good husband again."

"Husband?"

"Not now or in the immediate future, but you never know," I said with a big smile on my face. Luke started to smile too and looked happier.

"Still, what about this other driver? What happened?"

"I found out from the police that he was a family man as well and that his wife wanted to speak to me. I wasn't sure at first, but I decided that maybe it would be good to talk to her. After all, we were somehow in the same position and I thought it might help her as well. So, I told the police to give her my number and that it was okay if she wanted to call. A few days later the phone rang, and it was her."

"What did she say? How did she start a conversation like that? Christ, mate! What did you say to her?"

"It wasn't as awkward as you think. It wasn't as awkward as I thought either! She just introduced herself, and profoundly apologised for my loss, and said how sorry she was that Emily and Amy would never see their mum again. I thanked her and passed on my condolences regarding her husband. She then told me that her husband had had a heart attack whilst driving, which had caused him to lose control of the vehicle and subsequently crossed the central reservation causing the fatal crash. She has two boys aged fifteen and thirteen."

"God, I didn't even think about the story behind him, the other driver. She must be a bit messed up?"

"Yeah, I suppose so. And the more I talked to her, I realised that in many ways she has it worse than me. She has all the sadness and grief about losing her husband, and the father of her two boys, as I have about losing Cheryl, and the girls' mother. But she also seemed to be wrapped in guilt that her husband had caused not only his own death, but Cheryl's too. I couldn't let her keep thinking that way and told her that I do not blame anyone for this tragedy; and she needs to forgive her husband, and more importantly, herself. She thanked me and I told her if she ever wants to talk, to just call me."

"To just call you! How do you do it mate? I just couldn't do that. It would bring up all sorts of emotions for me that I just would not be able to cope with. How do you do it?"

"As I said earlier Luke, no one can prepare you for this sort of thing. And no one knows how they would really cope until they are faced with it. So, don't worry about it. I'm fine and you are fine and lets just move on, okay?" At that moment, Samantha arrived with our drinks.

"There you go boys, two pints of Stella and your change Luke."

"Hey Sam, you keep it. Thanks for bringing them over to us," replied Luke.

"Are you sure? Thanks Luke. How are you George?"

"Yeah, good thanks, Sam. How are you doing?"

"Yeah, okay, I think. You know I was thinking of you the other day. I was in Tesco's doing a bit of shopping and I looked down towards the end of the aisle and guess who I saw picking up a packet of frozen peas?"

"No idea I'm afraid Sam. Who was it?"

"Miss Bewley! You know, our old English teacher. Do you remember her?"

"Yes, I do. And I have to say the only reason I do remember her is because it was her English lessons that allowed me to sit next to you," I said hoping that Samantha had as fond a memory of those days as I did.

"Yeah, that's right. We used to sit together didn't we, after she split the whole class up. We used to chat about lots of things back then didn't we. I even thought that you might ask me out at one point, but I guess you weren't really interested in 'Skanky Samantha' were you," she said with a little smile forming across her lips.

"Skanky Samantha?" interjected Luke.

"Yeah, don't you remember that's what all the girls nicknamed me. Just because I wasn't one of the pretty, cool girls and wasn't exceptionally bright and clever like the geeky girls, I just got labelled 'Skanky Samantha' because they thought my red hair was dirty! Bloody cheek," she said, turning the smile into a bit of laugh.

"I thought you were great! And your hair was exceptionally beautiful. And I would have asked you out if I hadn't had the most terrible fear of rejection from you. It wasn't a case of not being interested, but a case of being too frightened you would say no," I said and smiled at Sam.

"You bloody fool George Hart! I would have loved to have been your girlfriend. You were so kind and thoughtful towards me, and every time you were with me, no one ever made any nasty comments to me. Not even Ben Wesley!"

"Ah, but that's not because of me. You have Luke here to thank for that," I said holding my hand out to Luke as a TV chat show host does when welcoming on a guest. "You see Luke put the 'frighteners' on Ben once, when I was having a spot of bother with that young man. Never bothered me again!" With that Samantha bent down so that she was level with Luke's face and gently kissed him on the cheek

"Thank you, Luke," she said and again gave him that infectious smile that she had. To be honest, for a microsecond I felt a tinge of jealousy that Sam had given Luke a kiss and not me. But this was soon to pass, when she turned from Luke to face me, bent down, and also gave me a soft kiss on the cheek. "Thank you too, George. If only, eh?" and with that she turned and started walking back to the bar.

"Cracking girl that Sam. I did fancy her myself, but I had an inkling you had a crush on her, so I left her alone," said Luke staring at Samantha walking away from us.

"Sorry mate. Didn't mean to ruin your chances." We looked at each other and started laughing.

We continued talking and catching up with what was going on in or lives. Sarah brought over more drinks and Luke told me how his son Ben was doing and the plans he and Sally had for the future. It was while he was talking about this subject that he suddenly stopped and realised that this might be upsetting me as 'future plans' was something that Cheryl and I had often talked about with Luke and Sally. About how we saw ourselves old and grey, living in a beachside villa somewhere in Spain; welcoming Emily and Amy, and their partners, and hopefully, their own children to our simple, idyllic retreat.

"Sorry George, I didn't mean to-"

"Hey mate, don't worry. I love hearing what you, Sally and Ben have planned and although you think it might upset me, let me tell you that it does completely the opposite. It makes me feel happy and so pleased for the both of you. So please, don't ever stop being you. Keep telling me everything as we have done since we were ten years old, Okay?"

"Thanks mate. So, what next then for you? Do you feel like getting back out there? You know, I mean getting active with, erm, you know, the ladies?"

"When you see something on tv or in a film about someone in my situation, most of the time the widower, or indeed widow seem to struggle with the thought of meeting someone new, or the thought of making love with anyone other than their dearly departed. Cheryl has been gone for over a year now, and I can honestly say that I have thought about other women for probably the last six months. You know the sort of thing; if I saw a pretty girl walking towards me I would think 'what would it be like to have sex with her' or 'I wonder what she looks like naked'. And do you know what? I don't feel guilty about that. I loved Cheryl with all my heart and while she was alive, I could never, ever imagine me being with anyone else for the rest of my life. But as much as I loved her and still do today, she's not coming back and I'm only human. I have needs, desires, wants! I'm sounding like an agony aunt now, I know. But the point I'm trying to make is, I have to make a new life for me and a new life for Emily and Amy. I can't just sit around and pine for Cheryl, and I'm absolutely certain that she wouldn't want me to. Do you understand?" I said looking into Luke's eyes hoping to get his approval of what I had just said.

"Abso-bloody-lutely mate!" came his response. "But just so that I'm very clear, that means you're interested in shagging again, right?" Once again, we both laughed out loud.

I shared with Luke the potential opportunities that might present themselves to me at my work. Although Luke seemed genuinely pleased and interested, I got the impression that he was a little worried that his best friend was going to desert him and leave for the untamed wilderness that was deepest Africa! I told him not to worry as nothing had been decided, and I had not even been offered anything yet. We continued talking, and at about 8:30 p.m. we decided that we should leave - Luke to go home to his beautiful wife and son, and me to my beautiful daughters, and the equally beautiful Martyna. After all, it was still her first day!

I Arrived at the gate to the house and just paused before entering. It was approaching 8:45 p.m. and I knew that the kids would already be in bed, probably not asleep yet, but in bed all the same. As I put my key in the door lock, I hesitated for a second and thought whether Martyna would be angry, or annoyed, or even upset, that I had not been there for her first dinner with the family. Perhaps it had been a little insensitive of me to go for a drink with Luke instead of going home for dinner with the girls and Martyna. The next thing I knew, I was in the local late-night Co-op, which was just down the road, buying a surprisingly, beautiful bunch of red roses, before running back home. As I entered the house, it was all noticeably quiet. I took off my coat, hung it up, removed my shoes and went into the kitchen.

To my surprise, Martyna was sitting at the breakfast bar, sipping a cup of peppermint tea.

"Hi George," she said with a big smile on her face. "I hope you have had a nice time with Luke. As it was my first day today, I made a traditional Polish meal for us, called Golabki. It's basically mincemeat with onions and rice, wrapped in a cabbage leaf. The girls absolutely loved it and really enjoyed helping to make it. I have left some for you, would you like me to get it for you?"

"I'm really sorry Martyna. It wasn't until I arrived here that I realised how incredibly insensitive I have been in not coming home for your first dinner with the family. I'm terribly sorry and as a way of an apology and a pathetic, desperate hope that you will forgive me, I bought these flowers for you," I replied and slowly handed them to her. To Martyna's credit, she took the flowers, gently sniffed them, looked back at me, and smiled.

"George, this is really thoughtful of you and I am deeply touched that you feel this way. But it really isn't necessary. I work for you and you owe me no explanations about where, or when, or who you meet. You let me know you were going to be late, and I really thank you for that. Some of my previous employers would not have been so thoughtful. Therefore, you have nothing to apologise for, and I have nothing to forgive you about. But thank you for the flowers, I really appreciate it," came the beautifully, soft, calm response from Martyna. "Now, do you want some dinner?"

"Thank you Martyna, but I will get it and maybe you can join me in a glass of wine? But first, I must just pop upstairs and say goodnight to Amy and Emily." With that, I left the kitchen and went upstairs to the girl's rooms. I looked in on each of them and they were both asleep. I carefully pulled their blankets up, and gently kissed their foreheads. I then proceeded back down to the kitchen, where Martyna had already prepared a plate of Golabki and was pouring out two glasses of an Australian chardonnay.

"Sorry George, I know you said you would get it, but it's no bother, really," said Martyna as I entered the kitchen.

"Thank you Martyna, and again, I'm really sorry. Tomorrow will be vastly different, I promise," was my somewhat grovelling response. We casually chatted as I devoured my meal, which incidentally was delicious, and both took another glass of wine through to the lounge and flopped on the settee.

"That was exceptionally good, the food I mean. What do you call it?"

"Golabki. It means 'Dove' or 'Pigeon'. We often eat it during the festive season or at family occasions like weddings. I'm glad you liked it."

"Again, I'm really sorry about missing dinner-"

"Please George, it really is okay, and the flowers are wonderful. No need to apologise anymore," came a smiling response from Martyna.

"Look, I'm sorry to have to dump this on you like this, But I had a visit from my boss in Frankfurt today. She is a lovely, understanding woman, who is also a Godmother to the girls, so knows all about our situation and the death of Cheryl. But the business world carries on and I must go to Frankfurt next week for a meeting to discuss the opportunity of opening some in-flight catering kitchens in certain cities on the African continent. I will probably fly out in the evening, stay the night, and fly back the next day after the meeting has finished. It means that you will be on your own with the girls. Now, Sally, Luke's wife, and Barbara, the girls' grandmother are both not far away and I will give you their contact details if anything happens. I'll brief them beforehand, and I'm sure that they would be only too pleased to help if necessary. Of course, you have met them both when you came for your fist interview, daunting as it may have seemed, they really did like you and agreed with me that you were the right person for the job."

"I'll be fine George, but I will take their telephone numbers and I will call them just to keep them in the loop and so that they don't worry. And you must not worry either. I've had a wonderful first day with the girls, and flowers from the boss as well! I'm sure Amy and Emily will look after me as much as I look after them," said Martyna, staring happily at the flowers I had given her. "What day next week?"

"I'll fly out on Tuesday evening and be back in time for dinner on Wednesday. Are you sure you'll be okay?"

"Of course. Now if you will excuse me, I'm feeling a little tired, so I will take a quick shower and then straight to bed. Good night George, see you in the morning."

"Good night Martyna, and thanks again - for everything." And with that Martyna went upstairs and I was left to finish my glass of chardonnay. As I sat there in silence, my thoughts turned to Cheryl and what she would be thinking about the day's events. The constant concerns for my wellbeing from my colleagues and customers; the obvious sadness in Tanja's voice when she first greeted me in my office; my drink with Luke in our old meeting place and finally, how well Martyna had done with Emily and Amy. I'm sure she was immensely proud of all of us and as I looked up to the ceiling, I raised my glass and softly whispered 'I love you babe and miss you so much. I hope you are happy with the choices I've made and remember, that the girls and I will never forget you, will never stop thinking about you and will always hold you close to our hearts.' With that, I finished my drink, placed the glass in the dishwasher and went to bed.

8

Unfortunately, due to an investment freeze by the company, the Africa expansion project was placed on hold and I didn't have to fly to Frankfurt for the meeting the following week.

Over the coming months heading towards Christmas, the girls, Martyna and I slowly but surely got into a routine, and we all felt extremely comfortable in each other's company. It was quite amazing to see how quickly Martyna had bonded with the girls and how quickly the girls trusted and took Martyna to their hearts. I have to say, that I too, became very fond of Martyna. It was almost as though we had become a proper family. We ate dinner together (my work permitting), we played games together, went for walks, had interesting conversations and Martyna had even started teaching the girls some Polish!

"Dobry wieczór ojcze. jaki był Twój dzień?" I would often be greeted with by Emily or Amy, as I entered the house after work, which meant 'Good evening father. How was your day?'

"Bardzo dobrze, dziękuję," I would reply in my best Polish accent, meaning 'Very good, thank you.' Martyna had also been giving me a few lines to learn as well! It was also easy and comfortable of an evening after the girls had gone to bed. Martyna and I would talk, just about anything really, or watch some tv together or even play chess. I have to say, she was particularly good at it, much better than me, but I did manage to win the odd game or two. Although it did cross my mind that she had let me win on those occasions! Some evenings, Martyna would just stay in her room and read or call her parents back in Poland. It was all extremely easy going, and we had developed a good relationship.

I hoped Christmas would be a lot different this year. Last year, Barbara and Derek had insisted that the girls and I stayed with them from Christmas Eve until the day after Boxing Day. Being our first Christmas without Cheryl, I thought it would be good for all of us to be together, so I agreed. Through no fault of anyone, it didn't turn out to be the best of Christmases. The girls were understandably upset about not having their mum around, and it was a very emotional time for everyone. I think what made it worse was Barbara, Derek, and I, all tried too hard to put on a smiling face for the girls. Trying to make Christmas the same as previous years when Cheryl was still with us. Follow the same routines; go to the children's mass service, make sausage rolls and bacon and onion rolls on Christmas Eve, lay out the stockings, prepare the turkey for the following day's feast (something the girls and Cheryl always did right from when the girls were old enough to sit in a highchair!), and so on. That was obviously impossible, and the girls realised this.

In some ways, I think they felt we were trying to carry on without recognising that their mum wasn't there anymore, almost as if we had forgotten about her. Although this wasn't the intention, I can understand in hindsight how this must have appeared to Emily and Amy. The fact that we were at their grandparents from Christmas Eve for three days also didn't help. We always spent Christmas at our house. Barbara and George were always invited and, on many occasions, did accept the invitation to be with us on Christmas Day. Boxing Day, however, was always at Barbara and Derek's house. It was like a second Christmas as they would keep the presents from them to the girls, and hand them out on that day. That got missed last year as we were already at their house and all the presents were opened on Christmas Day! It was another thing that caused concern and anxiety in the girls, something they were used to happening every Boxing Day, that just didn't happen last year. A lot of tears were shed by everyone over those three days and I wanted to make sure that we did things differently this year.

Towards the end of November, I had asked Martyna what her plans were for Christmas, and whether she was going home to Poland for the festivities. She told me that her parents were going to her older sister's and her husband, as usual to be close to the grandchildren. Martyna told me that as she pursued a career in child minding abroad, it was just inevitable that her parents would grow closer to Amelia and further apart from her. But she was okay with this and continued to be in regular contact with them. And she remained close to her sister too. She also adored her nephews and had pictures of the boys in her room.

"So, you will be staying here over Christmas?" I asked Martyna.

"Well, yes, if it is okay, George?" replied Martyna, somewhat apprehensively. "I could go and stay at a hotel or something, if Derek and Barbara are coming, it's no problem, really."

"Don't be silly, that's not why I was asking. I'm not sure what Barbara and Derek are doing this year, but either way, I would really enjoy having you here for Christmas, if you would like to join us? And don't worry, you will not need to check into a hotel. Also, you are not expected to work either! It's your vacation, so if you did have plans, then that's okay too."

"As I mentioned before George, my parents will go to my sister's place for Christmas. Amelia has invited me to go as well, but I won't this year. But I don't want to get in your way either. Christmas is always a busy time for families, so I suppose I could see what my friends are doing, and let you know. Is that okay George?"

I was a little disappointed that Martyna had not accepted my invitation as I knew the girls would have enjoyed having her around at Christmas. To be honest, I was disappointed for me too! But I understood and besides, Martyna was a young, incredibly attractive woman, why would she possibly want to spend Christmas with me and two children, when she could be having fun with her friends, and going to Christmas parties!

"I understand Martyna. But my offer is still there and will continue to be there. You are more than welcome to spend Christmas with us, so if you change your mind, we'd love to have you here. And listen, even if you have other plans, this is still your home, so please come and go as you want to, remember you are on vacation," I said, and I think I hid my disappointment from her quite well.

"Thank you, George," Martyna softly replied and smiled at me with those naturally deep, pink lips and looking at me with her gorgeous, green eyes.

The days leading up to Christmas were quite hectic. I had attended the company Christmas dinner, although I really didn't want to go. Each year, the company hired out a room in one of the local hotels, and the management teams from all the UK catering units attended for a three-course dinner and evening 'disco'. There were usually about a hundred or so people attending. Obviously, the previous year, I didn't go, but it was normally a good event and Cheryl and I had always enjoyed it in the past. It did feel strange this year, sitting at a table of couples, with me being the odd one out of nine people. Still, I managed to get through the three-course dinner without too much trouble, and to be fair to my colleagues, it was somewhat awkward for them as well. At least when dinner had finished, and after Frank had made his customary speech, thanking everyone for a great year and for their 'hard work, determination and loyalty to the company', I was able to get up from the table and move to the bar.

The music started and the usual suspects entered the dance floor to show off their dancing prowess. There were always a dozen girls and two guys that kicked off the dancing, and after another thirty minutes, and a few too many vodkas later, the dance floor usually filled up, leaving more space at the bar. I turned to the bartender and ordered a Jack Daniels and ice. I wasn't driving and had pre-booked a taxi to pick me up at 10:30 p.m. Although the event went on until midnight, I knew I wouldn't want to stay that long. I looked at my watch and it was 9:15 p.m. Only another hour or so, I thought to myself. My drink arrived and after thanking the bartender, I held the glass to my lips and took a sip.

"Hi, George," said a seductive voice behind me. I turned around.

"Hi, Sarah. How are you?"

"I'm lonely George, buy me a drink?"

"Of course, but you do know it's a free bar?"

"Just get me a drink, George. Disaronno and coke please," replied Sarah.

I ordered the drink and returned to looking at Sarah. And what a view. She looked stunning, like a film star straight off the red carpet at a film premier or an awards ceremony. She was wearing a silver, backless, almost frontless, and side-less dress, which I wasn't sure if she was in, trying to get out of; or out of, trying to get in! One thing was obvious - there was definitely no underwear being worn! Sarah's drink arrived and I handed it to her.

"There you go Sarah, one Disaronno and coke."

"Thanks George."

"I have to say Sarah, you look stunning. Just like a movie star. Can I have your autograph?"

"Stop it George," came the instant reply, and a smile ran across Sarah's lips. "One does one's best to look good," she continued, looking around the rest of the bar and dance area before adding,

"Which can't be said for the majority of people round here, present company accepted," she added graciously.

"So, why are you lonely Sarah? Didn't you come here tonight with your boyfriend? Or girlfriend?" I said.

"Although I have had some experience of girls George, I am actually looking for a man. So, in answer to your question, I, as indeed did you, came here alone tonight."

"So, you're looking for someone? Well, there are plenty guys out there that would bite their own arm off to be with you Sarah. I would say you have the pick of the bunch. Any of them would be thrilled to have you as their girlfriend."

"Thank you, George, you're too kind. Unfortunately, having the pick of the bunch is only good when the bunch is full, plentiful, plump, and ripe," she replied while looking at a group of blokes from the accounts department all demonstrating their 'air guitar' skills to the song that what was playing. "Not, as is the case here, the last pickings of the supermarket grape box - squashed, bruised, and sour tasting."

"I see what you mean," I said. "I suppose us guys here tonight are a bit of a let-down for you."

"Just to be clear, I don't include you in my critique of the men here tonight. You're not the most handsome man George, but you are kind and sincere - a good person. I saw how you were with your wife, how loving and how well you got on with each other. You know, you are the only man here tonight that I would ever consider being with," Sarah suggestively said.

"Well, I'll take the 'kind and sincere' bit as a compliment. Not too sure about 'not being the most handsome though', a bit strong I think," I said and smiled at Sarah. She smiled back and sipped her drink.

"You know what I mean George, and yes, it was all meant as a compliment. And I know you will never be interested in someone like me. And that's my enigma I suppose."

"What do you mean?"

"Well, because of the way I look," she said and pointed at her dress. "Men that are nice, kind and thoughtful are intimidated by me. They wouldn't dare to approach me and actually strike up a conversation. Therefore, I just get the good looking, dumb shits that think I'm an easy lay coming up to me, you know the type, with the 'hello darling, fancy a shag', mentality. And the stupid thing is, I tend to say yes! And that's not what I want."

"So, just to clarify, am I the dumb shit, good looking guy asking for a shag, or the boring, ugly, sincere guy that's too afraid to talk to you?"

"You're neither George. You are good looking, and I don't think you will ever ask me for a shag. And you always talk to me, and are kind to me," Sarah sincerely replied. "And then there is work. No one ever takes me seriously because of how I dress. I work bloody hard George and I could do so much more."

"I know you do, and I've said to Frank that there is much more to you than meets the eye. But he doesn't think you are interested."

"Well, I am interested. But I don't think I should have to compromise who I am and the way I dress to achieve the things I want to; in a way, that's discrimination, right?"

"I suppose so. It might not hurt though, to let Frank know you want to take on more responsibility."

"Yes, I suppose you are right. Thanks George."

"My pleasure Sarah, and you are right, as gorgeous as you are, and as much as every hormone in my body screams at me to ask you for a shag, I don't think it will ever happen. And not because I don't find you incredibly attractive. It's because I really respect you Sarah, your honesty and for who you are."

"Thank you, George," said Sarah, and she leant forward and kissed me on the cheek. "So how are you doing George, really? It must be extremely hard looking after the girls and trying to maintain normality in their lives?"

"Yes, it is. But I have Martyna now, a live-in child minder. She is wonderful, and the girls have grown quite fond of her. She's Polish and we have settled into a good routine."

"That's good George. It's good to have a grand-mother figure around, to help the girls."

"Oh, she's not old. Martyna is twenty-eight."

"Twenty-eight! So, you have a pretty, young girl looking after your children, do you?"

"Well, she is very pretty, so yes, I suppose I do!"

"And does she look after you as well?" said Sarah with a glint in her eye.

"No. Our relationship is purely employer / employee," I replied shaking my head in amusement.

"Can't blame a girl for asking," said Sarah.

The music had slowed, and Sarah asked me if I wanted to dance. It was the first time I had been in a situation where a girl had asked me to dance since Cheryl had died. After a slight hesitation, I agreed, and we hit the dance floor. Although we danced slowly, and in each other's arms, we were talking throughout and therefore, it wasn't considered a romantic dance, worthy of office gossip. At the end of the dance, we returned to the bar, continued talking and drinking until it was time for my ride home.

"Thanks for a lovely evening Sarah. And please don't worry. You will find the man of your dreams and I'll do what I can to help you progress at work," I said.

"Thanks George. I have had a lovely evening as well. Thanks for being, well, being you. You are a lovely man George Hart and I'm so pleased to call you my friend. But if you do ever fancy that shag, I'm up for it," replied Sarah, and she placed her arms around my neck and whispered gently in my ear. "I really mean it George, I could be out of this dress in three seconds," before giving me a gentle kiss on the cheek. As we let go of each other, Colin, a young guy from the accounts department, quite good looking, approached Sarah.

"Hey Sarah, fancy a dance and erm, and 'more' if you're interested?"

"Oh, fuck off, you arsehole!" was Sarah's instant reply, and I saw her walk off briskly to the Ladies.

I left in the taxi and made my way home arriving just before 11 p.m. Martyna was already in bed, so I quietly made my way upstairs, got undressed and flopped into bed. I had had a good evening after all!

9

Christmas Eve soon arrived and although it was hectic leading up to it, I had managed to get everything done in time. The food shopping, the presents for the girls, the presents for the grandparents from me and the girls, and presents for Luke, Sally, and little Ben. And of course, presents for Martyna from the girls and me! All in all, lots of presents! Martyna had informed me the week before, that she had decided to take me up on the offer of spending Christmas with us, if it was still okay? I was delighted and when I told Emily and Amy, they too were thrilled. Derek and Barbara had declined my offer to join us on Christmas Day, but they were expecting us on Boxing day as usual and to stay overnight. This also included Martyna, who was a little apprehensive at first, but in the end said she would join us.

Martyna joined the girls and I at the children's Christmas Mass at the local church and thoroughly enjoyed it. It reminded her of her own childhood and attending similar events back in Poland at this time of the year. The girls always loved it and took particular delight in singing the carols as boisterously as they could to impress Martyna.

We arrived back home about 5:30 p.m. and after taking their shoes and coats off, the girls ran off excitedly to their rooms to grab their Christmas stockings to hang up by the white, marble fireplace, which Cheryl and I had installed not long after we moved in a few years ago.

"They seem pretty excited, George," said Martyna as we made our way into the kitchen.

"Yes. It's great to see it. It was different last year and a little difficult, with it being the first Christmas without their mum. So, I'm pleased they seem to be happier. But I want to warn you, things could still get a bit emotional. I'll try to keep that away from you as much as I can. Sorry."

"Oh George. Please don't worry and please do not apologise. I'm only too glad to help in any way I can. If I can support the girls emotionally, then of course I will. It must be so confusing for them. This is such a happy time of the year, and yet for them, it must only magnify their terrible loss. I'm here for them, and you too George."

"Thanks, Martyna. It's a relief for me to know you are here. The girls adore you and although I always try my best to comfort them when they are down or sad, sometimes a woman's touch is what is needed. Unfortunately, try as I may to be a mother as well as a father to them, I come up short on the female side."

"Don't put yourself down George. You are a wonderful father, and both Emily and Amy love you unconditionally. You've done an unbelievable job, being both parents to them. Nobody could have done more." I looked into Martyna's green eyes and smiled at her.

"Right, let me prepare some dinner!" I said trying to close the subject and moved to the fridge to retrieve a huge platter of prawns, smoked salmon, lobster, gem lettuce, cucumbers, cherry tomatoes and lemon wedges, that I had prepared earlier in the day.

"Looks amazing, George," said Martyna. "I'll go and see what the girls are doing and meet you back here in five minutes, is that okay?"

"Perfect Martyna, just enough time for me to make the cocktail sauce," I replied.

Martyna disappeared out of the kitchen and I set about making the sauce. The prawn platter was something that Cheryl and I had traditionally done on Christmas Eve since before the children were born. And although it was a departure from the more traditional 'fish and chips' from the local 'chippy' as was the norm in my household when I was a kid, it was still 'fish' on Christmas Eve, just without the batter and the chips! And Emily and Amy also loved it too.

I laid the table and put my 'famous' cocktail sauce next to the platter in the centre of the table. I say 'famous' only because Cheryl had once commented that my sauce was so good, that I should bottle it and see if Peter Jones from 'Dragon's Den' would be interested in it, as he was with Levi Roots' 'Reggae, Reggae' sauce! Needless to say, it never happened! I cut some bread from a ciabatta loaf and filled a basket, again placing it on the table and completed the table with plates, cutlery, water glasses and two wine glasses for Martyna and I. I filled the water glasses and poured out two glasses of a South African, Chenin Blanc. As I finished pouring the wine, Emily, Amy, and Martyna entered the kitchen.

"We've hung our stockings on the fireplace in the lounge, Daddy," said Amy.

"Yes, Martyna helped us. Daddy, although we don't believe in Father Christmas anymore, we will still get something in our stocking, won't we?" asked Emily.

It was probably to do with last year's somewhat difficult Christmas, the reason why Emily and Amy stopped believing in Father Christmas. They asked me about it, and it was a tremendously tough decision I had to make. I did not really want the girls to stop believing in the magic of Christmas at their age (at the time they were seven and five). But on the other hand, I felt a sense of duty to never lie to them, especially as I needed their trust to make them believe that, although they had lost their mum, everything would be alright in the future. Lying to them was not really an option. So, I made the uncomfortable decision to tell them about Father Christmas not being real. To be fair, the girls took it really well. Amy even said that she knew he wasn't real because there was no way he could get to every single child in the world in one night. Quite astute for a five year old! Although Emily accepted it, she did think maybe I might be wrong.

"I think you'll just have to wait and see tomorrow morning," I said, trying to act mysterious.

"Daddy!" said Emily. "You're such a tease, I can't wait for tomorrow."

"Well, the sooner we have dinner, the sooner you can have your shower, the sooner I can read you a story and the sooner you can get to bed, which will mean the sooner tomorrow will be here," I replied. "Come on, sit up at the table, dinner's ready." The girls and Martyna sat down at the table.

"Thanks for dinner, Daddy," said Amy.

"Thanks for dinner, Daddy," said Emily. All three of us looked at Martyna. She looked somewhat quizzical, before realising what she needed to say.

"Erm, thanks for dinner Daddy," she replied. We all laughed and tucked in.

Dinner was a great success and Martyna was even complimentary about my cocktail sauce. We all had a nice time chatting, and you could feel the excitement growing with the girls in anticipation of the 'big day' tomorrow. It already felt so different to last year. A lot more relaxed, and the girls appeared more content, somehow less anxious.

Following dinner, I cleared the kitchen and set the dishwasher. I then asked the girls to go for their showers. The truth is the girls were very independent and had been for a long time. They knew how the shower worked, knew what temperature it needed to be, and knew that they had to test the water temperature with their hand before getting under the shower head. They knew how to wash themselves properly, apply shampoo and conditioner and how to dry themselves. They didn't need supervision. This in part was down to Cheryl and I teaching them these things from an early age. But also, over the last year or so and not having their mum around, the girls somehow sensed that I needed help and just took it upon themselves to be more independent.

Martyna went with them and I could hear her telling the girls that it would be a good idea to tidy their bedrooms, so the house was nice and smart for Christmas Day. I think she was secretly saying in code, put your old toys away as you might get some new ones tomorrow!

After I had cleared up, I went upstairs and into the girls' room. They had finished their showers, dressed in their pyjamas and Martyna was brushing Amy's hair.

"I'm ready for a story Daddy," said Emily. "Can we have 'The Polar Express'?"

"I think that would be a great choice, Emster. What do you think Amster?"

"Yeah!" came the excited reply from Amy. I went to their bookcase and scanned each shelf until I found 'The Polar Express' and pulled it out.

"Right, on my bed in ten seconds," I said, and Emily and I made a dash for my room. This is something I had done with the girls since they were old enough to listen to stories. Often, Cheryl would join us on our bed, and we would all cuddle up while I read a story. By the end of the story, the girls would be quite sleepy and when they were younger, I would carefully carry them to their beds without them waking up before re-joining Cheryl for a more 'grown up' cuddle. Nowadays, although still sleepy, I would walk them over to their beds for a final goodnight kiss.

"Have we finished?" Amy asked Martyna.

"You'll do, off you go," replied Martyna, and with that Amy jumped up and raced round to my room.

Although the girls did not believe in Father Christmas anymore, they did love hearing stories about him. Therefore, 'The Polar Express' was a great choice for Christmas Eve. It took about forty-five minutes to read the book and when I had finished, the girls were very tired. We snuggled up together on the bed, each of my shoulders, covered with the girls' heads.

"Daddy." said Emily.

"Yes, sweetheart."

"What do you miss about Mummy?" came Emily's response.

"That's a lovely question Emily. What do I miss about Mummy? Well, I miss lots of things. I miss Mummy's smile, especially waking up in the morning. It was always lovely to see Mummy's smile. And I miss Mummy's little nose, but luckily, I see that every day on your face, because Mummy gave that to you. And I miss Mummy's long blonde hair. But again, I see that in both of you," I said looking down from left to right at the tops of the girls heads. "I miss her laugh, her smell, the way she used to dance and sing to 'Take That' records. I miss watching tv with her, or just sitting in silence when she used to read her romantic novels, laying on the sofa with her head in my lap, while I listened to music on my headphones. But the one thing I really miss, is telling Mummy that I love her-, and her telling me, she loves me."

"I miss telling Mummy that as well," said Amy.

"What else do you girls miss about Mummy?"

"I miss Mummy saying goodnight to me. And I miss her cuddles and how she used to give me a big squeeze," said Emily.

"I miss Mummy's smell as well, Daddy," said Amy. "That's why I keep her scarf on my bed, because I can smell her before I go to sleep."

"Yes, I have one of Mummy's scarves too, and I do the same before I go to sleep," added Emily. "I just miss Mummy so much. I know we can never see her again, but I do hope she knows how much we love her."

"And I hope she is not lonely without us Daddy," said Amy.

"I think Mummy knows how we all feel about her and how much we miss her. And I also think she is immensely proud of you girls, her girls, and the way you have been so strong and helped me so much. And Mummy can't be lonely because she is not on her own. Grandad and Grandma are keeping her company, and I'm sure she is always watching over us and enjoying what you guys have been up to. I think Mummy is incredibly happy and laughs along with us when we play our games and have our 'tickle' fights. And she will always be with us in our hearts. That's where we keep Mummy, safe and protected and warm, and where she will always be for us when we need her."

"Do you still need Mummy, Daddy?" asked Amy.

"I will always need Mummy. You know, she was very wise, and I used to talk to her about everything, work, you guys, the decking I laid in the garden, and even that tree I chopped down. I always asked Mummy for advice and she always gave it to me. And do you know what, I still ask her for advice today."

"But how can she tell you what to do, if she isn't here?" asked Amy as she sat up and looked at me.

"Well, when I ask her a question, I remember the things she used to tell me, and from that, I can work out what she would tell me today. So, you see, it's just like she is still giving me advice today."

"I ask Mummy questions too. And I like to just talk to her sometimes. Is that silly Daddy?" said Emily.

"Of course, it isn't sweetheart. I think we all still talk to Mummy in our way. And it's not always just when we visit her grave. And there's nothing silly in that."

"That's good, because I talk to Mummy too," added Amy as she laid back down. I smiled and looked down at my little princesses.

"Ok girls, a big day tomorrow, so I think it is time for bed. Get a good night's sleep and please try not to get up too early tomorrow morning," I said and went to get up from the bed.

"Is 5 a.m. okay Daddy?" said Amy as she and Emily walked out of my room to theirs.

"Well, if we can do a bit later that would be better."

"I know, I was just joking. How about 5:30 a.m.?"

"You little monkeys," I said and chased them, as they laughed and shrieked loudly to their bedroom.

After tucking the girls into bed and saying goodnight, I made my way downstairs to the kitchen. As Martyna was not there, I assumed she was in the lounge, so went across to it to see if she would like a drink. The lounge was also empty. I went back to the kitchen and started to prepare the traditional homemade sausage, and bacon & onion rolls. I set up the frying pan, then chopped up streaky bacon and a red onion, adding it to the pan with a little olive oil and seasoning. Although I didn't mind making pastry; for ease, I had decided to purchase it.

I had just placed the rolls into the oven to bake, when Martyna entered the kitchen.

"Hi George. Baking?"

"Yes. Traditional Christmas Eve sausage rolls, and bacon and onion rolls. Wait until you smell them cooking, I guarantee, you will not be able to refuse them!"

"I'm sure I won't. Can't wait. George, I'm really sorry, but I was passing your room earlier when you were talking to the girls about your wife, their mum. I was extremely touched by how you dealt with their questions, and how you feel about your wife. You did very well George, I just wanted you to know that. And sorry for listening in, I know I shouldn't have, but I couldn't stop myself. Won't happen again, I promise."

"Thanks, Martyna. It's difficult for me to know what to say to their questions sometimes. I just try to be honest with them and give them as much comfort as I can. And no need to apologise Martyna. You are part of this family now. You are going to hear all sorts of things said, by me and the girls, so please don't worry. Now, would you like a Christmas Eve drink?"

"Yes, but please let me get it. What would you like?"

"I think I will have a Macallan whisky. It's in the cupboard in the lounge. It's an eighteen year-old single malt, expensive, and a Christmas gift from Tanja, my boss. As you probably know, Christmas Eve is the big celebration day in Germany, so I told Tanja, that I would open it tonight and toast her good health. Care to join me?"

"I think that's a splendid choice George, I'll go and get it." Martyna left the kitchen and within a minute or so, was back with the bottle of Macallan and two crystal cut whisky tumblers.

"I see you found the glasses as well."

"Yes. Do you want to pour it out?"

"No, no. Go ahead. Do you want ice? I never do. I remember my dad telling me once, that good whisky should be enjoyed without it being watered down with ice. He liked his whisky but could never afford a bottle like this. So, I'll drink to his health too."

"Without ice is good for me too, George," said Martyna as she cracked the seal and proceeded to pour out two glasses, around two fingers full. She handed me one of the glasses and looked into my eyes.

"Here's to you Tanja, thanks for the present and for all your understanding over the past eighteen months. And here's to you Dad, god bless you mate. And Thank you Martyna, for all you've done, and hopefully will continue to do for me, Emily, and Amy. Merry Christmas!" and I chinked my glass with Martyna's. We both took a sip. Wow! The whisky was incredible. Smooth, rich with hints of spice and clove.

"That's really nice George. I'm not a big whisky drinker, but this is wonderful," said Martyna.

"Certainly is. Now Martyna, do you think you can help me? I have some presents hidden away in the shed. I will go and get them, but I'm not sure the girls are asleep yet. Can you wait by the bottom of the stairs, and when I come in, just give me the nod if it is safe to take the presents through to the lounge? Is that okay?"

"Sure George, but do you need a hand getting the presents from the shed?"

"No, I'll be fine. Thanks, Martyna," I replied before heading to the back door in the kitchen, slipping on my Crocs and making my way out to the shed.

I retuned with four big, black, bin liners full of presents and still had to return to the shed to get the remaining two bin liners, plus a few carrier bags that contained some smaller presents for the girls' stockings. When I had brought all the presents into the kitchen, I made my way to the lounge, via the bottom of the stairs.

"All quiet?" I whispered to Martyna.

"Yes, all good," she whispered back to me. I crept passed her as quietly as I could with the bags I could carry, before returning and repeating the operation. Once all the bags were safely in the lounge, Martyna joined me, holding our glasses of the Macallan, which she had topped up.

"Hope you don't mind George, I topped them up."

"Good idea," I said, smiling at her. I began to arrange the presents for the girls under the tree. They ranged from games, puzzles, drawing and craft sets, model horses (they had somehow got into horses over the last year or so, and what they really wanted for Christmas was a horse of their own - not this year I'm afraid!), Lego, money boxes, watches, DVD's, books, diaries, and much, much more. I also filled the girls' stockings with little presents, not forgetting to add some walnuts and a satsuma. This was something I had always added to remember the past, and to be fair, the girls looked forward to seeing the nuts and satsuma in their stockings.

"There's a lot there George, the girls will be thrilled."

"I hope so. It's not expensive stuff, but I think they will enjoy the presents. I do sometimes feel a bit guilty that I haven't bought them enough, when they tell me what their friends get for Christmas and birthdays. You know, some of their friends get forty-inch flat screen tv's and top of the range iPads. Amy told me once that one of her friends got a scaled down version of a motorised double decker bus, for her birthday. A bus! She said they all went on it in the girl's garden at her birthday party. Incredible."

"Don't worry George, I think they will love what you've got them. I have also bought the girls something." Martyna held out a bag to me with presents inside it.

"It's not much, but again, I think they will like them and hopefully have some fun with them. There's also a little something in there for you George."

"Thank you Martyna. You really didn't have to get the girls anything. It's truly kind of you. They will be so pleased. As for me, you really shouldn't have. Thank you so much."

"It's my pleasure George. I also wanted to thank you for welcoming me into your family, and for how nice you have treated me. And for inviting me for Christmas. I feel very happy here."

"We're extremely glad to have you here Martyna, you don't need to thank me. And just so you know, there might be one or two presents amongst that lot for you, as you've also been a good girl this year, according to Santa that is!" I said and we laughed together.

After retrieving the sausage and bacon & onion rolls from the oven and sampling them while they were warm, Martyna and I settled into the lounge and talked for the next two hours until it was time for bed.

"Goodnight George, see you in the morning. Oh, what time will the girls be awake?"

"According to Amy, she'll be awake at 5:30 a.m. But it will probably be more like 7 a.m. They usually jump out of bed, run downstairs, see all the presents under the tree and then they grab their stockings and bring them up to our, sorry, my bed, and open them there. I know it sounds a bit strange, but you are more than welcome to join us for that if you want to."

"Thanks, George, see you in the morning." Martyna left the lounge and went to bed. I wasn't really sure if the 'thanks, George' that Martyna had said, meant that she would join us. But no big deal either way. I finished my third Macallan and headed up, feeling a little exhausted!

Christmas morning came and I was awoken by Emily and Amy charging into my bedroom, clutching their stockings.

"Daddy! Wake up! It's Christmas morning!" Emily shouted excitedly.

"We've got our stockings here, but Daddy, you should see the amount of presents downstairs under the tree! Thanks Daddy, we know it was you who put them there and not Father Christmas," said Amy.

"Yes, thank you Daddy," continued Emily. "Can we open our stockings?" she said as both the girls scrambled onto my bed. I pretended to be still asleep and snored loudly!

"Daddy!" the girls cried out in unison and they both jumped on me.

"Alright, alright. I'm awake!" I said and sat up giving the girls a cuddle and a big kiss. "Merry Christmas girls. And yes, you may open your stockings." There was a little tap on the bedroom door.

"Can I come in?" whispered Martyna. She was standing in the doorway wearing a pink and grey checked pyjama set. She looked wonderful, perfect even. She looked like some sort of pyjama model about to strut her stuff down the catwalk. Not at all like someone that had just got out of bed. And the pyjamas, although quite loose fitting, still showed off her incredible figure. After a short pause, due to me taking in this lovely vision in front of me, I finally remembered to respond to her.

"Yes, please come in Martyna. Merry Christmas," I said.

"Thank you, George. Merry Christmas to you too. And Merry Christmas Emily and Amy. What have you got there?" said Martyna, as she entered my bedroom and sat down at the end of the bed.

Now, when I go to bed, I never wear any clothing. Stark, bollock naked is how I like to sleep. Even on the coldest of nights, I would climb into bed unclothed. I quite liked it. Cheryl on the other hand was like most women. Always cold! And even though Cheryl would have an electric blanket on her side of the bed, within five minutes of me getting in, she would be over to my side for a 'warm up'. She nicknamed me 'Ready Brek' after the cereal as I kept her warm and 'once inside her', I gave her a hot glow! So, I was now sitting up in bed with my chest exposed and only a duvet to hide my modesty! Although it felt a bit awkward to me, Martyna didn't seem to mind at all.

"Hey Emily, can you pass me my shirt on the chair, over there," I said, pointing to where I had left my polo shirt from last night. Emily duly went over to the chair and then handed me my shirt, which I quickly put on. "Thanks Emily. Come on then, let's see what you have in your stockings."

The girls rummaged through their stockings, carefully unwrapping the presents, and showing Martyna what they had. Normally, they would be showing Cheryl and I, but because they knew it was me that had bought the presents, they seemed to be more interested in showing Martyna. Not that I minded at all. It gave me the opportunity to step back and enjoy the girls' excitement and happiness. It was great to see. And it also gave me a chance to look at Martyna. She looked incredibly beautiful, and it was wonderful to see how comfortable she was with the girls. Once the stockings were emptied of their contents, I asked the girls to go and get dressed. Martyna also left my bedroom, which allowed me to quickly jump in the shower.

Following a hearty breakfast, and me prepping the Christmas dinner; traditional roast turkey with all the trimmings, we all sat in the lounge, where Emily and Amy were eager to get started on the presents under the tree.

"Ok girls, go for it!" I said. Emily and Amy jumped up from the sofa and made their way to the tree, selected a present each, and then sat on the floor and opened them. There were many shrills of delight as each present was opened, and Martyna and I looked on in amusement at the girls faces, each time they opened a present that they really wanted. They opened the presents from Martyna with particular excitement and were overjoyed at receiving Shimmer 'n' Sparkle Ultimate Make Up Studio (for Emily) and a Playmobil Country Horse Grooming Station (for Amy). In addition, Martyna had bought each of the girls a large chocolate Santa, colouring books and hair bands and hair clips. I'm sure it meant a lot to Martyna to see them so happy. It seemed to take an eternity, but eventually only five presents remained.

"Here you are Martyna, these four presents are for you," said Emily, as she and Amy handed them over to her.

"Wow! Thank you, girls. Are you sure they are all for me?"

"Yes, your name is on them," said Amy with a big smile on her face.

"Well let's see. Shall I open this one first?" said Martyna. She picked up a small, soft package and read the label. "To Martyna.

Merry Christmas and thanks so much for looking after us. Lots of love, Emily and Amy," she said out loud, and began to open the present. "A scarf! Just what I wanted. I love it. It's beautiful girls, thank you so much, that will keep me lovely and warm," and Martyna gave the girls a big hug.

She then picked up another soft small package and again read the label, which basically read the same.

"Socks," Martyna said after opening it. "I always need socks, thank you again girls. The girls were as excited about giving Martyna presents as they were to receive their own. "Before I open the other two, why don't we let your dad open this one," said Martyna, as she handed one of the three remaining presents to Amy to give to me. Amy took the present and walked over to me, followed by Emily.

"Merry Christmas, Daddy," they both said and handed me the present.

"Thank you, girls," I said and looked at the label. It was written in Emily's best handwriting, and Amy had added her own name at the end. "To the best Daddy in the world, Merry Christmas and lots of love, from Emily and Amy," I read out loud. It brought a lump to my throat and I looked at Martyna and silently mouthed 'thank you' to her. She smiled back at me. "So, let's see what this is," I said and ripped into the wrapping paper. The unravelling of the paper revealed a thin rectangular box. I opened the box and was delighted to see a classic orange and blue spotted silk tie, and silver tie clip. "Thank you, girls. Just what I needed. It's a lovely present, and I shall wear it on my first day back in the office after Christmas. Come here," I said, and we had a group hug. It was quite emotional. Cheryl and I had always bought gifts for each other from the girls. Understandably, last year I didn't receive anything, and I wasn't expecting anything this year. I again looked at Martyna. I think she had a tear in her eye and just nodded at me, smiling.

"Can Martyna open her last two presents now, Daddy?" said Emily.

"I think that will be a great idea. Come on Martyna, your turn," I said, and the girls went and sat by her.

"Ok, let's have a look at this one," Martyna said picking up a small square, box shaped present. "To Martyna, Merry Christmas. Thanks for being a part of our family. Lots of love, Emily, Amy and George," she read out. She opened the present and was somewhat stunned to find an earring box, containing a set of small, silver and diamond earing studs. "Thank you, girls," she stuttered, before turning to me. "Thank you, George. Their lovely, really lovely."

"It's our pleasure Martyna," I replied. "One more to go."

"Erm, yes," Martyna said, a little flustered. Again, she read the label and proceeded to open the present. A slightly larger box, but still small. This time the content was a silver chain bracelet, with matching diamonds to the earrings. "George, this is too much, I-,"

"It's not as expensive as you might think, but hopefully it's not about the money. I just hope you like it for what it is," I said gently.

"It's so pretty Martyna," said Amy.

"And it matches your earrings," added Emily. "Try it all on."

"Thank you again, George. And thank you girls. I love the earrings and the bracelet. And of course, my socks and scarf!" Martyna put on the earrings and bracelet and looked at herself in the lounge mirror. "They are perfect," she said. Although I didn't say anything out loud, I found myself adding 'so are you Martyna.' Perfect for the girls, and maybe perfect for me.' As the girls left the lounge, taking some of their new toys with them, Martyna turned from the mirror, walked over to me, and gave me a soft kiss on my cheek.

"Thank you, George. Thanks for inviting me for Christmas. I love the presents and I'm having a wonderful time," she said. Although I was a little taken aback, I managed to respond.

"My pleasure Martyna. We're all glad to heave you here and thank you again for my present. Just what I needed."

The rest of the day was filled with fun, laughter, games, great food, and the obligatory walk in the afternoon to ease the digestion of the Christmas dinner. The girls had a lovely day, and it was so different to last year. Even though Emily and Amy mentioned their mum a lot throughout the day, it was always about happy memories and no tears were shed. It had been a wonderful Christmas Day for everyone.

10

Christmas came and went, and we all seemed to have a great time. Even staying at Derek and Barbara's on Boxing Day turned out to be very relaxing. To be honest, I thought that it might prove a little awkward with Martyna being there. But Derek and, more surprisingly, Barbara, took to Martyna, and treated her almost like one of the family. The girls, of course, loved being at their grandparent's house. It is so much bigger than ours, and they seemed to spend the entire time running around, pretending to be horses, or playing board games. The board games were not restricted to the children though. As soon as Derek found out that Martyna played chess, he immediately challenged her to a game. Derek was a good chess player and had beaten me on many occasions, but I knew how good Martyna was, and didn't think he had a chance! When the girls had gone to bed, the challenge was on. Derek took Martyna to his study for the 'Clash of the Titans,' while Barbara and I sat in the lounge talking. It was only after a few minutes of talking to Barbara that I realised that the spontaneous 'chess challenge' might not have been so 'spur of the moment' and more like a cunning plan to separate Martyna and me.

"So, George, how are you really getting on with Martyna?" was the opening line from Barbara.

"Yes, really well. She is extremely good with Emily and Amy. She shows them things and is always encouraging them to express themselves through art and crafts. She helps them with their homework. She takes them to school, picks them up. She works around the house and makes dinner for us all. I couldn't be more pleased."

"That's nice George. Good to hear Martyna is looking after my grandchildren so well. And you George, how do you get on with her?"

"Amazingly well. I thought that having another woman in the house after Cheryl, would be full of unease, awkwardness even embarrassment. But that couldn't be further from the truth. From Martyna's very first day, we just seemed to gel," I replied.

"That must have been a relief for you. And how has your relationship progressed?"

"What do you mean Barbara?"

"Well, what do you do of an evening?"

"We talk, watch tv sometimes. Martyna reads in her room, normal stuff really. Why are you asking?"

"No reason George. Simply curious, that's all. Does she have a boyfriend?"

"I don't think so. But it wouldn't matter to me, as long as it doesn't interfere with her time with the girls. Look Barbara, is there something I'm missing here? Is there a specific question you want to ask me?"

"George, you know me too well. And yes, I'm curious to know if you have grown fond of her. I know it's only been four months since she moved in, but she is an extremely attractive young woman. And from what you have told me, she is wonderful with the girls and appears to be wonderful for you. I was just wondering if she has designs on you, you know, made a pass at you or anything?" I smiled at Barbara trying to hide my surprise.

"Martyna is an attractive woman. And she is fantastic with the girls. But no, she hasn't made a pass at me and for that matter, I haven't made a pass at her either. She is very professional, dedicated to what she does, and does it very competently. I go to work each day happy and content that Martyna is looking after my children. I would be lost without her."

"I understand George. I'm sorry for prying. I'm just saying that I know how difficult these last eighteen months have been for you and the girls. And most of our focus has been on Emily and Amy. But I do realise how tough things have been for you. I want to let you know that, as hard as it is for me say, I do expect you to meet someone new. Someone to replace Cheryl and share your life and the girls lives. But I don't want that to affect our relationship, or mine and Derek's relationship with Emily and Amy," said Barbara remorsefully.

"Barbara, nobody will ever replace Cheryl," I said leaning into Barbara and reaching for her hand. "I think about her every day and will continue to think about her every day for the rest of my life. The girls and I talk about Cheryl constantly, and they too, know that their mum is always with them in their hearts. But you are right. I'm only human and I'm sure that one day I will find someone that I could possibly spend my life with. Not as a replacement for Cheryl, just a new chapter. And I think that's what Cheryl would want. But let me be perfectly clear, you and Derek have been more like parents to me rather than just in-laws. You've guided me, advised me, helped Cheryl and I become good parents; I would never jeopardise my relationship with you, let alone that of the girls. Please don't worry Barbara, you and Derek will always be important to us and will always play a full part in our lives."

Thank you, George," said Barbara and a tear started to roll down her cheek. We embraced, and she whispered to me, "Well at least you didn't choose that dreadful Hansen woman," and we both laughed.

It was not until the drive home and the girls were asleep in the back of the car, that Martyna informed me that Derek had given her a similar 'pep' talk, while they were playing chess. She found it all quite amusing.

The first few weeks back at work after the Christmas break was a bit slow. Not much seemed to be happening, which was typical for the time of year, and it meant I could get home earlier than usual and spend more time with Emily and Amy. January flew by, and before I knew it, we were hurtling towards the end of February. I was sitting in my office when my mobile rang. I looked down to see Tanja's name on the display.

"Hi Tanja, how are you?" I answered.

"Hi George. I'm good, you?"

"Yeah, all good. What's up?"

"I just got word from the board. It's on!"

"What's on?" I said somewhat confused.

"The Africa expansion project. It's on. I need you to come for a meeting next Wednesday. Fly in on Tuesday evening, meeting Wednesday morning, okay?"

"Sure, no problem," I said and after a few pleasantries, we ended the call. This could get interesting I thought!

Tuesday evening came around quickly, and every workday up until that day, Frank Stanley had been pestering me about any developments or 'whispers' I had heard about my upcoming meeting. "Have you found out who's attending the meeting? Let me know if Nigel mentions my name. You know how good a 'Country VP' I am, so put a few good words in for me," and stuff like that was all Frank could think about.

My flight was scheduled for take-off at 8:05 p.m. landing in Frankfurt at 10:10 p.m. local time. I left the office a little earlier in the day so that I could have dinner with Martyna and the girls, before taking a taxi to the airport. Martyna had prepared spaghetti bolognaise, a particular favourite for the girls and I must admit, mine as well! We had a fun dinner with both Emily and Amy filling me on the events of their day at school.

"We had English today and I had to write a poem about the seaside. It wasn't that difficult actually as I love the seaside, and Mrs Davis said, erm, how did she say it, yes 'you've captured the imagery and spirit of a day out at the seaside beautifully,' at least I think that's what she said," said Emily in her typical grown-up voice.

"Well done sweetheart, it sounds like you created a wonderful poem. I hope I can see it in your workbook when I go to the next parent teacher meeting."

"And then we had to make a 'bug hotel' and go outside and collect as many bugs as we could find," continued Emily.

"Did you find any worms?" enquired Amy.

"No, just earwigs, centipedes, an ant, and a caterpillar."

"Could have had one of these," said Amy holding up a strand of spaghetti from her plate. We all laughed and when I looked over at Martyna, although she was laughing, she was looking at Amy with total admiration. Martyna then caught me looking at her and held my gaze for a moment.

"You are quite right Amy! And it would have been the biggest worm in the entire bug hotel," said Martyna turning her attention away from me and looking at Amy. "And you need to tell daddy what you have been doing at school today."

"Well. I can't really remember much about what I did in the class, but I fell over at break time and had to see the first aid lady because I grazed both my knees."

"Oh sweetheart, how did you do that?" I asked.

"I was playing 'it' and Sarah Bartley was chasing me, so I was looking over my shoulder. And then this boy, Aiden I think his name is, ran past and must have kicked my foot, so I fell over and bashed my knees!"

"Don't worry Dad, I saw what happened and took Amy to the first aid lady," said a protective Emily, "and it was an accident, Aiden did say sorry."

"Well, that's good. Did you get cleaned up and did the lady put some antiseptic cream on your knees?" I asked Amy.

"No, she just got a wet paper towel and cleaned them for me."

"Don't worry, George, I looked at them when we got home and made sure that they were all clean," said Martyna. "And now, we need to clear up while daddy gets ready to leave for the airport," continued Martyna, as she started to clear the table.

I said my goodbyes to the girls and although they were a little bit sad, they understood that it was only for one night and I would be back tomorrow. Martyna promised to read them Frozen, one of their favourite books, so that took the edge off me leaving them.

"Thanks, Martyna. And remember, call me if you need anything and you also have Barbara and Sally's contact details. I called them both today and they are only too pleased to help if you need them."

"Thanks George. But don't worry, I'll be fine. Enjoy your trip and I'll see you tomorrow," and with that I was in the taxi and at the airport within twenty minutes.

After I had arrived at Heathrow's Terminal Two, checked in and passed through security, it was just after 7 p.m. Enough time for a quick drink in my usual Terminal Two pub, 'London's Pride', before boarding and settling into my business class seat. Although I had travelled all over the world doing this job, I was never one for engaging in conversation with the person sitting next to me on a flight. Whether it be a short haul into Europe, or a long haul to the States, I would always try to avoid going past the obligatory 'morning', 'afternoon' or 'evening' greeting. The indelible image of Steve Martin sitting in the middle seat between an elderly gentleman in the window seat, asleep with his head on Steve's right shoulder, and the late, great, and sadly missed, John Candy, squeezed into the aisle seat to Steve's left, with his nonstop chattering about himself, his likes, dislikes and, of course, removing his socks and waving them in Steve's face! This image had stayed with me since I first saw the film 'Planes, Trains and Automobiles' way back in the late eighties. One of my all-time favourite films! So, you can imagine my displeasure as I went to sit down in seat 2A, that there was someone sitting in 2C (at least they always block off the aisle seat in Business Class!). However, the person was a genuinely attractive, woman, late twenties, blonde hair, slim, very pretty face, large, preppy reading glasses; her head was bowed as she was reading a fictional book. A good sign I thought, into her book, shouldn't have too much of a problem here!

"Evening, I believe I'm in the window seat," I said very politely and with that the woman looked up at me, smiled and got up out of her seat to allow me into mine by the window.

"There you go," she said.

"Thank you." I sat down and made myself comfortable and fastened my seat belt. So far, so good! The Captain addressed the passengers over the PA system, and gave out the usual flight information before handing over to the cabin crew for the safety briefing. It had been raining a little and the wind was getting up a bit, but nothing to strong, and nothing for a seasoned traveller like me to worry about! However, it was at the point, as the cabin crew finished the safety demonstration, and were carrying out their last-minute seatbelt checks, that the woman beside me turned her head and smiled at me.

"Bit windy isn't it. I hope we will be okay. I'm not an experienced flyer and if I'm honest, a little bit scared of flying." She looked so calm, and spoke in a noticeably clear and precise manner, so much so, that the words she spoke didn't match the way they were being said!

"Don't worry, it's only a little bit of wind, nothing that this plane can't cope with," I answered in a reassuring way.

"Are you an experienced flyer then?" she quickly responded.

"Well, yes, I am really, I suppose. I mean, I've travelled this route on many, many occasions and done more long-haul flights than I care to remember; so yes, I would say I was an experienced flyer. But as I said, please don't worry, you're going to be fine," I said and gave her a comforting smile. The aircraft trundled down the taxi way, and before too long we were lined up at the start of the runway. With a roar of the engines, the aircraft started moving, slowly at first before gathering tremendous speed, and eventually leaving the earth for the night sky.

The amount of time we were airborne was approximately twenty-five seconds before the first bumps of turbulence occurred, making the aircraft shake a bit and drop slightly, nothing really that unusual. However, this sequence of events triggered something that I had never experienced in all my time of flying around the world. With a hard slap, the young woman sitting next to me slammed her left hand down hard onto my right thigh and let out a little shriek in frightened bewilderment before turning to me.

"I'm really sorry, but I can't let go of your leg right now," she hastily said in a fearful state, in complete contrast to the calm woman that had informed me she was a terrible flyer!

"Erm, that's okay," I replied trying not to alarm her. "But really, please don't worry, what just happened is perfectly normal, and we'll soon be above the clouds and the flight will probably be very smooth, okay?"

"If you say so. Again, I'm really sorry," she said continuing to squeeze my thigh. Now that's the first time that I have ever experienced that. And the fact that she had reached across the empty middle seat, made it even more remarkable. The flight levelled out, and the ride was much smoother. The woman eventually looked up at me and again apologised, before releasing her grip on my thigh.

"Are you okay?" I asked.

"Yes. But I really don't like flying. As I have almost molested you, I had better introduce myself. I'm Fiona Stephenson," and she reached out her hand.

"George Hart," I replied. "So, tell me, if you are such a nervous flyer, what are you doing on a flight to Frankfurt?"

"I'm relocating. I've just landed a job with rather large investment banking company. So hopefully, this will be the last flight for me for a while. The trouble is, I haven't yet found a place to live, so I'm going to be living out of a suitcase in a hotel until I find somewhere."

"I see. Do you speak German?"

"Yes, I'm fluent. Took it as a second subject at university as I did it at A level at school. It does help that my mum is German, and only ever talked to me in German. So, it really helped me," she replied. "And you, why are you travelling to Frankfurt?"

"I work in Sales and Marketing for the largest, global in-flight catering company, who just happen to be headquartered in Frankfurt. My job takes me all around the world to cities that my customers, the airlines, fly to, where we have catering facilities. I'm here for a meeting tomorrow to discuss expansion on the African continent. So, I'm only here for one night."

"Where are you staying?"

"I'm at the Sheraton, at the airport. Our headquarters are not far from the airport, not in the city, so it's convenient for a pickup tomorrow morning."

"So am I! The company have put me in the Sheraton to save me having to travel into the city tonight. That's a coincidence. They will also pick me up in the morning and show me around some apartments they have acquired, that I might like to rent. Pretty cool really. Then I have a two-day familiarisation on Thursday and Friday, before starting on Monday. Luckily, my mum is coming out for the weekend to keep me company and make sure I pick the right apartment."

"Cool," I said picking up on the young vibe of the conversation, "Have you been to Frankfurt before?"

"Only once for the interview. But I really didn't see too much. But I've read a lot about the city and my mum knows it quite well, so I think it will be great!"

"I don't know it that well, but there are some good restaurants and there always seems to be something going on down by the river. And I do like the Irish pub not far from the main 'barnhof' in the city centre. Some crazy nights in there in the past," I replied, turning my head away and remembering some of the nights I had spent in that particular bar with customers, before directing them to the local red-light district just a few streets away. You see, that is what some customers wanted when they were visiting your city, whether it be Frankfurt, London, Madrid, Johannesburg, New York, Paris, Rio, or Montreal! When customers travelled to see you away from their own country, away from their own dreary lives and quite often, dreary wives or husbands. They tended to want to explore the local cuisine (being in catering, that was expected), the local wine (again, expected) and the local strip bars and whore houses (became expected!). Now, although I would never entertain the prospect of sleeping with a prostitute, or anyone on my trips as Cheryl meant the world to me, I wasn't averse to sometimes taking the customers to the local strip joints. To me this was a bit of harmless fun, and if it helped smooth the relationship with the customer, then that's what needed to be done. But if they wanted anything else, they were on their own!

The remaining flight went smoothly, and Fiona eventually settled and read her book; a fictional piece entitled 'When it Rains' which she appeared to be completely absorbed in. It wasn't until we had landed, and the plane had come to a standstill at the jet bridge, that Fiona looked at me and said she was glad that the flight was over.

"Well, we are here now, safely landed and you can now start the next chapter in your life, here in Frankfurt!" I said with a smile on my face.

"Yes, thanks and again my apologies for earlier, you know, the leg grabbing business, really sorry. Although, I have to say, I did quite enjoy it," Fiona replied, looking at me and giving a flirty wink with her left eye.

"The truth be told, I quite enjoyed it too!" I said returning the winking gesture.

"Do you have checked luggage?" Fiona asked. "Only as we are going to the same hotel, I was wondering if we could go together. But you probably don't have checked luggage do you, being here just for the one night?"

"No, I only have hand luggage, but I will wait for you outside the terminal. The Sheraton is only a short walk, so when you get your luggage together, head outside and I will meet you, okay?"

"Really very kind of you George, I'll see you the other side," said Fiona.

Once we were through immigration, Fiona and I split up. She went to collect her checked luggage and I made the long walk through the terminal to the outside, trying to pass the many 'dithering' passengers that seemed incapable of walking any faster than a tortoise with arthritis! One of my pet hates, is the people at airports that seem to think that just because they have no desire to depart the airport as quickly as possible, everyone else should be held up by their leisureliness! Move over! Let people who have a purpose in life, get by you!

Once outside I started checking my messages on my phone while waiting for Fiona. Nothing from Martyna, so I guessed all was okay with the girls. It was a little after 10:45 p.m. by the time I had read all my messages and replied to most of them, when I felt a gentle tap on my back.

"Hey George, I finally got my bag. You all set?"

"Hi Fiona, yes all good. This way." I led Fiona in the direction of the short walk to the Sheraton. We chatted about the coldness of the weather in Frankfurt and how it would be nice to get to the warmth of the hotel. When we arrived some seven minutes later, we walked up to the reception desk.

"Is it a room for two? What name sir?" said the girl on reception in English, but with a heavy German accent. Both Fiona and I looked at each other, blushed slightly and smiled back at the girl.

"No. No erm-, I have a room booked under the name of Hart, and this young lady has a separate room booked under the name of Stephenson, I think?" I said turning to Fiona.

"Yes, that's right," she confirmed.

"My apologies, you just look like a great couple," came the reply from the girl, Annabel - I think her name tag said. A slight awkwardness ensued as the check-in process was carried out. Once checked-in, we walked to the elevator.

"I'm on the third floor George. What are you on?"

"I'm on the fifth," I replied.

"Shall we grab a drink in the bar, George? After all the help you've given me, and as a way of thanking you for letting me hold onto your leg, can I buy you a drink?"

"Yeah, why not," I said without really thinking about it, "let me just dump this in my room, check in at home, and I'll see you in the Sports Bar in fifteen minutes, okay?"

"Great!" came Fiona's excited reply, "I'll see you there." Fiona exited the lift on the third floor, and I carried on up to the fifth.

I made my way quickly to my room and once inside, dumped my overnight bag on the bed and immediately called home.

"Hi George, how are you? Have you arrived safely?" was the caring, soft spoken words Martyna said to me.

"Yes, thanks for asking Martyna. How are the girls, did they go to bed okay?"

"No problem. They are little angels. Amy kept asking if you were back tomorrow, and although I kept saying yes, it wasn't until Emily told her that you would be back, that she finally believed me. But she was great in the end and I thanked Emily for helping with that, you know, told her how much of a grown up girl she was. She was delighted with that!"

"Thanks for looking after them Martyna, I really think you are wonderful with the girls, and I know that only after this short amount of time, that they both think the world of you. Actually, me too, I also think the world of you."

"Stop it George, you'll have me blushing in a minute. Anyway, its late and I need to get to bed. Have a good night's sleep and we'll see you tomorrow for dinner. Take care."

"You too, take care Martyna and sleep well." As the call ended, I couldn't help but think of how wonderful Martyna was. How beautiful she was with those piercing, green eyes, and perfect figure. How amazing she was with Emily and Amy. How caring and kind she was to me. Was this girl beginning to have an effect on me? In such a short space of time, was I developing feelings for her? Did she have feelings for me?

"Stop it, George," I found myself saying out loud, "get changed and go and have that drink with Fiona!"

I walked into the Sports bar at the Sheraton hotel and immediately spotted Fiona sitting on a bar stool towards the end of the bar. She was wearing a short red skirt, red high heel shoes and a cream coloured 'v' neck blouse, which was slightly sheer, allowing just a glimpse of a pink 'push up' bra. This made a formidable cleavage appear at the base of the 'v' neck blouse! To be honest, she looked gorgeous!

"Hi Fiona. Wow! You look great. If I had known I would have dressed more formally instead of these tatty jeans and blazer," I said hoping that she wouldn't take my comments too offensively. Although I need not have worried!

"Thanks for the compliment, George. I like to look nice, and you look great as well. Thanks for agreeing to the drink. I hope it wasn't too forward. I know you said you had to 'check in at home' so I assume you are married, and I can now see your wedding ring. I suppose having a drink with a strange woman, who just so happened to grab your leg at 10,000 feet doesn't really feel right. But hey, you're here now, so what are you having?"

"Firstly, I really do mean you look great! Secondly, you are correct, I am wearing a wedding ring. But unfortunately, I am a widower." As I said the word 'widower' I suddenly realised that this was the first time since Cheryl's passing that I had actually used that word. It felt strange, alien, almost as if I were talking about someone else!

"Oh my god. I'm so sorry George. I never, well what I mean is, well, erm…,"

"It's perfectly okay," I said lifting my hand up to stop Fiona from talking, or at least trying to talk any more. "And I would like to thank you actually. You are the first person that I have ever struck up a conversation with on an aeroplane, and actually enjoyed it! You are the first person ever to grope my thigh, and yes, it wasn't a grab, it was a 'grope', which I really should have reported to the senior flight attendant, if not the Captain himself! Probably should have made a formal complaint regarding sexual harassment; and, you are the first person that I have ever introduced myself to as a widower," I said with a slight sadness in my voice. Fiona looked at me for a second with horror in her eyes, before it was replaced with a warm smile.

"Thank you, George. Now what about that drink?"

11

The alarm on my phone went off at 7 a.m. and I reluctantly turned over from the right side of my bed to turn it onto 'snooze', another ten minutes is what I needed! Although my head hurt a little, it was no big hangover, and nothing I couldn't handle with the aid of a couple of paracetamols and a glass of water! Come to think of it, how many drinks had I drunk last night with Fiona? And what happened between Fiona and me? I turned slowly over to my left side with a sense of anxiety and fear wondering what, or more to the point, who I would see! Nobody was there and relief filled my mind as I lightly exhaled before sitting upright with a stark sense of urgency! Images started flashing through my mind of Fiona and me standing outside her hotel room door; of Fiona leaning into me, and kissing me on the cheek, of Fiona opening her door and taking my hand before leading me into her room and the door closing behind us.

"Oh fuck!" What had I done? What had happened? Did we 'get it on' last night? I kept telling myself to think, think what had happened, think about the events of last night! And then through a moment of clarity, it all came back to me. Yes, that's right, Fiona had quite a bit to drink last night, really going for it, so much so that I could not, or indeed, did not want to keep up with her knowing I had a meeting this morning. When we had finally decided it was time to leave the bar, I almost had to assist her in walking to the elevator. Once outside her room, she had indeed kissed me on the cheek, and led me into her room only to collapse face down onto the bed. I slipped her shoes off, and gently turned her over and laid her into the bed. The room was quite dark, so I turned on a small desk light just in case Fiona woke up and was a little confused as to where she was.

"Thanks, George. Sorry for molesting you on the plane. And sorry for getting drunk. A real gentleman," came the soft mumbling from Fiona as she started to fall asleep.

"My pleasure, Fiona. Sleep well, and maybe I'll see you at breakfast tomorrow morning. If I don't, have a great start in Frankfurt, and maybe we will bump into each other again. Take care," I replied and left the room.

I got out of bed and jumped into the shower. Brushed my teeth and got dressed before heading down to the breakfast room. I sat at a table and ordered tea, and then went to the breakfast buffet bar and chose some toast and marmalade. I went back to my table and started to spread the marmalade on the toast. A waitress came over and placed a pot of hot water, a cup and saucer and two breakfast tea bags on the table.

"Danke schön," I called out to the waitress.

"Bitte kein Problem," came the instant response. I had just taken the first bite into the toast, with its delicious covering of orange marmalade, when I looked up and noticed Fiona standing in front of me.

"Do you mind if I join you?"

"No, not at all," I said through a mouthful of food. Fiona sat down, was instantly asked by the same waitress what she would like to drink, ordered coffee, and then looked at me.

"I'm really sorry George. Was I frightful last night? Did I embarrass myself and more importantly, you?"

"No harm done. We had a nice time, a few drinks, admittedly, one of us had a few too many drinks and then we went to our 'own' hotel rooms. Perfect evening," I said with a smile on my face.

"God, I'm so sorry. I don't normally behave like that. It must have been the combination of the flight and being in Germany on my own and, well and meeting such a nice man like you. And thanks for looking after me, you know taking my shoes off and putting me into bed. Although my skirt and blouse are ruined now. You could have taken them off?" said Fiona with a wink and a smile.

"Maybe another time. Wasn't right last night. But you did look beautiful, as indeed you do this morning. And if we had both been conscious, instead of just one of us, then who knows what might have happened. But for now, I hope we are friends?"

"Of course, George. To be honest, I feel like shit this morning, but I wanted to see you before you check-out in case I never saw you again." The waitress brought over Fiona's coffee and placed it on the table. "I'm going to drink this coffee and then go back to bed for a few hours before I have to meet my contact. But I wanted to see you and give you my number. From what I remember, you are a wonderful man with two adorable children, you showed me the photographs right? And I just wondered if there was any chance you wanted to maybe meet up again? I know, it is insane! We only met last night, I grabbed your leg on the plane, we had a few drinks and you tucked me into bed. But I feel we have a connection. Don't you?"

"Wow. A lot to take in over my tea, toast and marmalade!" I said with a smile and wink. "You are bright, attractive, funny, intelligent, and a very charming person. We had a lovely time last night just talking. And to be honest with you, you must be special because if you remember, I don't do the whole 'talking to my fellow passenger on planes' routine. Of course, I would love to stay in contact with you and gladly accept your contact number and will gladly give you mine. But…"

"I thought there would be a 'but' in there somewhere."

"But - I am not ready for a new relationship right now. I'm not ready for a relationship with anyone, let alone with someone that is living in a different country to me. I must think of my girls and although I honestly believe that they would take to you like a pig does to shit, it's not the right time. Sorry Fiona. But listen, you can grab my leg on any plane, anytime you want to, and I promise I won't tell the Captain, okay?" We both sat for a moment, looking into each other's eyes, smiling at one another.

I was staring down at the contact number Fiona had given to me, whilst waiting outside the hotel and had not noticed Tanja's car pull up. The driver's window slid down and Tanja called to me.

"Hey! Can I give you a ride?" she said suggestively as if picking up a gigolo!

"Hey Tanja. Sorry, I didn't see you there," I said, as I slipped Fiona's contact details into my pocket and got into her black E Class Mercedes. Once inside, we quickly embraced, and Tanja pulled away.

"How are my girls?" she said, in a grandmotherly sort of way that instantly gave me a feeling of comfort, which brought a smile to my face.

"They are doing great. Martyna is doing a wonderful job with them, and things seem to be settling down into a nice routine."

"And you?"

"You know me Tanja, as long as the girls are okay, I'm okay," I said in a slightly subdued way.

"I'm not convinced. But we will pick this up another time. Right now, I need to talk to you before the meeting. You know Nigel Colnbrooke will be in the meeting, well actually, he will be running the meeting. And you know how egocentric he can be. I know this rubs you up the wrong way, but I need you to be the 'old' George in there today. Calm, collected, not rising to his antagonistic views, staying factual, keeping on track. There will be the 'controlling' guys in the meeting as well as the Head of Mergers & Acquisitions, Heinz Mayer. If things go well, I would like you to work with Heinz and probably one of the controllers and do some visits to potential acquisitions in the Sub Sahara region. Is that something you would be okay with?"

"Firstly Tanja, you don't need to worry about me and Nigel. I know he is an arrogant prick and I know how to handle him."

"Yes, I know. But with everything you have been through and to a large extent, still going through, I just wanted to make sure you were okay with all of this?"

"No need to worry. And as for the visits, now that I have Martyna, I would be comfortable leaving the girls for three or four nights at a time. So please don't worry Tanja. You can trust me," I said; but instantly had the thought that although Martyna would be okay, Emily and Amy might not be. However, I did not think it was right to share this with Tanja just yet.

We arrived at the HQ office, which was situated in a small town ten minutes' drive east of the airport. Tanja parked the car in the underground car park, and we took the lifts to the fifth floor. This was the floor where the board sat. The board was made up of the CEO, Victor Brandt, a genuinely nice man, late fifties, very calm in his mannerisms, an intellectual, always interested in people, and a very steadying influence. Then there was Lars Schuller, COO, also late fifties, arrogant, pushy, never likes to be wrong, rarely takes notice of anyone else's opinion. Someone Nigel looked up to and aspired to be like! Lastly, there was Cristina Wagner, CFO, early fifties, very numbers driven, always presenting detailed analysis. A nice woman, worked well with Tanja, and was considered an ally!

Tanja and I exited the lift and made our way to the executive boardroom. As we arrived, we were greeted at the door by Alma Kohl, the CEO's personal assistant and diary keeper for the executive boardroom.

"Hi Tanja, Hi George. Coffee, tea and refreshments are set out inside. If you need anything, please let me know. Heinz is already inside, with someone from the controlling department, a girl, not sure of her name. We are still waiting for Nigel and Daniel to arrive."

"Daniel!" said Tanja in a startled way to suggest she was not altogether pleased about this, and immediately feeling a little embarrassed that it had come out this way!

"Yes, Nigel thought it would be good to get Daniel's input for the meeting," said Alma. Daniel Mulzer was Country VP Operations, Germany. One of Nigel's 'henchmen', deeply knowledgeable about operations, but very Germanic in his approach, often not seeing potential due to the lack of international experience, and always thinking everything should be like Germany, you know, run with military precision, and having infinite resources available. It was obvious, Nigel wanted Daniel at the meeting to ensure operations took the lead and had probably already earmarked Daniel as the man to lead the expansion in Africa, ahead of Frank Stanley in the UK! Additionally, it gave Nigel another 'voice' to back up his ideas and plans.

Alma left Tanja and I at the boardroom entrance door and before entering the room, I turned to Tanja.

"Don't worry. We know what Nigel's like. Let's just see how it goes, before we start to panic!"

"Panic is not the right choice of word to use right now, George," she said worriedly, as we went into the room.

We were greeted by Heinz. He, as usual, was very welcoming, a warm-hearted man, who I had a lot of time for. He never seemed to have any hidden agendas, was straight talking and would always present fair and impartial analysis of any mergers and acquisitions projects he was working on. I liked him a lot and I think the respect was mutual. We had worked together some years back when the company expanded in the UK and acquired some small regional airport caterers and had since periodically kept in touch with each other.

"Hello Tanja, great to see you. I hope you are doing well?" said Heinz after giving Tanja a kiss on both cheeks.

"Hey Heinz, good to see you too. I'm doing okay, you?" replied Tanja.

"Very good. And excited about this potential project! And Mr Hart! How are you?" he said turning from Tanja to shake my hand. It was just something that happened each time we met. Heinz addressing me as Mr Hart, and me addressing Heinz as Herr Mayer. Probably to do with the German culture of addressing people by the surname until being 'invited' to call each other on first name terms. But it only happened on the first occurrence each time we met. As soon as the formalities were out of the way, it would be back to Heinz and George.

"Very well Herr Mayer. Great to see you and glad you are doing well," came my response.

"George, I am so sorry about your recent loss. I cannot imagine what you have gone through and if there is anything I can do, please do not hesitate to ask." Although I would not really consider Heinz a close friend, I did understand the sentiments behind what he was saying and really appreciated his kind words.

"Thanks Heinz. It has been a rough year, but I am getting things back on track, and being back to work and some semblance of normality helps a lot," I replied, not realising that we had still been shaking hands all this time. We disengaged the handshake and made our way to the coffee station to join Tanja. It was at this point that I noticed the girl from Controlling in the room. As our eyes met across the boardroom, she got up from the chair she was sitting in at the table and made her way towards us. She was tall, elegant, with black hair, green eyes, wearing a knee-length grey skirt, white blouse, and matching grey suit jacket. Probably 34-24-34 figure and aged about twenty-five (yes, I know, but I can't help noticing things like this!) Her three inch heels made her appear taller than she was, and when she eventually made her way to us at the coffee station, I realised we were at eye level with each other.

"Ah, let me introduce you," said Heinz to this mystery woman in his customary friendly way. "This is Tanja Weber, VP of Sales for the EMEA Region." Tanja extended her hand which was reciprocated as the two ladies exchanged 'hellos'. "And this is my good friend and colleague, George Hart, Sales & Marketing Director also for EMEA, and of course reporting to Tanja," Heinz continued.

"And you are?" I said as I too extended my hand.

"Yes, sorry. This is Jana Muller, Manager of Controlling for Germany," continued Heinz.

"Very pleased to meet you George, it is okay to call you George?" Jana said in perfect English.

"Well, that's my name and I hope you don't mind me calling you Jana?"

"Not at all."

"Then, very pleased to meet you too, Jana," I said shaking her hand. At that moment, the door burst open (and I really mean, burst open as if to make the biggest impact possible), and in stepped Nigel and Daniel.

"Morning everyone!" said Nigel in his normal aggressive tone as if to say he had not got all day and was far too important to be here really! He proceeded to sit at the head of the boardroom table and opened up his Gucci briefcase, making sure everyone knew it was Gucci, placing it in such a way on the table that ensured the Gucci motif was prominent! He pulled out a two-inch-thick document, which he slammed on the table. Daniel sat in the chair on his right-hand side and proceeded to carry out the same actions, only pulling his document from an Armani bag!

"What a couple of arrogant pricks," I thought to myself and for one tiny second, I thought I may have said it out loud! However, I had not and just looked at Tanja. Her look back at me, told me that she had thought the same thing; and we both smiled at each other.

Heinz, Jana, Tanja, and I took our refreshments and sat down on either side on the boardroom table. It was a slightly old-fashioned boardroom by todays modernistic standards. Wood panelling was very prominent on the walls, the table was made from the finest ash and the chairs were very ornate, albeit a little uncomfortable. It could seat sixteen people comfortably, and there was a large screen on the wall at the end of the table used for presentations and video conferencing. Two, large, triangular-shaped conference call phones were placed at either end of the table and the company logo was proudly displayed down the length of one of the walls. Miniature flagpole table stands also adorned by the company logo, were dotted around the room.

"So, lets kick this off," said Nigel in his typical domineering fashion. "I think we all know why we are here. The board and I have decided that expansion into the African market is a way to grow the company, extend our global coverage and improve profitability." I looked at Tanja and again our telepathy was spot on. She also found the statement 'the board and I' that Nigel had used, very pretentious as we both knew the idea had originally come from the Sales Department, passed up to the board from Tanja through the CFO Cristina Wagner! But hey, let him have his five minutes.

"I have a report here," Nigel continued and waved his thick document in the air, "that gives a comprehensive overview of the African market, detailing the airlines operating there, flight and passenger volumes, local facilities and their capabilities, the competitive landscape, scope for expansion, market price, resource requirement and much, much more. I think today's meeting is simply a formality to decide who heads up this expansion project, in order to ensure financial and operational success. I have distributed this report to the board and I'm sure the board will concur with my findings and the way forward."

"I would like to say that I have assisted Nigel with this report and think that we could complete the first phase, which is four cities, within a time frame of six months," added Daniel.

"Thank you, Daniel and thank you for your support in producing the report. I know that we have not involved Sales to any great extent in the production of this report, but I think we have done a great job without your help," Nigel continued. "Obviously, we now need to involve the Sales Department so you can get the customers 'on board', after we have established ourselves in the identified start up cities." At that point, there was a quiet, almost timid knock on the boardroom door and before anyone could react, the door opened and in walked the CEO and CFO.

"Good morning everyone, sorry to disturb you like this, but both Cristina and I thought it would be a good idea to join you this morning. I hope you don't mind?" said Victor Brandt, CEO.

"Good morning everyone," continued Cristina, the CFO. "As you all know, this project is close to my heart. When it was first suggested by Tanja, I thought the idea had great potential and I am keen that we develop it, mindful of the risks and carrying out all necessary due diligence along the way." Everyone stood and one by one, shook the hands of both Victor and Cristina, before they both took their seats around the table. You could see that Nigel was a little bit shaken by this intrusion. Although he had a 'good' rapport with the board, it was primarily the COO, Lars Schuller, that he had most interaction with and, therefore, a more familiar relationship.

"Erm, well thank you for joining us," continued Nigel. "Shall we get started?" A brief nod of the head from Victor concurred that Nigel should indeed continue. "However, just to give a brief summary, I have just informed the team that we have produced a report," he said, again holding up the thick document that had been lying on the table, "that contains all the details required in order for us to move forward with this project, outlining the facts and figures to sustain profitability." This time Nigel turned to Cristina with a smug look on his face as if to say, 'you don't have to worry, I've done the numbers.' "The plan is for a phased approach incorporating the introduction of four locations to be up and running within the first six months," he continued, and finished the statement by this time turning to Victor for a sign of approval, which to be fair, was given with a smile and once again, a slight nod of Victor's head! This was my chance I thought!

"I have some questions," I said while looking down at my notepad, pretending to read some imaginary notes that I had made (in reality, just scribbles on the page!)

"Well, I don't think we need to bore both Victor and Cristina with the details right now," came the response from Daniel, which was quickly backed up by Nigel.

"Yes, it's not appropriate to go into details, George. All the information you need is in this report, which has already been sent to Lars Schuller (COO) and therefore, by proxy, to the board for approval."

"I understand that Nigel, but all the same, I do have some questions that I would like to get some answers to," I said. It was at this point that Victor looked at Nigel.

Victor was a great CEO. He was very balanced, considerate in his approach to all employees and always appeared to have time for me. This was probably due a chance meeting I had with him some years back. I was based in our catering facility close to Gatwick airport and was responsible for the sales for the UK. At the time, the Gatwick catering unit heavily relied on the charter airlines for revenue which amounted to over £20 million a year. These contracts were out for tender which if they were lost, would result in the closure of the facility. What was making the situation more desperate was the fact that our facility had seen no investment in the previous ten years and was looking old and tired. The competition on the other hand, had a new state of the art catering facility. Very appealing to our charter airlines.

Victor was at that time the SVP Global Operations and visited the facility to discuss the probability of closing the unit as it was unlikely we would retain the charter airline business. It was never an easy topic of discussion. Victor, like many of us, had worked in the catering facilities when he first started out. He knew the despair it would bring to many families if he had to close the facility and make people redundant. It weighed heavily on him. During the meeting with the facility General Manager, Victor asked me what my thoughts were. I took the opportunity to point out to Victor that, despite the tired, outdated look of the facility, and the lack of investment in equipment, trucks and IT, the employees and management did an exceptional job for the customers. The service was always on time, the quality of the food was never in question, and we had great communication and relationships with our customers. Price was always a determining factor for airlines in deciding where they placed their contracts, but as I explained to Victor, with a small amount of investment, combined with competitive pricing and given the exemplary performance of the facility, I believed that I could retain the contracts.

I proceeded to explain that the investments needed would pay for themselves in reduced labour costs and supply chain handling and overall, the profitability would improve, despite offering the customer a competitive price. Even back then Victor was a great man. A listener, a man driven by balanced judgement, a creative thinker and someone who treated everyone with respect. And he loved my pitch! He asked me to document the details as to what investment was required, produce the tender strategy plan, and personally send him the final proposed P&L. The businesses were retained on a new five year contract and the facility received its investment, improved profitability, and secured its medium-term future.

Although not friends, Victor and I enjoyed a mutual respect from that moment on, and over the years he would periodically give me a call out of the blue to ask for my opinion on something. Sometimes, he would act on it, sometimes not. But it was a nice feeling knowing that the top man in charge valued my input.

"I think it will not do any harm for George to ask his questions. And although you have sent the report to Lars; Cristina and I still have to agree it's content and sign off on it." Said Victor, without taking his eyes off Nigel.

"Thank you, Victor," I said before turning to Nigel. "Let's start with the airlines. What research does the report include regarding their future growth or possible downsize in the region? What are their current 'pain points' in the region? Is it logistics, product availability, hygiene standards, pricing? Are they generally happy with the current local operations or are they experiencing issues with delays, aircraft hits or loading failures?"

"Look George, we have carried out extensive research as to the numbers, you know, passenger loads, flights, meal services and the figures show that when you extrapolate that against the current selling prices, the returns are enormous. Costs for labour and produce are much less down there compared to the rest of the world."

"I am not questioning the pax loads and flight figures that currently operate. I'm sure your figures are correct. What I am questioning is the long-term sustainability. What I'm also questioning is what USP's (unique selling points) have been identified to attract customers; have we considered what we can do to alleviate pressure points for our potential customers? Does the report also consider the global nature of some of our customer contracts involving global volume discounts and pricing formulas? The independent caterer in some of these cities can charge what they like and get away with it because the airline doesn't have a choice, no leverage. The moment we are in situ, the airline can leverage other cities in the world that we cater them in, to reduce price and lower the market level. Has any of this been explored in the report? And this really is the tip of the iceberg. I have had some experience in South Africa dealing with the local catering company in Johannesburg. You have to first understand how business is done on this continent. There are always complications. Different rules, different legislation, cultures, political connotations, and business priorities. Don't get me wrong Nigel, I'm sure a lot of time and effort and a good deal of great information is included in the report. However, I think we are trying to run before we can even crawl, let alone walk!"

I had indeed been in Johannesburg a few years ago when I escorted one of my UK charter customers down there to visit the local catering company. My customer's airline was to begin seasonal charter flights to Johannesburg to take advantage of the rise in popularity of South Africa following the end of apartheid and the lucrative 'safari' market. I was asked to go as the company even back then, were trying to get a foot hold in the region by exploring any 'joint venture' opportunities. It was not particularly successful. The local catering company was owned by a wealthy elderly guy, who originated from Germany, was large in body mass and a character even larger than life itself! Not a racist, but with strong views on Black Economic Empowerment (BEE) which was a racially selective programme launched by the South African government to redress the inequalities of Apartheid by giving black (African, Coloureds, Indians, Chinese, Women and really any previously disadvantaged groups) South African citizens, economic privileges that were not available to White South Africans.

He wasn't really interested in a joint venture with anyone and more to the point, this small UK charter airline business, two flights a week, for a six month seasonal period! He was interested in the scheduled airlines, the BA's, Lufthansa's, KLM's, Virgin Atlantic's, and Qantas' of this world. The daily or twice daily, three class, full-service flights that yielded high profits. Because he was a 'one man' show, he gave those airlines the 'attention' they required to ensure they remained his customers even though he was charging high prices. He did what needed to be done without any hesitation as he answered only to himself. But that's how business was done in the region. A sort of 'you scratch my back and I'll scratch yours' mentality. I did quite admire him! In some respects, he was just operating the way the business used to operate twenty years ago all over the world, where relationships between supplier and customer where seen as the most important aspect of retaining business. Over time, price and economics changed all that in the northern hemisphere. Needless to say, it was not how I or my customer, was used to doing business and my customer eventually went with the competition. But it certainly was an eye opener for me.

I proceeded to ask several more valid questions, which were backed up by Tanja, Heinz, and Jana, who for the most junior person in the room, found confidence from my lead and began to contribute to the discussion. After about an hour of discussion, much of which was spent by Nigel and Daniel deflecting criticism of their report, Victor raised his hand in a way to suggest 'enough is enough'.

"I think this meeting was a great start in assessing the opportunity, raising questions and concerns, airing thoughts and ideas," said Victor, "and I would like to thank you all for your participation and to you, Nigel and Daniel, for the comprehensive report that you have created. However, as we have just witnessed, there are many unanswered questions and issues to consider before we make any final decision on this matter. I know that Heinz has made an initial contact with the current caterers in both Johannesburg and Addis Ababa regarding the opportunity of a joint venture with these businesses. Although these two cities are not included in the four identified in phase 1 of Nigel's report, I think it would be an appropriate way to proceed to explore this further and see where it takes us. I would like Tanja and George to instigate informative talks with the airlines to assess their interest and as George put it 'advise us of their pain points' within the region, so we can focus on providing services that help to alleviate them. If this can be done within the next two weeks, I would like to propose that we send some people to both Johannesburg and Addis Ababa to conduct a scouting mission, start preliminary negotiations and see where it leads us. Does everyone think this is a good way to proceed?"

"Of course, Victor, and I would like to suggest that both Daniel and I lead the visits to South Africa and Ghana," said Nigel.

"Ghana? Don't you mean South Africa and Ethiopia?" I said quizzically.

"Erm, yes, I meant Ethiopia, South Africa and Ethiopia," came the startled response from Nigel.

"We will decide in the coming weeks who will go," concluded Victor. And with that the meeting was adjourned.

Tanja and I went back to her office along with Heinz and Jana. For the first thirty seconds, nobody said anything. I think we were all collecting our thoughts before trying to articulate what we had just witnessed in the meeting.

"Look, it's very apparent that this is a good idea. And the potential is enormous if done correctly. But having that pair of 'twats' leading this, is not the right way to go about it. They can't be allowed to lead this project in Johannesburg and Addis. They are too arrogant to carry out negotiations and too stupid to ask the right questions. I think, you Tanja, Heinz, and Jana, should put yourself forward as the team to lead this. What do you think?" I said to the group.

"You are right, George. They are a couple of twats!" Tanja responded. "But you are wrong about the team. I have limited operational experience. I've never conducted hygiene audits or even worked in the facilities. I know a lot, don't get me wrong. But you know more. Therefore, I suggest the team is you, Heinz and Jana."

"I agree with you Tanja. And I agree with you, George. Those two are a couple of twats!" came the surprising comments from Heinz as we all turned to face him. After a subtle pause, we all laughed!

Tanja said her goodbyes to me and told me that she would be in contact soon with a plan to approach the airlines. Unfortunately, due to other meeting commitments, she was unable to give me a ride back to the airport to catch my flight. She slipped €50 into my hand and told me to buy the girls something nice at the airport and let them know how much she missed them. She then told me that Jana would take me to the airport.

I met Jana at the office reception, and she escorted me via the lifts to her car in the underground car par. We then set off on the ten-minute drive to the airport.

"Thanks for the ride Jana, I really appreciate it," I said, as Jana pulled out of the car park.

"My pleasure, George. You really handled Nigel and Daniel well today. They can be so difficult."

"Difficult? Is that another word for Twat?" I responded and we both laughed. We proceeded to talk freely for the remainder of the journey and although we had only just met a few hours before, we were amazingly comfortable in each other's company. Jana's English was perfect and for a German, she had good sense of humour. She was bright, interesting, and extremely attractive. She had a beautiful smile, and I couldn't help but notice her long legs as her skirt slightly rode up while she was driving!

"Take care George," she said as I got out of her car, "hopefully we will be in contact soon."

"Yes. And you too! Oh, and thanks for the lift back. Drive carefully, Jana," I replied, closing the passenger door, and giving her a wave as I stood there while she drove away. 'Nice girl' I thought to myself, someone who's company I really enjoy.

12

Once inside the airport, I made my way to a little toy shop that was situated just prior to the security check. I picked out two largish monkeys and thought to myself 'come on Kumbuka and Mjukuu, I'm sure 'Emster and Amster' will love you two' in reference to the monkeys we all loved at London Zoo. I paid for the toys with the €50 that Tanja had given me and made my way to the security hall, went through without making the x ray machines beep (a nice surprise as normally I forget something in my pocket or my watch which sets it off!) and continued through passport control. At this point my thoughts turned to Martyna. I was suddenly very aware that for the first time ever, I had left my children overnight with someone not related to me. Yes, the girls had stayed with Luke and Sally, but they were practically family. I looked at my watch. It was about 3:30 p.m. local time so Martyna would be getting ready to go and pick the girls up from school. I thought I would give her a quick call.

"Hey Martyna, how are you?"

"Hi George. Really good. A bit rushed as I must collect the girls soon and I have just laid out the kitchen table with some 'arty' things. I think the girls will have fun making some pasta necklaces when we get back!" was the cheerful response from Martyna.

"Sounds great! I won't keep you, just letting you know that I'm at the airport, the flight is on time, so I should be back about six-ish."

"No worries George. Thanks for letting me know. I thought we could have a lasagne for dinner tonight, keep the pasta theme going, is that okay for you? I'll make a salad to go with it."

"Wonderful, look forward to it and seeing you and the girls. Hope they have been okay?"

"They've been angels. Missing you, but we've managed to have some fun and they are great kids George. You should be immensely proud of them, and yourself."

"I am proud of them. Drive carefully, Martyna and see you soon," I said as I ended the call. My thoughts immediately turned to how wonderful Martyna was with Emily and Amy. I looked up and saw a confectionary shop and I quickly purchased a medium sized box of Lindt chocolates before heading to the gate, to wait for my flight.

The flight back was uneventful and the passenger sitting next to me didn't reach out and grab my thigh thirty seconds after take-off! Shame really, as she was quite an attractive woman! But I at least managed to revert to type and only greet the passenger with 'good afternoon', before retreating into silence for the remainder of the flight. After a quick call to Martyna upon landing, I made my way out through Terminal Two and proceeded to the taxi rank. There were always plenty of taxis at the airport, so I had no trouble climbing into one of the available black cabs and before long we were pulling up outside my house. I paid the driver, collected my things, and stepped out of the vehicle. The driver pulled away and I was left standing outside my front gate, staring at the house. For a split second my mind wandered, and I found myself thinking 'I hope Cheryl had a good time with the kids, I wonder if she has cooked a roast for dinner, I wonder what she is wearing' and-, 'It would be great to make love to her tonight.' Then the reality kicked in. Cheryl was not here to greet me. She would not have made a roast dinner, not be wearing any of her wonderful clothes and most definitely would not be making love with me tonight. Cheryl was gone. After letting out a huge sigh, I gathered myself together and made my way to the front door.

As soon as my key had turned in the lock, and before the door could fully open, I could hear both Emily and Amy rushing down the hall, calling out "Daddy's back!" in an overly excited fashion. After entering the house and immediately dropping my bags to the floor, I scooped up both girls in my arms and gave them a big hug, kissing them both gently on the lips.

"Hello, my darlings, I've missed you so much!" I said holding them tightly in my grasp.

"We've missed you too," Emily said. "But we have been good girls and had a lot of fun with Martyna."

"Yes Daddy, but we still missed the fun we have with you," continued Amy. I think she was trying to soften the blow that really, they had had a wonderful time without me!

"Well, I am so glad you've had a lovely time with Martyna. And now," I said while gently placing them back down to earth, "I have a present for you both from Tanja." I reached into my bag and pulled out the two cuddly monkeys. "This could be Kumbuka and Mjukuu."

"The monkeys from London Zoo!" they both cried out in unison.

"Yes, but you can call them whatever you want to, it was just an idea that I had, to call them after the monkeys at the zoo."

"I think we should call them Kumbuka and Mjukuu," Emily said.

"Yes, I agree," said Amy. "Is Aunty Tanja coming to see us?"

"Not now. She is terribly busy with her work. But she told me to tell you that she misses you both very much and wants to talk to you on skype this weekend. That would be nice, what do you think?"

"Yes, that would be very nice, and we can thank her for the monkeys," continued Amy.

"And I also have here a box of chocolates. But they are not for you two. They are for you to give to Martyna, as a thank you for looking after you while I was away."

"Can we give them to her now?" said Amy.

"Of course. Is Martyna in the kitchen?"

"Yes, we've been helping to make the lasagne." The girls turned and headed for the kitchen, with Emily holding the box of chocolates behind her back. I followed on behind them. As the girls and I entered the kitchen, I was hit by the wonderful smell of the lasagne emanating from the oven. A large bowl of salad had been prepared and was sitting in the middle of the kitchen table, along with four place settings and condiments. The thing that struck me more than anything, was how I was drawn to Martyna. She was busy preparing glasses of water for the table and had not yet looked up to see me, Emily and Amy standing in the doorway.

"Almost ready," she said, "if you want to take your seats, I will bring over the water, get the lasagne from the oven and then we can eat." It was at this point, Martyna finally looked up. "Is there something wrong?"

"No, I don't think so," I said. "But I think the girls have something to say." Martyna diverted her gaze from me and looked at the girls.

"Are you okay girls?"

"Yes Martyna. But we want to thank you for looking after us so nicely and playing with us and well, making us not miss Daddy too much," said Emily.

"Yes, so here is a present for you," continued Amy. The girls walked forward and gave Martyna the chocolates. Martyna was visibly moved by the girls' gesture and kneeled to give them both big hugs, while thanking them for their kind gift. Martyna then looked up at me and mouthed 'thank you, George' before returning to the 'group hug.' It was quite an emotional moment for me too! Emily and Amy looked so natural and comfortable hugging this woman. From the outside looking in, you could have even believed that this was just another normal mother and daughters' moment. A loving exchange between a parent and her children. And to be honest, in that moment, that is how it felt to me. Martyna was wonderful with the children. And she looked fantastic. She was wearing tight black jeans and a cream coloured, loose fitting 'poncho' jumper. The kitchen was warm, but I was sweating! Was I really starting to have feelings for this woman?

"I'm just going to get out of this suit, and I will be back shortly," I said and promptly exited the kitchen. I needed a few minutes alone. By the time I had returned to the kitchen, now dressed in my blue jeans and white polo shirt, the girls and Martyna were sitting up at the table and Martyna was dishing up the lasagne. It must have been hot for Martyna in the kitchen as well, as she had now disposed of the poncho jumper to reveal a white, round neck T shirt, that perfectly captured the outline of her breasts. It was getting hot again in the kitchen for me! Fortunately, the conversation had turned to favourite characters from the 'My Little Pony' movie. Emily's favourite was Princess Skystar, and Amy's was Twilight Sparkle.

"What's your favourite Martyna?" Amy asked.

"Well, it would have to be 'Pinkie Pie' because I love the colour pink."

"That's my second favourite character," said Emily "because pink is also my favourite colour. What's your favourite Daddy?" After a little pause and quick thinking, trying to remember the movie, a movie incidentally that the girls, Cheryl, and I had seen together, I managed to remember one of the characters.

"Erm, well, if I had to choose a favourite, it would have to be 'Applejack' because she is extremely hard working-, and I like apples!" With that I sat at the table and we continued to discuss movie characters, what the girls had done over the last twenty-four hours and just about anything else that families talk about at the dinner table.

The lasagne was perfect, not too wet, crispy parts around the edge and beautifully seasoned. Martyna certainly knew how to cook.

After dinner, I told Martyna to get some rest while I cleaned up the kitchen, set the dishwasher and then asked the girls to go for their showers. I waited for them in their bedroom, and once they were showered and dressed in their pyjamas, I told them they could choose a book that I would read to them. As usual, it was a tough choice between Frozen and Tangled - Tangled won the day! We went downstairs and sat on the sofa in the lounge. Martyna was already in the lounge, curled up on one the armchairs reading a book.

"Well, the girls are all done and I'm going to read them a story. Tangled!" I said holding the book up to Martyna.

"Lovely. Can I listen too?" came the reply from Martyna.

"Well, I was going to read it to them on my bed," I replied.

"Oh! Sorry George, I didn't mean to, you know-."

"Yeah! Can Martyna listen to the story with us daddy?" Emily said.

"I would really like that Daddy. You read the stories really well and it would be so nice for Martyna to listen to them too!" Amy chipped in!

"Well, look, Martyna is reading-" and I bent over to read the cover of the book she was holding, "The Mighty Angel, and I don't think she would really want to listen to me reading Tangled." The book Martyna was reading was a book by a Polish novelist called Jerzy Pilch, which was subsequently turned into a film. A romantic drama about a drunk, trying to beat alcoholism and finding love with a young woman. "She is probably really enjoying having time to herself, without having to look after you two monsters," I continued giving the girls a little tickle.

"If the girls would like me to listen to the story with you, I would love to." Martyna said. A brief, awkward silence followed, with me looking into Martyna's green eyes, opened mouthed.

"Ok, erm, let's go and read the story," I tentatively said as the girls cheered and raced out of the lounge and upstairs to my bedroom.

"Don't worry George, it will be okay," said Martyna as she walked past me and followed the girls upstairs.

"Not if I get a stiffy!" I muttered under my breath as she left the room.

By the time I had reached my bedroom, the girls were already on my bed. The bed was a large king size so there was plenty of room for all of us.

"In the middle Daddy, like normal," said Amy. As I approached the bed, Emily and Amy were lying next to each other and Martyna was lying on the right side of Emily. Martyna looked so relaxed and incredibly beautiful lying there. I squeezed in between Emily and Amy and they immediately snuggled up to me in eager anticipation of the story. Martyna snuggled up to Emily. I began to read the story.

I read the story in my usual way, making up different accents for the characters and adjusting my tone and speed of dialogue to enhance the suspense. And I need not have worried about Martyna being there, as by the time I had got to the second or third page, it just felt normal that we would all be lying on my bed while I read a story. By the end, the girls were very tired and ready for a good night's sleep.

"Daddy, I know it is only a story, but can you really have long, strong hair like Rapunzel and use it like rope?" asked Amy.

"Of course not, silly," came the instant response from Emily. "But it is a good question Amy, and I wondered the same thing until Mummy told me that it was only a story," Emily continued in a mature, supportive, 'big sisterly' way.

"Yes, it is only a story Amy. But hair can grow awfully long, and it can be extraordinarily strong. But I wouldn't go around letting yours out your bedroom window and trying to climb down it to the garden," I added. We all burst out laughing!

I walked the girls to their bedrooms, tucked them into bed and kissed them goodnight. As I came out of their room, I was about to go downstairs, but suddenly stopped. I turned around and went to my bedroom, slowly pushing the half-closed door wide open. The bed was empty. A sense of relief filled me, quickly followed by a sense of disappointment, and finally back to relief. What would I have done if Martyna had remained on the bed, waiting for my return? I shook my head, content in knowing that my final emotion of relief was the correct emotion. I made my way downstairs and went into the kitchen.

"Tea, George?" said Martyna who was filling the kettle.

"Erm, no. Could do with a glass of wine actually! Care to join me?"

"That would be nice. I used a bottle of Pinot Noir for the lasagne earlier, just a small drop obviously, do you fancy a glass of that?"

"Perfect."

"Go and sit down in the lounge and I will bring it in." I turned and made my way to the sofa. Martyna followed me in a few minutes later with the two glasses of wine and her box of chocolates.

"Thought we could have a few of these George. Thank you so much for your kind thought about the gift. But you really don't need to. I have grown so fond of the girls already in only this short space of time and I love being around them. You don't have to worry," Martyna said as she unwrapped the chocolate box, opened the lid and offered me first choice.

"I wanted to. It's only a small gesture, but it means the world to me that Emily and Amy are so well cared for by you," I said as I took a hazelnut whirl from the box.

"Not that one!" came a sharp reply from Martyna, before instantly following up with "just kidding," and breaking into a beautiful big smile.

"Funny," I said in a joking, sarcastic way and returned the smile.

"Anyway George, this is getting a bit serious don't you think?"

"What do you mean?" I replied.

"Well, if you remember, it was flowers on my first day, and now chocolates, anyone will think we were dating?" she said, again looking at me with those gorgeous green eyes and smiling through her pink lips. "Just kidding-, again," she continued.

"Funny" I said again. We continued to chat freely, drinking wine, and eating some more of Martyna's chocolates. It felt very natural to me to be around Martyna, and I got the same impression from her. We managed to talk about all sorts of things, ranging from where we grew up, went to school and our taste in music.

"You know, I never really asked you why you left your last employment?" I said. There followed a silence and an eerily cold frost seemed to enter the room.

"Erm, is it important?" Martyna asked.

"Well, no not really, as long as you didn't murder your last employer," I said in a jovial way trying to lighten the dark mood that had ensued. Martyna looked worried. "Hey, I didn't mean to pry. You... you didn't actually kill your last employer, did you?" I cautiously continued. Martyna looked at me. Her worried look still present on her face.

"Of course, not George."

"But something bad happened?" I enquired. There was a slight pause and finally Martyna let out a huge sigh.

"You might think badly of me. I should have told you before you hired me. But it was just a reaction. I would never do something like that normally. It just happened. Before I knew it, I had slapped his face."

"You hit the little boy you were looking after?"

"Oh my God! No George, not the children. I would never do anything like that to the children."

"Then who?"

"My employer and his wife were very wealthy. They didn't have much time for their children. I felt so sorry for them as they were great kids, just needed and wanted to be loved and talked to. The parents not only didn't have time for them, but they also didn't have time for each other either. Always, yelling and screaming at each other. I think they both had 'other people' they were seeing, but basically just stayed together for the money, you know, it seemed too difficult to get a divorce and go their own ways."

"It sounds like a difficult situation for both the children and you," I said.

"It was. It was truly awful, but I made the most of it, kept the children busy and out of their parents' way. But one day I was in kitchen, making coffee, when 'he' came up behind me and, rubbed himself against my body and slid his hands around my waist before reaching up and, grabbing my breasts," Martyna said in a slow, thoughtful way, starring into the distance as if she was replaying the whole incident in her mind. "I turned around and slapped him as hard as I could on his face."

"I'm so sorry Martyna. I had no idea. It must have been a terrible experience."

"It was. He pleaded for my forgiveness and begged me not to tell his wife. I obviously couldn't stay after that. He paid me off, gave me a good reference and I left. But I felt so sad for the children. They were particularly good kids and I think about them a lot," Martyna said in soft, quiet voice. Then she turned to me. "Does this make a difference to you hiring me?"

"Of course not, Martyna. You had a terrible experience. One that you should not have had to go through. It wasn't your fault. You are safe here, the girls think the world of you, I think the world of you and have absolutely no regrets about hiring you. In the short space of time that you have been here, you have already become part of the family."

"Thank you, George. If you don't mind, I would like to go to bed now." Martyna got up and went upstairs to bed.

I watched Martyna leave the room and then proceeded to the kitchen, filled my wine glass, and sat at the kitchen table. Poor Martyna. It must have been a terrible situation for her. Trying to do her best for the kids of parents who obviously didn't give a shit about them. And to top it all, having some rich, arrogant prick trying to grope her. I felt bad for her, and truly angry that there had been no come back for that arsehole. Martyna loses her job, the kids continue to suffer, his wife never knows, and he is free to continue his assault on the next unsuspecting child minder! "What a fucking prick," I found myself saying out loud. The only good thing was that because of this, Martyna applied to be our child minder. And I was extremely glad she did.

This revelation from Martyna also made me think about my feeling towards her. First and foremost, she was wonderful with Emily and Amy. Kind, gentle, funny, creative, loving, patient, understanding, caring, respectful and just wonderful! To me, Martyna was also all these things as well as beautiful, intelligent, honest, sexy, humble, generous, sexy, enthusiastic, sexy, talented, sexy and … sexy! Maybe I was beginning to have feelings other than those of just an employer! Okay,, let's analyse this. On the one hand, Martyna is the live-in child minder for my children. She does a great job, and the girls think the world of her. She helps me to get my life back to some sort of normality by allowing me to go back to work, knowing the girls are safe and well cared for in my absence. On the other hand, If I had met Martyna in a bar or club, I would have been instantly attracted to her (as most men would!) and would have plucked up the courage to talk to her. But now, Martyna is working for me and how would that work? After the experience at her last position, I'm sure she has no intention of getting involved with her boss. Also, she has become a constant in the girls' lives, what would happen if we split up? That would destroy the girls again. All these thoughts were going around in my head until finally, "Whoa!!!!" What was I thinking! I had known Martyna only six months. She probably had zero interest in me other than me being her employer and I was being completely irrational about all this. "What a fucking idiot!" I thought to myself and a semblance of a smile came across my lips. "Drink your wine and get to bed," I ordered myself.

13

Martyna was already in the kitchen, coffee brewed and placing bowls and spoons on the table for the girls' cereals. She looked up at me and smiled as I entered the room.

"Coffee, George?" she said.

"Yes, thanks Martyna. The girls will be down shortly. They are dressed and ready, but they're just discussing the important issues of the day, like 'will Miss Simmonds allow Emily to continue her school project on the importance of windmills' and 'will Amy get to be the break-time teacher assistant to Mrs Raven!' Oh, and will you join in with them again with the Justin Bieber song that always seems to play on the radio as you take them to school?" Martyna looked a little embarrassed as for a split second she thought about the three of them belting out 'Sorry' in the car on the way to school. Her smile got bigger!

"Sorry George, can't help it I'm afraid!"

"No worries Martyna," I said with an even bigger smile on my face.

"George, just before the girls are here, about last night, I wanted-"

"No need. As far as I am concerned, nothing has changed. You are wonderful with the girls; we all think the world of you, and you are now firmly part of this family. I am glad you told me about what happened and, I am sorry you had to go through that situation. It must have been terrible for you. And if you wanted to somehow make a complaint, I would be only too pleased to help you with that any way I can."

"Thank you, George. And thank you for the offer of support. But I just want to forget it and move on. I am really happy here with the girls and you. Thank you again, George," said Martyna with a sense of relief that nothing had changed between us.

"Besides, who else would I get that could teach the girls the words of that famous linguist, songwriter and all-round entertainer, Justin Bieber!" I said, and added "Certainly not Mrs Hansen," under my breath. We both laughed.

Following breakfast with the girls, I said my goodbyes and made my way to the office. I knew today would be a difficult day as I was positive that Frank Stanley would make a beeline for me as soon as I got in, to find out how the meeting had gone. I exited the lift on the third floor and greeted my colleagues as usual, stopping to have a brief chat with Gavin Preston.

"Morning Gavin, everything okay?"

"Yeah, great. We've had two catering delays on TUI in Manchester yesterday and a shit load of FAC's on my latest account, American Airlines regarding food quality out of Paris! So yeah, great day ahead for me," was Gavin's sarcastic response.

"I remember those days. But don't forget, nothing is always what it first seems to be. We always get stuck with the delay from the TUI Station Manager, whether it is our fault or not, so there's a good chance we did nothing wrong. As for the FAC's on American Airlines, I know we have just had a change of menu in CDG (Charles De Gaulle) that might have something to do with the crew writing us up. Maybe there was something wrong with the food or maybe the crew were just not expecting the change in meal service. I'm sure you'll get to the bottom of it."

"Yeah, I know-, thanks for the encouragement," came Gavin's response as he turned to pick the phone up and call our TUI account manager at the Manchester catering facility.

As I neared my office, Sarah Castle looked up from her desk and gave me a long, lingering stare. As I reached her desk, Sarah stood up to reveal she was wearing her customary, short skirt, pale blue, exposing those elegant, long legs and matching pale blue heels.

"Morning, Sarah," I said as I walked past her and into my office. Sarah followed in behind me and as I sat down at my desk, she stood in front of it and leaned over to me. She was wearing a white, blouse with small collars. The instant she leaned over my desk, most of her cleavage was exposed to me, and as always with Sarah, the half cup push-up bra she was wearing (or almost wearing, if you know what I mean), accentuated the fullness of her breasts, and I could see the top half of her areolas!

"Coffee, George?" she said.

"Yes, please Sarah," I said while still trying to avoid looking straight at her wonderful tits!

"White, no sugar?"

"Yep!"

"Anything else you fancy George," came a slow seductive response while all the time maintaining her 'bent over the desk' posture.

"Any Hobnobs?" I enquired somewhat nervously.

"I like Hob-Knobs. I'll see what I can do." And with that, Sarah turned and walked slowly out of my office, with that distinctive cat-walk manoeuvre. Once more, I could not take my eyes off her arse. Magnificent!

Within thirty seconds of Sarah's departure from my office, there was a knock on the open door and Frank was standing in the doorway.

"Got time for a quick chat George?" said Frank excitedly.

"Hi Frank. Come in." Frank walked in, closed the door behind him and made his way to the chair in front of my desk. After sitting down, he looked up at me nervously.

"Well, how did it go? What's the scoop?"

"Morning George," I said, "how are you doing? The kids okay? How's the new child minder working out? Did you see the game last night?" I continued sarcastically.

"Erm, yes, okay. Sorry, George. It's just that I'm excited and a little anxious to know what's going on."

"I know Frank. And I am the one that's sorry, I know how much this means to you."

"No, don't be silly. But, but what happened?"

"Well, I met with Tanja, Heinz, and a girl from Germany Controlling, Manager named Jana Muller, and of course, Nigel and Daniel."

"Nigel and Daniel? Daniel Mulzer, my counterpart for Germany?"

"Yes."

"Sneaky fucker. I knew Nigel was up to something with Daniel. He specifically said to me that although Daniel was helping him with some information gathering, he was not looking at him for a position as he was too 'German' in his approach. And all the time he was planning to shaft me and give the position to Daniel. What a fucking arse!" Frank ended angrily, raising his voice. At that precise moment, Sarah had walked into my office holding a mug of coffee and some chocolate hobnobs. I think she had just managed to catch the last part of Frank's outburst 'What a fucking arse' and I think she thought he was talking about 'her arse'. She slowly walked over to my desk, placed the coffee and biscuits down and turned to Frank.

"Would you like some coffee too?"

"Erm, no, thanks Sarah. Look-, I'm not sure what you heard, but I was talking about someone, not you, but someone else just then and not your, you know, your …"

"I'm sure you were, but I want you to know Frank, that I do have a great fucking arse!" she said and looked directly at me.

"Thank you, Sarah and thanks for the clarification," I said and with that, Sarah swivelled and walked towards my door, turning just before exiting and giving me a smile and one of her cheeky winks. I smiled at her.

"She fancies you George. You want to be careful there." I looked at Frank and sighed, shaking my head.

"Right, let's get down to it," I said and proceeded to tell Frank all about the meeting, the unexpected but most welcome additions of Victor Brandt and Cristina Wagner and the next steps. I also reassured Frank that we were at the early stages of the project and nothing had been decided regarding future roles in the region. He was comforted by this and was much calmer as he left my office some forty-five minutes later. Although, upon leaving my office, he was still upset enough to part my company with the words 'I'll never trust that sneaky cunt Nigel, ever again!' which I though was rather appropriate!

The remainder of the day saw me liaising with Tanja and making calls to my airline customers to set up meetings with them to discuss the opportunities in the African region. All the customers I made appointments with over the coming two weeks, seemed very enthusiastic about discussing their needs, issues with current caterers in the region and generally positive about my company's plan to enter the market. Good news I thought!

I left the office about 5:45 p.m. and made my way home. I had given Martyna the 'heads up' that I was on my way and she informed me that tonight's dinner was to be beef casserole, served with peas, carrots, cauliflower, and roasted potatoes. Excellent, I thought to myself as I got in the car and headed home. It was funny you know, I never really thought Martyna would do all the cooking during the week and keep the house in great shape as well. But as she explained, I pay her a full-time wage and when the girls are at school, she has time to do lots of things around the house. She doesn't mind doing those things and she loves to cook as well! But the weekends were always my responsibility. And just as well, as I loved to cook too!

I arrived at the house, parked the car, and went in. After greeting the girls, all three of them, I rushed upstairs, changed out of my suit into casuals, a quick spray of Lynx and I was ready for dinner. Dinner was indeed a culinary delight! Succulent, tender prices of beef in an onion gravy, accompanied by the crispiest of roast potatoes, and slightly 'al dente' cauliflower, carrots, and peas. Emily and Amy also enjoyed it immensely, and it wasn't long before the four plates on the kitchen table were empty.

"For dessert, I only have yoghurt I am afraid, hope that's okay?" said Martyna.

"Yeah, my favourite! Please can I have black cherry?" said Amy.

"I would like strawberry please, if we have it?" asked Emily.

"And you George?"

"Nothing for me thanks, Martyna. That meal was delicious, filling and I couldn't manage another thing," I said. Martyna gave an approving smile and went to the fridge to collect the yoghurts for the girls. She placed the requested flavours in front of Emily and Amy, placed a spoon down next to each pot and then started to clear the table of the empty dinner plates.

"Leave that Martyna, I'll do that," and I set about clearing up. Once the girls had completed dinner, I cleared down the kitchen, set the dishwasher on and made my way upstairs to see how the girls were doing. As usual, they were showered, teeth brushed and ready for a story. Martyna was in her room, but her door was open. I asked the girls to go and say goodnight to Martyna, which they duly did, and I heard them ask her if she wanted to again listen to 'Daddy's' story tonight. I heard Martyna say that although 'Daddy's stories are wonderful, she was a bit tired so would not listen to the story tonight. The girls came running back into my room and I read them a few chapters of the David Walliams book, 'Grandpa's Great Escape'. We snuggled up together and I opened the book began to read.

After tucking them into bed, kissing them goodnight and wishing them sweet dreams, I headed back downstairs. As I passed Martyna's door, I noticed it was now fully closed and I could hear her talking to someone, presumably on her mobile. I went to the kitchen and put the kettle on, pulled a cup from the cupboard and a tea bag from the tea caddy which was standing on the kitchen work top. After making a cup of tea, I sat at the kitchen table and was about to put my lips to the cup to take a sip, when my mobile rang. I picked up my mobile and looked at the number. It was a German number, nothing unusual, but not a number I recognised.

"George Hart," I said

"Hi George, this is Jana. I hope you don't mind me calling you at this late hour?"

"Hi Jana. No, no worries. How are you?"

"Well, I am a bit freaked out," Jana said. "Just got out of the shower and as I am drying myself, I notice this big spider looking at me, I dropped my towel, grabbed some tissue and decided to be brave and grab it. Thing is I missed and now I don't know where he has gone!"

"So, you are telling me you are standing there naked, chasing a spider around your bathroom?" Lucky old spider I thought!

"Pretty much, yeah," Jana continued "but that's not the reason I called you, even though I'm still only in my underwear."

"And why didn't you call me after you had got dressed?" I asked.

"Because it's so hot in my apartment, it's 9:30 p.m. and I'll be going to bed soon, so not worth getting dressed! But wanted to touch base with you about the meeting yesterday and let you know what I found out today." My mind was a bit confused! Firstly, I had the images of this extremely attractive woman, fumbling naked around her bathroom, trying to catch a spider, and then standing there, phone in hand wearing nothing but a bra and panties, talking to me. The thoughts brought a smile to my face, but I quickly moved on.

"Great. So, what did you find out today?"

"Well, you're not going to believe this but, Nigel went to see Lars Schuller today and basically complained that Victor and Cristina hijacked his meeting yesterday and belittled him in front of us. Can you believe that?"

"Unfortunately, yes I can. Nigel didn't get his own way yesterday and when that happens, he usually goes and complains to Lars. It's nothing to worry about."

"Are you sure? I heard that there were some raised voices in the Victor's office, you know what gossip is like in this place, and Lars walking out of Victor's office in a rage."

"Don't believe all you hear Jana. If I know anything about Victor, it's how great he is with people. He would have carefully and diplomatically explained the situation to Lars and wouldn't have let him leave his office in a rage. Don't worry, things will be fine."

"Are you sure George? Anyway, it was great to meet you yesterday and I am looking forward to working more closely with you. I think we can work well together, and I am looking forward to spending time with you in Africa and getting to know you better."

"Me too, Jana. Although, telling me about chasing a spider in your bathroom while naked and standing there talking to me in your 'Unterwäsche' (underwear), I feel I know you much better already!" I said with a hint of a laugh in my voice.

"Well, I am German, straight talking, and not afraid of my body, so get used to it!" came Jana's quick, flirtatious reply.

"I probably could get very used to it," I equally flirtatiously responded.

"Great. I'll call you tomorrow if I hear anything else, okay? You have my number now, so save it in your phone. You'll know it's me next time, and who knows what I will or will not be wearing. Have a great evening George, Bye." Jana hung up.

What a strange, unexpected, and yet thoroughly pleasant call that was. Was this girl really flirting with me because she liked me? Or was she flirting with me because she flirted with everyone? Did I care either way? Not really! And I had a quick flashback to thinking of her in the bathroom naked. Wow!

As I continued with my cup of tea, Martyna entered the kitchen.

"Do you fancy a cup of tea Martyna? Kettle's just boiled; I can make you one?"

"No thanks, George," she said as she slid into the chair next to me. "Can I ask you something George?"

"Of course, as long as it's not the one about where babies come from!" At this, Martyna smiled and rolled her gorgeous green eyes.

"Don't be silly," she said, "I was wondering if it was alright to go out on Saturday night?"

"Martyna! You work during the week for me. I don't expect you to work weekends, unless of course I am away on business, so of course it's alright if you want to go out on Saturday."

"Thank you, George."

"Where are you going? Up town, dinner, club?"

"Probably dinner, Covent Garden or something."

"Girl friend? Someone from the child-minding trade?"

"Friend, or at least could be," said Martyna. I looked at her quizzically. "If you must know, it's a blind date. Well, not actually a blind date. It's a friend of one of my girlfriends. I've met him before, you know in like a group of us, but never on our own. Don't know him that well at all really, so kind of like a blind date."

"That's great. Be careful though. You said it yourself, 'you don't really know him' so make sure you keep in public view!" I said all fatherly.

"Thanks Dad. But seriously, I'm not sure I want to go. It's been a while since I have had a boyfriend and what with starting a new job with you and the girls, I'm questioning whether this is a good time for all that."

"Hey Martyna. I can't tell you whether it's the right time or not. I can't tell you if this guy is the right guy or not. And I can't even tell you if, and when you do find the right person at the right time, that it will last forever. I know better than anyone that life is unpredictable, full of surprises, some great, memorable and some tragic, terrible. But what I can tell you is to make the most of every day and every opportunity to find happiness. Don't let things stop you from trying to do this, especially work, the girls or me. Don't make excuses, get out there and live life. If things don't work out, and you can be sure you will have your fair share of things that don't, the experience is not wasted. Don't fear making mistakes and don't let it put you off chasing your dreams and being happy. After Cheryl died, I hated the thought of starting again. Was I being disloyal? How could anyone replace her, what would the girls think, what would my in-laws think? All these sorts of questions went around in my head. But over time I have realised that none of that matters. You must continue to live. Respect the past but look to the future. So, I say 'go for it.'"

"Thanks George. You're right. And sorry. My problems are insignificant compared to yours."

"What do you mean? What problems? I have two wonderful daughters, I am financially secure, I have a job, a nice house, great friends and now I have a lovely, kind employee, whom I trust implicitly with the care of my children. I had a loving wife and although she is no longer physically here, I see her every day in Emily and Amy. Not just in looks, but their actions, mannerisms, words, kindness, and character. So no, I don't have problems and neither do you. Now, you sure you don't want that tea?"

"Go on then. I will. Thank you, George."

14

Saturday evening soon came around, and it seemed like Martyna had spent the entire day trying to decide what to wear for her blind date tonight. She appeared so preoccupied with the event, that even Emily and Amy were asking me if everything was alright with her.

"Martyna's going on a date tonight, so she wants to look her absolute best. You know what a date is, don't you girls?" I asked Emily and Amy.

"Of course, we do. It's like what Emily wants to go on with David Brightly at school," said Amy.

"Stop it, Amy!" was Emily's instant response. "That's not true Dad, honest, Amy's making it up."

"No, I'm not. You said that David wanted to be your boyfriend and asked his mum if she could take you both to McDonalds. That's kind of a date isn't it Daddy?"

"Well, yes I suppose it is. Sort of," I said trying to find the right words. "But it's okay," I turned to Emily. "Although you are a bit too young for boyfriends right now, if David wants to take you to dinner at McDonalds, with his mum of course, then that would be okay. But I would like to meet David and his mum first."

"It's okay Dad. I don't really like him anyway. He mucks about a lot in class, smells a bit and makes funny noises with his armpits."

Emily then turned to Amy. "So, he is not my boyfriend and I don't want to have a date with him," she continued.

"Sorry Emily. I didn't know you didn't like him anymore," Amy said apologetically.

"That's alright, Amy. But you should really talk to me before saying things like that to Dad. You'll get me in trouble."

"Nobody is in trouble," I said. "But girls, just remember, I am here for you guys. You can always talk to me about anything. I might not always have the right answers, but I will tell you what I think. And you know that this is something that I have been telling you since you were old enough to understand. I will never be angry with you about anything. So long as you always tell me the truth. You both understand how important it is to be honest. If you do something wrong, as we all do from time to time, you must own up to it, say you are sorry and then we can move on, fix things, learn to be better people. So never be nervous or scared of telling me the truth. I am always here to help you guys, okay?"

"We know Daddy. And we will always tell you the truth," said Emily. We had a group hug and Amy whispered in my ear 'I love you Daddy' to which I responded with 'I love you both so much too, my lovely sweethearts'.

I had made the girls and myself a chicken curry for dinner and the girls had begged me to make a very simple dessert, but one they absolutely adored. It was a kind of mousse packet mix that milk was added to. Butterscotch was their favourite flavour and it was something I had made for them since they were small. However, one time I had crushed up some chocolate pieces and hidden them below the surface of the mousse, prior to it setting. When I gave them the dessert, I told them that the dessert had some buried treasure hidden in it! They loved it, and from that day on it was known as 'Daddy's Treasure Hunt Dessert' and always featured a surprise hidden below the surface.

Martyna was obviously not having dinner with us tonight as she was eating out with her blind date. The girls and I had finished, and I had promised them that I would play a game or two of 'Kerplunk' with them once I had cleared down the kitchen. They were busy setting up the game on the kitchen table as I switched on the dishwasher and gave the worktops a last wipe down. As I turned to face the girls at the kitchen table, my eyes were drawn to Martyna standing in the doorway.

"What do you think, George? Do I look okay?" said Martyna a little nervously. I have to say, she took my breath away. Martyna was wearing an off the shoulder, short, black dress, adorned with small green and beige flower prints, black belt, heels and nervously held a cream clutch bag.

"You look stunning Martyna," I said, and in order to avoid staring any further at her I turned to the girls and said, "Look girls, look how beautiful Martyna looks."

"You look just like a princess. What's her name, the one married to William," said Amy.

"Princess Kate," said Emily.

"Yeah, Princess Kate."

"Thank you, girls, but I'm sure I don't really look as nice as Princess Kate."

"Actually Martyna, the girls are quite right. You do look like a princess. And I'm sure your date will think so too."

"Thank you, George." We all stood in silence for a few seconds with huge smiles on our faces.

"Well. I had better go."

"Yes Martyna. And please be careful. You have my number if you need anything. I'm not prying, and god knows I'm not your father, but what time do you think you will be back? You know, so I don't start worrying." I asked and immediately felt a little embarrassed about asking the question because maybe Martyna had planned to not come back at all tonight!

"Oh, should be back about 11:30 p.m. not too late."

"Thanks, Martyna," I said with relief.

She had ordered a taxi and after waving her off, the girls and I settled down for the 'Kerplunk' world championship! After all the sticks had been placed in the plastic tube and the marbles had been added, we all got our 'game faces' on, determined not to let any marbles fall when it was out turn to pull out the stick.

Once we had finished our game, which Emily became the 'new, undisputed, world 'Kerplunk' champion of the wooooorld' (yes, I had to announce it in the style of the legendary boxing announcer, Michael Buffer!), the girls had a shower, got ready into their pyjamas and I read them a story. By 8:45 p.m. I was back downstairs and sitting on the sofa with the tv remote control in hand. I was about to press the button to bring the tv to life when my mobile rang. I looked at the screen and discovered the call was from Jana.

"Hey Jana, how are you?"

"Hi George, I am okay, you?"

"Yeah, good. Just put the girls to bed so my evening is my own now."

"The girls?" came a startled surprise from Jana. "what girls?"

"I did tell you about my girls, when you dropped me off at the airport last week, do you remember?"

"Oh, sorry George, you mean your daughters. Yes. For a second there, I thought you were having some sort or sex orgy with a few girls."

"I wish, but sadly no. Just a quiet evening in, watching the tv. There is an old film on tonight that I have seen a few times, but it is one of my favourites. So, I think I might grab a beer and watch that."

"That seems a bit sad George. Wish I could be there to keep you company. What's the film called?"

"Funnily enough, Only the Lonely," I said. "Sounds strange, I know, but it's a comedy starring John Candy."

"Well maybe one day I'll get the chance to watch it with you and keep you company."

"Deal," I said. "What can I do for you?"

"Nothing really, just thought I would give you a call and see if you know when you're coming back to Frankfurt. I bumped into Tanja in the canteen yesterday and she said you had both made progress with the customers, meetings set up and that they all seemed extremely interested in what we are trying to do."

"Yeah. I've got some meetings next week and I should be back to Frankfurt probably the week after. Hopefully, with good news and we can then start to plan with Heinz and Tanja, regarding visiting the region."

"And Nigel and Daniel, don't forget!"

"How could I forget those two twats. But somehow, I think we could do this without their help. Let's just wait and see. Anyway, it's Saturday night, why aren't you out on the town, clubbing, drinking and having a great time?"

"Well, I am splitting up with my boyfriend. He doesn't know it yet, but I don't think there is much of a future with him. So, I didn't really feel like going out tonight. Thought I would give you a call instead."

I thought this was a little bit odd, as I had only met Jana last week. I would have thought she would have had many friends to talk to and go out with, rather than staying home on a Saturday night and calling me! But as we had hit it off quite well, I just went with the conversation.

"Well, thank you Jana. I'm very flattered. But I'm sure you would have had a much nicer time going out with your friends."

"Not really. It's hot and sticky outside and I've had a nice shower, relaxed and just catching up on a book I've started reading."

"Did the mysterious spider catch you again tonight? He really is a lucky little devil."

"No, not tonight. But if you think he is lucky, maybe you can be my spider one day. And yes, I'm sitting in my underwear again. But only because it's hot in here."

"Ok, I believe you. What's the book called?"

"Girl on a Train. It's quite good. I like reading English books. It helps my English and I think the stories are a lot better." We continued to chat for the next twenty minutes and by the time we had said our goodbyes, it felt like we had become much closer, very flirtatious with each other and almost as if there was something going on between us. As silly as it sounds, was I starting to have feelings for this girl as well as Martyna? I pushed these thoughts to the back of my mind, went to the kitchen, grabbed a bottle of beer from the fridge, returned to the sofa and switched on the tv. I found the channel showing the John Candy film, settled into the sofa and began to watch it.

As the closing credits started playing at the end of the film, I heard a noise coming from the front door and looked at my watch. It was a little after 11 p.m. I picked up the tv remote control and switched it off just as Martyna appeared in the doorway.

"Hey. Did you have a nice time?" I said.

"It was okay," came a slightly disheartened response. Martyna walked into the lounge and sat next to me on the sofa.

"Are you okay? Do you want to talk about it?"

"Yes, I'm fine. We had a nice meal, a little Italian place in Covent Garden," continued Martyna, "some conversation, a few drinks, but, there was no real connection between us. Don't get me wrong, Zak, the guy, is nice enough, but not really my type. A bit boring actually. Although he probably thought I was boring too."

"I can't imagine anyone finding you boring Martyna. I'm sorry things didn't turn out too well. Especially as I encouraged you to go."

"Thanks George. And no need to apologise. It's not your fault. You were right to encourage me to go. It helped me to see what I want right now, gave me some clarity. You know, most of the evening when Zak was talking, all I was thinking about was Emily and Amy and If they enjoyed their story tonight, I am sure you read them one, right?" she continued. "And what will we have for dinner tomorrow, will you cook your famous Sunday roast, beef, roast potatoes, cauliflower, carrots, peas, Yorkshire puddings and your wonderful gravy. And although it's my day off, what I would do with the girls, you know, play 'Guess Who' or 'Snakes & Ladders' or 'Operation' or just sit and talk with them. It made me realise that I'm not ready for a relationship yet. Certainly not with Zak."

"I'm glad you feel that way about the girls, Martyna. It's so comforting to me that you have this special bond and feeling for them. And maybe this Zak isn't the right guy, but there is definitely someone out there for you. You must not give up or let this family get in the way. Do you know what I mean?"

"Yes, George. But you and the girls 'do not get in the way'; this is where I feel the most comfortable. This is where I feel at home," she said looking contently at me.

"Okay. But keep trying, huh! Now, do you fancy a beer?"

"I do! But let me get it. Do you want one?"

"I do!" I said. Martyna left the lounge, and I heard her head upstairs. A few minutes later, I heard her coming down the stairs and she headed into the kitchen, opened the fridge, and returned to the lounge with two beer bottles. She had changed out of her pretty dress and was wearing tight, white leggings and a grey baggy 'I Love New York' sweatshirt. Again, she looked fantastic. No matter what she wore, she just had a way of looking beautiful, charming, sexy, and just made me think of what it would be like to hold her, kiss her, feel her body. That was stupid though! Martyna wasn't interested in me. She adored Emily and Amy and I would go as far as to say, she even loved them.

But that was what she was here for. The girls. Certainly not to fall in love with her boss! Especially after the experience she had with her previous employer. No, put these thoughts to the back of your mind George and do not spoil a good thing, I had to tell myself.

We sat on the sofa drinking our beers, talking, and laughing about lots of things. Martyna reminisced about how nervous she was at the first interview because Sally and Barbara had been present, like two pit bull terrier dogs, guarding me, their master. And how embarrassed she was on the first day, turning up with a big box of CDs and laughing to herself, watching me struggle to carry them up the stairs. We must have talked for a good hour before I said that it was about time for my bed. We both stood up and faced each other.

"Thanks for a wonderful evening George. I've really enjoyed it. So much better than the first part of my evening. Thank you" and she leaned into me and gave me a kiss on the cheek. I was a bit startled. She smiled at me, said 'Goodnight George', turned around, and headed for the stairs. This was the second time Martyna had done that. The first being on Christmas day when she thanked me for her presents. I touched my cheek with my fingers, smiled to myself and went to bed.

The next morning, I was up early, busy getting the breakfast ready for the girls and of course Martyna. As it was Sunday, I decided I would make pancakes, 'American' style. After making the batter mix, I fried off some streaky bacon making sure it was very crispy and put it in the oven to keep warm. I prepared the filter coffee and, laid the table being sure to remember the maple syrup, icing sugar dusting, honey, strawberries and most importantly as far Amy was concerned, the blueberries. Amy loved blueberries and felt they especially went well with pancakes. I had to agree with her! I then sat at the table and picked up the Sunday paper to read.

Martyna arrived at the kitchen dressed in the same white leggings and grey, baggy sweatshirt from the previous evening. Even with her hair not quite as pristine as it had been the night before, she still looked gorgeous, homely and with my heart skipping a beat, I thought back to last night's kiss on the cheek.

"Morning, Martyna. Coffee? I'll start the pancakes and maybe you can give the girls a shout, let them know breakfast will be in about fifteen minutes. I think they are playing 'horses' in their bedroom!"

"Morning George. Yes, thanks, coffee would be good. And looking forward to the pancakes. But before I call the girls, I just wanted to say thanks for cheering me up last night. And - sorry about the kiss on your cheek. I don't know why I did it, maybe the alcohol. Anyway, I hope you were not offended or read anything into it?"

"No worries. I'm glad you had a nice evening and I'm only too pleased to help bring a smile to your face," I said, trying hard to disguise my disappointment that 'I wasn't to read anything into the kiss.' Martyna gave me a relieved smile and turned to exit the kitchen to call up to the girls. As I watched her walk away from me, I realised at that second that I really did have more feelings for her than just that of an employer. As crazy as it sounded in my head, I think I was falling for her.

"Hooray! Pancakes!" came the squeal of delight from Emily and Amy as they sat down at the kitchen table for breakfast.

"Okay, girls take a pancake and help yourself to the toppings. And Amy, leave some blueberries for everyone else!" I said as I brought over to the table a large plate of pancakes. "There is some more batter mix left, so if we get through these and anyone wants some more, I can easily make some."

"Thanks Dad," said Emily.

"Thanks Daddy," said Amy.

"Thanks Daddy," said Martyna, looking at me. They all laughed.

"Enjoy," I said. "And after breakfast, I thought we could go to Gladstone Park for a walk, maybe take a football and a frisbee, what do you think?"

"That would be great Dad. I can practice my shooting and passing," Emily said.

"Me too," was Amy's response. "Are you coming Martyna?"

"You are more than welcome to join us, only if you want to though. Please don't feel you have to. It's your day off so If you have things to do, it's not a problem."

"Thank you, girls, and thank you George. I would love to come with you and show you my footballing skills that I learnt while watching the great Polish player, Robert Lewandowski on tv," Martyna said, looking up at everyone as we all looked back at her in astonishment. "And David Beckham of course," she added!

After finishing up breakfast and with the girls helping to clear away, and dry the dishes, we all got ready to go to the park. The weather was very warm so, shorts and T shirts were the order of the day. I packed a rucksack with a large bottle of water, a packet of shortbread biscuits (Emily and Amy's favourites) a pack of plasters (always handy to have with children around!), the frisbee and my old football. I say old, only because I had had it a few years. But it was in great condition, almost like new. It was a replica of the official 2010 South Africa World Cup ball. I remember watching England's clash against Germany with Cheryl. We sat on the sofa, with our beer bottles, not holding out much hope of a win following England's less than impressive start to the tournament. Cheryl and I both loved our football and we were gutted about England going out of the world cup so early.

I have always been good at football. I started playing at the age of eight for a local under twelve boys' team. My dad used to take me on Sunday mornings to the games and watch me from the side-lines. He always encouraged me but was never one of those parents that would be shouting and screaming at their kids to 'do this' and 'move there' and telling all the other kids to pass the ball to their son.

After a short ten-minute walk, we arrived at the park. Emily and Amy could not wait to get the ball out of my rucksack to start playing. No sooner had I taken off the rucksack and placed it on the ground, the football was out of it.

"I think we should have teams Daddy," said Amy.

"Yes Dad, maybe Amy and I will be on the same team, and you and Martyna can try to beat us," added Emily.

"I tell you what, Amy and I will start together on the same team and play against you and Martyna. And then after that we can swap partners, how's that?" I suggested. Martyna agreed and we made a goal by using my rucksack and the big bottle of water as the goalposts. Emily and Amy are good at football for their ages. Cheryl and I had always liked going to the park with the girls to kick a football around and they seemed to take to it from an early age. With the increasing television coverage of women's football, the girls became more and more interested, and I was seriously thinking of approaching a professional team to see if they would be willing to take the girls on - that's how good I thought they were!

It was not long before the inevitable happened. Amy passed the ball to me and as I approached the makeshift goal, Martyna can running at me. As I feinted to go one way and then actually went the other, Martyna stuck out her leg and tripped me over. Unfortunately for Martyna, she fell too. Fortunately for me, she fell right on top of me. Our eyes met, not more than ten centimetres apart, our bodies touching in a tangled, sweaty mess on the ground. I could feel her breasts pressed against my chest and the top of her right thigh wedged into my groin. We looked at each other for a full thirty minutes! In truth, it was probably no more than a couple of seconds. But I felt a connection with Martyna, a tingling of electricity, a happiness I had not felt since before Cheryl had died.

"Thanks for cushioning my fall George," she said with a cheeky smile on her face "and it's definitely not a penalty!" she continued as she lifted herself up from me, before offering me her hand to help me up.

"Penalty or not, it's definitely a Red Card," I said continuing to look deep into her eyes. She smiled and then we both looked to see what the girls were doing. They had stopped playing and were just staring at us. I couldn't imagine what they were thinking at that moment. Had they just witnessed something too? Did they also see the connection that I had just felt with Martyna? One thing is for sure, children are very intuitive. They instinctively know when things are good and bad. Ask any child whose parents have split up and they will tell you that they generally knew things were not right. And due to a child's natural innocence, I had the feeling a question or four, was coming! I had to act quick to avoid the awkwardness of the situation.

"Right, who wants an ice cream?" I said.

"Yeah!" came the harmonious response from both Emily and Amy. Maybe I had got away with it for now, but I'm sure there would still be some questions to come from the girls.

We made our way to a little café at the north entrance of the park and while Martyna stayed outside with Emily and Amy, I went in to get the ice creams for the girls and two coffees for Martyna and myself. After paying for my refreshments, I returned outside to find that Martyna and the girls had found a place to sit on the small walls, which formed the remains of Dollis Hill House, a nineteenth century, grade II listed farmhouse which was destroyed by fire in the 1990s. The building was finally demolished in 2012. I handed the girls their ice creams and Martyna one of the coffees.

"Well, that was a good game of football," I said.

"I think Martyna, and I won," said Emily. "But it doesn't matter who wins, so long as everyone had fun."

"Did you get a bruise on your leg when Martyna kicked you Daddy?" asked Amy.

"Well, let me see," and I looked down at my leg. "No. No bruises, although I think Martyna should have been sent off, don't you?"

"Yes. Daddy, can we walk around the walls, while we eat our ice cream?"

"Yes, but please be careful." As the girls got up and made their way around the ruins of Dollis House, I looked at Martyna and she looked back at me.

"Sorry about your leg George, I hope it really is okay?"

"I think I'll live. But Norman 'Bite Your Legs' Hunter has got nothing on you," I said referring to the legendary, Leeds United footballer of the sixties and seventies who terrorised centre forwards by kicking the shit out of them in every game! Martyna laughed.

"And thanks for breaking my fall. Quite an intimate moment. But purely accidental."

"I know it was accidental. And no need to thank me for saving you. I didn't really know much about it anyway. One minute I was about to go past you, square the ball to Amy for her to score, the next I'm on the ground, flat on my back, with this beautiful, sexy, Polish child minder, on top of me, rubbing my genitals with her thigh, pressing her ample breasts against me, looking lovingly into my eyes and about to give me a long passionate kiss, tongues and all," is what I thought about replying. What I actually said was "I know it was accidental. And no need to thank me for saving you. No harm done." And that was that! We continued to chat normally and after a few games of frisbee with the girls, we walked home. No more was said about the 'Red Card' incident.

15

After coming back from the park, the rest of the day was filled with playing games with the girls, making a Sunday roast, showers, stories and putting the girls to bed. Martyna was in her room, so I sat on the sofa in the lounge and started to think about my work schedule for the coming week. My phone rang and I looked down at the number. Again, a German number, but this time I didn't recognise it.

"George Hart," I answered.

"Hi George, this is Fiona, Fiona Stephenson. I hope you remember me?"

"Hi Fiona. Of course, I remember you. How can anyone forget the first and only time they have been molested on an aircraft," I said. "How are you? Have you settled into Frankfurt life yet?"

"I'm fine George and thanks for reminding me about my molesting tendencies towards unsuspecting airline passengers," Fiona replied. "But seriously, I am sorry about that. You have forgiven me, haven't you George?"

"Of course, Fiona. I'm only joking. So, this is a nice surprise. How have you been?"

"Well, if you remember, I told you I had my mother over for the weekend. We've chosen one of the apartments that the company have offered me, close to the city centre in Sachsenhausen, but it needs a few things doing to it, so I can't move in for a couple of weeks. So, I'm stuck at the Sheraton for a while."

"That's a shame. But I know Sachsenhausen and it's a nice area and convenient for the city. Good choice."

"Yeah, although my mum wanted me to choose another place in Bockenheim, north of the river. She said it would be quieter. So, we had a bit of an argument. But it's okay. I'm glad she has gone back home now though."

"I hope you didn't leave it in a bad way with your mum. If it is one thing I know, always try to resolve your issues at the time they happen. Sometimes 'tomorrow' never comes."

"What does that mean?"

"Never mind," I said. "Maybe I'll tell you about that another time. Anyway, what can I do for you?"

"Nothing really. I was just wondering if you were planning to come back to Frankfurt soon. And if you were, whether you fancied meeting for a drink or dinner maybe?"

"Well, nothing is planned for now. But my meeting last week went well and that means I should be back there within the next two weeks or so."

"That's great. Would you like to meet up? And I promise I won't get drunk this time. My head hurt for the rest of the day last week!" I thought for a moment and the pause although was brief, seemed to go on forever. I realised I had to say something in response!

"That would be nice Fiona, I would really like that. I have your number so will call you once I have confirmed my travel plans," I replied. After talking for a further fifteen minutes about how Fiona's job was going and things to do in Frankfurt, we ended the call and I reiterated that I would call Fiona once I had a confirmed date for my return to Frankfurt. After ending the call, I started to think about Fiona, the night I had put her to bed. Taking her shoes off and gently placing her in bed. Although nothing happened that night, she did look amazing, and we really did get on so well during our 'drunken' evening together. And she did tell me at breakfast the following morning how she felt we had a connection. Fiona was obviously attracted to me as I suppose, I was to her, and now she was calling me to see when I was coming back to Frankfurt. It had been over eighteen months since Cheryl's passing. Should I feel guilty if I wanted to take things a little further with Fiona? I didn't have time to reconcile this in my mind, before Martyna entered the lounge.

"You look thoughtful. Anything wrong?" asked Martyna.

"Erm, no not really. Just thinking about my schedule for the next few weeks. I'm sorry Martyna, but you do realise that I might have to go back to Frankfurt in the next couple of weeks and there is a possibility that I will have to go to Johannesburg and Addis Ababa for a few days. I'm really sorry."

"Don't worry George. You did explain that your job involves travel, at the interview. So, it's not a surprise for me and there is no need to apologise. I love being with Emily and Amy and I hope they enjoy being with me. So really, no problem."

"Thanks, Martyna. And yes, the girls love being with you too!" We talked for a while about the events of the day, the 'red card' incident, the girls, and Martyna also paid me great compliments on my cooking prowess. The roast dinner was excellent! Although Fiona had been in my mind following our telephone call, Martyna was the one now firmly at the forefront. Again, she was only wearing jeans and a vest top, but she looked stunning and always smelled 'fresh' as if she had just stepped out of the shower. And the great thing about Martyna, is that I don't think she ever realises how good she looks, no matter what she is wearing. She almost appears to deliberately 'dress down' in order not to be noticed, but in effect, it makes her more noticeable. This woman was beginning to stir serious emotions within me. And it felt natural, comfortable, and exactly right!

The next week or so I spent with my customers, gathering information about the intended Africa Region expansion, and liaising with Tanja. We decided that between us we had enough intelligence to arrange a follow up meeting with Nigel and Daniel, so Tanja set the wheels in motion. Once again, I would fly out to Frankfurt on Wednesday evening, for a meeting the following morning. Frank was a constant presence in my office during that time, making sure I had his back if any decisions would be made on the management team for the new region. But again, I told Frank that it was too early in the process for those decisions to be made. My comments didn't do anything to comfort him!

On the Monday before the meeting, I contacted Fiona.

"Hi Fiona, it's George."

"Hey George, great to hear from you. How are you?" said Fiona excitedly.

"I'm doing well, you?"

"Yes, settling into the job, you know, meeting lots of people, learning how things are done, oh-, and learning the office politics. That's always the fun bit, learning 'who doesn't get on with who' and 'who has backstabbed who' and very importantly 'who is sleeping with who!'"

"Sounds fascinating," I replied. "Something right out of Jerry Springer! Listen, I just wanted to let you know that I will be flying to Frankfurt this Wednesday evening again, usual routine, staying at the Sheraton, meeting Thursday morning."

"That's great George. Do you fancy meeting up? Unfortunately, my apartment is still not ready, so I am still at the Sheraton, same floor, same room! It would be great to see you. Please say yes."

"It sounds like a plan," I said. "And look, the flight I normally take is fully booked, so I am getting an earlier one. Should be at the hotel by 8 p.m. So, if you fancy dinner?"

"I would love that. I'll book a table at the 'Taverne' restaurant at the hotel. It's not great, but I have eaten there a few times and the food's okay. Can't wait to see you George. Let me know when you arrive, okay?"

"Will do, and thanks for booking the table. Dinner is on me though! Look forward to seeing you Fiona. Take care." And with that, I had a date for Wednesday night!

On the Tuesday, before flying out to Frankfurt I got a call while I was in my office from Jana.

"Hello George."

"Hi Jana, how are things?"

"Yes, good thanks. I just talked to Tanja and she said you were coming out tomorrow on an earlier flight, as your normal flight is fully booked."

"Yeah. I'm not sure if there is some convention going on in the city and that's why the flights are fully booked, but it doesn't really matter. I'm only glad I managed to get a hotel booking."

"I haven't heard of anything, but anyway, I was wondering if you wanted to get together for a drink or maybe dinner. I don't want you to be bored if you are arriving earlier than usual. What do you think?"

"Well, actually, I have already arranged to meet a friend for dinner. I say friend, but I only met her a few weeks ago on my last trip to Frankfurt. Funny story really, I-"

"Her!" was Jana's startled reply. "Did you say 'her?'"

"Yes, it's quite a funny story really. You see, I was sitting in my seat on the plane, and it had just taken off, when this hand suddenly…" I continued before again being interrupted.

"Oh! Well not to worry, I'll see you in the office on Thursday morning. Have a safe flight and enjoy your evening with your 'friend', bye." Jana hung up. I lowered my phone from my ear and just stared at it in a mild state of confusion. That felt extremely weird! My immediate, gut feeling was that there was a hint of jealousy in Jana's voice because I had arranged to have dinner with Fiona. How could that be? No, I must be wrong about that. "Stop it George, you idiot," I heard myself saying in my head. Not every girl you meet fancies you!

The following day, I was planning to leave the office early to pick the girls up from school. As I was going to have to leave before dinner to catch my flight to Frankfurt, I wanted to spend a little time with Emily and Amy. During the morning I had a meeting scheduled with a young girl who had just finished university and was applying for a junior sales position with the company. She was to meet with Hilary Smith (UK Human Resource VP) first, before having a 'Sales Introduction' with me. If she were successful in the interview, she would be working alongside Gavin Preston, who I knew would do a good job in showing her the ropes and looking after her. It was about 10:30 a.m. when the 'ping' of the lift could be heard and I looked up from my desk, through my open office door and along the walkway to the lifts in anticipation of seeing our potential new recruit. After a brief pause, the lift doors opened and a rather bemused young girl, looked up from her mobile phone. She stepped out of the lift, looked around, turned 180 degrees, and got back in. The doors closed. Fifteen seconds later, the doors opened again, and the same bemused looking girl again looked up, stepped out, looked around and once again, started to return to the lift. Only this time, she must have taken a fraction longer, because as she started to re-enter the lift, the doors closed, temporarily squashing her, before immediately springing back to the open position. It looked like something out of a Peter Sellars, Pink Panther movie! Inspector Clouseau trying to negotiate an exit from a rogue elevator! She immediately pulled herself away from the doors and although I was some twenty metres away and she had her back to her audience, I could hear her muttering to herself something about 'getting a grip'! It wasn't just me who was witnessing this comical display. I could see Sarah, Gavin and the whole team looking at this poor girl. And if I had x-ray vision and looked through the walls of the offices to my left, I'm sure I would have seen both Hilary and Frank staring at this girl, with smiles on their faces. She turned around and was met with eleven pairs of eyes staring at her.

"Quite tricky these lifts. Erm, do you know if Hilary Smith is on this floor, the HR lady?" she said trying hard not blush. Gavin stepped forward and escorted the charming young lady to Hilary's office. I felt sorry for her, but she was delightful, and I intuitively knew she would fit in with the group very well.

After about one hour, Hilary came to my door with Melanie in tow.

"Hi George. This is Melanie Simpson, who is applying for the sales position. Are you okay to give Melanie an overview of the sales department?"

"Hi Hilary. Hi Melanie. I'm George. Please do come in and take a seat." As Melanie walked over to my desk, she stumbled slightly because her high heeled shoes got caught in the carpet.

"Ow! Bugger that!" she said as her ankle twisted slightly. I rose from my chair to assist her, but she managed to recover in time, and we proceeded to shake hands. From the doorway I saw Hilary raise her eyes in disbelief!

"Would you like a coffee or tea?"

"Coffee, thank you, milk no sugar," said Melanie.

"Won't be a minute," I said as I went around Melanie and over to Hilary who was still waiting in the doorway. I walked outside my office with Hilary and turned to Sarah.

"Hey Sarah, can you get me two coffees please, my usual and the same for Melanie. Thanks." I then turned to Hilary. "So, what's she like?"

"She has an English degree and is very bright. She holds herself very well and is obviously intelligent and eager to learn. But she has this slight awkwardness about her, where you think anything can happen, if you know what I mean?"

"Not really."

"Well, you obviously saw the lift episode this morning, right? Funny as it was, it was also a bit cringing!"

"Yes, so?"

"And now the trip! Well, I don't know whether it is just nerves or if she is just accident prone, but I get the impression that she is one of those people who, if there is a lump of dog pooh on the street, she's the one that's going to tread in it, do you see what I mean now? And I'm just not sure if that is the right image for someone who is supposed to be 'customer facing' to represent the company."

"I'm sure she is fine. Probably just a bit nervous. Don't worry. Anyway, I think she is charming and will brighten the place up. And as you say, she is intelligent, eager to learn and I'm sure will turn out to be an asset for the company." I turned away from Hilary and re-entered my office.

"So, Melanie, how has it been so far? Has Hilary done the company bit, you know, history, facts and figures, all the good stuff to make you feel like we are a company you want to join? I expect you have a lot of questions? But firstly, and much more importantly, is it Melanie or Mel or don't you mind either way?"

"I don't mind. Most people call me Mel. My dad always calls me Mel or sometimes-" there was a short pause.

"Sometimes what?"

"Nothing, not important really. Just sometimes he calls me Meloney. Not sure why-, just does."

"Well, Mel it is then," I said. "So, any questions so far?"

"No, not now. There was quite a lot of information to take in and I'm sure there will be questions that come to me later. But for now, I'm okay." At that moment, Sarah entered the room with the two coffees and placed them on my desk.

"Thanks Sarah, really appreciate that."

"Anything for you George, you know that," said Sarah as she walked back out of my office, swinging those amazing hips from side to side.

"I realise that you have probably already been through this with Hilary but tell me a little about yourself?" I asked Mel.

"Well, after finishing sixth form I took a year out to get some work experience before going to university. I had passed my driving test, so I wanted a car and the only way to do that was to earn money. My dad bought me a little, old Corsa but of course I needed to be able to pay for the petrol, tax and insurance, so I got a job at the duty-free shop at Gatwick airport, in the perfumes department."

"So, you can drive, which is great, and I can see you have ambition. You know what you want and go for it! Tell me a little about your experiences at the duty free?"

"Well, although I had always had 'Saturday jobs' from the age of sixteen, this was my first full time position involving shift work. But I adapted well to that, I didn't mind the hours, the money was good, and I learnt a lot about myself."

"Really. What did you learn?" Mel paused for a short while before answering.

"I learnt how to handle people, you know, the general public. Although my Saturday jobs were in clothes stores, therefore already dealing with the public, it was nothing compared to the duty free. People can be so rude, arrogant, and just downright nasty! I suppose I was lacking a little in self-confidence when I went there, but I soon toughened up. You obviously saw the lift thing this morning, I'm sure everybody in the office did, well that's just typical me! I've never been able to shake that sort of thing off. The difference now is that I don't care about stuff like that anymore. It used to bother me, looking like a fool, but I just don't worry about it anymore."

"I did see it this morning, Mel. And I have to say, you handled it very well. And that's an ability that anybody taking on a sales role needs to have. Because, in this business, you never know what is going to be thrown at you, you never know what will happen from day to day, your customers change frequently, their moods differ and you are constantly the face of the company, often defending the actions of colleagues who have made mistakes, sometimes costing the airlines a lot of time and money. Therefore, you do need to have adaptability," I said giving Mel a reassuring smile. Mel smiled back and seemed to relax a little.

"You know, when I went for my interview for the duty-free job, when the interview had finished, I got up, shook hands with the interviewer and then tried to exit the office through the stationary cupboard! This caused a snigger from the interviewer and at the time I was devastated and thought there is no way I would get the job. But I did and I thought, well I'm not going to worry about stuff like that anymore. Another time, I was walking through the store, and someone had spilled a fizzy drink on the floor. Yes, it was me that walked into it, slipped, and fell over, legs in the air like some cartoon character falling over, much to the amusement of the customers and my colleagues alike. But again, it didn't bother me. I just got up, dusted myself down and got on with what I was doing. I got the feeling that each day the people sitting behind the CCTV cameras would be saying to themselves 'here she is again, I wonder what she is going to do today that we could send off to 'You've Been Framed', but still, I didn't care about it."

"What did you learn about the public and how to deal with them?" I said.

"Well, I learnt that although people in general are well balanced, polite and not out to cause offence, alcohol definitely has a negative effect on them and at the airport, alcohol is available twenty-four hours a day! It only takes a second for any perceived injustice to turn someone into a homicidal maniac! But seriously, buying is an emotive thing, you want to get value for money, you don't want to feel ripped off and you always want a bargain. I think that's true of any customer buying something, whether it be a product or a service. And therefore, I learnt that you must try and get to the reason for peoples' frustrations and where possible, because it wasn't always possible, try to match their expectations."

"Can you give me an example?" I said. Mel again thought for a second.

"A woman came up to me in the store, a little worse for wear due to drinking; it was only 9:30 a.m. Anyway, she was incredibly angry that she had earlier been charged full price on an item of perfume, which she had subsequently seen advertised for 'half the price' on the airline she was flying with and wanted to return the product immediately for a full refund. She obviously wanted to 'get the bargain' that the airline was offering. I informed her that so long as the perfume had not been used there would be no problem in issuing a refund. However, she had actually used the perfume already, and became very angry that this would invalidate a refund, to the extent she was shouting at me, telling me that I was ripping her off and that she would 'take this further', you know, all the usual things. I asked to see the advertisement for the airline product stating the price which was half of our price. She took out her phone and showed me the on-line advertisement. It was indeed the same product and exactly half the price. However, on closer inspection I realised that the quantity of the perfume was in fact less than half of our quantity. It was seventy millilitres as opposed to our one hundred and fifty millilitres. Once I pointed this out and told her that our product, the product she had purchased and used, was cheaper than the airline product due to the volume, the woman was all smiles again and thanked me for my help. I helped her realise she had not been ripped off and in fact got a bargain. Job done." With that, Mel leaned forward to pick up her coffee, misjudged the distance and knocked the full coffee cup flying all over my desk and onto my trousers! "Oh shit! I'm so sorry, let me help you," she continued and went to get up.

"Don't worry, I've got it," I said and pulled a box of tissues from my drawer to mop up the desk. At that moment, Sarah walked in also with some tissues. She must have heard the cup go flying.

"I've got it George," said Sarah and in an instant, she was mopping up all the spilled coffee from the table. "We'll have to get you out of those trousers, George," she continued with a suggestive look on her face. Without responding, I looked at her with an 'oh really' expression.

"Really sorry for that. I am a bit clumsy. Bollocks! I think I've ruined you suit. Shit! Sorry. And sorry for fucking swearing," said Mel.

"It's okay, it'll come out," I said reassuringly, and I looked at her. "You're not related to Mrs Hansen, child minder, by any chance, are you?" I said having a flashback to the child-minding interview with Mrs Hansen.

"No. Who is Mrs Hansen?" said Mel.

"Never mind," I said. "Look, let me just go to the bathroom and I will be back shortly. And don't worry, accidents happen."

"Need some help George?" said Sarah.

"I think I can manage, but you'll be the first to know if I can't." I left the office and went to the bathroom to try and wash off the coffee stains on my trousers. To be fair, most of it came out and I used the hand dryer to dry the crotch of my trousers before returning to the office. Mel was still sitting at my desk and Sarah had made her a new cup of coffee.

"I'm so sorry," said Mel as I entered my office.

"No harm done. Just don't chuck that one all over me, okay?" I said, giving Mel a comforting smile.

"And on top of that, I must apologise for the swearing. That's not really me at all. Can we start again?"

"No. Not really, I don't see the point of starting again."

"Oh," Mel said disappointedly. "Well, thanks for your time, sorry again about your trousers and I hope you find the right person for the position." With that, Mel stood up and offered me her hand to shake.

"What are you doing?"

"I'm… I'm leaving."

"Sit down Mel. I don't want to start again because I think you are perfect for the role. Besides, you can't walk out of here on your own, you'll never make it to the lifts without me to guide you," I said and started to laugh.

"You mean, you want me to have the position?"

"Yes. I think you are great. Enthusiastic, good business sense, bright personality, intelligent, resourceful, and most importantly, you don't take yourself too seriously. And by that, I mean you are confident in yourself; you don't worry about what other people think. And I like that a lot."

"Thanks George. I can call you George, right?"

"Of course. Now let me fill you in a bit about the role," I said and spent the next hour going through what the role involved, what Mel's responsibilities would be and the expectations of the company. By the end of the interview, Mel was incredibly happy and accepted the terms and conditions. And more importantly, there were no more mishaps for Mel - at least not today!

I left the office about 2 p.m. and called Martyna to let her know that I would pick up Emily and Amy from school. Martyna was fine with this and said she would prepare some snacks when we got home, as she knew I would have to leave for my flight before dinner. I arrived at the school approximately five minutes before the girls would be coming out, so I stood there with all the other mums, and a few dads, just minding my own business. I felt a tug on my arm.

"How are you getting on Sweetie?" It was the mum who had propositioned me at the school not long after Cheryl's passing, large chest, big sticking out nipples! I felt a little scared.

"Oh, not too bad. You know how it is."

"I recently noticed that your girls are being collected from school by a nice young woman, girlfriend is it?" she asked enquiringly.

"No! No, just a friend really, well child minder situation, you know, looks after the girls, looks after me."

"Oh-, and in what ways does she look after you then?"

"Bit of housework, cooking, that sort of thing," I hesitantly replied.

"So not in the 'physical' sense then. Remember Sweetie, I'm always here for you, if you are lonely or just need to release that pent up tension you might feel. Always here for you," and she smiled before looking down at her ample cleavage.

Luckily, I was literally saved by the bell, as the home time bell rang out and children began appearing from the doors of their classrooms. 'Thank fuck for that' I thought to myself! Emily and Amy recognised me instantly and both ran towards me at the same time. We had a group hug. On the way home we chatted about what they had done at school and I was so happy, because they were so happy. After the sadness and raw emotions that we, as a family, went through after Cheryl died, I really couldn't imagine a life of happiness for us. I knew time was a great healer, but to see them laughing and acting like any other normal children of their age, was a comforting experience.

Once home, Martyna had been true to her word and snacks had been laid out on the kitchen table. I quickly got changed and asked Martyna if she wouldn't mind taking my suit to the dry cleaners, after explaining about Mel and the coffee incident. Martyna of course, didn't mind at all. I had packed the night before, so brought down from upstairs my overnight bag and headed for the kitchen. I was ready to leave, once I had sampled the snacks and relaxed a bit with Emily, Amy and Martyna. The girls were happy in Martyna's company and I was happy to leave them with her.

16

I arrived at Heathrow airport and went through my usual routine ending up having a quick bottle of Budweiser at the London's Pride pub inside the terminal. The flight was announced, and I made my way to the gate and after a short wait, boarded the aircraft. I had booked my usual seat (2A) and was somewhat disappointed, as indeed I always was, when there was a fellow passenger sitting in 2C.

"Excuse me please, I'm in 2A," I said.

"Oh. No problem," said a middle aged, overweight man in an American accent. He struggled getting up from his seat and moved into the aisle, allowing me to pass him and get to my seat by the window. My arse had no sooner touched the base of the seat when my worst nightmare, well 'flying nightmare' happened.

"What about these Goddamn small seats on these short haul flights, huh? Jesus, you'd think the airlines would realise that it's not just skinny, little bitches that need to get to places to get shit done, am I right?" He continued. "You can fart as much as you like, because there just isn't no room for the little fucker to escape the seat! Once you're in, it's like your ass is clicked into place and you're sealed into the seat. God, I fucking hate these flights. Give me a long haul any day of the week." He lent across the middle seat, extended his right hand and said, "Jeez, where are my manners, I'm-" and before I heard another word, the name 'Del Griffiths' popped into my head. The character John Candy portrayed with such comic genius in one of my favourite films, 'Planes, Trains and Automobiles'.

"Nice to meet you Del," I said extending my hand to shake his, without even realising I had called him Del.

"No, not Del, I'm Pat Brunswick. Are you okay buddy?"

"Yes, sorry um, Pat. I was miles away."

"Fuck! For a second there I thought I'd got stuck with a fucking retard! No offence."

"None taken. You just reminded me of someone, that's all. I'm George, George Hart. So, what brings you to London and now on to Frankfurt?" I said, surprising myself that I had continued the conversation! This was the second flight in a row that I had started a conversation with my fellow passenger. First Fiona, and now Del, I mean Pat!

"Off to meet my wife. We are on a European vacation. It's our twenty-fifth wedding anniversary, so we are doing, England, Germany, Italy, Spain and then France and back to London before going home to Washington. Not really my bag, but the wife, you know, she kind of likes all the history and the architecture and all that bullshit, know what I'm saying?"

"Right. So, where is she?"

"Well, I'm a General in the United States Army and I had a meeting with one of my counterparts today at your 'Home Office' so Meryl, my wife, went ahead on an earlier flight. By chance, she met one of her friends in London yesterday who was also travelling to Frankfurt today. So, they went this morning together, to do some sightseeing or some shit like that and I'll meet her at the hotel later."

"A General. Wow! So, you're still active then, I mean if you met with the Home Office?"

"Yeah, but not for much longer. I'm fifty-five in a couple of weeks and will be retiring. God fucking knows what the hell I'm gonna do with my time once I finish. I know one thing though. I'd better find something to do otherwise I'll go crazy with all the shit Meryl's got lined up for me! I see you are married, so you know what I mean right?" Pat said looking at my left hand and spying my wedding ring. I should have just said 'yes' and left it at that. But for some reason, as loud and as obnoxious as he was and as much as it was against my nature to talk to strangers, particularly strangers on aircraft, I didn't!

"No. Not anymore."

"Divorced?"

"No. My wife was killed in a car crash just over eighteen months ago."

"Hey, I'm sorry buddy, I didn't mean to pry. There's me running my mouth off about my Meryl and our twenty-fifth wedding anniversary, shit I'm sorry man."

"Unfortunately, I didn't get twenty-five years. But what I did get, was a lovely, warm, beautiful person to share my life with. Someone I miss terribly and think about all the time. And someone I see every day in my two gorgeous daughters."

"You have children too! Man, that's tough. I'm a General, used to dealing with life and death situations, making decisions that affect the lives of thousands of people. I am supposed to be 'hardened' to situations and able to separate emotions, but shit, anything ever happened to Meryl and I'd be broken. I know I go on about her a bit, but that's all part of my 'bravado'. So sorry George."

"No need for apologies Pat. It wasn't your fault. It was nobody's fault. Just a silly accident," I said. "Do you have any kids?"

"No. Me and Meryl couldn't have any. We tried for a long time, then we found out that there was something wrong with Meryl, you know, a woman's thing. After that we talked about adopting, but somehow Meryl lost interest knowing that she couldn't have her own child. So, it's just us. But we're okay and my sister has two girls and a boy, teenagers now, and they visit us all the time. So, we're all good."

"I'm sorry for you both," I said, and we continued to talk for the rest of the flight, sharing our life stories and experiences, well as much as you can in an hour's flight! It was strange! This guy who I thought was going to be so annoying, turned out to be very funny, interesting, and genuine, a man who for some reason took to me as much as I did to him. Funnily enough, Pat and Meryl were staying at the airport Sheraton for one night before moving downtown to the Steigenberger Frankfurter Hof, a five-star hotel in the city centre.

"I can't believe you fucking thought I was going to be like John Candy. Fucking cock sucker," Pat said affectionately to me with a smile on his face as we swapped contact numbers and email addresses and said our goodbyes at the Sheraton hotel reception desk. "Maybe see you later for a drink, after dinner? I'd love Meryl to meet you."

"Well, as I told you, I'm having dinner with a friend tonight, but yeah, maybe we could meet in the bar for a nightcap."

"Oh yeah, that little 'hottie' you were telling me about. I'll look out for you. Take care George."

I checked-in and made my way to the hotel room. This time I was on the sixth floor, room 624. Once inside the room, I placed my overnight bag down and looked at my watch. It was 7:45 p.m. local time. I took out my phone and gave Fiona a quick call.

"Hi Fiona, it's George."

"Hey George. How are you? Are you here already?"

"Yes, just got to the room. Will just call the girls, take a quick shower and should be ready by 8:30 p.m. Is that okay for you?"

"Perfect George. Really looking forward to seeing you. Do you want me to come and scrub your back in the shower?"

"Erm, nice thought, but I think I can manage. Take care and I'll meet you at the bar, okay?"

"Sure thing. Shame about the shower. Enjoy, bye," and Fiona hung up. I smiled to myself as I laid the phone on my bed and kicked off my shoes. It really did seem like Fiona wanted a bit more than just dinner tonight. Was I ready for something more? Did I want something more? Did I need something more? Was it time to 'get back in the saddle' as they say! If anything did happen, how would I perform? After all, it had been a long time since I had enjoyed the intimacy of a woman. And even longer since I had enjoyed the intimacy of a woman that wasn't Cheryl. These thoughts buzzed around my mind for a few minutes before I realised that nothing would probably happen tonight and if it did, I told myself to just 'go with the flow' and let things be what they will be. I picked up my phone and called Martyna.

"Hi Martyna. How are things, all okay?"

"Hey George. Yes, all good here. The girls are in the shower and I promised them I would read them a story. Obviously, it will not be as good as how you read to them, but I said I would do my best," Martyna said and giggled.

"That's wonderful Martyna. And you don't need to worry. I've heard you reading to the girls before; you do a fine job. Thanks for being there with them. And thanks for being you. You don't know how much comfort it gives knowing that the girls are safe and happy when they're with you. It takes a lot of pressure off me and allows me to concentrate on work. One of the best decisions I've ever made, asking you to look after the girls."

"Stop it George, you don't have to keep thanking me. You know it's a pleasure for me too. Emily and Amy are great kids, and you are a great father. You should be proud of them and yourself. I'm only too glad to help but remember; you do still pay me. I'm not doing it for free. It is my job, however much I love it."

"You're making me blush now," I replied. But Maryna was right, and her last comment hit me a little hard. Although I had grown very fond on her and was beginning to have strong feelings for her, she was in all honesty an employee, who was there, looking after my kids because I paid her. Maybe she would never feel anything for me other than someone who was just a nice employer.

"You still there George?"

"Erm, yes. Listen, give the girls a big kiss from me and tell them I love and miss them very much. I'll give you a call tomorrow from the airport before my flight departs, okay?"

"Thanks George, and please don't worry. The girls are safe with me. They miss you too. See you tomorrow."

"Have a nice evening Martyna, take care and see you tomorrow." I hung up, placed the phone on the bed and got undressed. I took my shower gel and shampoo from my bath bag, walked into the bathroom, and entered the shower cubicle. As the water splashed all over me, I thought to myself 'well, let's see what happens tonight then!' and tried to push Martyna to the back of my mind.

I dried off and quickly got dressed. Jeans, pink polo shirt and a black formal blazer. A spray of 'Baldessarini', a quick check of my hair in the mirror and I was good to go! I looked at my watch and it was 8:25 p.m. "You'll do George. Remember, it's no big deal," I said to myself. Time to go. Never a good idea to keep a lady waiting.

Fiona was not in the sports bar as I entered, so I took a seat on the furthest bar stool at the end of the bar. I remembered that Fiona seemed fond of 'Pink Gin' at our last meeting, so I ordered a Pink Gin and tonic for her and a beer for me. What with another important meeting tomorrow, I wasn't going to be drinking heavily tonight! After a few minutes, I sensed someone approaching and turned to see Fiona walking towards me.

"Hey George, lovely to see you," she said as she leant into me and gave me a kiss on both cheeks. "Been waiting long?"

"Hi Fiona. Great to see you. No, only a few minutes, but enough time to order a pink G&T for you."

"Thanks George. But I won't be having to many of these tonight. Not like last time!"

Fiona looked amazing! Black high heels, skinny, tight, black jeans and a pale-yellow blouse, once again slightly see through that allowed a glimpse of her bra. Her shoulder length, blonde hair looked so soft and perfectly layered and she smelled magnificent. I found myself just staring at her for a few seconds.

"Anything the matter, George?"

"No. No, nothing's the matter. You look amazing!"

"Thanks George. Although, I decided to dress down after last time and take a leaf out of your book by wearing jeans. But thanks for the compliment. You look great too! And you smell wonderful."

"Thanks Fiona. So, tell me, how have you been getting on? Your apartment still not ready I take it?"

"Well, it's been really good actually. My colleagues all seem nice, but as I mentioned to you on the phone, it seems like it doesn't matter where you are in the world, 'office politics' is always part of daily life. But generally, I am happy with my choices."

"That's good to hear."

"And although the apartment is not ready yet, it will be soon, so I'm not too bothered. It's quite nice, two bedrooms so my mum can stay when she comes to visit, and my bedroom has an en-suite, which is always a blessing. And only a short walk into Frankfurt city centre. So again, I'm quite happy with everything."

"Sounds great. And has your mum forgiven you for taking the Sachsenhausen apartment?"

"Yes, we're all 'pals' again. You know what mums are like, they always think they know best don't they, so it's not surprising that we fight sometimes. But all good between us now."

"Actually, I don't really know what mums are like," I said rather sheepishly.

"Oh George. Don't tell me you lost your mum as well as your wife?"

"Yeah. But it was a while ago. I lost my dad to cancer when I was ten and it hit my mum quite badly. She had some mental problems and although she did her best for the next eight years, it just became too much for her. So, we were never that close, you know. I tried to help as much as I could after my dad died, but I was just a kid and didn't really know what to do for the best. We didn't have family close by, so it was kind of down to me."

"I'm so sorry George. Your wife, dad, and mum. What happened to your mum?" There was a slight pause before I looked up, directly at Fiona.

"She committed suicide."

"Oh my god. You poor soul," said Fiona, before she got off her bar stool and put her arms around my neck and gave me a very heartfelt hug. As Fiona relinquished her hold on me and moved back to her bar stool, I could see a tear rolling down her cheek. I reached into my pocket and handed her a handkerchief.

"Here," I said. "My dad always told me to keep a handkerchief in my pocket. He said it wasn't for blowing your nose on, but in case the occasion arrives when a lady might need it."

"Sounds like a real gentlemen," Fiona said softly as she wiped the tear away and handed me back the handkerchief.

"He was. But listen, that was all a long time ago. And although I miss them both a lot, and it saddens me that Emily and Amy never got the chance to meet their grandparents; life goes on. So, let's say we change the subject and have a lovely evening together, okay?"

"Thanks George. Your parents would be so proud of you," and another tear fell from her eye.

We drank up and made our way to the 'Taverne' restaurant within the hotel and was shown to our table by one of the waiters. Menus were hastily handed to us and we were asked for our drink orders.

"Just sparkling water for me," I said to the waiter. "What are you having Fiona?"

"Same for me," she replied, and I ordered a large bottle. "This is lovely George. Although this is only the second time, we have seen each other, well third if you're counting breakfast last time. But I'm hoping you're not as I must have looked a right mess at breakfast following my drunken behaviour the night before. Actually, let's forget about the night before as well!"

"You were lovely on the plane when you molested me, well grabbed my leg; you were lovely that night, although slightly inebriated; and you were lovely at breakfast, although slightly ungroomed and dishevelled. But the theme here is 'lovely' so please don't worry. Now what was you going to say?"

"Well, I was going to say that I know we don't know each other that well, however I feel really comfortable with you. I feel we have a connection."

"I think we do too. But let's not get too carried away. Let's enjoy dinner, get to know each other better and not worry about anything else. Is that okay?"

"Perfect George."

We ordered our meals and spent the next hour and a half talking openly about ourselves, our likes, dislikes, and it felt refreshing for me, as this was the first time, I had really opened up to anyone since Cheryl. I was pleasantly surprised about how much Fiona and I had in common, and I was genuinely warming to this captivating woman. Following the conclusion of our dinner, I paid the bill, much to Fiona's annoyance, as she wanted to at least pay half. However, I pointed out to her that I had said in our phone conversation that I would get dinner. Therefore, she conceded gracefully.

"Drink at the bar?" asked Fiona. "On me, this time!"

"Sure, why not. A nightcap would be good," and we made our way back to the sports bar. On entering the bar, I noticed Pat and Meryl, sitting at one of the tables. He recognised me instantly and stood up, beckoning me over to him.

"That's Pat and I assume that's his wife Meryl, you know, the guy I was telling you about earlier, on my flight over. I think he wants us to join him. Really sorry."

"No, don't be silly. It will be fun. Come on, let's go over."

"I did tell you, he swears a lot, didn't I?"

"Yes, it'll be fine, come on," Fiona replied and held onto my arm and dragged me over to Pat and Meryl's table.

"Well look at you George, you old wanker! And who is this pretty little young thing you are with?"

"Hi Pat. This is Fiona. Fiona, this is Pat and Meryl I believe?" I said going to shake Meryl's hand, while Pat was busy giving Fiona a 'familiar' hug! However, before I could get to Meryl, she had stood up and also embraced me in the same way Pat was embracing Fiona. Typical Americans!

Meryl was a tall, thin lady, and although in her late fifties, she was extremely attractive, elegant and you could instantly tell that she took pride in her appearance. A kind of Kim Basinger lookalike, with flowing blonde hair. My first impressions were of a kind, warm, lovely lady!

"Hi George. Pat has told me so much about you. I feel I know you already. I am so sorry about your wife and your two little girls, god bless them," said Meryl in a typical 'southern drawl' as she let go of me.

"Thank you, Meryl. It's lovely to meet you. Pat told me a lot about you too," I said, turning to Pat who had finally stopped molesting Fiona and let go of her!

"Please join us," said Pat.

"Yes, it would be so nice," continued Meryl. I looked at Fiona and she smiled at me before we all sat down at the table.

"Waiter!" Pat raised his arm and called to a waiter, who acknowledged him and quickly made his way to our table. "Now what will guys have to drink? Fiona?"

"I'll just have a glass of Prosecco."

"And you George?"

"I'll have a Spiced Rum and Coke, thank you."

"Meryl honey, do you want something else?"

"Yeah, Pat. This will be gone soon enough," Meryl said looking at her near empty glass of what looked like a Gin and Tonic. "I'll take another."

"So, two Gin and Tonics, a glass of Prosecco and a Spiced Rum and Coke. Thank you, Sonny," Pat said to the waiter, and he turned, and left our table.

"So," I said turning to Meryl, "Pat tells me you guys are on your twenty-five wedding anniversary trip. That's wonderful, congratulations. What are you going to do in Frankfurt?"

"Well, we're going to the 'Sanskansberg' Museum, one of the largest natural history museums in Germany."

"You mean Senckenberg?" interrupted Fiona.

"I don't know, whatever the fuck it's called," whispered Pat under his breath as he looked at me.

"Yes, sweetie, that's the one," continued Meryl. "And then we're going to the 'old town' to see the beautiful old timber buildings. It looks so picturesque in the brochures."

"The 'Romerberg'. Yes, if you like architecture, you'll love the 'Aldstadt' and there are also some lovely little museums tucked away in those buildings and around that area. Fascinating stuff," said Fiona.

"And then we're heading off to Berlin! Can't come to Germany and not go to Berlin. See the wall and all, and 'The Reichstag', again a beautiful building. Do a river tour as well; my friend Barbie told me that you get to see quite a lot on one of those tours."

"That sounds wonderful. I'm sure you'll both have a great time," I said and turned from Meryl to Pat, who was busy rolling his eyes. Meryl had just caught the end of the eye roll and gave him a hard stare.

"Yes, it will be wonderful," said Pat, feeling a little embarrassed about his negativity and a smile broke out on his face as he lovingly looked into Meryl's eyes.

The drinks arrived and once the waiter had left, we toasted each other with a 'Cheers', raising and clinking our glasses.

"So, what's the story with you two guys then?" asked Meryl. "Pat told me a little about you George, but he didn't mention you, Fiona." I jumped in!

"Well, we're just friends. We met in rather peculiar circumstances on a flight a few weeks ago, when Fiona molested me on an aircraft and I had to make a citizen's arrest and have the plane diverted to Paris," I replied. I was immediately slapped on the arm by Fiona and she embarrassingly looked at Pat and Meryl, who were a little stunned and open mouthed!

"Lucky bastard; and you had her arrested? I would have…" said Pat, before pausing and looking at Meryl. After an awkward second or two of silence, Pat again looked at me. "Are you fucking with us?"

"Yes. It is true Fiona grabbed my leg. But only because she is a nervous flyer, and a sudden bout of turbulence frightened her a little. But that's all." We all laughed, and Fiona and I told our short story of how we met. The evening went very well, and we all bonded. By the end of the night, you would have thought that Fiona and Meryl had been friends for many years. And to be honest, I can't remember the last time I laughed so much. Pat was a very funny guy and his brashness only succeeded in contributing to his indelible character.

"You two make a lovely couple. My very own Prince Harry and Meghan Markle! That's how I'm going to remember you guys," said Meryl.

"Well, I hope I've got more hair than Harry! And we're not really a couple," I responded, keeping my eyes on Meryl as I could sense that Fiona was looking at me. "But seriously, it's been a fantastic evening," I continued trying to change the subject. "It's been a pleasure to meet you both; you two are a wonderful couple. I can see why you have been together so long. You know each other so well and I think it's easy for anyone to see the great love and respect you have for each other. You're an inspiration for anyone who doubts whether marriage, or long-term relationships in general, actually do work these days. Enjoy the rest of your trip, and here's to another twenty-five years," I said raising my glass and saluting Pat and Meryl.

We all stood up and hugged each other, swapped contact details and Pat and Meryl were insistent that we should visit them in Washington, if we ever get out there. We would be warmly welcomed. We said our goodbyes and Fiona and I left the bar, leaving Pat and Meryl to finish their drinks. We walked in silence to the elevators and waited patiently for the doors to open. The sound of the 'ping' letting us know the doors were about to open, broke the silence and as they did, we both stepped inside.

"What floor are you on George?"

"Err, sixth," I replied. Fiona pressed the buttons for floors three and six and the doors began to shut. Before the elevator had begun to move, Fiona had turned around to face me and pushed me up against the back wall and immediately started passionately kissing me. Although a little taken aback, I found myself responding just as passionately. We were so busy kissing and touching each other's bodies that we didn't notice the 'ping' of the elevator as it arrived at the third floor. It was only when the doors started sliding open that we stopped and looked around to see if anyone were about to enter. Luckily for us, there was nobody waiting. Fiona grabbed my hand and marched me all the way to her room, only letting go to remove her door key card from her purse. She slid the card down the handle reader mechanism and opened the door.

Again, grabbing my hand she led me inside her room, hauled me over to the large double bed and fell backwards onto it, pulling me down on top of her. My jacket and polo shirt were off in an instant and it wasn't long before Fiona's yellow blouse was on the floor, closely followed by her bra, revealing her ample breasts and hard, erect, dark pink nipples. Fiona was busy tugging away at my jeans and I reciprocated by working on hers! In truth, it probably took about a minute for us to be completely naked although it felt like ten seconds, and fully into the throws of fervent love making. Our bodies seemed to fit so well together and there was no 'awkwardness' that sometimes accompanies the act of love making for the first time with someone new. I couldn't get over how wonderful Fiona's body felt against mine. Her breasts were spectacular, and I kissed her from head to toe, stopping longingly at her nipples and her vagina.

Although I am no expert at the art of Cunnilingus, I knew my way around a woman's body, and she shrieked with ecstasy as I pleasured her with my tongue. To be fair, Fiona also seemed experienced and reciprocated the act on me! I was a little nervous about how I would perform as it had been some time since I had been with a woman. I needn't have worried!

17

I awoke to the sound of my phone alarm buzzing and as I opened my eyes, looking up at the ceiling, I could sense I was not alone. I turned to my left and this beautiful, blonde creature was staring at me with a happy, warm smile on her face.

"Morning George," Fiona said softly.

"Morning Fiona," I replied. "Sleep okay?"

"Like a log darling, like a log. You?"

"Very well, thanks for asking. Are you okay?"

"I'm okay George. Last night was wonderful. To be honest it was much, much more than I had been dreaming about these past few weeks and let me tell you, I've been dreaming all sorts of things about you and me."

"Oh, great," I said nervously, wondering where this was going. However, I was genuinely surprised with what Fiona said next!

"Don't worry George. I know you are not ready for a relationship. I know you have your girls to consider, and I know that my living here in Frankfurt would be difficult. So, I don't expect anything from you George. As much as I would love for us to start seeing each other like a 'normal couple', I know that's not going to happen. Well, maybe not just yet anyway. Perhaps in the future, if you still want to, but not yet. I understand." I looked at Fiona with a certain amount of wonderment. This lovely girl, who I had just spent an amazing night with, who was fun, loving, intelligent and who I was instantly attracted to, had literally just 'let me off the hook.' There was no need for wriggling, no need for embarrassment and definitely no need to feel ashamed of our actions the night before.

"I had an amazing time last night Fiona. I don't just mean-, you know," I said, looking at the bed. "The whole evening, dinner, drinks in the bar, everything. You are an incredible person and deserve so much more than I can give you right now."

"Stop there George. I had a great night too. And I wouldn't change anything. I'll take last night for now and we can see what happens in the future. If there is no future, then so be it; there's no pressure from my side. And if there is someone out there who can give me more than you can, and he'd have to be some sort of 'Superman' to be able to compete with you last night, then maybe you will become just a memory. A happy, loving, warm, memory." We cuddled each other and lay there in silence for a few minutes.

"I need to go," I whispered softly.

"I know," said Fiona, tuning to face me and softly kissing my lips. After this short embrace, I got up and walked to where my clothes lie at the foot of the bed. I bent down to gather them up, forgetting that I was still totally naked.

"Nice arse, George," Fiona said in a slow seductive way as she sat up allowing the sheet to drop from her chest, exposing her impeccable breasts and once again, exacting nipples. I turned to face her with a wry smile on my face.

"Thanks. Nice tits," was my response and I could instantly feel myself becoming aroused. Fiona let her tongue suggestively dance around her lips as she looked directly at my growing penis and in a split second, I had leapt on top of her and we enjoyed another magical love making session.

I got back to my own room, showered, and quickly got dressed. I was due to be picked up by Tanja at 9:30 a.m. so still had plenty of time. I had arranged to meet Fiona for a coffee in the breakfast room at 9:15 a.m. so quickly made my way down to the reception to check out and then went to the breakfast room. Fiona was already there and waved me over to her table. As I sat down, a waitress arrived and took my coffee order.

"Hey George. You look good, smell good and I know you are good!"

"Hi Fiona. Listen, I just wanted to say thanks again for last night. Not just the physical stuff, I mean the whole evening. I really did have a great time with you."

"Me too George. You are a lovely man and if our circumstances were different, who knows where this could go. But for now, let's be good friends, no pressure about having a serious relationship. But let's just promise to stay in touch."

"You know Fiona, you are right, if circumstances were different, I would love to see how far we could go. You are a special person. And maybe one day I will not see the current obstacles that would hamper a relationship with you. Maybe I'm just deliberately putting obstacles in the way."

"Stop it George. You'll be giving me hope soon!"

"Sorry," I said and smiled.

We finished our coffees and said our goodbyes, embracing each other and committing to stay in touch and be good friends. I left the hotel and waited outside for Tanja to arrive. A car pulled up and although it wasn't Tanja's, I did recognise it. I opened the passenger door and jumped in.

"Hi Jana, this is a nice surprise," I said.

"Hi George. Yes, Tanja is a bit tied up, so I volunteered to come and get you," said Jana as she checked her mirrors and pulled away. "You look tired George, have a heavy night last night?"

"Something like that, yeah. But I'm all good and looking forward to the meeting. Any updates for me?"

"Did you meet your 'friend' last night?" continued Jana in a prying way that made me feel a little uncomfortable.

"Yes. I had a genuinely nice evening thank you. Now, any updates?"

"Oh, no, not really. Nigel and Daniel have reluctantly agreed to let you, Heinz and I go on the trip for the 'scouting' mission and Heinz has already set up meetings with contacts in Addis and Johannesburg. So, today's meeting is more of a formality, really. Putting the plan together and agreeing dates."

"That's good," I replied as I looked across at Jana's lovely long legs, which were on display due to the short skirt she was wearing. At that point, she seemed to notice me looking through her peripheral vision and slightly widened her legs, before averting her eyes from the road in front and looking to her right, directly at me. I just smiled.

We arrived at the office, parked the car, and made our way up to the boardroom. As usual, we were greeted by Alma Kohl, the diary keeper for the boardroom.

"Good morning, George, good morning Jana. The coffee station is set up inside. Victor, Lars and Cristina will all be joining you this morning," she said, showing us into the boardroom, before turning and exiting, closing the door behind her.

"Coffee! Great. Do you want one Jana?"

"Yes, thanks George. So, Lars is joining today. I wasn't expecting that. I hope it will be okay?"

"As long as Victor is present, Lars will be fine. And although Nigel will feel more comfortable, and in some respects 'cockier' with Lars in the room, Victor will not let him overstep the mark."

"I hope you are right George."

At that point, Tanja and Heinz entered the room and Tanja made a direct line for me.

"Hey George," she said, embracing me with a kiss on each cheek. "And how are my two favourite girls in the world?"

"Hi Tanja. They're doing great and actually asked me to give you this," I said, pulling a handwritten letter from my inside jacket pocket and handing it to her.

"Oh George. You know, your girls are just the best in the world. Is this what I think it is?"

"Could be. Yes, they wanted to write to you to thank you for the cuddly monkeys I got them on your behalf, the last time I was here. They love them so much and in Emily's words, wanted to write a heartfelt letter of thanks to their favourite Godparent," I said.

"That girl is just so grown up! I shall read it later and treasure it always. Can't wait to see them again. The next time I come to London, I am going to stay for the weekend, and I want to take them shopping. No excuses!"

"Thanks Tanja, they will absolutely love that."

"Mr Hart," said Heinz as he walked towards me and extended his right hand.

"Herr Mayer, a pleasure as always," I replied as we warmly shook hands. "How's the family, all good?"

"Yes, George. Thank you for asking. My son seems to grow taller each day, he will soon be taller than me! And what about you? How are your girls?"

"There doing fine, thank you." We continued to chat for a little longer before Nigel and Daniel entered the room closely followed by the COO, Lars Schuller.

"Morning everyone," said Nigel in a slightly unnerving, friendly way, which was not his normal typical persona. This was closely followed by Lars and Daniel also greeting everyone. A chorus of 'morning' from everyone else in the room was the response. Seconds later, Victor and Cristina entered the room and whole 'morning' episode was repeated!

After everyone had taken refreshments and had settled into a seat at the boardroom table, Nigel proceeded to run the meeting. To be fair, he did it very well, without any arrogance and laid out the plans for the upcoming visit to Addis Ababa and Johannesburg, who would be attending (Heinz, Jana, and myself), the desired outcomes, etc. In fact, it was a side of Nigel that I had never seen before. I kept looking at Tanja and Victor in amazement as Nigel was talking, and each time, they gave me a reassuring nod of their head as if to say; 'don't worry, we've had a chat with Nigel.' However, the bombshell was about to be dropped!

"In closing, I would just like to add," said Nigel, "that after some considerable thought and discussion with the board, it was decided that I should also accompany Heinz, Jana and George on the trip, acting in a purely 'advisory' role to support the initial discussions. I do hope this is okay for you all and I am looking forward to working with you to bring success to this project." I looked around the room at each board member and finally Tanja. They were all looking at me, not Heinz or Jana, just me! Nigel had me over a barrel. That's why he was being so nice. It had already been agreed by the board that he would be coming with us.

"All sounds great," I said looking at Nigel with a false smile on my face (what else could I do!). "I'm sure we will make this project successful, and I believe that we have the right team in place. Good job Nigel." Nigel smiled just as falsely back at me and the air of tension that had previously been in the room dispersed. As we all left the boardroom, Tanja asked to see me in her office. We walked in silence the few metres from the boardroom and after entering her office, Tanja closed the door.

"You knew, didn't you?" I asked.

"Yes. I'm sorry George, my hands were tied. And if I had told you before the meeting and given you time to think about it, who knows what you might have said. I'm sorry."

"Tanja, I've known you a long time and you know I respect you and your judgement. And if you're telling me that your hands were tied, I believe you. But that was a little below the belt. I would have expected you to have said something to me and not just let me walk into that. You know Nigel is a fucking idiot, a dangerous fucking idiot."

"I know George and again I am sorry. I had a long discussion with Victor. Lars was putting pressure on him about Nigel being involved and this is where this 'advisory' role came from. Victor asked me to 'make it happen' and so I agreed. But listen George, Victor has a lot of time and respect for you. He knows as well as I do that you can handle Nigel. And he wants to be informed immediately of anything that happens that could possibly jeopardise this project. So, I'm sorry and you are right, I should have trusted you. Forgive me?"

"You're forgiven. He is a twat though! And I'm not guaranteeing that I won't kill him down there if he steps out of line."

"Just make sure you hide the body well," said Tanja with a smile. "And just for the record, you didn't fool anyone with that smile you gave to Nigel. But I thought you handled it very well."

"Thanks. So, what happens now?"

"You're due to fly out not this Monday, but the following Monday. Travel out here on the Sunday, stay the night, and then travel Monday on Lufthansa with the rest of the team to Addis. You'll be there for two days doing a kitchen inspection and then meeting with the Ethiopian Airline officials who run the catering unit. They are Government owned and basically only cater for Ethiopian Airlines currently. They are as interested as we are in working together to attract new business through our international connections and know how. This one should be a win - win all-round. From there, you fly on Wednesday on Ethiopian Airlines to Jo'burg again for two days. Same 'MO' but this will be harder. The current caterer does very well, caters most of the international airlines that fly into the city. There is competition there, but they have their hands full with the national carrier."

"So, what's their incentive to do anything with us?"

"That's for you to find out, George."

"Yeah, no worries."

"You'll fly back overnight on Friday, arriving Saturday morning. You can take British Airways back, directly to London. I hope that's going to be okay with the girls and, what's her name, Marilyn or something?"

"Martyna," I said and suddenly realised that I had not thought about Martyna for a while. Obviously, Fiona had become more prominent in my mind due to the previous evening's events. However, the thought of Martyna gave me a slight guilty pain in my stomach, which was strange. I had no reason to feel guilty, well at least not because of Fiona. But I did!

There was a knock on Tanja's door and Heinz and Jana entered.

"Hope we are not disturbing you Tanja?" said Heinz.

"No, come in. I was just filling George in. I know this is a shock for you two as well, so I'll tell you what I have just told George. My hands were tied and if Nigel steps out of line, Victor has promised me he will intervene and get him the fuck out of the picture. Sorry I couldn't let you all in on it before the meeting."

"It is a bit of a shock," said Jana.

"A shock, yes. But I think we can handle it, right George?" said Heinz, looking at me for some reassurance.

"As Tanja said, she didn't have a choice and we do have the backing of Victor. We'll be fine and between us we'll make sure Nigel doesn't cause any trouble," I replied.

"I do know that Victor has spoken to Nigel and in no uncertain terms, has explained who is leading this project - you three. And about his 'advisory' role in this," said Tanja. "I don't think we need to worry, just make sure you keep Victor and I informed of anything that gives you cause for concern, okay?"

"He's still a twat though," Jana said, and we all smiled.

We discussed the logistics of the trip and Heinz gave us an update on the contacts he had made. We were to meet with the CEO of Ethiopian Airlines, who would introduce us to his senior management team and in turn, they would lead the facility tour and be present in the preliminary discussions. As for Johannesburg, we were to meet with the catering company's owner and his management team. Everything seemed to be set and an air of optimism had entered the room, even with Nigel being part of the group, we would still have a successful trip.

At the conclusion of the meeting, once again Jana offered to take me back to the airport. I have to say, I didn't mind at all. Any chance to see her legs while she was driving was alright by me!

"So, George, you will be coming in on the Sunday and we will all leave together on the Monday, right?" Jana said as she drove to the airport.

"Yes, that's right. A bit of a pain really, I could do with spending time with my girls on the Sunday, especially as I am going to be away for the week."

"Yes, it's probably not ideal for you. But listen, as you will be here anyway, do you fancy having dinner?"

"I'm not really sure what time I'll be getting into Frankfurt. You know, as I said, I would like to spend as much time as I can with the girls," I self-consciously replied. And instantly realising how pathetic it sounded, I quickly followed up with, "But it would be nice to have dinner with you. Let me see what the flight situation is, and I will let you know. Thanks Jana."

"You're welcome George. I understand about your girls. But if you can, and want to have dinner, I would really like that."

"What about your boyfriend," I asked.

"Well, I wasn't thinking of inviting him," replied Jana.

"No, I mean, won't he mind you having dinner with me?"

"Shouldn't think so, we split up a couple of days ago. He wasn't really for me, not my type."

We continued to chat freely until we arrived at the airport. Throughout the journey, I periodically looked across at Jana's legs as her short skirt seemed to be caught even higher up her thigh than usual and I could just glimpse the decorative pattern of the top of her stockings. I got the feeling that Jana knew I was looking and was making it as easy as she could to facilitate my view of her legs. As Jana pulled up outside Terminal 1 at Frankfurt airport and the car came to a standstill, I took one last look at her long, luscious legs.

"See something you like George?" said Jana provocatively as she turned to look at me. I looked up from her legs and directly into her eyes.

"Yeah, I do. Thanks for the lift Jana. Take care and see you in a few weeks," I said gently, smiling and giving her a quick wink of my eye as I exited the car. Without looking back, I strode off into the terminal. To be honest, it was more out of fear that I didn't look back at Jana than anything else! Was she impressed with my 'cool' action? Was she annoyed I hadn't followed up with something more physical like a kiss? Did she think I was an idiot? God only knows, but I didn't want to look back to find out!

The hour or so wait for my flight went quickly and it wasn't long before I was sitting in my seat on the aircraft waiting for the boarding to be completed. I gave Martyna a quick call to let her know I was about to depart and all being well, would be back home by about 6 p.m. for dinner. It was not until I heard Martyna's voice and subsequently ended the call, that I suddenly had the same guilty pain I had experienced earlier. However, this time I was starting to feel guilty about Fiona as well. The previous night I had enjoyed a wonderful evening in the company of a beautiful woman, had a fantastic session of love making, got away without any serious commitment other than being good friends, and here I was flirting with Jana (another beautiful woman). And to top it all off, I somehow had strong feelings for Martyna as well! What the fuck was going on with me! And then the inevitable happened. Cheryl popped into my mind. The feeling of unfaithfulness overwhelmed me, and I could feel my eyes dampening. Luckily for me there was still nobody sitting in the seat beside me, otherwise I think they would have immediately noticed my distress. Cheryl would be so disappointed in me. Flirting with Jana, casual sex with Fiona and feelings for the child minder!

"Was I right about you and Jennifer Parks?" I could hear Cheryl asking me in my head. "Have you never been faithful to me? My parents will be so upset with you George."

"Can you fasten your seat belt sir, thank you," said the flight attendant as she startled me from my trance. "Are you okay sir?"

"Yes, I'm fine, just got some dust in my eye, not that the aircraft is dirty, and you guys don't clean it properly, but just some dust.. miniscule amount… hardly any really, enough to make my eyes water though. Yes, I'm… I'm fine. Thank you," I bumbled out trying to cover my tracks. I hoped I had got away with it, and the flight attendant moved on. But that's one thing about flight attendants. Nothing was unusual for them. They must see so many strange things during their careers, so to what most others would seem weird or even bizarre, to them was just the norm. I decided to think about other things for the rest of my journey home and concentrate on Emily and Amy, pushing my guilt to the back of my mind.

18

I was greeted as usual by Emily and Amy as I entered the front door and after our initial hugs and kisses, I made my way into the kitchen. Martyna was standing by the hob, stirring a pot of something.

"Hi George. How was your trip?"

"Hi Martyna. Yeah, good thanks. I've got the dates for my trip to Addis and Jo'burg. I'll talk to you about that later if that's okay?"

"Sure, no problem. We're having chilli con carne. Rice is almost done, so it will be ready in about five minutes if you want to go and change."

"Thanks, I will," I replied thoughtfully. I was feeling a little ashamed of myself, talking to Martyna as I would normally do, knowing that I had spent the previous night with Fiona and was today, flirting with Jana. It felt like I was cheating on her. Stupid, I know, but that's how I felt! I turned slowly and walked out of the kitchen.

"You okay George? You seem a bit distracted. Anything wrong?"

"No Martyna. Everything is fine. I'll be down in a minute," I replied without turning to face Martyna, and continued my way upstairs to change. When I returned to the kitchen wearing jeans and a navy-blue polo shirt, Emily and Amy were busy setting the table with cutlery, place mats and four glasses. Emily then carefully poured out carbonated water from what seemed like a huge bottle into each glass and upon completion of the last glass, looked up at me and smiled.

"Well done 'Emster', no spills, great job sweetheart."

"Thanks Dad."

"I helped with the table Daddy," chipped in Amy.

"I know you did 'Amster', and what a lovely table it looks. All we need now is the glorious food that Martyna has kindly cooked for us, and we are all set."

"Take your seats. I'll bring it over," said Martyna and with that she brought over two smaller bowls of chilli and rice for the girls. "Be careful girls, it's a little hot, not because of the chilli, just because it's hot!" She returned to the kitchen worktop and brought over two larger bowls for me and her, gently placing them on the table. "Same for you George, it's hot, so don't burn your lips and tongue," she continued, waving her index finger at me, and gave me a 'mumsy' look.

"I'll be careful," I said as the girls giggled!

"I haven't made it too hot, in terms of the chilli, but If you think it's a bit too spicy, I have some sour cream here, that you can add on top, okay?" Martyna said pointing to the tub of sour cream.

"Thank you Martyna for dinner. It looks delicious. I'm really looking forward to this and enjoying my meal with my three favourite people," I said looking lovingly at Emily and Amy and then turning to Martyna and winking my left eye.

"Thank you Martyna," came the coordinated response from Emily and Amy, and we all tucked in. It was indeed a fine chilli con carne and although we were all chatting while eating, like any normal family meal, it wasn't long before all the bowls were empty.

"That was really nice," said Amy. "Daddy, did Mummy used to make a nice chilli like this?" I paused for a moment, looking at both Amy and Emily, before fixing on Amy.

"Mummy did make a lovely chilli Amy. And like Martyna, she used to make sure it was not too hot for you. Do you know how? Mummy always took the first taste from each of your bowls, just to test the temperature, and then feed you your first spoonful, before handing you the spoon and saying, 'you're good to go' and kissing the top of your heads," I said as I recalled in my mind Cheryl doing just that.

"I think I remember Mummy saying that" said Emily softly.

"Me too," added Amy.

"That's good," and I again paused for a second looking at both Emily and Amy. "Shall we visit Mummy's grave at the weekend, take her some lovely flowers and let her know how much we love her and think about her all the time?"

"That's a wonderful idea Dad. I would like that," said Emily.

"Can Martyna come with us?" asked Amy. This took me by surprise, and I wasn't sure how to react. We had visited Cheryl's grave many times since Martyna had been living with us, but the girls had never once asked if she could join us. I looked at Martyna, and she smiled at me.

"I'm not sure what Martyna has planned for the weekend, and-"

"Do you have anything planned for the weekend?" Emily asked Martyna before I could finish my sentence.

"No, not really."

"Would you like to come with us. I would like you to meet Mummy. I think she will be pleased that you have come to look after us. Please come with us?" continued Emily. I looked at Martyna and gave her a reassuring smile, letting her know that it was okay by me and obviously, the girls as well.

"Well, yes, it would be lovely to meet your mummy. Thank you, girls. But please excuse me a minute." Martyna, got up from the table and exited the kitchen in the direction of the downstairs cloakroom.

"Right, come on ladies, let's clear the table and I think there is ice cream in the freezer you can have, if you really want it?"

"Yeah!" came the loud response from the girls and they hurriedly helped to clear the table and put the dishes in the dishwasher. I pulled the ice cream from the freezer and prepared two portions for the girls.

"Grab two spoons Emily and sit back up at the table."

"Yes Dad," and with that both girls were back at the table as I put down their ice cream in front of them.

"Tuck in ladies," I said. "Just going to check on Martyna." I made my way to the cloakroom and gently knocked on the door.

"You okay Martyna?"

"Yes, be out in a minute," came Martyna's instant reply. I returned to the kitchen and sat with the girls.

"Is Martyna okay?" asked Amy.

"Yes, just needed to use the bathroom. She will be out soon. Listen girls, I need to tell you that I must go on a business trip to two countries in Africa which means I will be away for about a week. I'm really sorry, but unfortunately, I need to go."

"Is that where elephants and giraffe live?" said Amy.

"Yes sweetheart, that's right."

"Which countries?" asked Emily.

"Well, firstly I need to go to Addis Ababa which is the capital city of a country called Ethiopia, which is in the east of Africa. You remember which way is east?" Both Emily and Amy proceeded to recite the verse that I taught them from a young age how to remember the points of a compass.

"**N**ever, **E**at, **S**hredded **W**heat!" they both said using their index fingers to point up, right, down, and left.

"Correct. And then, I will travel all the way south to a city called Johannesburg in a country called South Africa. Now South Africa has three capitals, and Johannesburg isn't one of them, although it is the largest city."

"That's a bit weird," said Emily.

"Yes, it is! Martyna will look after you and although I will miss you so much, I will call you every day and you'll see, the week will go very quickly and before you know it, I will be back." Amy got up from her seat, walked over to me and put her arms around my neck.

"Don't worry Daddy, we love Martyna looking after us. We will be alright." Emily followed on behind Amy, also putting her arms around my neck.

"And we love you so much Dad," she said. We had a group hug! I looked up to see Martyna standing in the doorway. She had obviously heard Amy say that she loved Martyna looking after them and was clearly moved by it.

"Okay, girls, finish up your ice cream and thanks for a lovely cuddle. Hi Martyna, everything okay?"

"Perfect George."

Following dinner and after clearing down the kitchen, I went upstairs to see the girls. Both Emily and Amy had already showered and were waiting on my bed with book in hand, ready for a story.

"Martyna read to us last night and it was particularly good. But we do like your stories," said Amy.

"We've got 'The Lion King'. Hope it's okay?" said Emily holding up the book. I think she got the idea from our conversation earlier about Africa!

"That's fine sweetheart," I said and climbed on the bed to read the story.

After finishing the story, I tucked the girls into bed and said goodnight to them and made my way back downstairs. I entered the kitchen and found Martyna sitting at the kitchen table.

"Fancy a beer?"

"No thanks, George."

"You okay?" I said as I grabbed a beer from the fridge, before sitting at the kitchen table. There was a pause before Martyna turned and looked at me.

"So, when do you go on your business trip?" To be honest, it wasn't the question I was expecting.

"Two weeks' time. I fly to Frankfurt on the Sunday to meet up with my three colleagues and then we all fly to Addis Ababa on the Monday. We then go to Johannesburg on the Wednesday before flying overnight Friday, arriving back Saturday morning. Fortunately, I can fly directly from Jo'burg to London on the way back. Are you sure it will be okay? I can always ask Barbara to come and stay, help out, she would be a great help for you."

"No George, it's absolutely fine. It's a normal working week, without you being here, that's all. It will be no problem." There again was a pause. This time it was me to break the silence.

"Sorry about the girls earlier, you know, asking if you wanted to come to Cheryl's grave at the weekend. I know it was awkward for you. And you don't have to, I'm sure we can find a reason to 'get you out of it' if you would prefer not to come."

"George don't be silly. I was deeply touched at how the girls thought of me, about their desire for me to meet their mum. The fact that they were comfortable enough to want to show me where their mum is buried. That's why I had to excuse myself and go to the bathroom. If I hadn't, you would have seen the tears rolling down my face. They are such brave girls, a credit to you and your wife. They are kind and sensitive and always say whatever they are feeling. There's no pretence with them. And that's why I would be honoured to go with you to your wife's grave. It will also give me a chance to introduce myself to her. Let her know how wonderful her family is and how much I love working for you and being with Emily and Amy. Let her know not to worry about you guys. Let her know I will always do my absolute best for her family."

Chapter 18

"Thank you Martyna. We all feel the same way about you. And to be clear, you are part of the family now, whether you like it or not! I have said it a few times, but I want you to know that I really do mean it. You mean so much to Emily and Amy."

"I do like it George, a lot. And how much do I mean to you?"

"What do you mean?"

"Sorry George, forget that question," said Martyna as she rose from her chair.

"No! Please sit down," I said and grabbed Martyna's arm preventing her from leaving. Upon realising how it looked, I let it go immediately. Martyna sat back down and looked at me. "Look Martyna, you are the best I could have ever hoped for to look after my children. I was absolutely dreading the idea of sharing our lives with a total stranger. The thought that the girls would be unhappy or would make the new child minder unhappy by comparing her to their mother; tiptoeing around the house trying to avoid one another, awkward silences, no laughter in the house, frightened to ask for additional duties when I needed help; personal issues that I wouldn't want to deal with and someone who was shit at cooking! All these things and thousands more were going through my mind at the thought of appointing someone to look after my children. The first interview I carried out, was with you. And I knew instantly that you were the one. It didn't matter if the next dozen interviews were better qualified, more intelligent, more resourceful, and more anything else, and by the way, they weren't. I knew it was you who I wanted to help me with the girls. Even Barbara and Sally knew it. And we were all right. The girls love you, almost like their own mum. I realise how strange that might seem, but it's true. They will never forget their mum and will always ask questions about her, and I welcome that, encourage it and I'm so pleased that they are happy to do it. But they also have you in their hearts now too."

"What about you George?"

"I'm coming to me. You are an intelligent, caring, kind and generous person. You always put others first and you never complain about anything. I love watching you play with the girls, the laughter, creativeness and sheer joy that you seem to have as much as the girls do."

"That's true, I do."

"I'm not really sure what you are asking me. But if it's what I think it is, then yes, I have strong feelings for you. You are stunningly beautiful, sexy, and alluring. You light up the room when you enter it. And it doesn't matter what you are wearing, jeans, T shirt, dress, skirt, dungarees, or a black bin liner, you always look elegant, charming, and yes, sexy. And I admit, I was a little jealous of your blind date with Zak. I have grown very fond of you Martyna. But because of the relationship you have with Emily and Amy, I can't spoil that or place it in any form of jeopardy. If I had met you down the pub or at work or anywhere, I would be begging you to go out with me. And over time, after we had gotten to know one another, I would have introduced you to Emily and Amy. But you are the girls' child minder, someone they have grown to love and trust. What if we get together and decide in a month's time that it's no good? How would that be for Emily and Amy. I think the world of you Martyna and we seem to fit together very well at this level of our relationship. But even if I wanted to, I can't take our relationship further and risk what the girls have with you. I couldn't put them through that. It wouldn't be fair."

Martyna had not taken her eyes off me since I had begun talking.

"I understand George. And I wouldn't want to jeopardise the relationship I have with the girls either. You are right. I too, have strong feelings for you. From the first day I saw you, actually. You are also kind, thoughtful, caring, and generous. And you too, are also sexy, elegant and it doesn't matter what you wear either. But I understand the situation George. I'm sorry for bringing this up, probably was a bad time to do it. But I'm glad we have had this chat. I'm glad that what we each thought was happening, was indeed happening and not just our imagination, a fantasy. I only hope it hasn't harmed our current relationship. That would be terrible."

"We know how we feel about each other. That's a good thing. And what happens in the future is another thing. But for now, nothing has changed from my side," I said hoping that Martyna would agree.

"Nothing from my side either," said Martyna and she covered my hand with hers, looked at me, smiled and again rose from her seat. "I'm going to do some reading in my room George. Then I'll have a shower and go to bed. I'll see you in the morning. Goodnight George." Martyna left the kitchen. I watched her leave, sucked on my bottle of beer, and then went to the lounge, flopping down on the sofa.

I wasn't sure what to think about the events that had just played and went through the evening again in my mind, beginning with Martyna asking me if I was distracted. Of course, I was distracted, the night before I had had an amazing time with Fiona, a wonderful sex session, and earlier today, been treated to Jana's lovely legs and flirtatious conversation. Then, I was face to face with the woman that I really did seem to have feelings for. And on top of all that, there was Cheryl. I looked up at the ceiling and whispered to myself: -

"Cheryl, I hope you are listening. I love you so much and I wish you were here with me right now, sitting on this sofa, cuddling up, enjoying a beer, and maybe watching some tv. But I guess that's never going to happen again. So, I'm sat here alone, and as you already know, I slept with Fiona last night. I'm so sorry sweetheart, I hope you can forgive me. And then there's Jana and of course the lovely Martyna. Is all this too soon? It has been eighteen months now since I lost you. I am lonely and although the girls are great comfort to me, it's not the same as having you with me. Someone to talk to, someone to listen to, someone special to cook for, someone to curl up with on the sofa. And someone to be intimate with. I miss you darling and hope you understand. And I hope you understand about the girls wanting Martyna to meet you. I know you would have liked Martyna. All my love, sweetheart," and I kissed the fingers on my right hand and blew a kiss to the ceiling.

The next day passed like clockwork and seemed to go very quickly. Fortunately for me, Frank was not in work, so I didn't face the barrage of questions I was expecting. That evening, the girls and I decided that we would visit Cheryl's grave on the Saturday afternoon.

As I awoke Saturday morning and looked up from my bed, I could see that the sun was shining, and it was going to be a nice day. I looked at my phone to check the time and found that it was only 6:40 a.m. A bit early for a Saturday but gave me a good opportunity to go downstairs and prepare breakfast for everyone. There appeared to have been no 'fallout' between Martyna and I following our conversation on Thursday evening, and things were as they had always been between us.

I raced out of bed, used the bathroom, and then jumped in the shower. After drying myself and brushing my teeth, I dressed in shorts and a vest top and headed downstairs to the kitchen as quietly as I could in order not to wake anyone. Although the girls always seemed to get up early on the weekends, all was quiet. As I reached the kitchen, I saw Martyna sitting at the kitchen table holding a coffee cup to her lips, looking a little lost in thought. However, she noticed me almost immediately. She was wearing similar attire to me. Shorts and a vest top. And as with me, she wasn't wearing a bra either, which allowed her nipples to pierce through her top. She looked stunning as usual! I looked down at my own nipples, and although not the same density, they too were sticking through my top!

"Morning George. Would you like a coffee? It's freshly made."

"Yes, thanks. What are you doing up so early?" I said as I made my way to the cupboard housing the cups and poured myself a coffee.

"I thought I would be the only one up at this time and could make a start on breakfast."

"I didn't sleep too well last night, so thought I could start the breakfast. Seems like we both had the same idea." I sat down at the table and looked at Martyna.

"You okay?" I said.

"Yes, George I'm fine. I suppose I was a little bit nervous about today, about going to see your wife's grave, with you and the girls. But I know it will be okay. Emily and Amy will take care of me."

"It will be okay. And yes, the girls will take care of you, as will I! So, sit there, drink your coffee, relax, and let me get on with breakfast, okay?"

"Yes Sir, begging your pardon Sir!" Martyna jokingly replied, pretending to courtesy like an old-fashioned servant. We smiled at each other.

"Right! What the hell do we have for breakfast?" I said as I clapped my hands together and turned to face the cupboards and fridge. "Do you know if we have any English muffins?"

"Yes, there are some in the freezer, why?" asked Martyna.

"I fancy a bacon and egg 'Hart-Muffin', which for the uneducated in the room, is loosely based on a McDonalds egg McMuffin, well, solely based on a McDonalds egg McMuffin, but infinitely more delicious and you don't have to leave the house to get one! I know the girls will love it, how about you?"

"Sounds remarkable! I'm in, but only if I can help."

"Of course, you can. Now, let me grab that frying pan," I said as I bent over to reach the pan from the bottom of a cupboard.

"Nice arse," I immediately heard! But it wasn't said by Martyna. It was what I heard in my head and I replayed the moment with Fiona a few mornings ago, where I turned to Fiona, with her impeccable breasts and replied 'nice tits'. Only this time I turned to see Martyna smiling at me. Was she thinking 'nice arse' as well? I know I was still thinking 'nice tits' and I swear her nipples had got bigger!

"If you can find the muffins in the freezer and pop them in the oven, that would be a great help," I said trying to forget all my previous thoughts and concentrate on the breakfast.

"Aye, Aye Sir," Martyna continued in her subservient manner, and she put her coffee cup down on the table, got up from the chair and moved across the kitchen to the freezer. It was automatic and, in some respects, out of my control, but my gaze followed her movements, and I was struck by just how elegantly she moved. Without any support, her breasts gently 'bobbed' up and down as she walked to the freezer, and as she opened it with her back to me, I stared at her perfectly formed buttocks. 'Wow', I thought and hoped my total admiration for this girl's body, would not lead to an embarrassing erection in my shorts!

"Concentrate on the eggs and bacon, you fucking fool," I whispered to myself.

"What? Did you say something George?" said Martyna as she turned towards me, closing the freezer door, with the muffins in her hand. The coldness emanating from the freezer appeared to have made her nipples stand out even further!

"Yes, now for the eggs and bacon," I replied, turning away from Martyna, and placing the frying pan on the hob, hoping that it hadn't been too obvious that I had been watching her.

"I'll put these in the oven on a low heat and then go and wake the girls, okay George?"

"That will be great. I'll slow this down a bit, give them a bit of time. Ask them to meet here in the kitchen at 8 a.m. sharp!" I said in a military fashion.

"Aye, Aye Sir," and Martyna raised her hand in salute and smiled awaiting my response. As she did, her top rose a little from her waist to reveal a flawless, flat stomach and a ringed pierced naval. I tried hard not to look at it and maintain eye contact, and to my surprise, I managed to succeed, finally raising my right hand in salute back to her.

"Dismissed," I said and smiled. Martyna turned and left the kitchen and I heard her take the stairs up to the girls. I sat at the kitchen table somewhat relieved that I had managed to control the movements in my shorts and finished my coffee, deep in thought.

Later that afternoon, we arrived at the graveyard and made our way to over to Cheryl. It was a warm day, but Emily and Amy had insisted on wearing lovely dresses, as they wanted to look their best for their mum. I was wearing chinos and a polo shirt and Martyna was wearing white three-quarter length leggings and a red short sleeved blouse.

Fortunately, the plot I was offered at the time of Cheryl's death, was in a small corner along with a few other graves, right by a large oak tree which gave a nice shade from the sun. A park bench sat just off centre from the base of Cheryl's plot. It was close enough for us all to sit on and think about Cheryl in our own way or talk to each other about her. But also, just far enough away so that if Emily, Amy, or I wanted our 'own time' with Cheryl, we could do so without being heard.

As we approached Cheryl's grave, Emily, and Amy each took a red rose from the bunch I was carrying and then stood either side of Martyna. They both looked up at her and Emily, on Martyna's right side, offered up her left hand, and Amy on Martyna's left side, offered up her right hand. Without talking, Martyna took hold of the girls' hands and they all walked slowly to the foot of Cheryl's grave.

"Mummy, I would like to introduce you to Martyna. She is our child minder and looks after us when Dad is at work. We like Martyna very much and she helps us with our homework and always tries to make things fun," said Emily.

"I'm sure you will like her too Mummy. She even makes quite a nice chilli con carne as well," continued Amy.

"Hello Mrs Hart," said Martyna in a soft voice. "Very pleased to meet you. You have two incredibly beautiful, loving girls and I will always do my best for them. You must be enormously proud of them," said Martyna. Emily and Amy, let go of Martyna's hands and gently placed the roses close to Cheryl's headstone. I walked up behind Martyna and placed my hand on her shoulder.

"Emily, Amy, do you want a few minutes alone with mummy, so you can tell her all what you've been doing since the last time we were here?"

"Yes, thanks Dad," replied Emily.

"Martyna and I will just be over there on the bench, okay?" Martyna and I turned around and slowly walked back to the bench and sat down. I placed the remaining roses on the bench beside me and looked at Martyna.

"Are you okay? Difficult - I know."

"Yes and no," said Martyna. "Yes, I am okay and no, it's not difficult for me. It's incredibly sad that Emily and Amy have to grow up without their mother, and I can't imagine what that feels like for them, the pain, the terrible pain they must feel. And yet, here they are, talking to their mum, introducing me to her like she is still here. And that's because she is still here, very much a part of their lives, and especially important to them. As I am also sure Cheryl is still here for you," said Martyna turning to me. "So yes, I am okay George, I'm happy for the girls and you. And it's not difficult, I recognise and understand that the love and bond you three have with Cheryl, will always be there. It's a good thing. Although there must be sadness when you come here, for you and the girls. But I quite clearly see the happiness too."

"You're right Martyna. When I come here with the girls, my sadness is because of them. It weighs heavy on me because I know the special relationship they had with their mum. I know how much they loved her and continue to love her. To have that taken away in an instant, to not be able to say goodbye, to no longer have that special 'mummy' cuddle. It breaks my heart. But then I see them here, talking to Cheryl as if it's just a case of not seeing her for few days, like when they go and stay at their grandparents' house. It brings a smile to my face. And don't get me wrong, even though they appear strong, happy, and content, I'm not naïve enough to think that they won't need some sort of counselling in the future. It might just hit them like a freight train at any time."

"And you George, are you okay?"

"What do you mean, do I need counselling?" Martyna just looked at me with concern. "I am as fucked up as the rest of the population. We all have problems, concerns, whether it's relationships, financial security, the way we look, too fat, too thin, small dick, big dick! Whatever it is, we all have problems. But in answer to your question, yes, I'm okay, the girls are my rock, they keep me levelled and keep me sane. Although they are not the angels you think they are," I said breaking into a smile. "You do know they cheat at 'Kerplunk' don't you? Yeah, they half slide out a stick and if some marbles are about to fall, they push it back in, and choose another one - little cheats!" We both laughed. Emily and Amy started walking over to us on the bench.

"Daddy, can we show Martyna around the graveyard?" asked Amy.

"Well, it's a graveyard so there's not much to see," I replied.

"Yeah, but there is that bit down there, where the big headstone is, with an angel on top of it, that I would like to show Martyna. Can we?"

"I would love to see it Amy," said Martyna. She turned to me and whispered, "give you some time on your own, with your wife." Martyna set off with the girls and it was like they were on a field trip. I could hear them chatting about the headstones, the flowers and what sort of wildlife could be found here. I picked up the remaining roses and walked towards Cheryl.

"Hey sweetheart. How are you doing? I'm sure the girls told you all about their school projects, oh, and Emily is going on a school trip to the 'Natural History Museum' next week. Do you remember when we took the girls there when they were very young, I think they were four and two at the time. Do you remember Emily pointing at the skeleton of the Blue Whale and saying, 'that will make a lot of fish and chip suppers!' And Amy being sick all down her new outfit, that you had bought the previous day. What was it, yeah, that's right, it was a red sleeveless dress, and she had-"

"White tights on, with a white sweatshirt, her hair was tied back, it was so wild, I even struggled with it. She looked lovely," I could hear Cheryl saying to me.

"I love and miss you so much darling. Please don't judge me too harshly. It's tough here, on my own. Feels like before I met you. As a kid I always felt on my own. Dad checked out early, God bless him, and Mum, well, as you know, Mum tried but wasn't really there for me. So, it was always kind of lonely. And then I met you. You changed all that for me. You showed me true love. With your mum and dad, you showed me what a family should be all about. And you blessed us with our own family, two adorable children, who I see you in, every day. And I will fight every day to keep what you showed me alive and well, so that Emily and Amy have the best life they can possibly have, even if you are not physically here to share it with us. You know I would gladly swap places with you my love, but to be honest, I'm not sure what is more painful. At least your pain has ended. But I'm only human. And I need company. Female company. But the girls will always come first, you don't need to worry about that." I paused and stared down at Cheryl's headstone and in my mind could see her smiling up at me. I bent down and removed the dead flowers from the glass vase at the base of the headstone and replaced them with the red roses. "Sleep well sweetheart. Love you always." I kissed my fingers and touched the headstone, before standing back up. "See you again one day."

I looked up and saw Martyna, Emily and Amy in the distance, still busily chatting and started walking towards them, a single tear running down my cheek.

19

I got to work early on Monday morning to try and catch up on some tenders I needed to review prior to submission to the customers. Most people didn't arrive at the office until about 8:30 a.m. so as I had arrived at 7 a.m. I knew I would get at least ninety minutes without being disturbed. I headed for the coffee machine, made a fresh pot, and waited for it to be ready and once it was, I poured a cup, added milk, and went to my office.

I placed my coffee cup on the desk and took out my laptop, engaged it in its docking station and fired it up. I sat down, staring at the monitor, waiting for it to spring into life. Within a few seconds, and with me entering a few passwords, I was into the system. I picked up one of the tender documents lying in my 'in tray' and looked at the front cover. Just then my mobile rang. I checked the incoming number, and it was Tanja.

"Hi Tanja, how are you?"

"I'm good thanks George, you?"

"Yeah, all good, just about to review the British Airways tender for Washington, I have a good feeling about this one."

"Does that mean you're in the office already?"

"Yes, just arrived, thought I would take advantage of the peace and quiet," I replied.

"Good. Nice to see you're so keen. I thought you would still be at home, was hoping to say hello to the girls. But I can do that another time. Listen, the reason I'm calling so early is that I have to be at a meeting with the Finance group today. Cristina will be there and it's an all-day meeting to review where we are on our global budget, versus actual, so I won't get to call you today. But I wanted to let you know what I heard this morning. Nigel is trying to get Daniel added to the trip. I don't think Victor will agree, but I just wanted to make you aware in case you hear anything today."

"Daniel will have no impact on the trip so I agree, I can't see Victor authorising it. However, Nigel won't have any impact either and he's still going!"

"Yes - little twat that he is. Still, at least you know. If you hear anything, send me a text and I'll try to call you during a break," said Tanja.

"Will, do. And Tanja, thanks for letting me know. I really appreciate it."

"No problem George, enjoy your reading and talk to you soon." Tanja hung up and I put my phone down on the desk. Fucking Nigel, what a little prick! The thought quickly entered my mind that I shouldn't let Frank know about this, as he would be instantly put in a bad mood for the rest of the day, and I would be interrupted constantly by him wanting to vent his annoyance and seeking reassurance. I didn't need that today and anyway, Daniel going on the trip as well, would probably not happen.

I had managed to complete my review of the tenders and sign off on them before the office started filling up. At 9 a.m. Frank arrived in the office and upon seeing me sat at my desk, popped his head though my office doorway.

"Just going to grab a coffee, want a refill?" he said.

"Thanks Frank, that would be nice," I said and got up to hand him my cup. He met me halfway across my office and took the cup.

"Is it all right to have a quick chat George, when I come back with the coffee?"

"Sure, Frank. No problem," I said and returned to sit at my desk. A few minutes passed and Frank entered my office, put the two coffees on my desk and sat down.

"So, I heard that you are off soon, next week is it? Africa!"

"Yeah. It's only the early stages, Frank. Nothing has been decided yet and things might not work out down there. Don't worry mate, I'll keep you in the loop about what's going on."

"I heard Nigel is going too?"

"Yeah, sneaky little fucker managed to worm his way onto the trip. But again, don't worry, I'll let you know what's said when I get back."

"Thanks George. I also heard that Daniel is going as well?" News travels fast I thought!

"I heard that rumour too. But I don't think it's true. There's no need for Daniel to be there. To be honest, there's no need for Nigel to be there either. I'll do what I can for you Frank, again, don't worry," I said trying to reassure him.

"I know you will George. I just see this as a great opportunity. One I know I would be good at. Don't want to miss out, you know?"

"I know. Frank, there is something you could do for me. Sarah."

"What about Sarah?"

"I talked to her at the Christmas party."

"Yes, we all saw you talking to her, and dancing with her. Be careful there, George. That one has designs on you I think!"

"You know as well as I do, as attractive as Sarah is, there is nothing going on between us. But she did tell me that she wants to progress; she wants more responsibility. I've told you before, she is a bright girl and capable of a lot more."

"So, what do you have in mind?"

Chapter 19

"I could use someone here to coordinate things for the trip to Africa, to consolidate the reports, complete the overall presentation to the board on our findings, recommendations, that sort of thing."

"Yes, I suppose she could do that," said Frank.

"I would also need her to put together a company presentation that I can present to our prospective partners, you know the sort of thing; ideology of the company, values, facts and figures, all the good boring stuff, but vital in portraying the right image of the company."

"You think Sarah can do this sort of thing?" asked Frank.

"I think she is more than capable, and I also think she will surprise you on how efficient, conscientious and intelligent she is. All Sarah needs is encouragement and motivation."

"And longer skirts!" said Frank while lost in thought, probably about Sarah's legs. But with a quick flinch, he 'was back in the room.' "I'll let her know George, ask her to pop in and talk to you about it, okay?"

"Thanks Frank. I really appreciate it and I'm sure Sarah will too."

Within a few minutes of Frank informing Sarah of me needing her help, Sarah had knocked on my open door.

"Hi George, do you have a minute?"

"Hi Sarah, yes come in," I said beckoning her into my office. Sarah strode across my office, around my desk and bent over to my sitting position so that she was at eye level to me, allowing me to perfectly view down her loose-fitting top exposing her delightful breasts.

"I just wanted to thank you George. I won't let you down and whatever you need, I'm your girl, okay?" And with that she gave me a big hug. After releasing her hold, she stood upright and smiled at me.

"No worries Sarah. And I know you will do a good job. Listen, I'm a bit busy right now, but let's schedule a meeting for later today and I will fill you in on what support I'm looking for from you, is that alright?"

"I'll look at your diary and set it up. And again, thanks George," said Sarah, as she turned and exited my office with her usual catwalk style, perfect buttocks moving in harmony with her silky legs. Yes, I know I shouldn't be looking, but I just couldn't help myself!

The week went quickly and following my meeting with Sarah, she put together an amazing presentation for me to take on my trip. Sarah was also extremely excited about having to put together the board presentation upon my return. She took to her new responsibilities with eagerness and a real sense of pride in her work. Even though this had only been a week in the making, both Frank and Hilary had noticed an incredibly positive change in her. Even her skirts and dresses appeared to have grown six inches in length, much to my disappointment! As I was about to leave work on the Friday evening before my trip, my mobile rang, and I looked down to see Fiona's name on the display.

"Hi Fiona, how are you?" I answered.

"Hi George. I'm very well, how are you?"

"Yes, I've had a good week at work, busy, but good all the same. And now I have tomorrow with my girls."

"That's nice George. What are your plans for the weekend? Are you taking the girls somewhere nice?"

"Well, I only have tomorrow really as I have to fly to Frankfurt on Sunday." As soon as I said this, I felt a tinge of guilt that I hadn't let Fiona know I was going to be in Frankfurt on Sunday evening. This was mainly because I had agreed to have dinner with Jana. During the week Jana had called me and we had firmed up arrangements. She was going to pick me up at the airport, drive back to her place in the city, drop her car off and then walk to a local gastro pub for dinner. I was then going to take a cab back to the hotel at the airport.

"You're coming to Frankfurt on Sunday?" was Fiona's startled response. "Why didn't you let me know? Or are you trying to avoid me after our 'encounter' last time?"

"I'm really sorry Fiona. I'm flying out on Monday from Frankfurt to Addis Ababa with three of my colleagues for the start of a week-long trip taking in Addis and Johannesburg. Unfortunately, I am having dinner with one of them on Sunday evening, so wouldn't be able to see you. And no, I'm not trying to avoid you Fiona. Why would I do that. I hope you understand. I'm really sorry," I replied and genuinely felt sorry for her.

"That's okay George. It would have been lovely though. To see you I mean, catch up, and have copious amounts of sex with you. And I'm finally in my apartment! It would have been nice to show it to you. But I know the situation, so it's all good." I got a sense that she was smiling on the other end of the line. It made me smile also.

"Thanks for your understanding Fiona. And it would have been nice for me too. To see you I mean and catch up. The sex part would have been great as well!" Fiona laughed.

"So, you are going on a trip. I hope it goes well for you. Will the girls be alright for so long without you?" asked Fiona.

"Yes, they will be fine. And Martyna is wonderful with them," I replied. The mere mention of Martyna's name, popped her into my mind and suddenly I had a flashing loop of Jana's legs while she was driving, Fiona's breasts as she rose from the hotel room bed, and Martyna's lovely smile, amazing green eyes and gorgeous pierced navel! I paused for a second. "So, they will be fine without their old dad for a few days," I continued.

"Yes, I suppose they will. And from what you have told me about Martyna, I'm sure she will look after them very well. And by the way, you're not their 'old' dad."

"Thanks Fiona," I said, and we continued to chat for a bit longer. I ended the call by promising to let her know the next time I would be in Frankfurt. Fiona was happy with this and it just reiterated to me what a lovely person she was. What she really wanted was a serious relationship between us. However, she understood my situation, demanded absolutely nothing from me, and yet continued to care for me. Fiona was a fantastic woman, warm, genuine, and made me realise that I probably cared for her more than I was willing to accept!

The weekend went all too quickly and after a ten mile bike ride with Emily and Amy on Saturday morning, followed by a visit to the local swimming pool in the afternoon, we were all quite tired. Not tired enough for Emily and Amy though! As I stepped out of the shower on Saturday evening, dried myself and got dressed, Emily and Amy stood in the doorway of my bedroom.

"Daddy," said Amy.

"Yes Amster, what can I do for you?"

"Well, we were wondering if we could fix your hair up, like we used to do to Mummy," said Amy as they revealed a brush, hair bands, hair clips and 'scrunchies' that they were concealing behind their backs. It took me a little by surprise and I felt an overwhelming sense of sadness that these two little girls will never have the opportunity to do that sort of thing with their mum ever again. After a short pause, a smile came across my face.

"Well, I don't have as much as Mummy's beautiful, long blonde hair, but you are more than welcome to try and create a fantastic hairstyle for me."

"Yeah!" were the cries from the girls and I set off with them to their room, where they sat me down on the floor and proceeded to brush my hair, first this way, then that way; created bunches with multi coloured hair bands, put in hair clips with little pink bows on them, before finally fixing a scrunchie to the back of my head!

"So how do I look?" I asked.

"You look lovely Dad," said Emily. "But there is one thing missing."

"What's that?" I replied.

"Make up!" was Amy's instant response. "Can we put some lipstick and eye shadow and mascara on you, Daddy?"

"You know, from the Christmas present that Martyna got for me. Please Dad, it will be so much fun," cajoled Emily.

"If it will make me look nicer, then go ahead," I said, reluctantly agreeing to be 'made over.' After another ten minutes had passed of the girls busily working on my face, they finally stood back to admire their work.

"So, am I glamorous, gorgeous and totally beautiful?" I asked with a certain amount of trepidation. Silence ensued as the girls just stared at me.

"Wonderful!" shouted Amy as the silence was finally broken. "Come on, let's go and show Martyna!" The girls helped me to my feet and dragged me down the stairs. We burst into the kitchen to find Martyna sitting at the kitchen table, reading a magazine. She looked up in astonishment.

"Look Martyna, we've done Dad's hair and made him look beautiful," cried out Emily.

"What do you think Martyna?" said Amy.

"Yes, what do you think?" I also added, moving my head from left to right and then giving a little twirl. A smile raced across Martyna's face and I could see that as much as she thought the whole thing was a mixture of admiration for the girl's efforts and humour because of how I must have looked, she was also in some degree of shock!

"I think your dad looks fabulous!" she said. "Wow! I can't believe that this is your dad, no - this must be your older sister that I've not met before. What's your name Miss?" Martyna continued.

"It is daddy, it is," said Amy excitedly. "We just did his hair and then we put some make up on him."

"Don't be silly Amy," said Emily. "Martyna's pulling your leg. She knows it's him really, don't you Martyna?"

"Ah, now I see. Well, you girls did such a fine job, I was almost fooled. But now I can see it's your dad. An incredibly beautiful dad."

"Why thank you Martyna. One does one's best," I said remembering what Sarah had said to me at the Christmas party. "Now girls," I said turning to Emily and Amy. "I think it's time for bed. It's been a long day. Off you go and I'll be up in a minute." As the girls left the kitchen, Martyna burst into fits of uncontrollable laughter.

"It's not that funny," I said trying not to laugh as well.

"Can I take a picture, George. Stay there, let me get my phone," Martyna managed to say through her laughter.

"Only if you're quick. Might try my luck down at the docks tonight," I said which just made Martyna laugh even more. After taking my picture and calming down a little, Martyna walked up to me, reached out and smoothed a bit of rouge from my cheek.

"There, that's better," she said as she lowered her hand. "You know, I really admire you George Hart. Those girls love you so much and you do so much for them."

"Yeah, like leaving them for whole week," I solemnly replied, feeling guilty about having to go on the business trip.

"No George. Don't feel bad about that. They understand and it in no way affects how they feel about you. And besides, I'm here to look after them," Martyna said and smiled at me.

"Thanks, Martyna. I guess, it's time for another shower, get this shit off me!" I said and turned to go back upstairs and tuck the girls in. As I left the kitchen, Martyna called out to me.

"You look good as a woman George, but don't go trying on any of my clothes!" I turned, gave Martyna a sarcastic smile, and then continued upstairs.

The Sunday was relaxed and the girls, Martyna and I, enjoyed each other's company, playing games and doing some paintings. It was soon time for me to leave for the airport and I followed my usual routine at the terminal, stopping for a quick bottle of Budweiser at the airport bar. Once on-board the aircraft I settled into my seat and thought to myself 'I wonder who I'll get this time' thinking back to my previous two flights to Frankfurt and meeting Fiona and Pat.

Luckily for me, I had the row to myself! The flight was smooth and uneventful (always a good thing in my book), and it wasn't long before the aircraft touched down in Frankfurt. Before disembarking, I made a quick call to Jana to let her know I had landed. She was already at the airport and waiting outside in her car. I then called Martyna to let her know I had arrived safely and quickly had a chat with Emily and Amy. I made my way through immigration, out of the terminal and walked along the arrivals area. I noticed Jana's car. Jana saw me coming and got out to open the boot.

"Hey George," she said as I approached her. "Put you bags in here." I put my case, and rucksack containing my laptop and documents, into the boot and as I turned to Jana, she embraced me and kissed me on both cheeks. "Good flight?" she continued as she went round to the driver's side and got into the car. I got in the passenger seat.

"Yeah, it was a good flight. Hope you haven't been waiting long?"

"No. I looked to see when it was due to land, so timed it well. Traffic is fairly good today, being a Sunday, so it didn't take long."

"Great." I looked across at Jana's legs, as she started to pull the car away. Unfortunately for me, Jana was wearing three quarter length leggings. A bit of a disappointment, I have to say! "So, have you had a good weekend?" I asked Jana.

"Yes. Quite good. Met some friends yesterday evening, bit of dancing, drinking, you know. Then met some different friends for breakfast this morning. And now I'm seeing you for dinner. So, yes, a good weekend, I think. You?"

"Yeah, spent time with Emily and Amy. They did my hair for me yesterday and put make up on me, made me look pretty, so yes, a good weekend I think too."

"They put make up on you! Please tell me you got a picture. I've got to see that," said Jana smiling, but still keeping her eyes on the road in front. Jana made the short drive to the Sheraton so I could drop my bags and check in.

"I won't be long, okay?" I said.

"No worries, George. If I get moved on, I'll circle around and meet you back here," said Jana. Once I had checked-in, I went to my room and quickly freshened up, before returning to where Jana had dropped me of. She was still there.

"Sorry for the wait Jana."

"No worries George, you weren't long at all. You smell good though," she replied.

"Thanks, you do too. So, where are we going for dinner?"

"A little place I know quite well. The food is quite good, nothing too fancy, and I know the chef very well."

"That sounds great. I'm looking forward to it."

"So am I."

Jana drove to her apartment building, which was a fabulous block of eight apartments in a long line of other apartment blocks running along 'Karpfenweg', a road overlooking the river Main. She parked the car outside the apartment building, and we got out.

"Lovely view Jana. This place must cost a bit?"

"Yeah, my parents are quite well off. They bought it and I pay them a reduced rent for it. But, yeah, it's nice. Right, shall we go?"

"Yes. How far is it to the restaurant?"

"We're already here. I'm cooking tonight!" she said, and a broad smile came over her face.

"You mean, we're eating here in your apartment-, you're cooking?"

"Don't look so surprised George. I can cook," she said, still smiling.

"I don't doubt you can cook Jana, but I wasn't expecting to have dinner with you in your apartment."

"Is it okay though?" she said. I thought for a second.

"Perfectly fine with me, if you are sure?"

"Let's go. I'm on the top floor."

Once inside her apartment, Jana showed me around. She had a large, combined kitchen/diner, a large lounge area with fantastic views over the River Main, two bedrooms, the master having an en-suite and a family bathroom. All tastefully decorated, modern and pleasing to the eye. We walked into the kitchen, which faced away from the river and Jana picked up an apron and started to put it on.

"I've prepared most of it already George, but just need to finish off a few things," she said. "Take a seat at the table and I'll get you a drink. I thought a glass of white wine to start with?"

"Sounds great. But you seem like you're going to be busy. So, let me fix the drinks. Is the wine in the fridge?"

"Yes," Jana said pointing to the fridge. "Glasses are in that cupboard," she continued pointing to a cupboard opposite the fridge. "Thanks George."

"My pleasure, and no thanks required. Thank you for doing this. It's a lovely surprise and I'm looking forward to sampling your cooking."

"Well, as I said earlier, I know the chef - me, the food is quite good, but not too fancy."

"Well, I can smell something good coming from the oven. What are we having," I said as I opened the fridge and retrieved a bottle of Chardonnay. "Is this the wine you mentioned?"

"Yes, that's it. We're having pork knuckle, Creamed mashed potatoes and red cabbage. I prefer a white wine with pork."

"So, do I. The meal sounds fantastic. So, we're having 'schweinshaxen'," I said in my best German accent. "Is there anything I can do to help?"

"No, thank you George. Pour the wine, sit down at the table and I'll just finish off the potatoes, and then plate up. Maybe you can get the cutlery from this drawer here," Jana said, pointing to drawer by the side of her. "And your German accent was 'Sehr Gute'," she continued.

I placed the bottle of wine on the kitchen surface, retrieved two glasses from the cupboard and poured out the wine. I placed the bottle back in the fridge and made my way to the drawer by Jana to get the cutlery. She was preparing the potatoes on the work surface above the drawer and therefore had her back to me. Her white leggings looked every bit as sexy as the short skirts I was used to seeing her in, and perfectly outlined her long legs and hugged her firm buttocks.

"Excuse me," I said as I went to open the drawer. Jana shuffled slightly to her right to allow me to open the drawer and take out the cutlery. "Are we having dessert? Shall I get spoons out as well?"

"I have some ice cream for dessert. I was going to make something, but I ran out of time. Sorry."

"Again, no need to apologise Jana. Ice cream is perfect," I said as I added two dessert spoons to the knives and forks, I had already taken from the drawer. I looked at Jana, and she looked back at me. We both smiled.

I made my way to the dining table and set the cutlery, and side plates that Jana had additionally asked me to grab from another cupboard. I placed our wine glasses on the table and then sat down.

"Right," Jana said, "I hope you enjoy this." She brought over two plates of hot food that looked very appetising.

"Looks fantastic Jana. Thank you so much."

"My pleasure George. Guten appetite."

"Guten appetite."

The food was indeed as good as it looked. The pork was tender, the potatoes smooth and creamy and although, I'm not the greatest red cabbage fan, it tasted sweet and was a fine accompaniment for the pork. We talked freely over dinner and to my surprise, none of the conversation was about work. All personal stuff. Likes, dislikes, music, food, cars, and all sorts of things. It was a very pleasant meal and Jana's company was very engaging.

"Thank you, Jana. I'm absolutely stuffed now," I said as I finished my last mouthful of ice cream. "That was wonderful."

"Glad you liked it George. I'm rather full myself now. Let me clear this away and we can relax in the lounge."

"No, you go and relax, and I'll clear this away," I said and got up to clear to the table of the empty dishes.

"Ok George. Just stack it in the dishwasher. I've already set it up. All you have to do, is close the door and press the start button. I'll go and fix us some drinks in the lounge." Jana got up, winked at me, and left the kitchen for the lounge.

I took the dishes over to the dishwasher and placed them inside and pressed the start button. The dishwasher startled into life as I wiped down the kitchen surfaces and the dining table. I filled the sink with hot water and a squirt of washing up liquid and rinsed through the wine glasses and cutlery. Once I had dried them and put them away, I took a last look around the kitchen and it was all clean, neat, and tidy. I made my way to the lounge.

On entering the lounge, Jana was sitting on the sofa with her back to me. It was a high-backed sofa, so I could only see the back of the top of her head.

"So, what drinks have you prepared," I said as I made my way around the sofa and sat down beside her. It was as I sat down that I noticed Jana had changed. There she was, sitting on the sofa… in her underwear! Red bra and matching French knickers. Her long, slender legs that I had admired so much in her car, were now completely visible to me, from her toes right up to her French knickers! Nice, toned stomach, with a small mole to the left of her concave naval, and her medium sized breasts, perfectly cupped in the underwired bra, just pushing them up slightly to produce an endearing cleavage. Yes, I was looking! In fact, I wasn't just looking, I was staring!

"Sorry, George. But I have told you before how hot it gets in my apartment. Hope you don't mind?" she said as she looked directly into my eyes and smiled.

"Erm, no. I don't mind, I, erm, I'm cool with that. Actually, I'm not cool at all, it is rather hot in here isn't it," I said a little flustered and stuttering, not knowing how to react and finally averting my stare. "No air conditioning?" I asked looking around the room.

"No. I don't like to use the air conditioning. But listen, if you are hot too, you can always strip down to your underwear as well. I don't mind," Jana said calmly with a hint of seduction in her voice. "Here," she continued and handed me a glass tumbler. "Cognac okay for you?"

"Sure," I said nervously and took the glass from her.

"Cheers!" said Jana and clinked my glass. I took a sip of the cognac and wondered what was going to happen next.

"Again, thanks for dinner," I said turning to Jana and staring at her breasts. She noticed me looking at them. "It was really nice of you and I enjoyed the-."

"I have asked you before, but I will ask you again George. See anything you like?" Jana interrupted.

"Lots," was my surprisingly short answer.

"Do you want to fuck?" Jana replied. "I know it's against the old saying 'don't fuck the company,' but I'm game if you are?"

"Yeah, let's fuck," I said and placed the glass down on the coffee table in front of the sofa. Jana, did the same with her glass and then stood up to reveal her full beauty, beckoning me to stand as well. As I stood up, she passionately kissed me, and I could feel her breasts pressing against my chest. She then took my hand and led me to her bedroom, closing the door behind her.

I took an Uber back to my hotel, arriving just after midnight. Once in my room, I took a quick shower and while the water rained down on me, I re-lived the moments of the evening with Jana. From the moment she picked me up, right through to the sex we had enjoyed. We did things, that I had never done before, things that most men fantasize about, but rarely get to experience for real. It wasn't 'love making' as it had felt with Fiona, wonderful, full of emotion and a mix of gentleness and energy. No. This was 'sex', high energy, different positions, toys, handcuffs, blind folds! A completely different experience for me. Not necessarily better, but different and just as enjoyable. I finished my shower and got into bed. I was to meet Heinz, Nigel and of course Jana at the departure gate in the morning. The flight was at 11:30 a.m. so I had to be at the airport approximately ninety minutes before that. I looked at my phone. The time was approaching 12:35 a.m. Plenty of time to have breakfast in the morning before walking the short walk to the terminal. It had been an extremely eventful evening. I rolled over and went to sleep.

20

The alarm awoke me from my sleep and I quickly shut it off before pausing for a few seconds. The first thought that came to mind was Jana! What an incredible evening! This happy thought was short lived as I immediately wondered how she will react to me today and more importantly, for the next five days of our business trip together! We had left each other on particularly good terms last night, so there was no reason to think that it would be problematic. However, before last night, I hadn't known Jana intimately. That had all changed now and changed in a very eccentric way! I guess I would find out soon enough, so decided not to worry about it.

I got up, showered, dressed, and packed my bag. I headed down for breakfast and had my usual toast and coffee. It felt a bit odd, not seeing Fiona at breakfast as I had done on my previous two visits. My mind drifted to her and I was envisaging her sitting at a kitchen table in her new apartment, silk dressing gown loosely fitted around her, large reading glasses on, coffee cup in one hand, newspaper in the other (probably 'Die Welt'), before getting ready for work. To be honest I felt a little ashamed. Although Fiona and I had promised each other nothing and made no commitment to each other, I somehow felt that my evening with Jana was kind of like cheating on her. That again made me briefly question my feelings for Fiona. Did Fiona really mean more than just a friend to me?

It was too early in the morning to think too much about my situation with Fiona and so I tried to put her to the back of my mind. I had a full week of work ahead of me, that twat Nigel to contend with and an upcoming reconnection with Jana that I was a little apprehensive about.

I finished my breakfast, went back to my room, and packed the few remaining items into my case. I looked at my watch, which incidentally, I never changed to read the local time. For some reason, I always left it on the English time and then calculated the local time. It was 8:20 a.m. 9:20 a.m. local time. I took a last look around the room before exiting and heading down to reception to check-out.

I arrived at the airport, passed through security and passport control, and made my way to the departure gate. Although, we had all been given passes to the Business Class lounge, the thought of spending any more time with Nigel than I really had to just didn't appeal to me. Therefore, as I reached the departure gate, I took a seat close by and got out my phone. It was now 10:30 a.m. and I knew that Martyna would be back from taking the girls to school, so I called her.

"Hi George, how are you? Are you at the airport?"

"Hi Martyna. Yes, I'm fine. At the gate and the flight looks like it will leave on time, so all good. How are you?"

"Yes, very well George. The girls seemed a little bit 'down' this morning as you were not here. I hope you don't mind, but to cheer them up a bit, I told them that today we would go to Pizza Hut for dinner. Only today George, just to get them over the first day, I hope it's okay with you?"

"That's great Martyna. No problem. In fact, I wish I were coming with you. Not really looking forward to being away from the girls for so long, going to miss them a lot," I said regrettably.

"They are going to miss you too George, me too. And don't worry about the girls, I'll look after them and make sure the time goes quickly. Before they know it, you'll be back," replied Martyna.

"You will miss me too?" I asked as if I hadn't quite heard Martyna properly.

"Of course, George," said Martyna and there was a slightly awkward pause. "So, did you manage to get a good night's sleep, it's quite a long flight to Addis, right?" asked Martyna, trying to change the subject. I immediately thought of Jana and some of the crazy things we had been doing last night.

"Yes, not a bad night's sleep, you know, thinking about the business trip, so a bit of tossing and turning, well turning, no tossing, you know what I mean," I embarrassingly replied. "Well, erm, listen, I will call you when I land in Addis. Have a lovely time with the girls at Pizza Hut, tell them I love them very much and can't wait to be home with them - and you Martyna."

"Thanks George, I will. Take care and have a safe flight."

As I put my phone down on the seat next to me, I looked up and saw Jana walking towards me.

"Morning George. We thought you might have got lost. We have been waiting for you in the Business Class lounge."

"Morning Jana. Well, the least time I have to spend with that fuckwit Nigel, the better. And I had a few calls to make, so decided to make better use of my time, than just the usual small talk with that twat," I said rather grumpily.

"Woke up in a good mood this morning, I see," replied Jana sarcastically.

"Sorry Jana. How are you?"

"All good George. I slept like a baby. Thanks for last night. I had a great time. You?"

"Yes, I had a great time too. Thanks for making me dinner, and, well, you know. Are we okay? You know, cool?"

"As a cucumber, isn't that the English saying?" Jana replied with a smile on her face. "Look George, I think you know I was attracted to you from the moment I saw you. I just went with my instincts last night and, luckily enough for me, you reciprocated my advances. We're both adults, no current relationships, well at least that's what you told me. So, we both had a good time, and I'm hoping we might be able to continue what we started last night, during the business trip, no strings attached! So, what do you think?" Jana continued with the same smile on her face and with such confidence. I suddenly remembered chatting to Jana in her car on the way back to the airport from one of the meetings and telling her that I was single.

"You're right Jana. We're both adults and single. But I'm not looking for any serious relationship right now," I said with slight hint of contrition. This was due to a few reasons. Firstly, I felt a bit guilty about telling this girl standing in front of me that although last night was fantastic, I didn't want a serious relationship with her. Secondly, since I had told Jana I was single, I had slept with Fiona. Thirdly, even though Fiona and I had agreed to be friends, I felt I had been disloyal to her. And lastly, I had strong feelings for Martyna! What a fucking mess!

"Me neither George. But I'm up for some fun if you are? And don't worry, I know how to be discreet. Our colleagues will not find out. And if you're not, so be it. You don't have to worry about coming home one day to find your kids 'bunny' boiling in a pot. I'm a 'little out there' when it comes to sex, but I'm not mad!"

"Thanks Jana," I said smiling back at her. "Let's see how the trip goes, okay?"

"Fine by me," she said, before looking over her shoulder. "Heinz and Nigel will be here soon. Luckily, Victor blocked Daniel from joining us. I think we have been split up in the seating. So, no cosy cuddles under the blankets for me and you unfortunately," Jana said with a suggestive wink. Again, I smiled at her. It appeared that our previous evening's exploits had not caused any disharmony to our working relationship!

A few minutes passed before we spotted Heinz and Nigel walking towards us.

"Mr Hart. A pleasure as always. How are you my friend?" said Heinz, shaking my hand.

"Herr Mayer, I am very well. And you?"

"I'm good George. Looking forward to the trip. How's the family?"

"Yes, all good Heinz. I think the girls will miss me, probably not as much as I will miss them though. And how is Patricia and your son Ulrich?"

"Both good. We had a lovely family meal last night and I've promised to take Ulrich to the football game on the Saturday that we return. Frankfurt is playing Mainz in the local derby! He can't wait."

"Morning George," interrupted Nigel. "Couldn't find your way to the lounge?" What I really wanted to reply was 'oh fuck off you condescending, annoying little prick!' However, my common sense prevailed and instead I calmly replied.

"Just had some calls to make and to be honest, the Business Class lounge is usually full of pretentious 'wannabes', talking shit and pretending to be something they're not. Can't really be doing with all that. Did you enjoy your coffee?" The tension in the air went up a notch and I could sense Jana and Heinz looking at each other. Meanwhile, Nigel was still looking at me, furrowed brow, eyes narrowed, like some gunslinger in a Western movie, not sure when to draw his pistol in a duel.

"Yes, I did enjoy the coffee," Nigel replied, and a smile returned to his face easing the tension between us. "I think it's time to board. Unfortunately, we are all sitting separately," he continued.

"Oh, how unfortunate," I caustically replied.

"Yes," said Nigel still smiling at me, albeit through gritted teeth. It was obvious to both of us that I knew that he knew that I wasn't disappointed at all by the seating arrangements! "See you on-board." Nigel turned away and walked up to the Business Class boarding gate.

"Sorry about that Heinz, Jana. He just pisses me off so much, the arrogant mother fucker," I said.

"Going to be an interesting trip!" replied Heinz and he smiled at me. "Don't worry George, it will be okay."

"Yes, I know. And I won't let him get to me. Sorry again Heinz, Jana," I said looking at them both. "Let's get on board."

We boarded the aircraft and indeed were all spread out in the Business Class cabin. That was fine by me, as I have previously mentioned, I'm not a big fan of talking to my fellow passengers. I had a window seat in the last row of the cabin (8A) and luckily enough, an empty seat by the side of me. Nigel was in row one, as expected, while Heinz and Jana were in rows three and four, respectively.

After settling into my seat and following the Captain's announcement, the crew completed the safety demonstration on the Airbus A350. There was a slight delay waiting for incoming planes to land, but nothing too lengthy and it wasn't too long before we were airborne and heading for Addis Ababa.

Following the drinks and meal service, I decided to try and get some sleep on the flight, catch up a bit for missing out last night! I reclined the seat, put a blanket over me and closed my eyes. Normally, I slept well on aircraft. Even on the shortest of flights, I could sometimes be snoozing prior to take off! And it wasn't long before the soothing rhythm of the aircraft and purring noise coming from the engines had done the trick and I was asleep.

I was awoken by a tapping on my thigh and in a daze, I initially thought the contact with my thigh was coming from under the blanket. I looked to my right to see Jana sitting in the seat next to me with her hand on my thigh. Luckily enough (or unluckily enough depending on how you view it), her hand was on top of the blanket.

"Don't worry George, I'm not molesting you. Well, not just yet anyway," said Jana.

"Shame," I said rather groggily. "What's the matter, everything alright?" I asked.

"Yes. Just thought I would see how you are and let you know we've got about thirty minutes until we land. I went to the bathroom earlier and thought you could join me, but unfortunately you were asleep. So, I thought I would just wake you prior to landing. Hope that was okay?"

"Yep. That's cool. Thanks. I mean about waking me up, not going to the toilet with you, or I mean, thanks for letting me sleep. You know what I mean," I said somewhat confusingly.

"I think so. Anyway, Nigel has done nothing but try to chat up the pretty young flight attendant the whole flight. Not too sure how he got on. I think he's given her the 'I'm an important executive' spiel. Maybe she fell for it, maybe she didn't. Might find out later as I think the crew are staying at the same hotel as us. Speaking of hotels, we're staying at the Radisson Blu Hotel, quite nice from what I've heard and only about a fifteen minute drive from the airport. As for Heinz, I saw him using his laptop for about an hour before he tried to sleep."

"Thanks for the update. And what about you? Manage to get any sleep?"

"Not really. A bit tired now though. I talked to Heinz just after take-off and went through the itinerary with him. Seems like there is a hotel shuttle bus from the airport, so we must take that. As it will be about 8 p.m. by the time we get there and we'll all be quite tired, Heinz thinks it will be a good idea to check-in, and then meet in the bar for a quick drink and maybe something to eat, before having an early night. We are due to be picked up at 9 a.m. tomorrow and taken to the catering facility for the tour. But I guess you know all that already." By the time Jana had finished talking, I had fully restored my seat to the upright position.

"Yes, I read the communication Heinz sent out last week with the itinerary attached to it. So, I'm not sure why you are going over it again with me. Or is it just my company you were seeking?" I asked and smiled at her.

"I guess I'm a bit nervous, that's all. I've been on a few business trips, but not for this long and not this important. You will help me George, won't you?"

"Of course. There's nothing to worry about. Heinz and I will do most of the talking, that is if Nigel sticks to his role and keeps his fucking nose out of things."

"Thanks George. And yes, I was seeking your company. Maybe tonight as well?" Jana got up from the seat beside me and went back to her own seat.

The landing was smooth and being in Business Class, we didn't have long to wait to exit the aircraft. We congregated prior to going through immigration and once through, made our way out of the airport to the hotel shuttle bus stands, via customs control. As we all only had 'carry on' luggage, we were fortunate enough to avoid the gathering masses at the baggage reclaim area!

"It's this way, come on," said Nigel with an authoritative tone in his voice as if he was the Scout Master, leading his cubs on an orienteering expedition. I just thought he was a total prick! "Yes, the stand should be just over there," he continued.

"I'm not sure it is," said a hesitant Heinz. "I think it is the other way actually."

"Nonsense, Heinz. It's definitely this way."

"Nigel!" I said quite abruptly, to get his attention as he started heading off in quite clearly the wrong direction.

"What George, what do you want?" came Nigel's frustrated response.

"The sign up there quite clearly states that the Radisson Blu Hotel shuttle bus is this way," I said firstly pointing to the sign and then pointing in the opposite way to which Nigel was heading. Nigel looked up at the sign, then back to me, before fixing his stare at Heinz.

"Well, why didn't you say Heinz," said Nigel. "I hope we haven't missed it now."

"I did try to tell you but-" commented Heinz, but before he could finish his sentence, Nigel had hurriedly walked back past us and was now heading in the right direction. Heinz and I looked at each other, smiled and shook our heads, hoping this wasn't a sign of things to come.

While we waited for the shuttle bus, I quickly called Martyna to let her know I had arrived safely. She sounded really pleased to hear my voice and briefly told me about how much the girls had enjoyed Pizza Hut. I told her I didn't have much time and would call tomorrow and talk to the girls. It was lovely to hear Martyna's voice and listen to her talk so excitedly about Emily and Amy.

Once on the hotel shuttle bus, it didn't take long to arrive at the hotel. We passed through the hotel security including a metal detection machine for us and an x-ray machine for our luggage and made our way to reception. Nigel, as always, lead the way and checked-in first.

"See you in the bar in fifteen minutes," he said and rushed away to the elevators. It had taken him ten minutes to check-in. If it took the rest of us the same amount of time, he'd be sitting in the bar on his own! And indeed, it did take quite a long time for the rest of us to check-in, me being the last. But quite frankly, I wasn't exactly worried about not being on time for Nigel.

I made my way to the fifth floor and found my room. I was in room 525. It was a nice hotel, so I was expecting a good room and wasn't disappointed. Large bed, a sort of separate living area with a sofa, armchair, TV and mini bar, and a nice bathroom, with a largish bath and large walk-in shower. I looked out of the window, and although it was dark, I had a view of the UNECA Conference Centre. It was a genuinely nice, clean, and tidy room. I unpacked my suit and dress shirts for the next two days, my toiletries and underwear. Just before going down to the bar to join the others, I brushed my teeth and gave myself a quick spray of 'Baldessarini' before checking my appearance in the bathroom mirror. "Looking good George", I said to myself and then left the room.

As I entered the bar, I saw Jana, Heinz and Nigel sitting around a large glass coffee table to the side of the bar with two leather sofas either side of it. Heinz and Jana had taken up one sofa, leaving me with a space next to Nigel. 'Thanks a lot guys,' I thought to myself as I sat down next to Nigel.

"Sorry I'm late, check-in was a nightmare," I said.

"We got you a beer George," said Heinz. "Hope that's okay?"

"Perfect, thank you Heinz."

"And we've ordered some snacks, chicken wings, pizza bites, satay, tempura prawns, that sort of thing," added Jana.

"Sounds great. Thank you. So, how are your rooms, all okay?"

"Yeah, great," replied Heinz.

"Not bad," said Jana. Nigel said nothing and hadn't even looked up from his phone since I had sat down. He just sat there typing away with a big smile on his face.

"And how's your room Nigel?" I asked.

"What? What was that?" came a flustered response from Nigel. "My room did you say? Yes, it's nice, large comfy bed and a jacuzzi bath, very satisfactory. In fact, I'm feeling rather tired. I think I'm going to head up if you don't mind. See you at breakfast, 8:30 a.m." Nigel got up, still smiling, and still looking at his phone. "Good night," he said and made his way to the elevators. As he left, I turned to Heinz and Jana.

"What was all that about?"

"I don't know George. But he barely said two words to us either. Has been on that phone for the last ten minutes," said Heinz.

"I think I know," said Jana. "Just before I got to the bar, I saw Nigel with that flight attendant from our flight, the young girl. It looked like they were 'getting along' very well if you know what I mean. My guess is that they are meeting in his room for a little rendezvous, perhaps to try out the jacuzzi." Heinz and I looked at Jana before looking at each other. We all pulled the same face of horror as the thought of Nigel's naked body entered our minds.

"Well, more food for us then," I said, taking the mood to a more auspicious and pleasant level.

The drinks and food arrived, and we had an enjoyable evening discussing the agenda for the next two days. After the initial introductions with our hosts, Heinz and Jana would work on the numbers while I focussed on the kitchen audit. I hadn't got a clue what Nigel would do! Then we would meet up late afternoon to put the finishing touches to our meeting presentation. This would take place the following morning, before flying to Johannesburg in the afternoon, arriving around 7 p.m. on Wednesday evening. The food that Jana had ordered was good and was enough to satisfy us all. Good job Nigel had gone to bed, or whatever it was he was doing, otherwise there might not have been enough!

"Well, Jana and George, I think it is time for my bed. We have a lot to do tomorrow, so I want to be well rested," said Heinz. "Sleep well and I will see you at breakfast. Guten Nacht."

"Good night Heinz and sleep well," I answered.

"Guten Nacht, Heinz," said Jana. After Heinz had left, Jana turned to me. "Another drink George?" I looked at my watch, and it was 8:40 p.m. back home, so with the time difference it was 10:40 p.m. here in Addis Ababa.

"I'm game if you are?" I replied.

"Yes. I'll have another glass of Chardonnay. Another beer for you?" said Jana as she summoned over a waiter and placed our order. It wasn't long before the drinks arrived and we 'clinked' glasses in a toast to a successful trip.

"So, George, are you up for some fun tonight?" asked Jana.

"What kind of fun do you mean?"

"Well, maybe not as physically demanding as last night, I'm a bit tired myself," Jana added before continuing. "But if you wanted to get together, lie down naked on the bed and see what happens, then I think that would be nice." I took a long drink of my beer before placing it down on the glass table that separated us, and then looked up at Jana.

"You know, I can't quite work you out Jana. I've only known you a few weeks and as far as work goes, you are very professional, diligent, hardworking, and great with numbers. You are risk averse and analyse everything to death. However, you appear to be the opposite in your private life. Adventurous, spontaneous, carefree and uninhibited."

"Work is work. But my personal life is for living. I see what I want, and I try to get it. If I do, great. If I don't, I try for something else. I'm driven to succeed. My mum was, and still is a controlling person. She drummed into me and my siblings that 'being first' is the only way to succeed and to never admit to defeat. At first, it made me want to rebel against her and do what I wanted to do. But it also taught me to be strong and I decided from quite an early age, I wasn't going to do anything that I didn't want to do. So now I look at how I can take advantage of situations for my benefit."

"What do you mean?"

"Take work for example. I'm not as good at my job as everyone thinks. But I use my looks and my legs, to get noticed and then I just bullshit my way through even when I don't know the answers. It gives me exposure; people think I know what I'm talking about and I get to advance. I use this," Jana said, pointing to her body, "to get ahead."

"And it doesn't matter to you that someone more deserving, yet less attractive, is overlooked?"

"No. Sounds callous, but that's who I am."

"Ok. Good to know," I said nodding my head slowly.

"Does that mean you don't want to fuck me?"

"You say what you mean don't you! No. Erm, it doesn't mean that I don't want to, you know. But it gives me a better understanding of you, that's all," I said thoughtfully.

"Look George, I'm genuinely attracted to you. I haven't been flirting with you since the first day I met you, just to try and get on this business trip."

"So, you have been flirting with me since the moment we first met?"

"Well, at least from the moment I gave you a ride back to the airport in my car. I knew you were looking at my legs and have been looking at them ever since."

"True," I said somewhat begrudgingly. "And what about calling me and telling me you're sitting in your underwear? Was that all part of the plan to get me interested?"

"It is hot in my apartment George, as you now know. And yes, I do sit there some nights in my underwear. But I suppose telling you that on the phone was another way to flirt with you without being physically in the same room," answered Jana.

"So, you are attracted to me?" I asked.

"Yes. But I'm not interested in fairy tales, falling in love, kids, and the outdated concept of marriage. As I said, I see what I want, and I go after it. And right now, George Hart, you are what I want!" I looked thoughtfully at Jana before breaking into a smile.

"Refreshingly honest, I have to admit. They say that twenty-four hours is a long time in politics. It's a bloody lifetime with you," I said still smiling at Jana.

"So, do you want to fuck me or not?"

"Drink up, and let's go," I said leaning over the glass table to reach my beer.

We finished our drinks and made our way up to my room. Once inside, Jana entered the bathroom, so I took off my jacket and sat down on the sofa. After a few minutes, I could hear the shower running and as I looked over to the bathroom, Jana appeared at the bathroom door naked.

"Join me?" she softly asked me, before heading back inside the bathroom. I got up from the sofa and made my way to the bathroom. Jana was already in the shower, soaping up her body, paying particular attention to her breasts, nipples, and completely shaved vagina, while all the time she was staring at me. I left the bathroom and took off all my clothes. I returned and stepped into the shower with Jana.

She immediately started to wash my body, my back, chest, and arms, before kneeling to wash my feet. She worked her way up to my balls and semi erect penis, carefully washing and caressing them. Then she took my penis in her mouth, slowly and sensually kissing, sucking, and licking it. It wasn't long before my penis was rock hard. I looked down and took hold of Jana's shoulders, gently lifting her upwards, passionately kissing her lips before moving on to her breasts and firm nipples. I reached for the back of her left thigh with my right hand, tenderly lifted her leg and pushed my penis towards her. She gave out a squeal of delight as I penetrated her vagina and we rhythmically rocked in the shower together.

After sex in the shower, we went into the bedroom to continue our lovemaking, before cuddling up together and falling asleep. It wasn't quite the early night we probably both needed, but it was definitely a night to remember.

21

I opened my eyes to the sound of the wake-up alarm from my mobile phone, and looked across to where Jana had been, to find nobody lying next to me. I switched the alarm off and sat up in the bed. Another interesting night I thought to myself! Different to the previous night with Jana which was all about fantasy and pure sexual delight. Last night was gentler, more emotional, and more like love making. A different side to her, that I found much more appealing.

I didn't have time to dwell on this as a busy day ensued, so I tried to forget about Jana, and jumped in the shower. However, as soon as I was in the shower, the memories of last night came flooding back to me. Jana soaping her body, almost playing with her herself before turning her attention to me. I smiled to myself and again tried to push last night's events to the back of my mind.

It was a little after 8:30 a.m. when I entered the breakfast room and saw Jana and Heinz sitting at a freshly laid table, white table linen, silver cutlery and a central floral display of blue hydrangea.

"Morning guys," I said as I sat down at the table, opposite Jana.

"Good morning George," said Heinz.

"Morning George," said Jana. "Sleep well?"

"Surprisingly, quite well actually," I replied looking directly at Jana.

266

"Why surprisingly?" Jana pushed me, still locking eye contact with me.

"After all the tension," and I paused and then turned my head to look at Heinz, "between Nigel and me yesterday, I had a lot of things going on my mind. So, I was surprised how easily I got to sleep." I then turned back to look at Jana. "I suppose I was just tired."

"Tea or coffee sir?" a waitress said to me in a perfect English accent as she approached our table. I looked at both Jana and Heinz, inviting them to answer.

"It's okay George, we've already given our orders," Heinz responded.

"I'll have coffee please," I said to the waitress.

"Help yourself to the buffet sir," she said as she vacated the area.

"Some news George," said Heinz.

"Oh yeah, what's that?" I replied.

"Nigel is sick and will not be joining us at the catering facility today. He sends his apologies. He thinks it must have been something he ate last night, although he didn't eat anything here, so it must have been on the flight. He said he will rest up today in his room and join us later when we get back to the hotel."

"He's sick? Well, that's a shame. As you know, I don't have much time for Nigel, and to be honest, I'm not sure what value he is adding to this trip, but I wouldn't wish him ill health, especially in a foreign country. Does he need anything? Doctor, medicine?"

"He said he will be okay. He has some medication he brought with him, so will just take it easy today."

"Ok, well I guess it's just the three of us today. Shall we get some breakfast?" We all stood up and made our way over to the breakfast buffet. It was a marvellous spread of hot and cold food items, eggs prepared four ways, bacon, sausages, mushrooms, tomatoes, hash browns, toast, bagels, fruit, cereals, cold meats, cheeses and so many other different items. Heinz made his way to the healthy food section, fruit, yoghurt, etc., while I went over to the hot section. As I was loading up some mushrooms onto my plate, Jana tapped me on the shoulder.

"You okay George?" she asked.

"Yes. You?"

"Yes. Sorry I wasn't there when you woke up this morning, but I needed to get a shower and get ready, so I didn't want to disturb you. Don't think I just used you and then left you," said Jana smiling at me.

"That's okay Jana. I understand, and I thought that's why you had left. But if you did just 'use me' and 'leave me', then that's okay too. I had a great time. I hope you did as well. But after talking to you last night, I think I have a better understanding of who you are and know that what we have done over the last two nights, is just sex. Great sex, but all the same, just sex. So really there is no need to explain anything. I'm cool."

"Thanks George. Also, I thought you might want to know that I saw that flight attendant leaving Nigel's room this morning at 6:30 a.m. I was going back to my room from yours when I saw her leaving a room along the corridor. I didn't think much of it until I saw Nigel step out of the room and kiss her. Don't worry, he didn't see me and by the time I walked past his room, he had already gone back inside."

"The old fucker!" I said slowly. "You know, I don't blame him for getting it on with the flight attendant, but to feign illness because he is probably tired, the old fart, that's a bit out of order. Still, nothing we can do about it and in many ways, I think it works out better for us. We can get on today without any interference."

"Yes, I agree. Anyway, I'll see you back at the table." With that Jana turned and joined Heinz at the healthy section of the buffet.

We finished our breakfast and went to Reception, ready for our lift. Just before 9 a.m. a tall black man with rounded glasses and a balding head entered the hotel reception, wearing a navy-blue suit, white shirt, and a red tie. He had an Ethiopian Airlines name tag dangling around his neck attached to a lanyard.

"This must be the guy," I said to Heinz and we started to walk towards him.

"Hello. My name is Kofi. I am the General Manager for the Ethiopian Airlines Catering unit. Are you my special friends from Germany?" the man said in a broad African accent with a big smile on his face revealing his pearly white teeth.

"Hello Kofi. Yes, we are. It's a pleasure to meet you. Let me introduce you to the team," I said. "This Jana Muller our Controlling Manager and this Heinz Mayer, our Head of Mergers and Acquisitions." Kofi exchanged greetings and handshakes with Jana and Heinz. "And I am George Hart, Sales and Marketing Director. Again, a pleasure to meet you."

"Please come this way," said Kofi and he led us from the reception to a white Toyota minibus that was waiting outside. The driver was standing by the opened sliding rear door, ready to assist anyone that needed help getting in. Luckily, none of us did! Jana looked a little shocked. I think she was expecting a luxury limo, a Mercedes or BMW. It was a relatively new vehicle, clean inside, and well looked after. However, it did have a large dent in the rear panel.

"That's normal," both Heinz and I said at the same time to Jana, to try and comfort her growing distress level. Once inside and seated, the driver closed the door and made his way around to the driver's seat.

"The journey will take around fifteen minutes. Please put on your safety belts," said Kofi. "My driver is excellent, but not all drivers are at the same level." Jana wasted no time in putting her belt on and really looked nervous. Heinz and I smiled at each other as we had both had experience of the African way, as we also put our belts on.

"Thanks Kofi," I said. "So how long have you worked for Ethiopian Airlines?"

"Well, Mr Hart, I have been working for the company since I came back from England after my studies. So, it must be twenty-five years now. I started as a 'packer', packing items into trolleys. But I have moved all around the facility in my time."

"That's great Kofi. So, you are really experienced with the operation. Oh, and please, call me George," I replied.

"Thank you, George. Yes, I have been General Manager for the last three years and I am excited to have the opportunity to learn more from you and your company, and to welcome new customers to our facility."

"Do you have much involvement with the financial side of the business?" asked Heinz.

"I do, but only in the preparation of the figures. Reporting, you could say, Mr Mayer."

"Please, as with George, please call me Heinz."

"And I'm Jana," added Jana.

"You are all truly kind. Thank you. Now during your stay, if you need anything, please do not hesitate to let me know. I am here to assist you with everything. If you have questions, please ask them. If I do not know, I will find somebody who does."

"Thanks Kofi, we really appreciate it," said Heinz.

"I do have a question myself. I was told that there would be four persons. A 'Mr Nigel Colnbrooke' is missing?"

"Yes, unfortunately Nigel is not feeling too well today, so will not be joining us. However, if he is feeling better tomorrow, he will attend our meeting with your Board," I said.

"Does he need any medical attention?" a concerned Kofi asked. "We have excellent Doctors here and I can arrange for one to see him if you would like me to?"

"I think he will be okay. We'll check on him later and if he's not feeling any better, we'll let you know. But thanks for your concern," I replied.

The rest of the short journey went relatively quickly and luckily without any incidents to further alarm Jana! We soon arrived at the catering facility and Kofi led us through the main entrance where we were greeted by a smartly dressed middle aged woman who asked us to sign the visitors journal and issued us with visitor passes attached to lanyards.

"Please make sure you wear your visitor passes at all times while you are our guests here at our facility," said the woman, who Kofi explained was 'Desta', his assistant.

"If I am not available at any time, please find Desta and she will also assist you with whatever you need," said Kofi.

"Pleased to me meet you Desta. I'm George, this is Jana and this is Heinz," I said introducing the team to Desta. After the introductions, Kofi lead us up some stairs to the 1st floor of the building, along a long corridor, past a large boardroom (which looked like something out of a 1950's 'men only' golf club), and to large double doors at the end of the corridor.

"Mr Ahmed, our CEO and Chairman of the Board wanted to welcome you before you start your day. Please just wait here one moment," said Kofi, as he lightly knocked on the door and went inside. I could hear him talking to a woman, before he reappeared at the door and beckoned Jana, Heinz, and myself into the room. "This is Neela, the personal assistant to Mr Ahmed, she will take us through to see Mr Ahmed," said Kofi. Neela was a young girl, very pretty and had a poise and professional manner that appeared way beyond her years.

"This way, please," said Neela and she walked towards another set of double doors, knocked, opened the doors, and announced us as we entered the room.

"Ahh, please, please come in," said a rather excited small man, wearing a dark blue suit, white shirt, and pale pink tie. Mr Ahmed, rose from his huge green leather executive chair and made his way around his large ornate, highly polished desk, to greet us with handshakes. His office was massive, fully oak panelled, with large paintings adorning three of the walls. I have to say, although it was very outdated, at the same time it was incredibly impressive. "My name is Aman Ahmed, but please call me Aman. I am the CEO of Ethiopian Airlines and welcome you to our catering facility," Aman continued.

"Thank you, Aman. I'm George Hart, this is Jana Muller and Heinz Mayer. But please call us, Jana, Heinz, and George. Thank you for inviting us here. We are all very much looking forward to working with you and your team," I replied.

"Please, come and sit down," said Aman as he ushered us over to a mini boardroom table, which had a coffee station set up on it, and trays of sweet pastries and bread rolls. As we sat down, Neela, starting with Jana, asked us all if we would like coffee or tea and then gave the orders to a second woman, who proceeded to deliver to drinks to us.

"So, tell me George, how was your stay last night?" said Aman.

"Very nice," I said without looking at Jana and hoping I was not blushing. "The hotel is very comfortable, and although we arrived quite late, we did manage to have a bite to eat before getting an early night." Just about got away with that one I thought!

"I'm so glad. But what about Mr Colnbrooke? Kofi tells me he is ill?"

"Yes, unfortunately, Nigel wasn't feeling too good this morning, so has decided to take the day to get some rest and hopefully he will join us for the meeting tomorrow."

"That is unfortunate. If he needs any medical assistance, please let me know immediately and I will ensure that he receives the best help available. He is the most senior person amongst you, isn't he?"

"Well, in title yes. But he is only here in an advisory capacity. We have Heinz who is our Head of Mergers and Acquisitions," I said turning to Heinz, "and Jana who is our Controlling Manager. Heinz and Jana will be working today on the administrative and 'numbers' side of things, and I will carry out an appraisal of the catering facility operations. You do not need to worry that Nigel isn't here. Everything is covered." Aman looked at me and then broke into a smile.

"I get a good feeling from your team, George. Now, I have made an office down the corridor available to you, for Jana and Heinz to work from. Neela will assist you with any information, documents and arrange for you to meet with the Financial Director. George, Kofi will lead you on the tour of the facility and around the operations. I do hope you will all be able to join me for dinner tonight. I have a booked a private room at the hotel you are staying at; the food is unbelievably delicious."

"That sounds wonderful Aman, we would be delighted to accept you offer for dinner," I replied.

We finished our coffees and talked for a while with Aman. He was a very well-educated man who had studied at Oxford University and lived in London for many years. His father was the Ethiopian Ambassador for the UK and with that, it had brought Aman many privileges, including meeting royalty, film stars and sporting heroes. Although I hadn't noticed it when I first entered his office, Aman showed me a framed photograph of himself and Price Charles shaking hands at a charity function, which he kept on a cabinet behind his desk.

"Very nice man, Price Charles. Sometimes a little misunderstood, talking to plants and all that, but a genuinely nice man," is how Aman described him. I had to smile!

We all left Aman's office and were shown into a small office along the corridor which we could use as a base. Kofi and I put on our white coats and hair nets ready for the tour and Heinz and Jana set up their laptops in readiness for the financial analysis they would be conducting. As we had left Aman's office, he again reiterated that he was there to help and if we needed anything, we were only to ask. He also confirmed that he would see us back at the hotel this evening for dinner at 7:30 p.m. Before I left with Kofi for the tour, I asked Jana if she would contact Nigel during the day to find out if he was feeling better and to let him know about dinner tonight with Aman. She said she would, albeit a little begrudgingly.

"Where would you like to start, George?" said Kofi as we walked down the stairs from the office.

"Let's start at the 'dish room'. I would like to see the off-loading of the dirty catering then and follow the process around the facility. Is that okay for you Kofi?"

"This is very good George. This way," replied Kofi and he led me out of the office building and around the side of the catering facility to the 'off-load' dock where the catering trucks returned from the planes with the dirty catering trolleys and equipment. Kofi was deeply knowledgeable and talked me through the process and also introduced me to the Supervisor in charge of the dish room. He went through the sorting process (flatware, chinaware, glass, etc..) and the trash removal before showing me the trolley wash area and the dishwasher machine.

"We currently have only one machine and it is quite old. We do realise that to attract additional business, we will need to invest in two new machines and retire this one," said Kofi. I nodded in agreement and smiled at him, while continuing to make my notes. We then made our way to the equipment stores area where all the clean equipment was held until ready to be used in production. This was a much quieter area than the dishwash room we had come from with all the noise of the washing machines and the general chatter of the people working in there. We walked down a long corridor which had 'caged meshing' from floor to ceiling either side of it, containing the catering equipment. As we were walking, I started to hear a sort of 'moaning' noise, as if somebody were hurt and trying to attract attention. It was only faint, but I looked at Kofi for some reassurance.

"Do you hear that Kofi?" I asked.

"That's nothing George," he dismissively replied, and we continued walking. The noise became louder the further we walked along the corridor and the noise was now more distinct and more of a 'pleasurable' tone. We stopped at an open gate in the meshing and the noise was quite loud by now.

"Sorry Kofi, but what is that noise?" I again asked in a more concerned manner.

"No, I am the one who is sorry George. It is Alfred and Edna. They are in their fifties you know! But, well, they like to, well, fuck! And they have been here so long, over thirty years, and have always fucked each other at work. It's kind of become a habit for them. I had told them we had visitors today and to not fuck today. But they have obviously not listened to me. They are good workers, trusted people, exceptionally reliable. And as I said, they have been here a long time. So, we kind of, how you say, 'turn a blind eye' if you know what I mean?" I slowly shook my head in disbelief and then a smile came over my face.

"Alfred and Edna eh! So, they're 'doing it' right now are they?"

"Yes. Sorry George. I'm hoping that this will not go into your report. It is very embarrassing."

"I didn't hear a thing," I replied and started to continue walking. However, I was stopped in my tracks when I heard "Good morning Mr Kofi," shouted out from within the caged area.

"Good morning Alfred," came Kofi's nonchalant response and he lifted his hand to wave back at Alfred. I looked into the cage and saw a small middle-aged man, with is trousers around his ankles, arse exposed, bending over a large woman who was leaning on a table, also with her huge arse exposed, taking her from behind. She, who I presumed must have been Edna, never said a word and continued to moan in delight as Alfred continued to 'pump' her from behind, while waving back at us and revealing a 'toothless' smile.

"Let's move on," said an uncomfortable Kofi, and we made our way along the corridor in silence for a few seconds. I thought the whole thing was hilarious, but I could see that Kofi was in some distress about what we had just seen.

"Kofi," I said turning to him. "As I said, I didn't hear anything," and I smiled reassuringly at him. He nodded at me and smiled back. "I saw a hell of a lot though! Too much for me and quite frightening!" I continued and we both laughed.

The rest of the tour took in the other departments, hot and cold kitchens, tray set up area, bakery, yes, they had an on-site bakery! I always found it to be one of my favourite places in a catering facility. Most catering facilities over the years had done away with on-site bakeries or pastry departments, instead opting to outsource these items. From a financial perspective in the Western world, it made sense. It was more cost effective to outsource. But areas of the world where labour costs were cheaper, it was more beneficial to have this department in-house, especially if you had a particularly good pastry chef. And I have to say, the smells coming from the pastry department were very pleasing.

Kofi introduced me to the pastry chef, a guy called Salana. He was respectful but was not a very friendly person. Extremely strict with his staff and hot on hygiene and standards. However, Kofi informed me that he was not well liked and never shared his knowledge, particularly the HACCP (Hazard Analysis and Critical Control Points) he learned while studying in Switzerland. However, he was an exceptional pastry chef and the products were extremely good. It was quite ironic really, because Kofi explained to me that the name Salana means 'sunshine, warmth or extremely bright'. Bright he certainly was, warm he certainly wasn't!

I had completed my tour of the facility by 3 p.m. and went back to the office that Heinz and Jana had been working in. Kofi took me to a 'street food' area for lunch and we had a traditional dish called

'Doro Wat' which means chicken stew. It was like a chicken curry and although smelled very tasty, I was wary of the lack of hygiene involved in making it. The last thing I needed was to be ill! Therefore, I declined to taste it, which Kofi respectfully understood the reasons why.

"How are you guys doing," I said as I entered the office where Heinz and Jana were.

"Yes, very well George," answered Heinz. "I think we are about done here. We've got all the information we needed, and I think Jana is just finishing off the analysis," he continued and looked at Jana.

"Yes. I'm just about done. Maybe we can spend an hour or so back at the hotel to review the day?" said Jana.

"Sounds like a plan to me. Did you manage to get hold of Nigel?"

"Yes. He is feeling much better and will join us for dinner tonight. He wasn't going to, but when I told him that it was the CEO of Ethiopian Airlines that had invited us, he suddenly felt much better! Total twat, that man," said a frustrated Jana.

"Flight attendant has left, has she?" I replied.

"Flight attendant, what flight attendant?" asked Heinz.

"Doesn't matter," came the unified response from both Jana and me.

"Probably. Anyway, how has your day been George?" Jana continued.

"Yeah. Good. There are a lot of issues, particularly around hygiene, and HACCP. And there are some security issues too. As you know, you enter the facility 'landside' but once you are inside, you have direct access to the airport apron, and to be honest, I think there are some flaws in the system that our international customers would not be impressed with. But I'm no expert on security, so we will have to get a full analysis done by someone in the that department from Frankfurt."

"I know who to contact about that," said Heinz.

"Good. But let's discuss this back at the hotel. Shall we make a move back?" Both Heinz and Jana nodded in agreement, so I exited the office and walked down the corridor towards Aman's office. I gently knocked on the door and entered to find Neela sitting at her desk.

"Hi Neela. We are about done, and I was wondering if you could arrange for transport back to the hotel? Also, I would like to say thank you to Aman for his hospitality and that of his team today, if that's possible?"

"Hi George. I will see if Mr Ahmed is free." Neela got up from her seat and knocked on the double doors leading to Aman's office, before entering. A few seconds later, Aman walked out from his office and extended his hand to me.

"Hello George. I trust you have had a particularly good day and you and your colleagues have been well looked after?"

"Hello Aman. Yes, thank you very much for all your support and the support of your team. I have had a 'particularly' good day with Kofi and having just talked to Heinz and Jana, they have also enjoyed the day and have found everyone most helpful."

"I am so pleased and hope that this will assist in our discussions tomorrow. Now, Neela will arrange for the driver to take you back to the hotel. Unfortunately, Kofi is a little busy right now, but we will see you all later for dinner."

"Thank you again Aman and yes we look forward to seeing you later," I replied and after releasing his handshake, I turned to walk back to the office where Heinz and Jana were busy packing up their things. Within a few minutes, Neela appeared and informed me that our driver was waiting outside the main entrance for us. We thanked Neela and made our way out of the building to the main entrance and sure enough the same vehicle and driver that had brought us here this morning, was waiting to take us back.

The journey back was a little quiet. I think Jana and Heinz had had an intense day and were feeling a bit tired. Obviously, Jana must have been tired after the previous two nights of sexual exertion with me, I thought to myself, hoping that was indeed the case! We arrived safely back at the hotel and after thanking our driver we made our way into the hotel foyer.

"Ok guys, what would you like to do? It's 3:40 p.m. so what we could do is have a meeting now to discuss the day and ready ourselves for tomorrow's meeting with their Board, or we can freshen up now and meet prior to dinner tonight. What would you like to do?" I asked Jana and Heinz.

"Personally, I would like to finish up now and then get a few hours rest before dinner, if that's okay with you two?" replied Heinz.

"That's fine with me," agreed Jana.

"Ok, let's take a seat over there," I said, pointing to a table close to the bar area. Jana, will you give Nigel a call and see if he is 'well enough' to join us?" Jana looked at me and sighed as if to say 'why the fuck do I have to call him' but eventually removed her phone from her bag and called Nigel. Heinz and I made our way over to the table and sat down.

"Are you okay Heinz?" I said, as Heinz looked a little weary when he sat down.

"A little tired, but we've had a good day. We got all the financial information we needed, and I think we will be able to construct a deal for this one, which would be beneficial for both parties. Unless you tell me that the facility is terrible and needs €5 million of investment!"

"Well, there are some investments required in equipment, dishwash machine, freezers and the holding chiller will need to be enlarged substantially. But the main areas of concern are more around training on hygiene, safety, and security. Portion control is also a huge issue if what I witnessed today is anything to go by!" Jana came over to the table and sat down next to me.

"Is he coming down?" asked Heinz.

"No. He's feeling much better but feels he can leave the summarizing to us. He wants us to brief him at breakfast tomorrow before the meeting. He said he was going to use the gym now and would see us for dinner. And that was that, total arsehole and a waste of space!" Both Heinz and I smiled.

We went through our notes of the day and by the end of our discussion, we had a very good idea of what needed to be done in order to bring the facility up to international standards and what sort of partnership scenario could be proposed. The object of tomorrow's meeting was not to make any offer, but instead to present ways in which to move forward towards an offer based on today's analysis of the financial and physical state of the catering facility.

"Well, if you'll excuse me, I am going to my room to get some rest for tonight," said Heinz as he got up from his seat and said goodbye to Jana and me.

"See you later Heinz," I replied, "and thanks for all the work today, you did a great job." As Heinz left us for the elevators, Jana turned to me.

"So, George, what do you want to do?" she said and smiled at me.

"Well first, I need to go and call my girls and see what they've been up to. And then I must check my emails and then I will call Tanja to fill her in on today. And by the time that's all done, I'll need to take a shower in readiness for dinner tonight."

"The shower bit sounds interesting, fancy some company?" said Jana with raised eyebrows.

"Don't take this the wrong way Jana, but as much as I loved taking a shower with you, I'm not sure we will have the time. Can we leave that idea for now?"

"For now," she replied and smiled. "Right, well I'm going to do the same and I'll see you down here for dinner about 7:15 p.m. okay?"

"Thanks Jana and again, thanks for all your work today. The analysis looks really good and I think once we get back to Frankfurt, we will be in a position to formalise an offer that our board will have no hesitation in signing off."

"My pleasure George, and hopefully both our pleasures later tonight!" Jana replied, collecting her things before heading to the elevators. I just sat there for a few minutes thinking of how 'pleasurable' it had been with Jana over the previous two nights, but could I really cope with another one? More importantly, where was all this leading?

22

I called the girls and had a long conversation with them about their day and asked them if they were behaving for Martyna. They promised me they were and after a quick conversation with Martyna, she assured me everything was fine and the girls were once again, just like angels! Although it had only been a couple of days, it was lovely to hear the girls voices. It was also genuinely nice to hear Martyna's voice too. I then called Tanja and filled her in on the day and about Nigel's 'illness' to which the phrase 'fucking twat' was uttered by Tanja. Seemed like it was becoming something of a saying whenever Nigel's name was mentioned!

After finishing my call with Tanja, I looked through my emails, answering anything that was urgent. There was an email from Hilary Smith advising me that Melanie Simpson, the girl that had applied for the sales position, had accepted the offer of employment and was due to start on the Monday I got back. Hilary was asking if I could create some sort of induction schedule for her. I forwarded the email to Gavin Preston and asked him to pull out our usual induction schedule, update it and let Hilary have it. Gavin was a good guy and I knew he would be able to take care of this in my absence. I completed my email inbox review, checked the time, and realised that

I only had twenty-five minutes until we were supposed to meet for dinner. I quickly took a shower and got myself ready.

I wasn't too sure if the evening attire was to be formal or casual, so I opted for a more formal approach (a suit) but without a tie. I made my way down to the bar area and saw Heinz, Jana and Nigel standing together, Heinz and Jana talking, while Nigel again 'played' with his cell phone! Nigel and Heinz had dressed like me, so I felt good about my clothing decision. Jana, on the other hand had dressed rather formally and was wearing a short, low cut black cocktail dress. I must admit, she looked dazzling and my thoughts turned to the body beneath the dress! 'Be professional' I thought to myself.

"Evening everyone," I said as I approached the group.

"Evening George," was the response from Heinz and Jana. Nothing from Nigel as he was too busy grinning at his cell phone.

"Evening Nigel," I said forcing him to recognise I was there, standing next to him.

"Oh, evening George. Sorry, was lost in my thoughts."

"And how are you feeling Nigel, better?" I enquired.

"How am I feeling? Oh, yes, much better thank you. Not sure what it was, probably something I ate on the plane. But all good now." I looked at Jana and winked. "So, Heinz and Jana have just informed me that the day went well, and you got everything you needed. The financials look good and your kitchen tour didn't highlight any problems," Nigel continued.

"I never quite said that Nigel," interrupted Heinz.

"Oh, didn't you? Well, if there are problems, let me know and I will sort them out with this 'Aman' character. Need to show them who is in charge round here. If they want my, I mean our help, then they're bloody well going to have to pull their finger out. Leave it to me," Nigel said in his typical brash way.

"Erm, Nigel. That's not what I said either," again replied Heinz.

"Well, what the hell did you say?" asked a frustrated Nigel.

"I think Nigel, you may have misunderstood," I said trying to restore some semblance of sanity to the conversation. "We did have a good day today. Our hosts were most helpful, kind, generous and supportive. Heinz and Jana met with their CFO and received the information they required to complete the financial study, which I believe has yielded a favourable result. This means that from a commercial perspective, we should be able to make a strong case to our Board for making an offer to Ethiopian Airlines about their catering facility. And talking of the facility, although there are several issues including hygiene and safety, production planning, portion control and security, they are not insurmountable and with a little investment and training, can be corrected. So, there is no need for any 'strong arm' tactics, no need to destabilize the relationship we have developed today and no need for any egos to be on display when we meet with Aman for dinner. He is an intelligent, well-educated, and respected man. So, let's just be professional, courteous and enjoy the evening and his company, okay?" Nigel looked at me with the same look he gave me at the airport in Frankfurt before we departed for Addis Ababa - eyes slightly narrowed, that furrowed brow returning to his forehead.

"Thanks for the concise appraisal of the day, George. Yes, let's be professional and enjoy the evening. After all, I am here to support you guys," said Nigel in a vaguely sly manner as if he had some ulterior motive. I looked at him and I think he knew I would be watching how he behaved tonight.

Aman called out as he entered the bar and made his way briskly over to us. He was wearing the same suit he had been wearing at the office but had now dispensed with his tie, making him appear a little more casual. It fitted with what we were all wearing (not of course, Jana though!).

"Jana, Heinz and of course George, how are you my friends?" Aman said and shook our hands.

"We are all very well Aman, and you?" I replied.

"Yes, very well. And this must be Mr Colnbrooke. A pleasure to meet you," said Aman shaking Nigel's hand.

"Very nice to meet you too, Mr Ahmed, but please call me Nigel."

"And you my friend must call me Aman. Now, let me introduce you to Kofi, my General Manager, his wife Desta, and my wife Neela," said Aman as he turned and ushered Kofi, Desta and Neela towards Nigel. Nigel was taken aback by Neela's beauty and you could instantly tell he was attracted to her.

"Delighted to meet you all and especially you Neela," he said holding on to her hand a lot longer than anyone else's he had shaken.

I pulled Kofi over to one side and looked at him quizzically!

"So, you and Desta are married?" I said.

"Yes George. I didn't want to say anything this morning when Desta gave you your passes. We keep our private life and work life very separate and very professional."

"More so than Alfred and Edna then," I replied and the image of Alfred 'banging' Edna from behind, briefly entered my mind. Kofi smiled. "And what about Aman and Neela?"

"Yes, they have been married only a short time. But again, very professional at work."

"She's got to be thirty years younger than Aman, right?" I cautiously asked.

"She is only twenty-two. Aman is in his fifties. But it's not uncommon. Aman thought it would be a good idea to invite our wives to ensure Jana did not feel uncomfortable with only men being at the dinner table. I hope that's okay?"

"No problem at all. I'm sure Jana really appreciates the thought. I will thank Aman privately, later. Thanks for filling me in Kofi."

"My pleasure. Now, let's get that private room for dinner." Kofi went to talk to one the hotel staff. As I looked back towards the group,

Jana was busily chatting to Desta, Heinz was engaged in conversation with Aman and poor Neela was left in the company of Nigel. I felt it was my duty to rescue her, so I walked over to them and interrupted Nigel mid-sentence.

"Hi Neela. How long have you and Aman been married?" I said trying to reiterate to Nigel that Neela was indeed married to Aman, in case that fact had escaped him, even though Aman had introduced her as his wife!

"Only for six months. But we love each other very much and I am so happy to be with him," she replied. Nigel looked at me, slightly annoyed and then looked back to Neela.

"So, you like older men then, do you?" Nigel asked in a very creepy, skin crawling sort of way.

"No Nigel. I don't like older men. I 'love' one older man. That's all," was Neela's calm and very precise riposte! It did the trick as Nigel just stood there, opened mouthed imitating a large seabass!

"Let's go and find where we are eating," I said and escorted Neela away from Nigel and back to the others in the group. Kofi returned a few seconds later and asked everyone to follow him to a secluded side room, just off the main restaurant. Inside the room was a medium sized round table, laid for eight people with white linen, silver ware, glasses, and a beautiful centrepiece floral display. Aman invited people to sit down and we took our places helped by the ever-attentive waiters and waitresses. Of course, Nigel made a bee line for Neela and sat down next to her, with Aman on her other side. Next to Aman was Desta, followed by me, then Kofi, Jana, Heinz and finally Nigel again completing the circle.

Drinks orders were swiftly taken, and light chatter ensued as the menus were passed out. Aman was trying to engage Nigel in conversation, but Nigel only had eyes and ears for Neela. This did appear to upset Aman slightly, not because he thought Nigel was potentially 'hitting' on his wife, but because he expected more from the senior man in our party. More presence, more professionalism, more intellect and a little more respect. Therefore, I engaged with Aman as much as possible during the evening and I found him a remarkably interesting man. He had some great stories to tell about his time in London and fascinating tales about his encounters with Tom Cruise, Harrison Ford, and Dame Helen Mirren! In fact, everyone seemed to participate freely in conversation with each other, even Neela, on the occasions she managed to escape Nigel's boring dialogue.

Jana was glad of the additional female company and made a conscious attempt to engage with Neela to lighten the burden that she obviously felt having Nigel sitting next to her. Regrettably, the more Nigel had to drink, the more apparent it became that he was trying to 'hit' on Neela. It was almost embarrassing! Fortunately, our newfound friends put it down to the drink and politely laughed it away. However, all in all, it was a nice evening and everyone appeared to have enjoyed themselves. As the evening ended and everyone had said their goodbyes, Aman came to shake my hand.

"I have had a genuinely nice evening George. Although, I have to say that Nigel is not the man I was expecting. I hope you do not think I am speaking out of turn when I say he is a fool, a jester. He is not very respectful and for someone in his position, I find him disengaged, not very intellectual or stimulating company. Some people, whose circles I move in, would describe him as rude. If this is the type of person that your company thinks highly of, it greatly concerns me. I have to ask myself, are you the right partners for my company?"

"Aman, off the record, I completely agree with you on your observations about Nigel. And I can only apologise for his less than impressive behaviour tonight. Please also pass on my apologies to Neela. Although a difficult situation for her, I thought she handled it with dignity, assurance and with great poise. You quite rightly must be extremely proud of her. But please don't think that Nigel typifies the senior management team or in fact any level of management in our company. The work that Heinz and Jana have done today and the way they have conducted themselves paints a far truer picture of what our company represents. We are excited at the prospect of working together with you and feel there are many things we can learn from each other. It may have been the alcohol, or the fact that Nigel has been unwell today that caused his behaviour. Let's not rush into any conclusive judgements just yet," I replied.

"You, on the other hand, are a gentlemen George. And you are right, I think you have a great team in Heinz and Jana. I think I really could do business with you. Thank you for kind words and for your reassurances. Now, tomorrow's meeting; any surprises from what you and your team witnessed today?" Once again, the image of Alfred and Edna entered my head.

"No Aman, no surprises. I think there is a great opportunity here for both of our companies," I said and smiled, shaking Aman's hand. "Have a safe journey home and I will see you tomorrow morning."

"Thank you, George. I look forward to seeing you in the morning."

Aman, Neela, Kofi and Desta left the hotel and we all returned to the bar, taking up the same sofas we had occupied the previous evening. Nigel sat there again staring at his cell phone. This time with a far more anguished look on his face. I looked at both Heinz and then Jana inquisitively and they both just shrugged their shoulders.

"Anyone for a nightcap?" I asked.

"Not for me George, I think I'll get to bed. Big day tomorrow. Guten Nacht," said Heinz.

"I think I will go up as well," said Jana and she gave me a nod as if to say, 'join me' and dump this arsehole. I discretely nodded back at her. "Good night George, good night Nigel," she continued and headed for the elevators.

"Good night Jana," I replied. Still nothing from Nigel.

"Well, if you don't want a nightcap, I might as well-," but before I had finished, Nigel replied.

"Bourbon and ice," he said and at last looked up from his phone and stared at me.

"Sorry?"

"I'll have a bourbon and ice."

"Right," I said and waved over a waiter.

"Two large bourbons and ice please," I requested from the waiter and he hurriedly retreated to the bar.

"You think you are better than me, don't you George?" said Nigel slurring some of his words. "Well, you're not," he continued. "Just remember, I'm the senior person on this trip. I'm the S-P-V- of Global 'operations', not you."

"You mean SVP of Global Operations," I said sarcastically.

"That's what I said, wasn't it?" he again slurred.

"Look Nigel, you are a bit worse for wear, in fact you're drunk! Do you really want to get into this right now? Because I'll tell you, I'm up for it if you are?" At that moment, the drinks arrived and the waiter hastily put them down on the table, sensing that there was about to be a heated discussion between his two patrons before again quickly heading back to the safety of the bar. Nigel picked up the glass closest to him and slumped back into the sofa.

"I do my best," he said, again slurring his words.

"That's just it Nigel, you don't do your best. You're always looking for an angle in anything you do. Always looking to see the best way for you to come out looking great in any given circumstance. And if that means using people, then you just do it, no regrets, no conscience."

"Is that what you think?"

"It's what I know Nigel. And the fact that I don't play your stupid fucking games, and tend to distance myself from you, gets up your nose, doesn't it?"

"Yes, it does!" Nigel said in a raised voice. A few of the remaining people in the bar areas looked around and then focused their stares at us. I lifted my hand to them and then gestured that we would keep the noise down. "Every time I have worked on a project with you, or even just been in the same meeting as you, you always try to belittle me, catch me out, put me down in front of my subordinates. Why do you do that George?"

"I do it to let you know that you can't manipulate me in the same way you manipulate everyone else around you. Let's face it Nigel, you're a nasty piece of work. You use fear and intimidation to get what you want and when that doesn't work, you use a 'carrot' approach, whereby you imply people will get promotions if they do what you want them to. And then suddenly, someone else gets the job after they've helped you to get ahead. That's really fucking nasty, Nigel." He looked at me and let out a big sigh.

"I never started out like that," Nigel said staring into his glass of bourbon. "Do you know, I started in the 'tray set up' area as a sixteen year-old kid, in our Dusseldorf kitchen. I loved it. six of us on a belt, putting together thousands of trays each day. We used to sing old 'Beatles' songs as we worked, you know 'Love Me Do', 'Hard Day's Night' and my favourite 'Help!' I had a great supervisor, Thomas. He told me if I were genuinely interested, that he would push for me to work in other departments to gain experience and help me to develop. And he did! By the time I was twenty-five I was the Operations Manager, second in command to the General Manager. That's when it all started to go wrong."

"Well look Nigel, if your wanting to explain yourself and take a trip down memory lane, I really couldn't give a shit! You can't blame others, you have to look at yourself," I replied and stood up to leave.

"Wait! Sit down. Please," said Nigel. I looked at him and slowly returned to my place on the sofa opposite him. At that moment, my phone 'buzzed' in my pocket. I took it out and looked at the text message I had just received. It was from Jana and read; I'm in room 358, ditch Nigel and come up for some fun! I looked up from my phone at Nigel and saw this desperate, dishevelled figure sitting in front of me.

"I'm tired Nigel. But if you've got something to say, carry on," I said and picked up my bourbon, taking a sip.

"The GM in Dusseldorf was Lars Schuller," continued Nigel. "He set me on this path of 'doing what it takes' to succeed. He told me that you must trample on people and take advantage of those around you to get to the top, because if you don't someone else will. And only when you get to the top, can you relax a bit, because people will automatically do everything to impress you once you've made it, you don't need to use them anymore, they instinctively go the extra mile for you."

"That's one way to do it, I suppose. A completely 'shit' way, but nonetheless, a way. I prefer to work with people, encourage them to fulfil their potential, coach and support them, understand their motives, ambition. And reward them for what they do, and not 'what they do that makes me look good', do you understand that?"

"Of course, I do. That's how I climbed the ranks in the Dusseldorf facility. I worked hard, respected peoples' abilities, collaborated, did what was best for the unit. If I 'shone' as a result, it was just a bonus. But I had good people above me, until I was the Operations Manager and Lars became my direct boss. That's when it all changed."

"How did it change?"

"Lars wanted promotion. To get it he needed to have the best functioning facility, most productive, cost efficient and most profitable. Just told me to make it happen and he would look after me. I did it! It was only later that I discovered that he took all the credit for my, and my team's hard work and ideas which made the Dusseldorf facility a shining light, a jewel in the crown of the company. All of which he had no input on at all. Once he was promoted, a new GM was installed, not me! And so, I began to realise, he had just used me for his own gain. That was how this 'world' worked! So, I thought I would do exactly the same."

"So, you're telling me that because of the way Lars treated you, you decided that you would be a complete arsehole to everyone for the rest of your career, or until you at least reached the top! Didn't you think about a different way to approach it?"

"No. That seemed to be the only way to get to the top," Nigel replied and followed this by finishing his bourbon. "Waiter, two more of these," he said loudly, gesticulating to the nearest waiter. I finished mine too.

"I may not be as high ranking as you are Nigel, but I am happy about who I am. And although there is always a separation between work and home life, the personality of a person will generally not differ between them. I am as happy with the person I am in work as I am in my personal life." The drinks arrived and placed once again on the table that separated us.

"You are right George. I am going through a divorce with my wife. I have treated her terribly for many years, not physically you understand, but just been a terrible husband and father, I have two boys you know."

"Sorry, I didn't know."

"Again, I did the same as I did at work. I just used her to get where I needed to be. She was my childhood sweetheart, stood by me when I was nothing, helped me through my studies. She was very bright and intelligent. But she sacrificed herself to support me. You see in Germany you need to present an image. You need to be 'steroty-, streotyp-, stereotypic-."

"You mean stereotypical?" I interjected trying to help.

"Yes George, yes. The man is always career minded, but needs a wife, two children, family dog, holidays in the Alps, two cars, a nice four door saloon and 'VW' bus for the wife to drive the kids about in.

I wasn't interested in my wife's needs, I just needed her to look after the children and keep the house nice, while I concentrated on my career. I stayed out late with my friends, got drunk, fucked other women and I did what whatever I wanted. I know it is not quite like that these days, but back then, that's how it was. And now, she is divorcing me and taking the children. And for the first time ever, I realise just how much I need and want my family," Nigel said, taking a large gulp of his bourbon.

"If you are trying to make me feel sorry for you Nigel - it's working," I said and we both smiled at each other, which was probably the first time that had happened since I had known him. "Do you love your wife and children?"

"Very much. But I think I have blown it now. As I probably have with the company after tonight's performance. I am sure that you will have something to say to Tanja and probably Victor about my behaviour tonight. And even if you don't, I think Aman will write a letter of complaint," Nigel said with a hint of dejection in his voice.

"The question is, do you want to change? Do you want to be the man you started out as? Or do you want to continue being this arrogant, self-righteous, annoying, manipulating, nasty little prick that I have always thought you were? No offence," I said downing my bourbon. "Waiter, two more of these," I called out to the waiter, who duly responded by bringing two more glasses of bourbon to the table. "In fact, just bring the bottle," I said to him and I looked up at Nigel, who nodded his approval.

"I don't think I will get any further with the company, if I manage to avoid any shit from this evening. So, I don't have to be a, how did you put it, 'a nasty little prick' anymore. And by the way, no offence was taken. So, yes! I want my wife back; I want my children back and I want back my self-respect. But change isn't easy, and lots of people will not be forgiving of my previous ways. Tanja, your boss, I've done some terrible things to her to make her look bad. And of course, you

George. I've tried to fuck around with you for a long time, not quite succeeded, but I have always tried."

"Yes, you old fucker, you have," I replied. "But you have to start somewhere. And I would suggest you start tomorrow morning with Aman and Neela. You were a complete dick tonight. Not only did you snub Aman, who by the way is a proud, interesting, courteous man, but you treated his wife like she was some 'good time girl' that you could slobber over all night. You were dreadful, embarrassing and completely out of order."

"Was I really that bad?" said Nigel as he lifted his glass to his lips.

"Fucking terrible. It was like watching an old grandad lust after his grandson's girlfriend. What were you thinking?" and once again we both smiled, more in disbelief about Nigel's behaviour than any comical element attached to his evening's behaviour.

"So, what shall I do?"

"If I were you, I would ask for a few minutes with Aman and Neela before the meeting starts tomorrow. Apologise profoundly and ask for their forgiveness. Blame your behaviour on the medicine you were taking for your illness-"

"What illness?"

"The one that kept you away from today's visit! As you are in such an honest mood Nigel, we'll come back to that one," I said with an air of authority. "Tell him the mixture of the medicine and alcohol caused a reaction and affected your behaviour. I have two catering truck models with me, you know the nice ones, cast iron, about twenty centimetres long to give as gifts for here and Jo'burg, I suggest you give it to Aman. He may refuse it at first, as is the culture here, but offer it to him up to three times. Hopefully, he will accept it and your apology."

"You think he will really want to see me and give me the chance to apologise?"

"To be honest Nigel, I don't know. But you can only try. And if he does, don't blow it by trying to interfere with our presentation afterwards. Leave it to Jana, Heinz and myself."

"Thank you, George," said Nigel and we both finished our drinks, before pouring another round from the bottle.

"Now, about this illness today Nigel, what the fuck was all that about?"

"I wasn't really ill."

"You don't say! We all knew you wasn't. We just weren't sure why you feigned it. Well?"

"Do you remember the little flight attendant on our flight, the brunette, quite busty?"

"Yeah," I said eager to learn the rest of the story, even though it was clear from what Jana witnessed this morning when she left my room, what happened.

"We sort of got together last night and she didn't leave my room until about 6:30 a.m. I pride myself on staying relatively fit, but she wore me out all night. I was so tired, I just needed to sleep for few hours; I was totally fucked - literally!" explained Nigel. I had to smile while shaking my head in some sort of misplaced admiration for this guy. A few drinks and I knew more about Nigel in half an hour than I did in the previous ten years of knowing him!

"Can I be honest with you?" I said.

"You always are George, go ahead."

"I don't blame you for getting it together with the flight attendant. You're separated from your wife, what you do in your own time, is up to you. But, to let it affect your work, and by that, I mean feigning illness today, is a shitty thing to do. As you already know, I didn't want you here on this trip; I didn't think you were needed and definitely could not contribute anything of any worth to the team. But you're here now. And you've made a crap start, lying and insulting Aman, and worst of all, trying to get off with his beautiful young wife! But as

I said, you're here now so from tomorrow, start making a difference. Don't be an arrogant prick, getting in the way and making people feel uncomfortable. Do your job. And do it well, with respect and clarity, support the team and help us, rather than putting on your usual air of superiority that just rubs everyone up the wrong way."

Nigel looked at me with an acceptance that indeed it was time for change. He picked up his glass and lifted it towards me. I reciprocated the gesture with my own glass.

"To new beginnings, George," he said and he clinked his glass against mine before we both downed the remaining contents of our glasses. Nigel then poured another round from the bottle of bourbon. "And by the way George, when I said you could be honest, I didn't think you would be that honest!" he continued, again smiling at me and giggling.

We then spent the next hour talking about his personal life and how things had been so different with his wife in the early part of his career. I also asked him about his name. After all it wasn't a typical German name. He explained to me that his father was English and in the military; stationed in Paderborn. His mother was German, but they decided that although they were living in Germany, that they wanted him to be named after his English grandfather who at the time of his birth, had recently died. Hence Nigel! Obviously, Colnbrooke was his father's surname.

The time went so quickly, as did the bourbon and I completely forgot about Jana. By the time we left the bar, we were very drunk and all I wanted was my bed and a few hours' sleep. My apology to Jana would have to wait until the next day!

23

The noise of my phone alarm was not very welcomed by me and as soon as I opened my eyes, I realised that the paracetamol was urgently needed! My head was thumping and to be honest, I felt like shit. However, over the years I had become accustomed to this feeling the morning before a big presentation. It seemed to happen quite often on attending a company seminar or important customer meeting where I was expected to make a presentation, I would be the last person to leave the bar the night before. However, ever the professional, I knew that a couple of paracetamols, and a fifteen minute shower was all I needed to get 'into gear' and be ready to put on a professional performance!

Although still feeling a little worse for wear, I went down for breakfast to meet up with the others. However, I suddenly thought about last night. Nigel and I had enjoyed a frank and honest discussion. He had 'opened up' to me about his private life, the troubles with his wife and family, and I now had a much better idea of why his business behaviour was, well, the way it was! My hope was that he would have remembered our conversation and would somehow try to make amends for his behaviour with Aman and Neela, and improve his attitude towards myself, Jana, and Heinz. And speaking of Jana, I had completely forgotten about her last night. I wondered what her reaction would be towards me this morning. I guess I wouldn't have long to find out.

As I entered the breakfast room, I saw Heinz, Jana and surprisingly Nigel sitting at a table. Nigel saw me and waved me over. Jana and Heinz looked over to me, Heinz with a smile on his face, Jana not! Could be awkward I thought.

"Morning George, how are you? Sleep well?" said Nigel all very chipper and friendly.

"Morning everyone. Erm, yes. Yes, I slept okay, you?"

"Yes, George. Thanks again for last night, I really appreciated your advice. Now, I'm going to get something to eat," said Nigel and he got up from his chair and headed for the breakfast buffet. Heinz, Jana, and I all followed him with our eyes before Jana and Heinz turned to me.

"What did you two do last night?" said Heinz very slowly and suspiciously.

"What?"

"You heard. What did you and Nigel do last night? Because whatever it was, Nigel seems to be a different, no, a better person than he was only just yesterday! What did you do to Nigel?" again asked Heinz.

"We had a few drinks, well quite a lot of drinks. We argued, we shouted, then we talked. I told him a few things, he told me a few things, I sprinkled some fairy dust over him and voila! A new Nigel!" I said with a smile on my face. All the time Jana was just staring at me.

"Well, I won't get too carried away just yet, but he certainly is a different person. He has apologised to Jana and me this morning for his behaviour last night and has pledged his full support! This is a dream, right? I'm getting something to eat," said Heinz in disbelief and he too got up from his chair and headed for the breakfast buffet. I looked at Jana, who was still staring at me.

"Look, I'm really sorry Jana. Nigel and I just got into things last night and it didn't feel right to just leave him. I know that sounds strange, given that I don't like him, but we somehow ended up at some middle ground last night and I'm hoping that maybe I got through to him about his less than appealing behaviour. I'm really sorry Jana."

"No need to apologise George. We are not joined at the hip. I am glad though, that your no show was due to your enlightening conversation with Nigel, and not because you didn't want to be with me. I trust that's true, right?"

"As you say Jana, we're not joined at the hip. And yes, I had an opportunity to get through to Nigel last night in a way that I might never get again, so wanted to see it through. But I should have texted you, to let you know. Sorry about that."

"You didn't answer the question George."

"What question?" Jana sighed and tilted her head to one side as if to emphasise what she was about to say.

"It wasn't because you just didn't want to be with me?" I paused slightly and let out a little sigh myself.

"We have enjoyed two wonderful nights together prior to last night. To be honest with you, I think I might have needed a night on my own."

"Not eating?" said Nigel as he placed a plate of cheese and cold meats down on the table and sat down.

"Yes, I'm just going to get something now," said Jana and she got up still looking at me, before turning and walking to the buffet.

"George, I've had a word with Jana and Heinz, you know, sort of apologised to them. As drunk as I was last night, I feel revitalised, ready to get stuck in and support you guys wherever I can. Don't worry, I'm not going to interfere with the presentation and meeting today. But remember, I'm here to support you guys with whatever you need. George-, George?"

"Sorry Nigel, I was miles away. Probably all the bourbon last night. Glad to hear you're onboard. Just going to get some food," I replied and headed off after Jana.

"You okay?" I asked as I stood next to Jana at the fresh cut fruit section of the buffet.

"Yes. Why? Shouldn't I be?"

"You seem a bit off with me. Look, I have apologised for not letting you know that I was with Nigel, but you seem to be more concerned about if I just didn't want to be with you last night."

"Well?" asked Jana.

"Well, what?"

"Did you not want to be with me last night?"

"I suppose not. I'm not sure what you want Jana. You were the one that said we are adults and not joined at the hip and well, just having fun. Why is it such a big deal for you if I decided to stay and talk to Nigel last night?"

"It's not George. And don't worry, I'm being stupid," Jana said apologetically. "Sorry George. And anyway, whatever you talked about with Nigel last night seems to have had a dramatic effect on him. He was actually nice to Heinz and me this morning! Forgive me George?"

"Nothing to apologise for. I hope we are cool?"

"Yes, we're cool. Now I need some food," she said and proceeded to add some fresh melon to the strawberries, kiwi and guava fruit that was already on her plate. "Are you having 'healthy' this morning as well George?"

"Not bloody likely! I need some sausage and bacon to settle my stomach after last night," I said and headed off to the hot food section.

When I returned to the table, Heinz, Jana, and Nigel were already busy tucking into their breakfasts. Nigel was praising the work that we had done the previous day (even though he had no idea what we had done!) and kept reassuring us of his support and the fact that things would be vastly different from now on. A positive step I thought, but only time would tell if this was to be the case. After finishing breakfast, we made our way back to our rooms to collect our things and gathered back down in the lobby to check-out. As we entered the lobby, I saw Kofi sitting in the foyer.

"Good morning Kofi," I called out. "Just checking-out and we will be right with you."

"Take your time George, I'm a little early. I just wanted to make sure I was here on time for you."

"Thanks Kofi, won't be long." We all checked-out and made our way over to Kofi, and after the greetings and handshakes, Kofi led us outside to our waiting vehicle and driver. Jana, Heinz, and I got in, but Nigel hung back and caught Kofi's attention.

"Look Kofi, I don't quite know what came over me last night. You must think I am some sort of complete idiot and worse still, and arrogant, unpleasant, and despicable man. I would like to apologise to you and your lovely wife Desta for my poor behaviour and hope you can forgive me and we can start again. I of course will apologise in person to Desta when I see her."

"Mr. Colnbrooke-"

"No, please call me Nigel."

"Nigel, thank you for your apology. It means a lot to me as I am sure it will mean a lot to Desta. But you really need to talk to Aman."

"Yes, I fully intend to. But as you were here, I wanted to personally apologise to you too!" replied Nigel and I saw him extend his hand, more in friendship than in a formal sense. Kofi responded and smiled at him and then Nigel got into the vehicle.

"Good start Nigel," I whispered to him as he sat down and put his seat belt on.

The journey went smoothly and although there was not much talking during the short journey, everyone felt confident about the upcoming meeting. Even Nigel, looked more confident after his discussion with Kofi went so well.

"Do you have that model of our truck?" Nigel asked me.

"Yes. It's in my bag. I'll give it to you when we get there, okay?"

"Thanks George. I really appreciate your help."

"No worries Nigel. I hope it goes well. Good luck," I said, feeling a small sense of pride in Nigel's newfound conduct. Although I had to remind myself not to get carried away. After all, it had only been a few hours!

We arrived at the catering facility and as per the previous day, Kofi led us into the building where we met Desta, who had once again had prepared our visitor passes. Without hesitation, Nigel walked straight over to her, while Kofi instructed us to hang back. Although I couldn't hear exactly what Nigel was saying, he appeared to be very profound in his apology to Desta and by the time he had finished talking, Desta was smiling and shaking his hand. A particularly good sign I thought, and I looked at Kofi, who gave a nod of approval about Nigel's effort to make amends for last night.

"Of course, the bigger challenge will be with Aman and Neela," Kofi whispered to me as we approached Desta for our passes.

"Good morning Desta. How are you today?" I said.

"Very well George. And even better now," she replied and smiled at Nigel.

"Glad to hear it. Thank you again for all your help and support during our visit." Heinz and Jana briefly chatted with Desta while picking up their passes and Nigel, Kofi and myself stood together.

"Kofi, do you think you could ask Aman if I could have a few minutes of his time before the meeting starts?" asked Nigel.

"I think that might be a very good idea. I will take you all up to the boardroom, and then Nigel, you can come with me to Aman's office. I don't know if he will see you, but I will try," replied Kofi.

"Thank you, Kofi," Nigel answered. Kofi escorted us up the stairs and into the boardroom and explained to Jana how the boardroom IT equipment worked so that we could present on the large screen. He then beckoned Nigel to follow him, and they both started to leave the room.

"Don't forget this Nigel," I said and handed him the catering truck model that I had retrieved from my bag.

"Thanks George, wish me luck eh!" he replied and I acknowledged him with a nod of my head. Jana approached and stood beside me watching Kofi and Nigel disappear out of the room.

"What's all that about?" she said.

"I told Nigel last night, that if he wanted to change the way he was, he needed to start right away. And start by apologising for his behaviour towards his hosts. He already started this morning with Kofi and Desta, now comes the big test. Aman was really upset with him last night, so I'm not sure if Nigel's apology will be accepted."

"And what about us?"

"Look Jana, I thought we already had this conversation this morning about us," I said quietly so Heinz couldn't hear me.

"No, not 'us', I mean you, Heinz, and me. I know he was quite nice to us this morning, but he hasn't apologised to us has he."

"Oh! Yes, sorry Jana, I see what you mean. He told me he had apologised to you and Heinz this morning at breakfast, is that not true?"

"He apologised for his behaviour last night, but not for being a complete twat for the rest of the time." And right there, that 'twat' saying was being used again about Nigel!

"Well, let's just take one step at a time. This is all very new for Nigel also."

"So, what's the plan George?" asked Heinz. "As we discussed, you do the presentation of the company, and then straight into your operation findings. Then Jana and I will do the financial segment," Heinz continued.

"Sounds good to me. Jana, you have my presentation on your PC, right?" I asked.

"Yes George. It will be ready to go when you start."

"Thanks Jana." We continued to chat amongst ourselves for a few minutes, before the door or the boardroom opened and in stepped Aman and Nigel, laughing and in deep conversation with each other.

"And that is how Price Charles got his nickname of 'the loony prince', but you didn't hear that from me!" said Aman laughing loudly with Nigel. "Good morning Jana, Heinz and George. I hope you slept well. I was just telling Nigel that I have some herbal remedies to help you sleep at night if you would like to try some?" We all looked at Nigel.

"Yes, I was telling Aman that I couldn't sleep very well last night, obviously because of my awful behaviour, but also because of the mix of medicine and unfortunately, alcohol that I had consumed. Aman kindly offered me his wisdom and advice on how to prevent insomnia, for which I am incredibly grateful," came Nigel's response.

"Good morning Aman. Thank you, but I slept very well as always. But I will keep your offer in mind. I trust everything is okay?" I said shaking Aman's hand.

"Very good George. Nigel has explained a few things, apologised to both Neela and I, and we are in a good position to move on. And thanks for your help with Nigel, he also told me how supportive you have been to him. You are an honourable man George. By the way, the offer of the herbal remedy is here when you need it," Aman said and gave me a wink. I think Nigel must have told him how much alcohol we had consumed last night!

"Now, I would like to present to you the Executive Board of Ethiopian Airlines," continued Aman and he proceeded to introduce us to the three people standing behind him. First was the Chief

Finance Officer who Jana and Heinz had met the previous day, called Yelekal. Next was a woman called Afia, who was the Chief Human Resource Officer and lastly was another man called Semere whose position was Chief Operations Officer. After the introductions and hand shaking, Aman invited us to have some tea or coffee and again there were trays of sweet pastries from the in-house pastry department. Having witnessed the pastry chef the day before, I knew that they were going to be good and hygienically prepared.

Following some small talk, Aman invited us to sit down at the boardroom table for the meeting to begin. We had previously distributed an agenda, therefore I stood up and walked to the head of the table where the large presentation screen was located, ready to open the meeting by giving my presentation about our company. However, before I could say anything, Nigel stood up and walked over to me.

"Before George starts the meeting by giving you all an overview of our company, I would just like to say a few words if I may," said Nigel. I took a step back to give Nigel the floor. "Although unfortunately, I could not participate yesterday due to a sudden illness, I wanted to thank you Aman, and of course, all your team for the hospitality and assistance afforded to Jana, Heinz and George. It has been greatly appreciated and enabled the team to do a thorough appraisal of the opportunity that presents itself here in Addis Ababa for our two companies to work together. I might not have got off to the best of starts," continued Nigel, looking directly at Aman, "but please be assured that I take this opportunity very seriously and would be honoured to support a decision to move forward with this project, should that be the case. As we all know, the team are only here today to present our findings and to answer any questions you may have, about the potential to move forward together. Therefore, although no decisions can be made today, I feel it is especially important for any future collaboration between our two companies, that honesty prevails and whatever is discussed today is not meant to be taken personally, but reverently and as a factual basis to which future decisions can be built on. Now, I will hand you over to George," said Nigel as he looked at me and smiled, before returning to his chair.

"Sorry, George to interrupt," said Aman, "but I too, would like to echo Nigel's remarks and comments. Thank you, Nigel. We have been pleased to welcome you here over the last two days and we also look forward to pursuing this opportunity further. The word 'honesty' that Nigel used is also extremely important to us. Therefore, we do not expect you to be saying nice things about our facility, if indeed, you have witnessed things that need improvement. We want to attract new international airlines to this city and recognise the need to update our systems, procedures, and practices to meet the demands of these potential customers. So please, present your appraisal and do not hold back on anything that needs to be addressed. Now George, please continue."

"Thank you, Aman, and thank you Nigel," I said before giving Jana the nod to display the first slide of my presentation.

The presentation lasted about thirty minutes and I found myself thinking what a fantastic job Sarah had done on it and to make sure I let her know when I got back to my office. Following some questions, we decided to have a short 'comfort' break, for people to refill their coffee cups and use the bathroom. During the break, Nigel came over to talk to me.

"Sorry George, I didn't mean to interrupt you first thing, but I wanted to say something, before letting you guys get on with things. I hope that was okay?"

"No worries Nigel. You did a good job. And thanks for not interrupting during the presentation. I take it things went well with Aman and Neela this morning, right?"

"Yes. Even better than I could have ever imagined really. You were right George. Aman is a fantastic man; he is gracious, respectful, highly intelligent and I love his stories. The one about Prince Charles is hilarious! As for Neela, well she is incredibly beautiful. And very forgiving of my behaviour towards her last night. A lovely woman. By the way, great job with the presentation. I think even I learned a few things about the company that I didn't know before!" said Nigel with a smile on his face.

"Well, I'm glad things worked out well. And you seem a bit happier too. I like this new Nigel, let's hope he is here to stay."

"I like this new Nigel too and he's here to stay! Only it's not the new Nigel, it's the old Nigel that's come back. Thanks again George," Nigel replied.

When we reconvened, I presented my findings about the facility. I went over in some detail, the areas of concern relating to hygiene and sanitation, portion control in production and the security issues, particularly the ease of access to the apron of the airport from the facility. I also presented a list of new equipment requirements, some of which they were already aware of (Kofi had previously pointed out that two new dishwasher machines were required to replace the current ageing one) including new 'walk in' fridges and freezers (the current ones were not maintaining the correct temperatures), new oven range in the hot kitchen, including a combi oven, 'bratt' pans and a new six ring burner (the current one had half of its burners inoperable, and the ovens appeared incapable of maintaining temperature), and a new blast chiller.

I also discussed new working practices that would incorporate 'lean' manufacturing techniques to improve productivity and reduce cycle time, all of which Aman and Kofi found most fascinating. I ended on a positive, by commending the pastry chef (Salana) on his wonderful pastries and his knowledge and organisation of hygiene in that department, which pleased Kofi. I also thanked Kofi for his help and the time he spent with me yesterday. Additionally, I praised him for his knowledge of the facility. Although the Ethiopian Airlines board might have already known how good Kofi was at his job, I felt it wouldn't do any harm to reiterate it! Another thing that pleased Kofi tremendously was the fact that I had not included any mention of Alfred and Edna 'doing it doggy style' in the middle of the airline stores area!

After finishing my presentation and answering the questions posed by Aman and his team, Heinz stepped up to present his financial appraisal of the business, ably assisted by Jana. It was clear from the numbers, that with the increased sales from new customers, and our expertise with new procedures to drive productivity and efficiency, there was a great opportunity to create a very profitable business here in Addis Ababa. It was an opportunity that was not lost on Aman. He could see it too!

As the meeting concluded and everyone was busily engaging in small talk, Aman pulled me to one side and asked me to follow him to his office. As we entered, he closed the door behind him. I immediately noticed the model truck that Nigel had given to Aman earlier, proudly displayed on his large desk.

"George, my friend. I wanted to personally thank you for your time and that of the entire team over the last two days. From what has been presented today, I see a wonderful opportunity for our companies to work together, in partnership and friendship. I have a lot to discuss with my fellow board members and we will await something from you on how to proceed after you have met with your board. But please try to impress upon your organisation, that we are extremely positive about entering into a partnership with you."

"Thank you, Aman. Off the record, I also believe there is massive potential here to develop something extremely special. But at the end of the day, I will not be deciding what happens. I will, of course, be able to influence and will be presenting the facts accordingly."

"Thank you, George," Aman said, smiling and shaking my hand, before turning and reaching for a box that was lying on his desk. "This is for you George," and he handed me the box.

"Aman, thank you so much, but there is no need for gifts. Your hospitality and kindness, support and well, forgiveness regarding Nigel, is what matters most," I replied.

"Please George, this is a token of my personal appreciation. Whatever happens, I have been greatly impressed by your leadership of the team, your veneration of our facility and my people, and your desire to help your colleagues, even when they might be beyond help!" said Aman, referring to Nigel. "However, you persevered and brought him back to the 'good side' which has impressed me more than you know. So please take this gift as a personal thanks from me."

"Thank you," I said as I received the box from Aman. "should I open it now, or?" I quizzically asked Aman.

"Yes, please open it," replied Aman. I opened the box to reveal a beautiful tribal wood carving of a man, with a pipe and walking stick, about thirty centimetres tall. "This is from my personal collection of wood carvings George, made from 'teak', probably around the 1950's. And I would like you to have this one."

"Aman, this is wonderful and I am profoundly grateful for your generosity. But I can't accept this. It would be wrong of me to accept this and in some way give you the impression that it would cement some sort of agreement between our two companies.

"George, I understand how you feel. However, I do not see this as an insurance policy, taken out to ensure an agreement is reached. I offer you this as a gesture of my friendship, regardless of the business outcome. You will always be very welcome here in Addis Ababa by me, whether it is as a business associate, or as my very good friend,"

"Thank you, Aman, it's truly wonderful and I am very happy that you consider me a friend, as in turn, I consider you also," I replied and shook Aman's hand.

"Now, let me get your transport organised to get you back to the airport. You have a flight to catch, Johannesburg I believe. Be careful there George, it can be a dangerous city!"

"I know. I have been before so will be careful."

"Oh, by the way, I know you are travelling on our airline to Jo'burg, so I have secured you all upgrades to First Class."

"Thank you again Aman, very generous of you, and much appreciated," I replied.

We left Aman's office and re-joined everyone in the boardroom, before saying our goodbyes to Aman and his board. Kofi escorted us down the stairs, stopping at Desta's office to hand in our visitor passes and say our goodbyes to her. As we exited the building, our transport and driver was waiting for us and as Nigel, Jana and Heinz entered the vehicle, Kofi pulled me to one side.

"I wanted to thank you George, for not mentioning, you know, about Alfred and Edna. I really appreciate it."

"No problem Kofi. But you do realise that they can't carry on doing, well, doing what they do. If you want to attract new customers, things will have to change and as sad as it might be for Alfred and Edna, they'll just have to find somewhere else to fuck each other's brains out!" Kofi smiled.

"I will talk to them again and make it truly clear George, don't worry. Thank you again."

"No. Thank you Kofi, and Desta, Neela, definitely Aman and everyone else here. You have made us feel so welcomed and given us so much support. You have a great team here and I think there is a fantastic opportunity for both our companies. Let's keep our fingers crossed. Take care Kofi and hopefully I will see you soon."

"Take care George," replied Kofi and we shook hands. I then climbed into the van and Kofi, slid the door shut, and we off to the airport ready for the next phase.

"What was all that about Alfred and Edna?" asked Nigel as the van pulled away.

"Just some Ethiopian folklore about a young couple in love, who let nothing stand in their way," I replied and once again the toothless smile of Alfred came to my mind as he took his beautiful Edna from behind!

24

We arrived at the airport and after thanking the driver, we passed through security (this was just to enter the airport!) before I led the team to the Ethiopian Airlines check-in desk.

"We don't need to go to the check-in desk, George, we are already checked-in," said Jana.

"I know, but Aman has arranged First Class upgrades for us, and told me to get our tickets changed at the First-Class check-in desk."

"Great!" said Nigel. "That's really nice of him."

After collecting new tickets, we made our way through security and passport control to the 'Cloud Nine' lounge, that Aman had also arranged for us to gain entry in to. It was a nice lounge, comfortable and served an array of hot and cold snacks, beverages and had wifi availability. Although the snacks looked appetising enough, I wasn't too sure of the hygiene practices in Addis Ababa, based on my experience in the catering facility and therefore, just stuck to a can of coke. I warned the others about my concerns and they heeded my advice.

It was approaching 1:30 p.m. so we only had a forty-five minute wait for our flight. The duration was five and a half and with Jo'burg being the same time as Frankfurt, it meant that all being well and no delays, we would arrive at approximately 6:45 p.m. local time. We were booked into the 'Emperors Palace Hotel' which was not far from the airport and had a shuttle bus service. I had stayed there on my previous visit to Johannesburg and it was a nice, high class hotel. It was also a casino complex, shopping mall and had a multitude of restaurants. It would be great timing, because I would be able to call the girls when we arrived as they would not yet have gone to bed. I was looking forward to talking to them, and somehow, really looking forward to talking with Martyna as well. At that moment, my cell phone 'buzzed' and I took it out from my inside pocket. It was a text message from Fiona!

"Hi George. Hope you are having a great time? Missing you a bit (lots actually) but Mum here to keep me company (or drive me mad! LoL). Call me if you can, or want to? Always happy to hear from you. Take care x." It was a lovely message to receive from Fiona and made me think again about what I was doing with Jana. Fiona was a terrific person, as was Martyna and Jana too, in her own way. I was eighteen months down the road from losing the love of my life, and here I was having deep feelings for two wonderful women, one of whom I had slept with, and having great sex with a third!

"Everything okay George?" asked Jana.

"What?"

"Everything okay? You look deep in thought?"

"Yes, sorry Jana, miles away."

"It's time to board, we need to go," she continued. We all got up and took a short walk to the gate, and of course being in First Class, we did not have to wait too long to board the aircraft. We were all seated in Row 2. Heinz and I in 2A and 2B respectively, and across the aisle, Nigel, and Jana in 2C and 2D, Jana being by the window. We settled into our seats and prepared for take-off.

"Heinz, I hope you don't mind, but I'm going to try to get some sleep on this flight. Sorry for being boring, but I'm dead tired," I said.

"No problem George. I will catch up on some work and then try to get some sleep too. You probably need it after last night and whatever you did with Nigel. But whatever it was you said to him, I'm extremely glad. It seems to have had a positive effect."

"Thanks Heinz," I replied and made myself comfortable. As the flight departed and headed for South Africa, I reclined my seat and in no time, I was asleep.

I awoke startled and opened my eyes. Heinz was looking at me.

"You must have heard the announcement that we will be landing soon. I was just about to give you a nudge, but you awoke anyway," said Heinz.

"Are we nearly there already then?" I asked.

"Yes. You've slept the whole flight. You must have been tired. I hope you can sleep tonight."

"So do I," I whispered under my breath, thinking that Jana might want to continue our exhaustive sex sessions. I put the seat into the upright position and, straightened myself out and then looked across at Jana and Nigel. Although I couldn't hear what they were saying, they were deep in conversation and huddled together.

"They've been like that the whole flight. Plenty of flirting going on from both of them," said Heinz quietly.

"Really. Maybe Nigel hasn't changed as much as we thought."

"Neither has Jana," replied Heinz.

"Jana! What do you mean Heinz?"

"Don't get me wrong. I like Jana and she is good at what she does. But I have known her for a while now and she knows how to flirt with the right people to advance herself and her career; flash her legs, wear low cut tops, that sort of thing. Whether or not she takes it any further than flirting, I don't know. But I would be wary of her if I were you George. I've seen the way she's been looking at you on this trip. I'm surprised you haven't noticed." I turned my attention from Jana and Nigel and looked back at Heinz.

"Can't say I have noticed," I said in a big effort to avoid the truth about what Jana and I have already been up to on this trip. I hoped I got away with it!

"Well, just be careful," Heinz replied and returned to reading his newspaper. I again looked across at Jana and Nigel and this time, Jana caught my gaze, smiled, and then returned to talking with Nigel before laughing quite loudly. Once again, she looked back at me. It appeared to be a deliberate attempt to make me jealous. The thing was, right at that second, I did feel a tinge of jealousy. I smiled back at her before bending forward to find my shoes in readiness for landing and the slight touch of jealousy faded instantly.

The landing was smooth and it wasn't long before we were inside the terminal building and making our way through passport control. Again, one of the perks of flying in First Class is being able to exit the aircraft before the other classes get to disembark and try to beat the queues in the arrival hall! Although that didn't quite happen as the airport was terribly busy, we still managed to get through quite quickly and made our way to the hotel shuttle bus stands. I took out my phone and looked at the time. It was a little past 7:20 p.m. local time, which meant 6:20 p.m. in London. I would have plenty of time to call the girls when we got to the hotel. I then started to type a text message.

"Texting home George? Checking in?" said Jana sarcastically.

"Actually I'm just sending Aman a quick text to thank him for the upgrades and again to thank him for his hospitality over the last two days," I replied very calmly.

"Oh," came a somewhat embarrassed response from Jana.

"But if you must know, yes, I will be texting my girls and letting them know that I will call them when I get to the hotel. I miss them a lot and can't wait to speak to them," I continued.

"Good idea George," added Nigel, "I think I will also send Aman a quick text too; you know to thank him for his understanding and all that." I nodded my head in approval at Nigel.

"Okay, I think we need to get on board that bus over there," said Heinz pointing to an American style hotel shuttle bus, with 'Emperor's Palace' emblazoned down the side, and we all made our way over to it. As we walked over, I hung back a little so that I could talk to Jana.

"Are you okay Jana?" I asked.

"Yes. Why shouldn't I be?"

"Well, you're acting kind of strange. I'm not sure what is going on, but I hope everything is alright?"

"I can spend time with Nigel just as much as you can. Don't get jealous about it," Jana replied and quickened her pace to catch up with the others. I stopped in my tracks and was a tad confused about Jana's response. I continued over to the bus. It was quite full and Jana had sat next to Heinz.

"George, over here," called out Nigel, "I've saved you a seat." I waved in acknowledgement to Nigel and made my way over to him and sat down. We were about three rows behind Jana and Heinz. The doors closed and the driver started the engine before pulling away.

"Thanks for saving me a seat Nigel," I said.

"No worries George. I texted Aman and got an instant reply. You know, I feel so much better. Better about this trip, you guys and most importantly, better about myself. Do you know, young Jana there," he continued pointing at Jana, "was flirting with me the entire flight."

"Really," I said pretending to be surprised.

"Yes. And do you know, as pretty and attractive as she is, I just wasn't interested."

"Not interested, you?" I said somewhat startled.

"A leopard doesn't change his spots overnight and I admit, I was rather flattered by it, but whereas I would have followed this sort of thing up in the past, I'm just not interested now. And do you know why George?"

"Haven't got a clue," I replied.

"Because I love my wife and when we get back, I'm going to do all I can to stop this stupid bloody divorce and show her how much I care for her and the children. That's why!"

"Good for you Nigel, good for you."

"And in no small way, is my change of outlook down to you. I have wasted so much time fucking people over and being a total dickhead-"

"And fucking other women," I interrupted. Nigel looked at me slightly annoyed. "Sorry Nigel," I added. He smiled.

"Yes, and fucking other women," he conceded, "but now I know what I want and the person I need to be to get it. And the thing is, it's not an 'act', it's the person I used to be. And you've made me realise that George. You! Thank you."

"Glad to be of service," I replied and smiled at him.

The journey took a little over five minutes before the bus pulled up outside the impressive Emperor's Palace Hotel, with its proud ornamental fountains in full flow. Although the bus was quite full, there were a lot of check-in desks available in the decadently, lavish arrivals area, so it wasn't long before we had all been given our room cards. Heinz and I were the last to receive our door cards and we had both watched Jana and Nigel walk to the elevators arm in arm as they went to their rooms.

"Nigel's going to have some fun tonight," said Heinz.

"I don't think so. He's changed," I said. "He wants to make a go of things with his wife and family and he wants to do right by the company."

"What the fuck did you do with Nigel last night?" said a stunned Heinz. I must admit, I was stunned too! I had never heard Heinz use the 'fuck' word in all the years I had worked with him. I shook my head and smiled.

"Nothing, mothing at all," I said.

I got to my room and dumped my bags on the bed. It was a fantastic room, well equipped, large double bed and very tastefully decorated. I slipped my shoes off, took off my jacket and sat down on the bed. I pulled my phone out and was about to make a call home, when I suddenly realised, I had not responded to Fiona's text message. I opened my text messages and immediately saw a new one from Aman, in response to the one I had sent him earlier. Then I re-read Fiona's message-

"Hi George. Hope you are having a great time? Missing you a bit (lots actually) but Mum here to keep me company (or drive me mad! LoL). Call me if you can, or want to? Always happy to hear from you. Take care x."

I began typing and before long I had clicked the send button. I paused for a second and reflected on my feelings for Fiona. She was beautiful, intelligent, with long blonde hair, and those large reading glasses that gave her the look of a shy librarian. And she was interested in me, cared for me, wanted to form a relationship with me. Why was I so reluctant to commit anything to this wonderful girl? I thought to myself that when this trip is over, I need to do some serious thinking about my life, my future, the girls, and who I would like to be a part of it all. For now, though, I needed to call the girls.

"Hi Martyna, how are you?"

"Hi George. We are all fine. I'll get the girls for you, hold on a minute," came Martyna's cheerful reply. A few seconds passed.

"Hello Dad, where are you?" said an excited Emily.

"Hi Emster, I'm in a hotel in Johannesburg. Do you remember which country that is in?"

"Of course, Dad, it's South Africa."

"That's right. So, how are you sweetheart?"

"I'm fine. School has been good and Martyna has let us do some baking with her this afternoon."

"That's great, what did you bake?"

"It was sourdough rye bread, I think."

"It sounds delicious. Have you tried some already?"

"Yes. We had some when it was still warm. We will save you some for when you get home."

"Thanks Emily. I'm really looking forward to coming home and now, I also have your bread to look forward to."

"I can't wait to see you Dad. But not long now, so I guess I can wait a few more days," said a very grown-up Emily. "Do you want to talk to Amy?"

"Yes, but only if we have finished."

"Well, I have to brush my teeth and get ready for bed, so I will hand you over to Amy. Bye Dad, love you lots!" With that the line fell silent for a few seconds and I briefly reflected on how grown-up Emily seemed. And of course, how happy she was in Martyna's company. The 'love you lots' comment made me smile.

"Hello Daddy," said Amy.

"Hello sweetie. How are you?"

"I'm okay," she said seemingly a little sad.

"Are you sure, you sound a little down. Is there anything wrong?" I pressed.

"Well, I'm missing you a lot. When are you coming home?"

"It's Wednesday evening, so I have two more days here, before flying home overnight and arriving Saturday morning. Don't worry sweetheart, it will go quickly and before you know it, I'll be with you and Emily and we can have a big group hug."

"That would be good. I've been missing Mummy too," Amy replied. This brought a lump to my throat. Not too many times over the last year and a half, had either Emily or Amy said that they were missing their mum. And now, me being away from them must have triggered something in Amy. Maybe she felt like I had abandoned her now.

"That's okay Amy. We all miss Mummy sometimes and I'm definitely missing you and Emily. But I will be home soon sweetheart and maybe on Sunday, we can go and visit Mummy, take her some flowers, and talk to her. You can tell her all about the bread you've made with Martyna."

"That would be nice. I would like that daddy," replied a happier Amy. "The bread tasted really nice, I think you will like it," she continued.

"I'm sure I will. How has school been?"

"Ok, I suppose. Miss Raven got a bit cross with me today because I spilt some water on the floor and Charlotte Smith slipped on it and fell over and hurt her knee. It was an accident Daddy, honestly!"

"I know it was sweetheart. And I'm sure Miss Raven does too. Try not to worry about it too much. You're a good girl and Miss Raven knows that. Everything will be fine tomorrow, you wait and see," I said, trying my best to comfort Amy.

"Ok. Do you want to talk to Martyna? We have to go to bed soon and Martyna has promised to read us Frozen Two!" Amy said excitedly and much more like her normal cheerful self.

"Ok sweetheart. I love you so much, and Emily too. Have a lovely story with Martyna, and I will see you soon." I blew two kisses down the phone, one each for Amy and Emily. Amy responded by doing the same.

"Hi again George," said Martyna. "So, how are you? The trip going well?"

"Hey Martyna. I'm good thanks and the trip has been good so far, thanks for asking. Amy seemed a little upset, missing her mum a bit-"

"I know George. But don't worry. I could see she was a little upset as I picked them up from school. Amy said that her teacher was cross with her for spilling some water or something like that. I didn't want to make a big thing about it at the time, but I will have a word with

Miss Raven tomorrow morning, once I've dropped the girls off, just to see what happened."

"Thanks, Martyna. I know Miss Raven quite well and I'm sure she didn't mean to be cross with Amy. Maybe Amy got the wrong idea, and well, she said she misses her mum and maybe that had something to do with it as well."

"Yes, I think you are right. I've tried to take her mind off her mum, but I have also encouraged her to talk about her with me, if she wants to. I hope that's okay George, I don't want to step on your toes."

"No, that's fine Martyna. Thank you for that. I don't want Amy or Emily ever feeling that they cannot talk about Cheryl to me and if you're happy to let them talk to you about her as well, then that's great."

"No need to thank me George. The girls mean so much to me and I'll do whatever I can for them."

"Thank you Martyna and how are you?"

"I'm very good! We made bread today, as I'm sure the girls told you. A secret Polish recipe for sourdough and rye bread, I hope you like it."

"I'm sure I will. What's so secret about it?"

"I'm afraid I can't tell you that, otherwise I will have to kill you!" replied Martyna with a slight giggle.

"Okay, I get the picture."

"And tomorrow, we are going to London Zoo after I pick them up from school. They said they really like going there and can't wait to see the monkeys!" I smiled to myself, thinking back to the time when I took the girls to the zoo, to let them know about Martyna.

"That sounds awesome. I wish I were coming too!"

"Next time George, next time," Martyna replied.

"But what I really meant, was how are you?"

"I'm good George. Miss having you around. The house, even with the lovely noise of the girls, seems a little empty without you. By the way, I have another date on Saturday night. I hope that's okay with you. It was a last-minute thing arranged by one of my girlfriends, you know, another blind date. Let's hope it's better than the last one."

"Yes, let's hope," I said slowly, feeling a little crushed inside.

"So, will it be okay then for the time off, the date on Saturday?"

"Yes, no problem, no problem," I repeated. "Well, I suppose I had better let you get to your reading of Frozen Two, you can't keep the girls waiting. Thanks again for all your help Martyna and for looking after the girls. Take care."

"You too George, bye," and Martyna hung up. I put my phone down on the bed. I should have been thinking about Amy and how I can best comfort her, support her and let her know that everything will be okay. Instead, I just felt forlorn, empty, and lonely. Lonely at the thought of Martyna finding love on her blind date. Lonely at the thought of Martyna moving on with her life, a life that might not include me and more importantly at this moment in time, a life that might not include Emily and Amy. At that moment, my phone rang.

"Hi George," said Tanja.

"Hey Tanja, how are you?" I answered.

"I'm fine George, but more importantly, how are you doing?"

"Yeah, I'm good. I just talked with the girls and they are doing well. I think Amy is missing me a bit, but I'll be home soon and I'm sure she will be okay."

"That's good to hear. That reminds me, I must look in my diary and book this London weekend so I can take the girls shopping. I'll let you know something next week."

"No worries, they will be pleased to see you as always."

"How did it go today with the Ethiopian Board meeting? And more to the point, how was Nigel?"

"It went very well. I think we have a great opportunity to partner with them and to get a foothold in the region. They are great people, willing to learn and I think we have built a good level of trust with them over the last two days," I replied.

"That's good news George. Victor will be pleased to hear that. Do you have something in mind, in terms of a proposal yet?"

"Yes. Based on the work that Heinz and Jana carried out with the numbers, and from what I saw operationally regarding the requirements to bring the facility to a standard that would be acceptable for international airlines, I have an idea of the sort of offer that we could make."

"Sounds great George. Now, how was Nigel?"

"Nigel was particularly good. I know that sounds extremely strange coming from me, but I have to give him credit."

"Are you shitting me or what George?" came the startled reply from Tanja. I smiled to myself. Over the years of knowing Tanja, I had become accustomed to her ways, her mannerisms and could almost predict with one hundred per cent accuracy how she would react in any given circumstance. And although, she could swear and use profanities as good as any of us, it always made me smile when I heard her use expressions that would not normally be associated with someone of her grace and elegance.

"No, I'm not 'shitting' you. To be honest Tanja, it's a long story. And Nigel did not get off the greatest of starts, as I told you yesterday with the 'faked illness' thing. It even got worse than that last night at dinner with the Ethiopian Airlines CEO and his wife. But things change, people change, and I think Nigel is someone who can actually help us achieve something on this trip." There was a short silence.

"Are you on medication George?" said Tanja. I laughed.

"No Tanja, I'm not on medication. Look, I'll tell you all about it when I get back. But for now, all you need to know is we are okay and Nigel is doing okay as well."

"Well, as you know, I trust you implicitly George. And if you say things are good, then I believe you. But I can't wait to hear what you have to say about that fucking idiot Nigel - just can't wait!" Once again, I laughed and I could sense a slight giggle in Tanja's voice too.

"I'll call you tomorrow Tanja and give you an update on Jo'burg, okay?"

"Okay George, take care and talk to you tomorrow," said Tanja and she hung up. Although Tanja was my boss, and Godparent to Emily and Amy, our relationship was more like that of a brother and older sister. And I was extremely grateful for it.

I took a quick shower, put on some casual clothes, and made my way down to the reception area where we had arranged to meet. To be honest, I had forgotten how big this complex was. There were so many gaming areas, large conference facilities, a theatre and cinema complex and a whole 'indoor' street of shops and restaurants. It was truly exceptional.

As I approached the reception area, I saw Nigel and Heinz talking and made my way over to them.

"Hi Nigel, Heinz," I said as I approached them.

"Hi George," replied Nigel. "This is a great place George. You have been here before, right?"

"Yes, I have stayed here once before. It's extremely nice with lots of things to keep you occupied - gambling, shopping, marvellous restaurants. Far too much to experience for just a short two-night stay."

"Do you have anywhere in mind to eat?" asked Heinz.

"Well, there are restaurants of all styles here; Italian, Chinese, Indian, whatever you want really. But I know a nice place called 'Tribes' which is fairly traditional but does cater for local African dishes as well. However, it is entirely up to you guys, I'm happy to eat anything," I replied. "No Jana?" I asked, looking at Nigel.

"No. Actually, she is bothering me a little bit. Not sure what she's up to really. But she has been flirting with me quite a lot. As you know, I'm no stranger to the 'flirting game' so I know when someone's interested. Do you know anything George?"

"No Nigel, not at all. But be careful," I said with a smile on my face and I turned and winked at Heinz.

"Don't worry George, Jana is not in my plans. However, I might have to have a quiet word with her later, put her straight about a few things."

"Here she comes now," said Heinz, looking in the direction of the elevators. We all looked around to see Jana walking towards us wearing heels, a tiny, short lilac skirt and a sleeveless beige lowcut blouse. She looked terrific!

"Good evening gentlemen," she said as she approached us.

"Hi Jana," we all responded in unison.

"So, what's the plan," Jana continued, "I'm quite hungry, has anyone any ideas about dinner?"

"George was just saying that there is a wonderful array of restaurants here, all extremely good. We just need to decide what we want. However, he recommends a place called 'Tribes' if we want more traditional but with some local African dishes. Any thoughts?" replied Heinz.

"That sounds good. Lead on George," said Jana looking at me and giving me a wink.

"Right, this way," I replied and we headed off in the direction of the restaurant. We walked through the complex, passing the gaming areas and through some of the shopping sections. Nigel, it seemed had deliberately ignored Jana and latched onto Heinz as we walked, leaving Jana and I together, walking a few metres behind them in silence. Jana finally broke that silence.

"You look nice George, smell nice too," she said.

"Thanks. You look terrific, smell terrific too!" I replied.

"It's a shame you won't be seeing what I've got on under this outfit later. Maybe Nigel will though."

"Okay," I nonchalantly replied. However, the thought had crossed my mind that Jana was in fact wearing nothing under her outer garments!

"Yes, Nigel is in the night of his life tonight," Jana continued.

"Good," I again replied unbothered by anything Jana was saying.

"Of course, he probably won't be able to keep up with me, but it will be fun all the same," Jana said trying to generate some reaction from me.

"Yep," I continued in my non caring tone. At this point Jana stopped walking and grabbed my arm.

"Come on George, you must be jealous a bit!" she snapped.

"On the contrary, I'm not jealous at all. However, I am a bit intrigued as to why you think I might be and why you are going to all this effort to try and make me jealous?" I replied.

"You know why," Jana said angrily.

"No, I don't."

"You stood me up last night. I was waiting for you, and you stood me up. And the worst part is that you stood me up for that fucking twat," she said pointing a Nigel a few metres ahead of us.

"I thought we talked about this at breakfast this morning. I'm sorry that I didn't let you know. I should have done. But I'm not apologising for talking to Nigel last night. He was in a desperate state. He had fucked up the whole evening with Aman and Neela, was worried about his job, and becoming more and more depressed about his life in general. So yes, we talked, said some harsh things that needed to be said, cleared the air a little bit and yes, I suppose to some extent we bonded. And I think he realises what he needs to do and the sort of person he needs to be, to stop being the fucking twat we all think he is! And since last night, he's been doing a good job. No. I don't apologise for talking to Nigel last night!" Jana looked stunned and ashamed of herself.

"Sorry George," she said as her eyes started to glaze over.

"You don't need to apologise Jana; you just need to listen. Listen to what I said this morning and listen to me now. We had a fantastic couple of nights together, well at least I thought they were fantastic. And if we have more fantastic nights together, then that would be nice. But I don't see us as a 'couple' in a traditional relationship. You said it yourself about just having some fun, not being tied at the hip and all that!" I said sternly.

"I know George, I'm sorry. Forgive me?"

"Nothing to forgive," I whispered softly, raising my finger to wipe away a tear that had formed on Jana's right eye, while keeping an eye on Nigel and Heinz, who by now were a good ten metres in front of us.

"Is this the place George?" called out Heinz as we approached the restaurant.

"Yes, that's it," I replied and we went inside. We were lucky that we didn't have to wait to be seated as usually, a booking was the only way to guarantee a table. The restaurant was as I had remembered. Decked out in African ornaments and detailed wood carvings, and subdued lighting, almost as if you were sitting outside to dine.

The meal was wonderful and everyone enjoyed their choice of food. The service was again as I had remembered, first class and Nigel left a hefty tip when paying for our evening. I must say, Nigel was on good form again. He was engaging and interesting, but not hogging the limelight and allowing everyone a turn at talking. Had this man really become such a changed person in the last twenty-four hours? Was it purely down to the conversation I had had with him last night? I really didn't know. But what I did know is that I liked this new Nigel. The arrogance seemed to have gone, the selfishness and rudeness he had possessed only just yesterday had also disappeared. He looked happier in himself!

"Right. I'm going to go and do a bit of gambling. Nothing too serious, a bit of blackjack and maybe a few spins on the roulette wheel. Who's up for that?" asked Nigel as we exited the restaurant.

"I will join you for a few hands of blackjack," replied Heinz, "it is one of my guilty pleasures I'm afraid." Jana and I looked at each other in surprise as this was an unexpected announcement from Heinz, before turning back to the two of them.

"Listen guys, I am a bit tired after last night," I said looking at Nigel. Nigel smiled back at me. "I'm going to have an early night, but good luck with the blackjack and try not to lose your shirt!" I continued.

"Jana? What about you?" asked Nigel.

"Erm, no. I think I will get an early night too. Be fresh for tomorrow. But have fun gentlemen and try not to lose too much money," Jana replied.

"Okay, see you for breakfast?" asked Nigel.

"Look, I'm quite sure that our hosts will lay on something when we get there, so I'm going to skip breakfast. Need to start looking after my waistline!" I said.

"Good idea George. Let's just meet at the front of the hotel. Pick up is at 9 a.m." Nigel replied. "Get some rest and I'll see you tomorrow." Nigel and Heinz headed off to the gaming areas leaving Jana and I alone. We turned and started to walk in the other direction towards the hotel rooms.

"Are you really tired George?" asked Jana as we approached the elevators.

"Yes. I really am tired. Nigel and I drank a lot of alcohol last night and I probably saw my bed at around 4 a.m. this morning."

"You would never have known based on your performance in the meeting. Great presentation, you held everyone's attention and I think in the space of two days you have managed to develop a solid relationship with Aman. Ever the professional even if you did feel like shit this morning!"

"Thanks for the compliments and yes, I did feel like shit this morning."

"So, you don't want some company tonight?" again asked Jana. The elevator arrived and we got in.

"Jana, I can't have you behaving like you have today-"

"I'm really sorry George. I got carried away. It won't happen again, I promise. We are friends who like to have some fun together, that's all. No ties, no complications," Jana interrupted.

"I am really tired…" and again before I could finish my sentence, Jana turned to face me and pressed her body up against mine.

"I can take really good care of you George. You don't have to do anything," she said softly, her lips inches from mine.

We entered her hotel room and Jana told me to lie on the bed. She slowly and carefully undressed me until I was lying there in just my Calvin Klein's. She then stood up at the end of the bed and kicked off her shoes. She unbuttoned her beige blouse and slipped it off, allowing it to drop to the floor, revealing her strapless white bra. She took her right hand up behind her back and unclasped it, again allowing it to drop to the floor. I stared at her beautiful breasts and her nipples started to harden. She unzipped her tiny lilac skirt, undone the button and with both hands pushed it to the floor. A tiny string white thong was now all she was wearing. Jana looked incredible and I could feel myself becoming aroused. She leant down at the bottom of the bed and began softly kissing my feet before working her way up my legs, paying particular attention to my inner thighs. When she reached my 'Calvin's' she stopped and looked up at me. She grabbed my underwear in both hands and slowly began to pull them down, encouraging me to lift my bottom to ease the process, revealing my fully erect manhood.

Jana was as good as her word and did take 'really good care of me' that night. It was again, another side of her that hadn't come through on the previous occasions we had been intimate with each other. She was gentle, soft, slow moving, and precise in her management of my body. She was in total control and I willingly gave in to her, allowing her to do whatever she wanted with me. It was another memorable evening which ended with us falling asleep in each other's arms.

25

It was 8:50 a.m. when I arrived at the entrance of the hotel and waved at Heinz, who was standing just outside. I had left Jana's room a couple of hours earlier, leaving her peacefully sleeping, to go to my room, shower and get ready for the day ahead.

"Morning George," Heinz greeted me. "Did you manage to catch up on your sleep?"

"Yes, thank you Heinz. I did sleep very well," I replied and it was actually true! Following the gentle intimacy between Jana and I; I had fallen into a deep sleep and felt so much better for it. "So how much money did you win last night then?" I asked.

"As I said last night George, blackjack is one of my guilty pleasures, and unfortunately at least last night anyway, I wasn't particularly good at it. Lost about €200. Not too bad," replied Heinz.

"Sorry to hear that. But as you say, it's not too bad."

"Being a numbers man it is a little puzzling as to why I play the game. The odds are stacked against the player, so you know the likelihood is that you will lose. But I just love to play! The trick is to know when to stop. Not go beyond your limit. It's a pity Nigel doesn't know that."

"Really! How much did Nigel lose?"

"Lose! Nigel didn't lose. He just kept winning and winning and winning some more. I kept telling him to stop, because the chances are, he was going to lose it all. But he didn't! I think he must have been about €5,000 up when I finally left him and went to bed about 12:30 a.m."

"So, you are telling me that you don't know how it ended up for Nigel last night?"

"That's right. I can't wait to ask him this morning," replied Heinz. At that moment, Jana approached us.

"Morning Heinz, morning George," she said.

"Good morning Jana, sleep well?" asked Heinz.

"Very well thank you Heinz. You?"

"Yes, although I was just telling George about Nigel last night. Can't wait to see him this morning." With that Heinz filled Jana in on his evening with Nigel. Luckily, Jana didn't reciprocate and tell Heinz about her evening with me! A few moments passed and Nigel joined us.

"Good morning Nigel," I said. "Have a good night last night?"

"Morning George, morning everyone. Yes, as a matter of fact, we had a wonderful night, didn't we Heinz," he replied looking at Heinz.

"Well, I didn't do too well, but I'm interested to know how you ended up. When I left you, I think you must have been about €5,000 ahead," said Heinz.

"Well, when you went to bed, I only played a few more hands and then went over to the roulette tables. You are right, I had won over R100,000 (South African Rand - just over €5,000) on that blackjack table. I'm sure they thought I was cheating. But the truth is, I am quite a good player and just got lucky last night. But little did I know that my luck was about to get even better. Betting on 'reds and blacks' and 'odds and evens' I managed to double my winnings in about half an hour. Ended up with over R200,000! So, don't worry

Heinz, I've got your stake money for tonight," Nigel said with a smile on his face. We all laughed.

A car pulled up and a medium built white man with jet black hair got out. I recognised him from my previous visit a few years ago. It was the General Manager of the catering facility.

"Hello George, good to see you," said the man offering his right hand out to me. There was a slight pause as I was struggling to remember the guy's name. Then it came to me.

"Hello Simon," I said. "Good to see you too. This is Nigel, Heinz and Jana," I continued as I introduced everyone. Simon Parks was an English guy who had been in Johannesburg for about ten years. He was in his early fifties but was one of those guys who was never comfortable about getting older. Therefore, he dyed his hair, drove a little sports car and if I remembered correctly, had married a local girl, exceptionally beautiful and half his age! I had found him to be a little sly, and almost 'schoolboy' like in his manner when I was here last time. But he was knowledgeable and had gained experience in the airline industry through previously working for Virgin Atlantic.

We got into Simon's car and although it was a big SUV, it was still a little tight in the back for Heinz, Jana, and me. Jana sat in the middle and I could feel her thighs against mine. She looked at me just once as we made our way to the catering facility, giving me an infectious smile. Nigel sat in the front and was busily chatting to Simon. It was only a short five minute journey before we arrived. Simon showed us in through the reception, up a set of stairs and into the boardroom. Once again, as in Addis Ababa, coffee and tea pots, pastries and bread rolls, cold cuts of meats and cheeses, were laid out on the boardroom table.

"Please, help yourself. I'm just going to organise your visitor passes and I will collect the rest of the team. Won't be long," said Simon and he left the room.

"Seems like a nice guy," said Nigel.

"Can be quite charming," added Jana.

"Very experienced," chipped in Heinz.

"Yes. All of the above. But can also be a bit devious, sneaky, and arrogant," I replied. "You have to remember these guys answer to the owner. As long as they make money, the owner isn't that interested in how it is done. From my experience from the last time, I was here, it was like one big 'boys club'. It's a different world. Sure, I think they work hard, but I think they play even harder. Try not to be drawn in too much and see through some of the bravado. Simon's rather good at that!"

"Thanks for the pep talk George," said Nigel. "Right, who wants coffee, I could murder one right now!" he continued and made his way over to the coffee pot, pouring out a cup.

"Yes, good idea," agreed Heinz and he went and stood with Nigel. Jana also said yes as did I, therefore Nigel became 'mum' and poured out four cups. We also tucked into the pastries, which were delicious and were a welcome relief to our stomachs as we had all missed breakfast.

The boardroom door opened and Simon entered being followed by his colleagues I recognised from my previous visit. The first person was Mark Fischer, the Operations Director, and the person basically in charge of the operations, including production, transport, hygiene, stores and the dishwash. He was white, mid-forties, a German native, but again had been living in Johannesburg for about ten years, married to a local woman and had two children, a boy and a girl, I think. I didn't like Mark very much either. His style of management was aggressive and could almost be considered bullying towards the employees. He also seemed to be proud of being able to take home food items from the facility for personal use. I know this because he told me on my previous visit! Steaks, kilos of prawns, whole sides of salmon, anything he fancied, he just took. He knew that as part of the senior management team, his car would not be subject to a vehicle search, as every other car is when it leaves the premises. To me, it was just theft! Although Simon never mentioned it, I'm fairly sure that he did the same thing.

The second person behind Simon was David Emeradis, the Finance Director. He was in his late fifties, white and originally from Zimbabwe. Again, another sly sneaky sort of guy. Normally, people in financial positions are very precise, proud of what they do and are 'sticklers' for details and procedures. David was none of that! I often wondered if he was manipulating the figures and 'creaming' money of the top for his own personal gain. This is something I had forgotten to mention to Jana. However, I would make sure that I did.

Then came a black lady, mid-thirties called Honesty Mkwumbala. Her position was HR Director. She was married and lived in a very well-off neighbourhood in a large house. Her husband also had a particularly good job and they had managed to work hard to achieve their wealth. This did cause some friction in the kitchen amongst the predominantly black workforce, as they sometimes thought of Honesty as a 'traitor', someone who had sold her soul to the white supremacy. To be fair, Honesty was, as her name, very honest in her approach to things and was impartial regardless of anyone's colour. I liked her a lot.

The last person was a young white guy, mid-twenties called Bruce Mellor. Bruce was South African and the Sales & Customer Service Manager. Although Bruce was not part of the senior management team, he had developed good relationships with the customers and was integral to the success of the business. When I first met Bruce, he appeared to be heavily influenced by the senior team, particularly Simon and David. But as I talked to him, I got the impression that he knew there were things going on in the business that he disagreed with but was powerless to act against. He would be someone I would need to get close to if I wanted to find out what was really going on in the facility.

"Let me introduce you to David, Mark, Honesty and Bruce," said Simon. Everyone greeted one another, and as I had known these people from before, I had a quick chat with each of them. They all seemed genuinely pleased to see me and we all mingled drinking tea and coffee for a few minutes.

"Is Gert not joining us?" I asked Simon. Gert Schneider was the owner, another German national, a large man with an almost Santa Clause type appearance, in his seventies who had been in South Africa for over thirties years. He was a chef by trade, white, quite condescending, and was married to a black national. There was no diplomacy with Gert. He said what he thought at the time, no thinking or weighing up a situation, straight to the point. However, he was exceptionally good with the customers and always made sure they were well looked after when they visited.

"Yes. He's just on a call now. A few minutes, that' all," replied Simon. Everyone started to take their seats at the boardroom table and it quickly looked like a 'them and us' situation as Nigel, Heinz and Jana sat together down one end and Simon, Mark, David, Honesty and Bruce all sat together down the other end. I noticed a gap between Honesty and Bruce and seized the chance to sit in between them.

"All right if I sit here?" I asked sitting down anyway.

"Yeah, no worries," said Bruce. At that moment, the boardroom door opened and Gert walked in.

"Sorry for being late, but business doesn't stop just because we have visitors from Germany!" said Gert. However, 'Guten Morgen und willkommen in meiner bescheidenen Catering-Einrichtung', which roughly translated means 'Good morning and welcome to my humble catering facility.' All the Germans in the room smiled. Gert then turned and looked at me.

"Hello George. Good to see you again. Hope you are not bringing me any more of that charter business nonsense. We want real customers down here, customers that make us a lot of money. How's your wife and family?" It was a typical brash opening from Gert and a particularly painful one for me, asking about Cheryl and the girls. The previous time I was here, Gert had asked me if I was married and had family. At that time, the girls were very young; I think Emily was three and Amy was one - still a baby really.

"The girls are fine, doing really well," I replied and left it at that. I didn't feel the need or have the inclination to divulge any further details about my family at that moment. Nigel appeared to have sensed the tension in my response and duly stepped in.

"From what I have seen already Gert, you seem to have built a fantastic facility and have a good team of people around you. I am looking forward to the tour of the unit," said Nigel.

"Yes. I am enormously proud of what I have here. But my team know I can't go on forever, none of us are getting any younger and that's why I am looking for potential buyers. I would sell to one of this lot if they had the money. But they don't," Gert continued, looking around the table at the members of his team. Again, it was another example of the directness and honesty this man exuded which at that precise moment, was not altogether welcomed by his team. "So that's why you have been invited here. For you to see if you think I have the right set up for your large international organisation," he said sarcastically, "and for me to see if you have the right amount of money to buy it." Nigel smiled at Gert.

"Yes, well let's get started then," said Nigel, who I must say handled the situation very well, without taking any of the bait that Gert was throwing out.

"Nigel and I will conduct an audit of the facility and review the operational aspects of the business and Heinz and Jana would like to go through the financials and administrative areas of the business," I said. "I believe that the necessary NDA (Non-Disclosure Agreement) was signed by both parties a few weeks back."

"Yes. I have it here," piped up David, the Finance Director

"You can use this room as your base and I have arranged lunch in here for 1 p.m." said Simon. "Mark will lead the unit tour and David and his team will be available to Heinz and Jana for any questions and support regarding the financials."

"Thank you, Simon," I replied. "So, we are ready when you are."

We quickly finished our drinks and Simon brought over two white coats and hair nets for Nigel and me to wear on the tour. There was a natural 'hubbub' of noise from the various conversations in the room and out the corner of my eye I noticed Nigel talking to Gert in German. Although I knew a few words in German, I was by no means fluent in the language, so couldn't make out what they were talking about. I just had a feeling that it was a little suspicious and maybe Nigel was slipping back into his old sneaky, devious ways in some form. As we were about to leave the boardroom, Gert came over to me.

"George, can I see you in my office for a minute before you start the tour?" said Gert.

"Sure," I replied and we came out of the boardroom and into his office a few doors down. Gert closed the door behind us and asked me to sit down.

"I just wanted to apologise for, well for asking about your family. I had no idea about you losing your wife in such a tragic way. Please forgive me," said a very sincere Gert. It knocked me back as I hadn't expected Gert to be apologising and I had already forgotten about his earlier enquiry about my family.

"There is no need to apologise Gert. You weren't to know and I haven't taken any offence from your question."

"Thank you, George. If it is any consolation, I know how you feel. Before I came to South Africa, I was living in Munich. I was married to a beautiful, sweet German girl called Eva." Gert turned away from me, paused for second and looked out of his window. "She was also killed in an automobile accident. Completely ripped me apart. We didn't have any children, but the thought of not ever seeing my wife again just broke me. I needed to do something drastic in my life. That's when I came to Johannesburg." Gert turned around again to face me. "I just want you to know that I feel your pain. And with two little girls to look after, it must be exceedingly difficult for you."

"I am sorry to hear about your loss Gert. And thank you for sharing that with me. I don't know if the pain will ever go away completely. It does diminish each day, little by little. I try my best to put it to one side and concentrate on my girls. They lost their mother and nobody deserves to go through that at such a young age. They are a great comfort to me and the way they have coped is a credit to their mother," I replied. For such a big powerful man, Gert looked a little shaken and I could see a wetness forming around his eyes. I think he was still thinking about Eva.

"If you want a new start George, let me know. I can help," Gert said, wiping his eyes with a handkerchief.

"If you don't mind me asking, how did you know about my wife?" I asked.

"Nigel pulled me to one side and let me know. He wasn't nasty about it, he just wanted to let me know. Out of protection for you, I think. I am glad he did."

We left Gert's office and returned to the boardroom. Jana and Heinz were busy setting up their laptops and were already in deep conversation with David and Bruce. Nigel was talking with Mark and Simon. Honesty had left the room. As Nigel saw me, he made his excuses with Mark and Simon and headed over to me.

"Look, I'm really sorry George, but I have to tell you that I told Gert about…" I lifted my hand to stop Nigel mid-sentence.

"I know. And thank you Nigel, I really appreciate your concern. We've just had a nice chat and everything is fine. Thanks again mate," I said. Nigel smiled and returned to Mark and Simon. I gestured to

Jana to come over to me for a quick chat before Nigel and I left for the facility tour. In a huddle, so nobody could hear, I let her know of my suspicions of David and to be extra vigilant in her appraisal of the figures. She shook her head in acknowledgement and understanding of what I was saying. I then looked into her eyes.

"Are you okay?" I asked.

"Yes. Really good George, really good," she replied with a smile on her face. "Hope you are too?"

"No, not really," I replied. "I think we need to talk. Later, on our own. Would that be okay?"

"Of course. And yes, we do need to talk."

The rest of the day went very well. Nigel and I were shown everything in the operation and the facility was well run, exceptionally clean and it looked as though all the relevant HACCP regulations were being adhered to, as well as hygiene practices being maintained. Security of the premises building was tightly controlled (unless you happened to be a member of the senior management team!) and generally, the physical structure of the buildings (there was a separate office block and bakery department, which also housed the canteen on the first floor away from the main building) were in good shape. Nigel was a little disturbed by the large number of employees. I could see him thinking that this would be an obvious area where the reduction in employees would yield savings to the bottom line and he eventually made the comment to me when we were alone.

"That's an area of potential savings, the number of employees. Far too many in my opinion," said Nigel.

"On the face of it Nigel, you're right. And I'm sure back in your days in the Dusseldorf facility, you would have half the number of employees for the volume of business that this facility turns out. But it is not as simple as that. You see labour costs in the production areas are incredibly low. Therefore, you must analyse the most cost-effective way of buying product. For example, in Europe we mainly buy in ready prepared vegetables, meat and poultry, deserts, bread, pastries etc. Ready to go into production and final assembly. Obviously, that comes at a higher food cost. Here in Johannesburg, it is often more cost effective to have your own in-house butchery, bakery, vegetable prep area. Then you buy in unprepared products and employ low-cost labour to prepare the items for production. There is sometimes a problem with consistency of product when you work this way, but if it is controlled properly, the benefits can allow flexibility, offer USP's (Unique Selling Points) to the customers and be financially rewarding."

"Thanks, George. Never thought of it that way. Good point."

"But you are still right Nigel. The number of employees does on the face of it, look too high. All I'm saying is, we need to keep an open mind."

We finished the day and ended up back in the boardroom. Heinz and Jana were wrapping up and putting their laptops away. I had already typed up my notes from the tour and we were getting ready to leave.

"I hope you have had a good day?" said Simon as he entered the room.

"Yes, thank you Simon and thanks to your team. Everyone has been most helpful and I think we have had a very insightful day," I replied.

"That's good. I have arranged a dinner tonight at a place called 'Kitamu'. It's an African restaurant about a twenty-five minute drive from here. I will take you back to the hotel so you can freshen up and then we can go from there. Is that okay?"

"That sounds great," said Nigel. "Will Gert be joining us?"

"Unfortunately, not. Gert has other commitments tonight; he sends his apologies and hopes you have a nice time. He will see you all in the morning for the debrief, replied Simon. "But Mark, David and Bruce will join us."

"Thank you again Simon," I said and we all left the boardroom following Simon down to the car for our lift back to the hotel.

Once at the hotel, I quickly made my way to my room as I wanted to take a quick shower and make a call to the girls before dinner. We had been given thirty minutes before Simon would be back to pick us up again. I picked up my cell phone and dialled home.

"Hey George, how are you?" answered Martyna. The sound of Martyna's voice again caught me off guard. I really missed hearing her, talking to her of an evening and I immediately thought about her upcoming date on Saturday night.

"I'm good Martyna. How are you?"

"Fine George. I'll just get the girls." I could hear Martyna telling Amy that it was me on the phone.

"Hello daddy. Have you seen any lions or elephants?" said Amy.

"Hello sweetheart. No, I haven't seen any animals yet. I probably won't either. But I'll tell you what. One day we will all come to South Africa and go on a Safari, where we will see lions and giraffe and elephants, rhino's, cheaters, buffalo, elk, and many, many, more. How does that sound?"

"That sounds wonderful Daddy. What's an elk?"

"It's like a big deer, with large antlers. Anyway, how are you sweetheart, how was school today?"

"It was good. Miss Raven wasn't cross with me anymore and I wrote a poem about animals you find on a farm. I didn't think it was very good, but Miss Raven liked it and read it out to the class. When are you coming home?"

"I fly home tomorrow evening and will be back with you guys Saturday morning. I'm so glad you had a nice day at school and I'm sure your poem was fantastic. Maybe you can ask Miss Raven if you can bring it home for the weekend so I can read it. Have you still been missing Mummy?" I asked tentatively.

"A bit. But I'm okay and can't wait to see her on Sunday. Martyna said that maybe I could paint a picture of Mummy and take it with me. I miss you too Daddy." Again, I had a sad feeling. A feeling that I was letting down Amy and Emily, by being here in Johannesburg.

"I'll be back soon sweetheart. Can't wait to play 'Kerplunk' with you and 'Frozen Snakes and Ladders', and lots of other games. And I can't wait to see Mummy too. I'm sure she will love a painting from you, of her," I said and could feel a tear running down the side of my face.

"Thanks Daddy. Love you lots! I'll pass you over to Emily, byyyyeee!"

"Love you to sweetheart," I just managed to reply before Emily picked up the phone.

"Hello Dad. I need to tell you something, well two things actually," said Emily in a confident manner.

"Hello Emster. Wow, two things eh! Well, I hope they are good things," I said with a smile on my face even though Emily couldn't see it!

"Well, one is good and one is not so good," she replied rather cautiously. "The first thing is that I had to stand up in assembly today and give a presentation on 'Monkeys', it's a project that I and Chelsea Picking have been working on for about two weeks. But Chelsea was too scared to do it, so I did it on my own!"

"That's wonderful sweetheart! How did it go?"

"It went very well. Miss Simmonds gave me ten merits for it and said I did a 'beautiful' job. Even the head teacher invited me to her office and told me how proud she was of me for presenting such an 'informative' and 'interesting' piece of work. She also said I was very brave for doing it on my own," continued an excited Emily.

"Well, I'm enormously proud of you too Emily. Well done sweetheart. Maybe you can show me what you presented when I get back?" I asked.

"Yes, I will do the presentation for you, Amy and Martyna, although Amy has already seen it in assembly. Dad, speaking of Amy, she seemed a bit down the last few days, so I've been cheering her up. We played 'horses' and I even let her beat me at 'Hungry Hippos' and 'Operation'," continued Emily. "I talked to her about Mummy as well because she said she missed her," said Emily, her mood subdued a little.

"She is incredibly lucky to have a big sister like you Emily. Thank you for looking out for Amy and for cheering her up. And how are you feeling about Mummy, are you missing her too?"

"I always miss her. And I always will. But she's not coming back, so I try to remember my 'happy times' with her. Our cuddles, kisses, dressing up like a princess day, and things like that. I know you miss Mummy too, Dad. But we have each other and if I don't have a Mummy, at least I have the best Dad in the world," The tears were streaming down my face by now. My little girl was suddenly, not quite so little. Very brave, very grown up.

"Thank you, sweetheart. And I have the best daughters in the world too. And you are absolutely right; we have each other and together we are a strong family." As I was saying this to Emily, it struck me that Emily had been using 'Dad' instead of 'Daddy' for a while now. Another indication that she was indeed growing up!

"Now Dad, I have something else to tell you. I was helping Martyna with the drying up and a glass slipped out of my hand and smashed on the floor-"

"Are you okay? You didn't hurt yourself or cut yourself?" I interrupted.

"No Dad, it was okay and Martyna made sure I hadn't hurt myself and asked me to join Amy in the lounge, while she cleared it all up. I'm really sorry, it was a complete accident."

"Sweetheart, of course it was an accident and accidents happen. There is no need to say sorry, I'm just so glad you are not hurt. And thanks, by the way, for helping Martyna with the washing up. Was Martyna okay?"

"Yes, she was great. She said the same as you, accidents happen. It was a little bit scary when it happened because it made a big crash sound. But after Martyna had cleared it up, she came and gave us both a big cuddle. I said to her that I should tell you and she said that would be a good thing to do, so I did."

"Thank you for letting me know Emster, and don't worry about it. As long you are okay, that's all that matters. Glasses can be replaced, Emily's and Amy's can't!"

"Neither can Martyna's," added Emily. "I've got to go now, but lovely speaking to you Dad. Love you," again finishing in such a grown-up way.

"Love you too darling," I replied.

"Hi George," said Martyna. "I guess you heard about the glass. Sorry about that, Emily asked if she could help with the drying up and I said yes, but to be careful. Total accident, but my fault really."

"Hi Martyna. Please don't worry. Accidents happen, right? Nobody's fault. Amy seemed a little better, did you speak to her teacher?"

"Yes. Miss Raven wasn't aware that Amy thought she was cross with her. So, I think she made a special effort towards Amy today. It seemed to do the trick. And Amy seems more settled. I did suggest that maybe she paints a picture of her mum to take on Sunday. Hope that was okay?"

"Very good idea Martyna, thank you."

"So, how are you? Did you have a good day?" asked Martyna.

"Yeah, all good thanks. In fact, I'm running a little late; need to quickly have a shower before going out to dinner."

"Very nice. I hope you enjoy yourself. Don't let me keep you George if you are in a hurry, I understand. Looking forward to seeing you on Saturday."

"Me too Martyna. Thanks again for looking after the girls, I really do appreciate it. And sorry I can't talk for longer. Take care."

I hung up and reflected on my call. Amy, still a little sad about things and missing her mum. Emily, ever so grown up and developing more and more confidence every day. And Martyna-, beautiful Martyna. Wonderful with the girls, keeping my family going, sensitive, kind, caring and going on a blind date on Saturday night! And I wondered what Emily meant when she said 'neither can Martyna's' when I mentioned that Emily's and Amy's can't be replaced! I needed to take a shower.

I took one last look in the mirror before adding a quick spray of Baldessarini and then headed for the reception. As I was about to enter the elevator on my floor, I heard Jana call out. I held the lift back and waited for her.

"Thanks George. You smell nice, again!"

"Thanks. Just the usual I'm afraid."

"It works for me," Jana replied with a cheeky smile. The elevator doors closed and we began our descent to the ground floor.

"So, what did you want to talk about George?" asked Jana.

"I don't think we have time to discuss anything now, but basically I wanted to talk about us." Jana looked thoughtfully at the floor before turning to me.

"You probably mean 'not us', don't you?" The elevator stopped and we stepped outside seeing Heinz and Nigel directly ahead of us.

"Let's talk later, okay?" I whispered to Jana out of earshot of Heinz and Nigel.

"Okay," Jana agreed.

The restaurant that Simon had chosen was wonderful. The atmosphere, quality of the food and service was exceptional, and I have to admit, the company was also extremely good. Simon was a touch 'brash' and arrogant, as I had remembered him before. But Nigel was giving as good as he got and I think was rather enjoying 'sparring' with him. Mark was trying really hard to impress Jana with his food knowledge. David was seeking to find out from Heinz if there was anything he should be worried about in the financials, and myself and Bruce just had a great time chatting about anything and everything, drinking beer! It was a genuinely nice, fun evening.

By the time we got back to the hotel, it was 10:30 p.m. Nigel and Heinz headed for the gaming areas and once again, Jana and I declined. Instead, we headed for a bar in the complex. After being seated and ordering some drinks, Jana turned to me.

"That was a nice evening. Mark's a bit of a twat though. If he's not careful, he could take that title from Nigel," she said. I smiled.

"You're not far wrong there," I replied.

"So, what's up George? What's bothering you?" At that moment, our drinks arrived. Jana had ordered a house red wine and I had a spiced rum and coke. I waited for the waiter to leave the table before turning to Jana.

"It's difficult Jana. I don't really know where to begin. I do know that I have had a fantastic time with you this week, starting last Sunday in your apartment."

"I have to say, your face was a picture when you saw me sitting in my underwear," Jana said smiling at me. I smiled back.

"I know. I didn't know where to look! All I knew, was that I wanted to look! You are extremely beautiful, funny and very, very sexy."

"Is this where the 'but' bit comes in George? Is this the bit where you say, 'we're not right for each other' and 'it's best we stop this' whatever this is, 'before it goes too far' something along those lines George?" I looked away from Jana and stared at my drink on the table.

"You know, I was talking to my kids earlier, before we left for the restaurant. My eldest, Emily, she's not quite nine yet and she was telling me about her day at school; about how brave she had been giving a presentation in front of the whole school in assembly. She was so proud of herself, as I was of her too. And then she felt the need to tell me that she had broken a glass, dropped it on the floor while drying the dinner things. She felt guilty about it, even though it was a complete accident. And after that, she told me how she had tried to comfort her little sister Amy, she's six, because she was missing her mum, by playing with her and letting her win the board games. Trying to make her happy. I was, am so proud of her. She told me that she misses her mum every day too, but she wanted to help her sister.

And then there's Amy. She had a bad day at school yesterday and thought her teacher was angry with her. Turns out, the teacher wasn't angry at all, but Amy didn't know. But really, it had nothing to do with that. Amy was just missing her mum - a lot. So, I promised to take the girls to their mum's grave on Sunday. It's something we do regularly but I hadn't planned to this weekend. We go there so the girls, and me as it happens, can talk to Cheryl, my wife, their mum; tell her about our day, how we feel, our plans, whatever really. Whatever we want to. It must sound stupid to you. Christ, if anyone told me this, I would think they are off their head! But it's a way for all of us to cope with the fact that we will never see her again. Amy's going to paint a picture of her mum to take on Sunday with us. And I think we will play games in the afternoon, before having a Sunday tea, sandwiches, crisps, cake and of course a cup of tea!" I turned and looked at Jana. Tears had started to fall from her eyes and I could again feel my eyes moistening over. "This is my life Jana. A life with two wonderful, brave little girls who need me, rely on me, take up my time. They are my focus and the most important thing to me."

"I understand George," Jana said while searching for a tissue in her handbag. I reached into my pocket and handed Jana a handkerchief.

"You are a wonderful woman, and I know we both agreed that this was 'a bit of fun'. But if we continue, it will start being something else and that's something that I couldn't put you through. You are young, gorgeous, adventurous; god knows you're adventurous! You don't want to be with someone like me, that has baggage and will always be putting my daughters needs before yours. I can't do the things you can do at the drop of a hat or live a life like yours. The girls will always come first. I really do hope you understand. You're amazing, but we need to stop this, before it really starts." I looked at Jana and smiled. Through her tears, she smiled back.

"I do understand George. And my tears are not for us. They are for your daughters. I can't imagine what it must be like for them. Or you, really. But you are right, we can't continue like this. I've had a lovely time with you and I want you to know that if circumstances were different, I think we could have made something incredibly special and long lasting of our relationship." She leaned forward and kissed my cheek. I grabbed hold of her hand and gently squeezed it and we sat in silence for a few minutes.

As I went to bed alone, I thought about the conversation I had just had with Jana. It was a perfectly accurate assessment of my circumstances. How could I put Jana or anyone in a position where they would always come second behind Emily and Amy? That included Fiona and Martyna as well. The conversation I had had with the girls earlier somehow put my life back into perspective. I had lived a life totally devoted to the girls since Cheryl's passing. However, recently I had been intimate with Fiona and Jana. And I liked their company, liked their warmth and care. And definitely loved the sex. And my feelings for Martyna were more than that of just an employer. But I could now see that it would be unfair to ask anyone to be involved with me, knowing that I would not be able to devote the time and effort that a full, loving, physical relationship deserves. Well at least if it was to be a successful relationship. I had a lot to think about!

26

The debrief meeting went well and I think Gert was pleased with the compliments regarding his facility and professionalism of his team. David Emeradis, the Finance Director, looked a little anxious and you could almost see a bead of sweat dripping from his forehead when Heinz gave his assessment of the financials. Although Heinz did not allude to anything being 'suspect' regarding the figures, he did tell me prior to the meeting, that something didn't quite 'add up' and he and Jana would dig a little deeper once they got back to Frankfurt. Maybe it was nothing, but when Heinz had a 'feeling' about things not being right, his suspicions were normally confirmed.

Before leaving for the airport, I had a chance to have quick chat with Gert, 'one on one' in his office. I think I had struck a chord with him the previous day when he learned of Cheryl's death and probably more by the fact that it had been caused by a road accident.

"George, thank you for coming. I am pleased that you found my facility up to standard. I knew you would though, we're not a 'tin pot' cowboy outfit here. We do things properly, well at least in terms of the operation. Don't ask me what goes on behind closed doors because I'm not going to tell you," said Gert in his usual forthright manner. "However, I wanted to let you know that I meant what I said yesterday. If you need a break, a different environment, somewhere that doesn't constantly remind you of your past, then this is as good a place as any to come. Your girls would love it here too. The outdoor life, the weather, the cost of living; you would live like Royalty, just like your good old Queen Elizabeth. I can help you with all of that."

"Sorry Gert, but are you offering me a job?" I replied.

"I've seen how you handle yourself George. I know how you are with customers. You know, I've had customers here that mention your name in conversation, all positive stuff. And from what Simon tells me, snivelling little prick that he is, you know your way around the kitchen. Now don't get me wrong, I don't want any more of you pompous, 'plum in your mouth' bastard Brits here. But for you, I would make an exception. So yes, I could offer you a job. Or even if you just wanted a vacation out here, I could help with that too. Safari, Sun City, Cape Town, The Garden Route, anything you want."

"Well, that's something to think about." I replied a little surprised.

"Yes. But I don't need an answer now. Just think about it, okay?"

"But you're selling up Gert, you're 'not getting any younger' I think were the words you used yesterday," I said, trying to coax some explanation from Gert for this sudden offer of a job.

"Things can change!" was Gert's immediate response. I felt that I needed to push this a little further.

"Can I ask you something Gert?"

"Sure, as long as it's not the one about where babies come from," he replied and he chuckled to himself. I used that line with Martyna when she told me about her first blind date! And just as Gert found it funny now, I had thought so back then. Problem was, it just wasn't funny!

"What really is your motivation for selling the business?" Gert turned away from me and looked deep in thought. A few seconds passed before he responded.

"What I said yesterday was true. I'm not getting any younger. I've recently had some health issues and it made me step back a bit, take stock of my life and think about what I really want to do now I've reached the 'twilight' years. I've been working hard all my life George; always running around trying to be better, improve myself, achieve something and of course, make more money. So, it's hard to just suddenly stop and think about a life where I don't have to go to work, I don't have to entertain customers and I don't get the thrill of winning new business."

"I understand that Gert, and I'm sorry to hear about your health issues-" I replied before Gert quickly interjected.

"Nobody knows about that George, and I trust you will keep it that way," he said turning and raising the index finger of his right hand at me. I nodded my head in acknowledgement.

"If you are selling, how can you offer me a job?" I continued.

"I can always influence the buyer, as part of the deal, who I think would be right for certain positions. No guarantees of course, but I am known for my negotiating skills."

"I see."

"I'm not sure you really do George. Things are done differently in Africa."

"I get that Gert; I am aware of how 'differently' deals can be struck in this part of the world. But I like to think that I can progress my career based on my own merits, my own hard work and recognition of that hard work from my peers and the powers that be, within the company."

"You mean from people like Victor Brandt and Lars Schuller?"

"You know Victor and Lars?" I asked.

"Yes. I've known Victor over forty years. He worked as an apprentice in my restaurant in Munich. We kept in touch for a while before I moved here. Victor is a nice man, thoughtful, decent, caring. But he won't be in his current position much longer. He will already be thinking about retirement. Then it will be left to the likes of Lars. Scheming, using people, manipulative little prick that he is. In fact, he would do very well here in South Africa, especially in the political scene!"

"So, you know Lars as well?"

"Not as well as Victor, but yes, I know him. Devious little shit!" exclaimed Gert and I could tell there must have been some bad history between them. I decided it was probably not the right time to pursue this. "You see George, you're willing to let people like Lars control your destiny, pick you up, play with you and cast you aside when they see no further use for you. Whereas I'm not willing to play that game!"

"You're wrong Gert!" I said defiantly. "I may want to be recognised for my work, for my knowledge and my management style that I believe promotes a culture of expression and personal growth, but I am not naïve. I know how people like Lars operate and I don't associate myself with it or people like that. I also know my own worth. And that means I will always have choices. To stay, go, start something new. I won't allow myself to be dictated to by someone like Lars."

"Good for you George, I'm glad you have strong belief in yourself," said Gert with a smile peering through his greyish white beard. "To get back to your original question, about my motivation for selling, it's purely money. Sure, there are the health reasons, but as I said, that's between you and me. I have a great business here that makes a lot of money and like you George, I know my worth too! So, you can tell Victor and Lars that if they want my business, they're going to have to pay the right price for it," continued Gert, and again he smiled at me.

"I get the message Gert," I replied, smiling back at him and in some way having admiration for this old git's conviction.

"They might tell you that they will be able to 'bluff me' by saying they will open a facility in Johannesburg in direct competition if I

353

don't sell to them at a reduced price. Well, tell them I have contacts and can make the granting of a license exceedingly difficult, if not impossible for them to secure. And even if they did get the license, it could take five or ten years. I'm just saying, you know."

"I hear what you're saying Gert," I replied.

We shook hands and left his office to re-join Nigel, Heinz, and Jana in the boardroom. Simon, David, Mark, and Honesty were also present and they were all busily engaged in conversation as Gert and I entered the room. When Nigel saw Gert and I, he came over and asked if he could have a quick word with me. We moved to the end of the boardroom out of earshot from anyone else.

"How did it go?" asked Nigel.

"Yes, very well. From the work that Heinz and Jana have done and from our experience yesterday on the tour, I think we have enough information to be able to put something together when we get back to Frankfurt for the board to look at."

"Great work George. By the way, the presentation this morning was splendid. I think you and Heinz and Jana, have created the right impression and gives us a solid foundation with Gert and his team."

"Thanks Nigel. But you have also contributed on this trip and I want to thank you for your help and support. I must admit, I didn't want you here. I wasn't sure of your agenda and I didn't think you would add anything. I was wrong."

"No George. I was wrong. And have been for a long time now. Thanks to you and a bottle of bourbon, I can now see things much clearer. Fuck that twat Lars! We'll do this thing the right way from now on. As a team. Thanks again George," replied Nigel in what I thought was one of the sincerest things anyone has ever said to me in the workplace. Wow - a complete change for Nigel!

After saying our goodbyes, Simon drove us to the airport. I was really looking forward to going home and seeing Emily and Amy. Martyna too if I'm honest, even though the thought of her having a successful blind date on Saturday night filled me with dread. We said our goodbyes to Simon and made our way through the airport. Nigel, Jana and Heinz, were booked on the Lufthansa flight back to Frankfurt which left Johannesburg some ninety minutes before my flight to London. We decided to get a quick drink in a bar before we went our separate ways and while Nigel and Heinz went to buy the drinks, it gave Jana and I chance to talk for the first time since the evening before.

"How are you Jana," I asked.

"Not that good George, I have to say," was her saddened response. "Don't worry, I still understand about last night and agree about us, or the lack of us. And I know I shouldn't be surprised as it was me that only wanted a 'bit of fun', nothing serious. However, you are a nice, decent man George. And a tiny piece of me will always love you and think about what might have been."

"I'm sorry Jana, I shouldn't have let 'us' go as far as it did. It was only a few nights, a few great, magical nights. However, I should have prevented anything from happening."

"I suppose me saying that I will tell everyone about us and make a scene at work, won't change your mind will it?" Jana replied in a somewhat 'joking' fashion. Well, at least I hoped it was a joke. I smiled and shook my head.

"Not really Jana, and I hope that was a joke?"

"You're probably too old for me anyway," she replied and smiled back at me. "Oh George. I feel empty, let down. German men are so immature, scripted, and competitive. Probably because they are so insecure and usually 'mummy's boys.' You are different. Confident in yourself. Know how to treat a woman and more importantly, how to please a woman."

"You'll find someone very soon, I'm sure of that. Someone when you least expect it. Someone who will blow you away and melt your heart. And someone that will know, appreciate and forever hold dear how fortunate they are to have someone as wonderful and beautiful as you in their life."

"Stop it George, you'll have me crying again," replied Jana and she placed her hand on top of mine. We looked into each other's eyes and it felt like a sense of closure on our amazing, but short week together.

Heinz and Nigel came back with the drinks and we made a short call to Tanja to let her know how things had gone. It was agreed that I would work on the proposals during the following week, with the support of Jana and Heinz, and then go to Frankfurt for two days the week after, to finalise the proposals and present our recommendations to the board. Tanja was rather surprised to hear Nigel on the call and even more surprised, or disturbed, I'm not quite sure which, that he had input and was praising the work carried out by the team. She was so concerned that after Nigel, Heinz and Jana had left to catch their flight, she called me back for a 'one on one' conversation.

"So now that twat has gone to catch his flight, what really happened?" was Tanja's opening statement.

"Exactly what we just told you. More to the point, exactly what Nigel just told you," I replied.

"George, I was brought up a Catholic, and while I am somewhat divorced from the whole religion thing these days, I am still inclined to believe in miracles, heaven and hell and the holy trinity. But what you are telling me about Nigel is totally un-fucking-believable!" I laughed out loud and I could sense even Tanja had a smile on her face.

"You'll see next week. I think he wants to have a chat with you," I said through my laughter.

"I can't fucking wait," Tanja replied. We talked a little more about the trip and Tanja asked after Emily and Amy before we said our goodbyes and arranged to call each other the following week.

I thought I would look around the duty free and try to find some presents for the girls and Martyna. I manged to find a place selling beautifully embroidered cushions, so bought one each for Emily and Amy. One had a lion cub on it and the other an elephant calf. They looked fantastic and I could see the girls using them to sit on when they played on the floor. I also managed to find some African print pencil cases and two small wooden carvings of a hippopotamus and a giraffe. Again, I was sure the girls would like these.

I then turned my attention to Martyna. I tried to think of what brand of perfume she used but was struggling. Could I remember the smell? No, not really. And then it came to me. I had seen a diamond shaped, gold bottle of perfume on the kitchen table a few months back. The bottle looked very cool and was called-, was called-, what the fuck was it called? Miss something, no, woman, no that wasn't right either. Got it! Lady something. Armed with this information, I headed to the perfume counter where a pretty, young girl knew exactly what I was talking about from my description.

"Lady Million by Paco Rabanne is what I think you mean sir," she said when I described the bottle to her. Yes, Lady Million. That was it. When she brought over the box and showed me the contents, I knew I had the right perfume.

"It's a very seductive type of scent sir," said the girl, "for your wife?" she asked. I looked at my left hand and saw my wedding ring. The girl must have noticed it as Fiona had also done so the first night, I had a drink with her in the Sheraton hotel.

"Erm, no not for my wife," I replied hesitantly.

"Say no more sir," said the girl knowingly, as if I was buying the perfume for a mistress!

"No, erm, no it's not what you think-" I protested.

"As I said sir, none of my business," she interrupted and handed me a bag with the perfume in it. I just smiled, paid for the perfume, and left the shop feeling a little embarrassed.

As I was flying in Business Class, it allowed me automatic access to the British Airways lounge. I thought I might as well make use of it as I had about an hour to kill before boarding. I made my way to the lounge, showed my boarding card to the receptionist, and gained entry. The lounge was quite large and had areas with tables and chairs, as well as a quieter area where you could sit and work. Although I wasn't going to be working, the quieter area suited me, so I found a nice spot tucked out of the way and put my bags down, claiming my territory! I went to the bar area and poured myself a beer and helped myself to a few freshly cut sandwiches from a large serving tray, placing them on a plate. A few olives and some crisps and I was all set.

I made my way back to my seat and placed the food and drink by the side table. The beer tasted great, cold refreshing and was just what I needed. I proceeded to eat the sandwiches, olives and crisps and felt very relaxed. The beer had soon been dispensed with and I thought I would get one more before boarding the flight. As I returned to my seat with my beer, I noticed a woman sitting in the seat next to mine. Flat soled shoes, tight denim jeans and reading a Financial Times newspaper, that was so big, it obscured her face and the top half of her body. All I could see above the woman's waistline was a pair of arms, covered by a white, close fit, long sleeved sweater, and the huge newspaper. I wasn't too impressed as I had just wanted to relax and dearly hoped that this person wouldn't strike up a conversation with me. I was wrong!

"Hello George," the person said. I looked to my right where this person was sitting and was immediately hit by the aroma of Coco Mademoiselle. The newspaper was lowered and there sitting next to me was Jennifer Parks! "Fancy seeing you here," she said.

"Jesus! Hi Jen. What are you doing here?" I said and was genuinely pleased to see her. She looked just as I remembered the last time, I saw her, in the coffee shop in Chelsea, a few weeks before

Cheryl died. That thought struck me for a second, but I soon put it to one side.

"I saw you from across the room and then when you went to get another beer, I thought I would surprise you."

"Well, you certainly have. Great to see you," I said and we embraced with a hug. "So, what the hell are you doing here?" I asked.

"Another photo-shoot. It's a follow up from a couple of years ago. I think I told you about it the last time we met. It was in that café in Chelsea, right?"

"Yeah, I think it was," I replied trying to be a little vague. "That's great. You didn't get into any trouble then, with the locals?"

"No, they remembered me from last time. Treated me like a queen actually! Got some great photos and I should make a lot of money from this," Jennifer said with a satisfied smile on her face, revealing those pearly white teeth surrounded by her plump red lips. Her demeanour then suddenly changed and she looked a little sad.

"What's up?" I asked.

"Sorry George, I forgot. I bumped into Luke a few months back and was asking after you. He told me about Cheryl. God, I'm so sorry George. When Luke told me about the night before, the row between you and Cheryl, and because it was about me, I-, I'm just so sorry George. You must hate me."

"Jen. It wasn't you fault. It was nobody's fault. Just a stupid bloody accident. A case of being in the wrong place at the wrong time. You have nothing to be sorry about and nothing to feel guilty about. Things just happen like this sometimes. I hope Luke didn't make you feel like it was your fault?"

"No, he didn't. In fact, he still believes it's all his fault. For mentioning my name in front of Cheryl. From what I can tell, it's really eating him up inside. He feels responsible." I hadn't seen Luke in few months and made a mental note to see him as soon as possible next week.

"I didn't know Luke felt that way. I'll talk to him. None of you are to blame."

"How are you coping?" Jen asked.

"It's better now than it was and I'm sure it will get easier as more time passes. But it has been difficult. The girls have been wonderful. Brave and a great comfort to me. Although, I'm sure that the full impact of them losing their mum has not really materialised yet. I think we still have some difficult times ahead of us. But we are a family and are open with each other and we'll get through it together." Jen leaned across and squeezed my hand to comfort me. There followed a slight pause and a short, awkward silence.

Although it seems a ridiculous thing to think about, my mind turned to the row Cheryl and I had that night. Cheryl had no reason to feel insecure about our relationship; we loved each other, wanted to be together and had a wonderful family life. Cheryl trusted me implicitly as I did her and she was never jealous of any other woman. Except Jennifer. I think it was because it was so 'close to us' when we were at university and it wasn't long after Jen and I had finished our brief fling, that I got together with Cheryl. Although Cheryl never mentioned it, I'm sure that they must have seen each other around campus and maybe it was just too much for Cheryl and that's why Jen got stuck in her mind.

"You're on your way back to London, then?" Jen said finally breaking the silence.

"Yes. I have been on a business trip with a few colleagues from Germany. We flew out of Frankfurt on Monday to Addis Ababa and from there to here on Wednesday."

"Wow. Ethiopia. I bet that was an experience?"

"Yeah. But as usual on these trips, I don't get to see much. In your job, when you visit different countries, you soak up the culture, capture the real spirit of the country and take pictures that reveal to the viewer a taste of what life is really like for the locals. When I travel,

I see an airport, a hotel, a catering facility and a restaurant if I'm lucky!" I replied.

"I still bet you had a nice time though," said Jen, smiling from my previous comment.

"Yes, I have and can't complain."

"So, what were you doing in Addis and Jo'burg?" Jen continued.

"My colleagues and I visited two local catering operations with a view to either buying or forming some sort of joint venture. The company has an expansion strategy that is targeting the African continent."

"Sounds exciting. So, you might end up spending a lot of time in this part of the world then," said Jen.

"Maybe. We'll see."

We continued to chat until our flight was called for boarding. Although we were sitting in different rows, I had an empty seat next to me and Jen asked me if I minded if she swapped it for her original seat so we could travel together. I didn't mind at all. In fact, it was great to see her and from the first moment she had said 'Hello George' in the lounge, we were extremely relaxed in each other's company.

After take-off and the flight attendant had completed the first drinks service, I still had Cheryl and more to the point, Cheryl's total dislike for Jen, on my mind. Although Jen and I were talking about lots of different things, I still couldn't shake this from head. I seized the moment.

"Jen, I hope you don't mind, but can I talk to you about Cheryl?" Jennifer was a little surprised. She looked away from me and down at her drink, a sparkling white wine.

"Why, George," she finally answered.

"I don't know. I suppose it bothers me that Cheryl had such a dislike for you and was so jealous of you. Cheryl was never jealous of anyone and trusted me one hundred per cent. And I never had any interest in anyone else after getting together with her. So, I don't understand why she got so upset the night before she died, when Luke mentioned your name. And until seeing you today, I never really thought about it too much. But I guess, I'm-, I'm missing something."

"Oh my God! You don't know do you?" said a stunned and somewhat flustered Jen.

"Know what?" I replied, my intrigue beginning to build. Jen took a long 'gulp' of her drink and pressed the flight attendant button. The flight attendant arrived instantly and Jen waved her glass at her.

"Another one of these please," she said. "And you better get him another Bloody Mary," she continued, pointing at me. The flight attendant wheeled away to get the drinks.

"What's the matter Jen. What's going on?"

"She never told you, did she?"

"Told me what? Did you guys have a fight at Uni?" The flight attendant returned with our drinks and after we had both said a quick 'thankyou' we were again alone. "Well? Did you and Cheryl have a fight?"

"Yes," said Jen, and looked away from me. I could sense that she was replaying a scene in her mind. A scene I was hoping she would relay to me.

"Go on," I encouraged her.

"It was in the ladies toilets; do you remember the toilets on the ground floor or the King Henry Building?"

"Yes," I replied, although I hadn't really got a clue what toilets she was talking about!

"Well, I was in there one day, washing my hands when Cheryl walked in and just started having a right go at me. Screaming at me! It was so bad, that the girls coming out of the toilet cubicles didn't even bother washing their hands, they just left immediately," said Jen taking another gulp of sparkling wine.

"And?" I said eagerly wanting to find out more.

"Well, I wasn't standing for that, so I gave as good as I got. We had an almighty stand up shouting match. Fortunately, we didn't come to blows, although I was awfully close to punching her. Sorry George."

"No, don't worry," I said. "Was it really intense?"

"Yes. We went at it for about five minutes. She was yelling at me to stay away from you. I told her that I wouldn't talk to you, but she wouldn't believe me. I ended up telling her to 'fuck off' and leave me alone. Such a shame really."

"So that's why she hated you. You had a big row over me and Cheryl thought you were still interested in me," I said in slow realisation of what had been eating at Cheryl all these years.

"No George," said Jen.

"What? What do you mean no George?" Jen looked even more horrified.

"You really don't know George, do you?"

"What the fuck are you on about Jen? What don't I know?" Jen's glass emptied faster than Superman on crack! She placed the glass down and turned to me.

"Cheryl and I were friends before she ever met you. More than just friends. After you and I had finished, Cheryl was a great comfort to me. I know we didn't have anything too serious, and it didn't last very long, and that's probably why you never met her as my friend when we were together. But any breakup leaves you feeling vulnerable for a while. Cheryl was there for me. And one thing led to another, and we started 'being together' as a couple."

"Sorry Jen, you've lost me. Are you telling me that in between me being with you and me being with Cheryl, that you and Cheryl got it together?" I asked, slightly agitated.

"Yes," Jen replied slowly, waiting for my reaction. I was shocked, angry, sad, confused, interested, curious even, but most of all relieved all at the same time. I wasn't sure why I felt relieved, maybe I was subconsciously thinking Jen was about to tell me something far worse! However, with all these emotions running through me, none of them prompted me to say any words! I just looked at Jen. "Sorry George, I thought she would have eventually told you," Jen continued. "Say something George, say something," she pressed. I let out a deep sigh.

"Thanks for telling me," I said slowly, and I smiled at Jen. "Cheryl never told me any of that."

"It wasn't for long and I think we both knew that we preferred a man, but it was still incredibly beautiful and something that I will always look back on with happiness. And then Cheryl met you. You must have told her about me and how we had a fling. I guess she wanted to make sure you never found out that she had also been with me, another girl! That's why she was screaming at me in the toilets. Telling me to stay away from you. Not because I wanted you back or anything. She just didn't want me to casually tell you in conversation that she and I had been fucking each other's brains out." Again, Jen paused and looked at me. "Sorry George. That was a bit insensitive of me. But look, it was a long time ago, and I know she loved you so much. I think she also knew how perfect you thought she was and didn't want to destroy the image you had of her. Something I have probably just done in the last ten minutes! God I'm so sorry George."

"Please stop apologising Jen. There's no need to apologise. It's a lot to take in, but it makes sense now why Cheryl asked me never to talk to you or see you or have anything to do with you. I was so in love with her, that I never really stopped and asked myself why she would be like that." Again, Jen reached out her hand and gently squeezed mine.

"Don't think badly of her George, we were all very young back then," Jen said softly.

"I don't think badly of her, or you either. In fact, I am happy that she had a different kind of experience in her life. It made no difference to us, our life together and makes no difference to how I feel about her even now, now she's no longer with us. I do feel incredibly sad though. Sad that Cheryl felt she needed to hide this from me. Admittedly, a bit of a shock, but it wouldn't have made me love her any less or change how much I wanted to be with her. And she carried this needless burden for so many years. That's what saddens me."

"I know it is no consolation, but I have never told anybody about me and Cheryl and I never will. Not because it was sleazy or because I am embarrassed about it, but because it was special for me and I believe special for her too. Just us."

"Thanks Jen. Thanks for telling me. I'm sorry Cheryl yelled at you. I know how that can be when she gets into one!" I said smiling.

So, Cheryl was never jealous of Jennifer and the only reason that she was so insistent on me never talking to Jen or having any contact with her, was to preserve her secret. A secret lesbian affair that she had enjoyed with Jen all those years ago and before I had ever met her. I dearly wish that Cheryl had told me and in doing so, I could have lifted her fear of me finding out. It made me look at myself and wonder what I had done or indeed not done, to make Cheryl feel she couldn't trust me enough to share this secret. I didn't have the answer.

27

The flight finally landed at Heathrow airport after a long eleven hours. I say long, but the time appeared to go quite quickly as Jennifer and I talked for most of the flight. And although Jen's revelation about her and Cheryl played on my mind, I managed to suppress those thoughts and really enjoyed her company for the rest of the journey. She was still as gorgeous as she ever was; funny, eloquent and had that strong self-belief and confidence that made me think it was not very surprising to hear about her having had a lesbian experience. It was just a slightly weird feeling that it had been with Cheryl!

We continued talking through customs and finally out of the arrivals' door into the terminal. Although it took me a short while, I suddenly noticed two A4 size home-made posters with the words 'Welcome Home Daddy' painted on them in bright colours. The posters started coming towards me at a fair pace closely followed by the two little girls holding them.

"Welcome home Dad," shouted Emily and Amy as they raced towards me. It was a wonderful surprise to see my two girls running towards me; I dropped my bags as they approached and bent down to give them a big hug.

"Hey sweethearts, this is a lovely surprise," I said, giving them both a big kiss. They clung on to me so tightly I thought they would squeeze the air out of me! To anyone watching, they must have thought I had been away for months, years even!

I looked up and saw Martyna slowly walking towards us. She had a delightful smile on her face and I think she intuitively knew how extremely happy I was. In all the years that I have been travelling, nobody had ever met me at Arrivals when I had returned. It was always a case of either rushing to the taxi stand or finding my way to the airport car parks to get home as quickly as I could. I had often thought how nice it would be to have been met by someone, like you see in the romantic films, where the wife and kids meet the husband, the excitement of the kids seeing their dad and then that moment where the wife and husband embrace for that slow, loving kiss. Well, I definitely had the excitement of the kids! But unfortunately, there was no loving kiss. Don't get me wrong, I didn't blame Cheryl for not meeting me or think badly of her because she had never done that. I knew she had her hands full with the girls and besides, I always got my slow, loving kiss when I entered the house!

"Hi George," said Martyna.

"Hi Martyna," I replied. "Thank you. This is fantastic. Why?"

"Why not?" she replied, again smiling.

"It was Martyna's idea Dad, and then Amy and I decided to paint these posters for you," said Emily. "Who's this?" I had quite forgotten that Jennifer was standing next to me!

"Erm, this is Jennifer," I said turning to Jen. "Jen, this Emily and Amy, my daughters."

"Hello Emily, hello Amy," Jen replied.

"Hello Jennifer," the girls said in unison.

"Jen and I used to go to school together when we were only a little older than you are now," I said. "And Jen was also a close friend of your mum," I said, looking at Jen with a reassuring smile. She smiled back at me.

"So, you knew Mummy?" asked Amy. Before answering, Jen again looked at me. I nodded.

"Yes, I knew your mum. We were friends when she was at university," said Jen softly.

"Where are my manners, Sorry. Jen this is Martyna, my-, who helps me with the girls. Martyna, this is Jennifer," I said. I'm not sure why I had hesitated to introduce Martyna as my live-in nanny! Stupid really, but maybe I thought of Martyna as much more than that. The two women exchanged hellos and shook each other's hands.

"Well look, I had better get going George," Jen said, looking at her watch.

"Can we give Jennifer a lift," asked Emily. I thought this was rather sweet of Emily as she had never met Jennifer before.

"No, it's okay, I have my car in the car park, but thank you Emily for the thought. It was lovely to meet you all. Have a wonderful weekend with your dad," replied Jen. Martyna must have sensed something in Jen's voice, a need to 'exit the scene' quickly.

"Come on girls, let's get a bottle of water for the drive home. Nice to meet you Jennifer," she said and ushered the girls to the nearest WH Smiths.

"You can see Cheryl in both of them," said Jen sadly as she watched the girls walking away, holding Martyna's hands.

"I know."

"Their eyes, the nose, the mouth."

"I know," I again replied.

"Thanks George. For introducing me as Cheryl's friend. That was nice."

"You were. And much more. I'm sorry things turned out the way they did between you and Cheryl. And if I had known, it would have made no difference to Cheryl and me. We could have all been friends." Jen smiled at me.

"You would have just wanted a threesome, wouldn't you?" she said, as her smile widened. I smiled back and for an absolute mini-second, that's all, I swear, the threesome thought ran through my mind!

Jen and I said our goodbyes with hugs and kisses, and we promised each other to stay in touch. I made my way over to Martyna and the girls and we set off to the car park. Although the girls were excited and were used to me bringing them back gifts from my trips, they never once asked to see what was in my bags. They sat in the back of Martyna's car, chatting and giggling and I sat in the front passenger seat. It felt really good to be home.

"Thanks again for the surprise Martyna. Nobody has ever met me at the airport before. It was fantastic to see the girls. And the posters were great. Thanks again. Oh, and it was great to see you too."

"George, please stop thanking me. Besides, it was as much the girls' idea as mine. It's good to have you home."

"Have you missed me then?" I asked. Martyna, looked to her left at me and smiled, before returning her eyes to the road ahead.

"Of course, I've missed you. I've had to put the rubbish out on my own, a bulb needs replacing in the lounge and the car needs a service." I slowly turned to my right to look at Martyna. She looked to her left and our eyes met. We both smiled.

It was only after I had dropped my bags in the hallway as we entered the house, that the girls realised that maybe they might contain something for them.

"Daddy, it doesn't matter if you didn't, I would still love you anyway, but did you buy us anything from Africa?" said Amy very cutely.

"Amy, you mustn't ask Dad if he bought us anything, he does so much for us anyway," came a frosty, very grown-up riposte from Emily.

"It's okay Emily," I said before turning to Amy. "So, you would still love me anyway, would you?" I said.

"Yes Daddy, certainly," came the immediate response from Amy.

"Well, that's good then. But yes, I have got you guys something. Go and sit in the lounge and I'll be in there in a minute. The girls quickly made their way to the lounge. Martyna had already walked down the hallway to the kitchen and had put the kettle on.

"Coffee George?" she asked as I entered the kitchen.

"Sounds good, please," I replied. "I'm just going to go upstairs and change and sort out my laundry. Won't be long. Meet you in you in the lounge, alright?"

"No problem," Martyna replied and I made my way upstairs. After a few minutes I returned to the lounge with three duty free bags, where the 'ladies' were patiently waiting. Emily and Amy were sitting on the sofa and I sat in between them. Martyna was sitting in one of the armchairs.

"Well ladies, this bag is for you, and this bag in for you," I said, handing the girls their gifts. They excitedly dived into the bags, before pulling out the embroidered cushions.

"Wow Daddy, this is great," said Amy as she looked at the lion cub on the cushion. "I'll call him Simba," she continued.

"And I'm going to call mine Dumbo," added Emily as she looked at the elephant calf on her cushion. "Thank you, Dad."

"You're welcome sweetheart," I replied. The girls then pulled out their pencil cases and the wooden carvings, both of which they were thrilled with. They each said thank you and gave me a kiss and hug before Amy finally noticed the third bag, I had brought into the room with me.

"What's in this bag Daddy?" she asked.

"This bag is for Martyna. Can you give it to her for me?" Amy picked up the bag and walked over to a surprised Martyna.

"Thank you, Amy," she said. "George, you didn't have to buy me anything."

"I know I didn't have to. But I wanted to," I said. Martyna looked into the bag and pulled out the perfume.

"Thank you, George," she said, looking at me with that infectious smile on her face. "How did you know?"

"What is it Martyna?" asked Amy.

"It's my favourite perfume," answered Martyna, before turning to me. "How did you know?" she asked again.

"I could say that I have a 'nose' for perfume and I remembered the aromatic smells as you walk into a room and went around sniffing dozens of bottles until I found the right one. That, of course, would be lying though. You left your current bottle on the kitchen table a few months back and I remembered the distinctive shape of the bottle. All I had to do was describe the bottle to the lady on the perfume counter and hey presto!"

Thank you, George, it's really sweet of you." Martyna got up from the chair and came over to me. She bent down to me and gently kissed me on the cheek. I was somewhat surprised at this and it felt a little awkward, especially in front of the girls. However, the girls, didn't even appear to notice that Martyna had just kissed me on the cheek. They were too busy sitting on their cushions and playing with their new wooden carved animals!

"My pleasure Martyna, you are more than welcome," I replied. Martyna left the lounge and I could hear her walk up the stairs, presumably to put her perfume in her room. "So, girls, what are we going to do today then?" I asked. This brought shrieks of excitement from Emily and Amy as we decided to plan the rest of the day.

Once the dinner things had been cleared away and the girls were upstairs having their showers, I was beginning to feel very tired. It had been a long day and I kept forgetting that I had flown over night back from Johannesburg and therefore had not had a proper night's sleep. In fact, no sleep at all as Jennifer and I had talked for most of the flight. The girls and I had been for a walk in the local park in the afternoon, taking a football with us to have a 'kick about' before coming home and playing a few games of Buckaroo and Jenga. Martyna had her own plans for the afternoon and due to her impending dinner date, had also skipped dinner with us. I knew she would be leaving soon and as much as I tried not to feel too jealous, I somehow did! As I finished tidying up the kitchen and putting everything away, Martyna appeared in the doorway.

"You okay George?" she said.

"Yeah, great. Feeling a little tired now. Will be nice to have an early night and it's always nice to get back into your own bed," I replied.

"Jennifer seemed nice. I bet that was a big surprise, seeing her at the airport and all that. I guess you had a lot to catch up on."

"Yes, we certainly did," I said looking away from Martyna deep in thought about Cheryl and Jen.

"Are you sure you are okay George?" I turned back to Martyna and smiled.

"So, let me have a look at you," I said, trying to change the subject. "Wow! You look stunning Martyna, absolutely stunning," and she did! She was wearing a pale blue, high neck, sleeveless, knee length cocktail dress. She was also wearing the diamond earrings and matching silver chain bracelet that I had given her at Christmas. The dress, although not tight fitting, still accentuated her wonderful figure and because she had somehow styled her hair differently, in essence 'put her hair up' it had the effect of showing off more of her beautiful face. And of course, I could smell the 'Lady Million' perfume that she had on. And to be fair, it was a very fitting name of perfume for her as she I thought she looked like one in a million; a billion actually!

"Thank you, George," she replied. "Are you sure you are okay about me going out tonight, with you being tired and it being your first night home?"

"Of course, Martyna. I'll read to the girls, and get them to bed early, relax with a beer in front of the telly and then get an early night myself. You do remember that I'm taking the girls to the cemetery tomorrow, don't you? You are more than welcome to join us if you would like to."

"Yes, I remember. I would love to come," Martyna replied softly. There was a slight, almost uneasy pause before Martyna continued. "George, do you remember the conversation we had a few weeks back about our feelings for each other?" I turned from cleaning down the kitchen work surface and looked directly at Martyna.

"Yes," I said resignedly, briefly reflecting on it. Again, there was a silent pause.

"I don't have to go out tonight if you-" but before Martyna could finish her sentence I had already replied.

"Of course, you must go out on your date. You never know, this could be the start of something incredibly special, a new beginning, the first chapter of the rest of your life. It could be your last 'first' kiss. And you look amazing Martyna, so I'm sure whoever your date is, will fall instantly head over heels in love with you," I blurted out somewhat sarcastically, ending with a false smile, before averting my gaze from Martyna and returning to my chore of wiping the kitchen surface.

"Ok George. I'm leaving now. Say goodnight to the girls for me and I'll see you later," Martyna replied sadly, and she slowly turned to walk down the hallway to the front door. As soon as she had turned, a bombardment of thoughts entered my mind. What would she have said if I had let her finish her sentence? "I don't have to go out if you-what?" If I am too tired, if I am too jealous, if I am too stupid, if I am too incapable of telling this lovely woman how much I am in love with her? What? Should I run down the hallway and apologise for my less than benevolent behaviour, tell her to have a wonderful time, give her my blessing, not that she needs my blessing. Or should I try to stop her from going out by giving her a big passionate kiss and proclaiming my undying love for her? What did Martyna expect or more importantly want me to do? Did she want me to tell her not to go out on this date? Did she want me to confess my true feelings for her?

In the end, I did and said nothing, hearing only the front door open and close as Martyna left the house. What a fucking idiot I had just been!

After reading to the girls and putting them to bed, I slumped on the sofa with a bottle of beer in hand, taking a large swig before placing it on the coffee table. After reflecting on the conversation with Martyna and my mixed-up emotions, I knew I needed to talk to someone. That someone was Luke. Not just about me and my problems, but also to try and ease his burden of the responsibility that he felt for Cheryl's death. I took out my phone and was about to call him when it rang. I looked at the display and saw the name Barbara.

"Hi Barbara, how are you?"

"Hey George, I'm fine. Just thought I would call to make sure you got back okay. How was it?"

"Thanks Barbara, it was all good. I met some nice people and I think the company will have a great opportunity to expand in the region."

"Sounds exciting! Glad it was a good trip. I bet the girls were glad to see you?"

"Yes, and Martyna brought them to the airport to meet me. It was so nice seeing them excitedly running over to me as I came through the arrival's hall. We've been for a walk this afternoon and played games. Oh, and tomorrow we are going to visit Cheryl." I replied.

"That's nice George, say hello from me and tell her dad and I will visit during the week," Barbara said mournfully.

"So, how's Derek, all okay?"

"Yes, he's fine, pottering around the garden, moaning about the state of the world and generally getting under my feet. So yes, all good!"

"Glad to hear it."

"George, the other reason I'm calling is I was wondering if we could have the girls next weekend; I could pick them up from school on the Friday and they can stay Friday and Saturday night. You can drive up on Sunday afternoon, stay for tea. Bring Martyna if you want to. We haven't had them here for a while and we miss them terribly. What do you think?"

"Sounds like a plan Barbara. I've got no problems with it."

"And maybe you can go out with Luke and Sally. I don't think you've been out for a while George. You need to get out there and have some fun!" Fortunately, Barbara had no idea of the fun I had just had with Jana over the previous week!

"Yeah, maybe. I was about to call Luke when you rang, so I'll see if they are available next week."

"If not, maybe you can take Martyna out for dinner?" came a slightly 'fishing' response from Barbara. I smiled to myself at the thought of taking her to dinner. That would be nice if it ever happened!

"I'll call you in the week to firm up the arrangements," I said changing the subject.

After a few minutes of general chit chat, we ended our call and I again turned my thoughts to Luke. I pressed his speed dial number on my phone.

"Hey Luke, how are you doing?" I asked as Luke answered my call.

"Hey George, great to hear from you mate. You're back then. How was it?" I had previously told him in a quick text that morning that I was back from a trip to Africa and would call him in the evening.

"Yeah, all good mate, all good. Listen I was wondering if you've got time for a quick chat and a beer after work on Monday?"

"Erm, well I've got some shit to do, but hey fuck it! I'll move some things around. Always have time for my 'homie!' You okay though?"

"Yeah, fine. It's just we haven't seen each other for a while and I'm missing my dose of intellectual conversation with you. You know, about football, cricket, girls, top ten female celebrity arses and other such hot topics of the day," I replied. Luke laughed.

"Great. Well look, I'll meet you in the 'usual' at about 5:45 p.m. - is that okay for you?"

"Sounds great. See you then mate, take care." We ended the call and in some respects, I felt some relief. I knew that Luke was the one person who would understand what I am going through right now and would be able to give me some advice. It also felt good that I would hopefully be able to finally put his mind at rest regarding Cheryl. I switched on the television and continued to drink my beer, flicking in between channels. I finally settled on a channel showing an old comedy film called 'Stir Crazy' starring Gene Wilder and Richard Pryor. I had seen it many times but as I wasn't going to be up long, it was an easy enough watch that didn't require my full attention.

I awoke to the movement of my arm and looked up to see Martyna gently shaking it.

"You must have fallen asleep George," she softly said, smiling at me and looking at me through her gorgeous green eyes.

"God, sorry Martyna," I said in a slight daze. "What time is it?"

"A little after 1 a.m. You should probably get to bed."

"Martyna," I said still looking into her eyes. "I want to apologise to you. My behaviour before you went out this evening was terrible. You didn't deserve that. I hope you can forgive me?"

"Nothing to forgive George," Martyna whispered to me and again a broad smile ran across her face. "I understand," she continued.

"Did you have a nice time?" I asked somewhat tentatively.

"Yes." Upon hearing her reply, I was overcome with a profound sense of dejection. Martyna continued "Jack is a nice man; we have a lot in common and he was a gentleman the whole night. We had a lovely meal, then went for a few drinks at a late-night bar. He was attentive, made me feel at ease, he is extremely good looking and I would be a fool not to see him again. But-, do I feel about Jack, the way I feel about you? No," she said, shaking her head.

There was a slight pause before she again continued. "I'm tired George, I think it's time for bed." Martyna helped me up from the sofa, kissed me on the cheek and left the lounge. I sat back down on the sofa and remained there for a good five minutes, gathering my thoughts, and trying to make sense of everything. It was too late in the day to for me to really take in all the thoughts running around in my mind, so I decided to head up to bed. Tomorrow was another day and hopefully a day that would bring me some sense of clarity. Talking to Cheryl might help. But I needed to make things right with Martyna one way or the other. If she indeed would let me.

28

Not surprisingly, I didn't sleep too well and was up early on the Sunday morning. I took a quick shower and headed downstairs to the kitchen in my shorts and vest top. Once there, I made a fresh pot of coffee and sat at the kitchen table lost in my thoughts. It was a little after 6:30 a.m. when I heard footsteps coming down the stairs. I looked up at the doorway waiting to find out who it was. To my surprise and I have to say, a little bit of relief, it was Emily.

"Morning Dad."

"Morning sweetheart," I quietly said back to her. "Come and sit here and give me a cuddle," I continued and beckoned Emily over to me to sit on my lap. We had a tight hold of each other and it felt really good to cuddle with her.

"Why are you up so early Dad?" Emily finally said after letting me go.

"I think my body clock is upside down because I missed a night's sleep when I flew back from Johannesburg."

"Is that what they call 'jetlag?'" asked Emily.

"Yes. How did you know that?"

"I heard you telling Mum that one time when you came back from a trip to America." I smiled at her.

"Anyway, what are you doing up so early?"

"I couldn't sleep very well either."

"Why, was you thinking about something?"

"Yes."

"Was it Mummy?"

"No."

"No! Well do you want to tell me what it was? Maybe I can help," I said hoping to comfort Emily somewhat.

"Martyna went on her blind date last night, didn't she?"

"Yes," I said, wondering where this was leading.

"I wonder if she had a nice time?" Emily said gazing out across the kitchen as if in some sort of trance.

"I think she did," I replied. "Why do you ask?" Emily turned to face me.

"Because I am scared that if she finds someone and falls in love with them, that she will not want to be our nanny anymore. And we would have to start all over again," Emily said with a heavy heart.

"Oh sweetheart," I said cuddling her back up to me. "We can't prevent Martyna from finding someone to love and having a wonderful future, just because we want her to be our nanny. Martyna is an amazing person and we all love her very much. But she too, deserves happiness and I'm sure that even if she did meet a man, fell in love with him and decided to move on with her life, she would always keep in touch with you and Amy."

"And you Dad, and you."

"Maybe me too. But the point is, things change over time and we can't stop situations from developing just because we want them to stay the same. That wouldn't be fair. And anyway, one day, you and Amy are going to be all grown up and want to leave me to go and live your own lives too. That's what happens. But it doesn't mean we won't still see each other and talk to each other and still love each other."

"But it's not fair. We lose Mum, find Martyna and then lose Martyna."

"Did you feel like this when I called last week and you said that 'Martyna's are not replaceable either' when we were talking about the broken glass?"

"Yes. I don't want Martyna to leave. Amy and I are a bit worried about it."

"Look Emily, first of all, it was a 'first date' last night. Even if the guy that Martyna met turns out to be someone that she would like to get to know much better, these things take time. She is not going to leave us anytime soon, I'm quite sure of that. So, you have nothing to worry about right now, and really nothing to worry about at all. We all love Martyna being here, but she is not our slave or pet. She is a lovely, kind, generous person who will at some stage find someone to share her life with and will eventually move on from being your nanny. And when that day happens, we will all be happy for her and thankful for the time she spent with us. Please don't worry about it, Emily." We hugged again.

"Why can't you marry Martyna, Dad?" came a muffled reply from Emily. We disengaged our hug and I looked at Emily and gave her a warm smile. Before I could answer, Emily continued. "I've seen the way you look at her, I know you like her. And I've seen the way Martyna looks at you. I know Martyna would not be a replacement for Mum, but she makes Amy and me happy, and I think she makes you happy too. Isn't that enough Dad, I mean, to marry someone?" I looked at my little girl in amazement! When did she become so grown up and perceptive about the things going on around her? I was taken aback and was struggling to find the right words to respond to Emily, who had quite clearly worked out an obvious solution to her problem!

"Happiness is a very big and important part of the reason why two people decide to get married. But it is not the only reason. Love, compatibility, physical attraction, and lots of other things also play a part. Sometimes, these things are instant; as soon as you meet someone, you immediately know these things and have these feelings.

Sometimes, they grow stronger over time. And sometimes, they fade over time. Martyna certainly makes me happy as she also makes you happy. But all the other things and feelings also need to be there. And most importantly, need to be felt by both people. It can't just be one-sided."

"But do you feel that way about Martyna?" said Emily. I paused, again smiled at Emily, and drew her in close to me.

"I think I need to get the breakfast going," I said, changing the subject.

"Dad!" came a disappointing response from Emily.

"Morning George, morning Emily," said Martyna as she entered the kitchen. It took me by surprise! I had no idea how long Martyna had been there and if she had listened to any of the conversation that Emily and I had just had.

"Morning Martyna," I said somewhat startled. "Coffee is freshly brewed if you want a cup?"

"Thanks, I will," Martyna replied and she sat down at the kitchen table. I slid Emily on to the chair next to me and made my way to the coffee pot, pouring Martyna a cup.

"Morning Martyna," said Emily. "Did you have a nice time last night?"

"Yes, thank you Emily. I did," Martyna replied before looking at me and smiling. She then returned to Emily. "You look tired Emily, why are you up so early?"

"Yes, I am a bit tired. Maybe I'll go back to bed and see if I can sleep some more." Emily got up and went back upstairs. I brought Martyna's coffee over to the table and placed it in front of her before sitting in the chair opposite.

"Again, I'm really sorry about yesterday Martyna. I feel terrible, embarrassed and a little foolish. Please accept my apology?"

"There is no need to apologise, but it is accepted, so no more needs to be said," came the gracious response from Martyna who continued to look at me and smile.

"Thank you. So, how was it really, the date? Jack, I think you said his name was. Do you think you will see him again?" I said getting up from the table and walking over to the coffee pot to refill my cup.

"I heard your conversation with Emily."

"Did he take you somewhere nice? I'm sure he did, after all you looked stunning last night and-," I continued.

"I heard your conversation with Emily," Martyna repeated, stopping me in my tracks. I stood there frozen, coffee cup in hand, with my back to Martyna. The silence was deafening and appeared to continue for an age!

"Sorry Martyna," I finally replied, still with my back to her. "Emily was worried about you leaving her and Amy."

"And you George, are you worried about me leaving you?" Once again, the silent pause was excruciating. I slowly turned around to face Martyna. She was still smiling at me and looking deep into my eyes as she sat there in her pyjamas clasping her coffee cup.

"Can we talk about this later?" I slowly asked her. "Maybe when the girls are in bed and over a glass of wine?"

"Of course, George," Martyna replied, still smiling. "And please, let's not make it spoil our day. Everything is okay," she continued. "I'm going to have a shower and get dressed. Are you making breakfast?"

"Yes, full English okay with you?"

"Perfect George. I like a full English," she replied with an air of suggestiveness. "Although I should be looking after my figure," she continued as she got up from the chair, extended her arms and did a full 360-degree turn, to show off her body. And what a body it was! Martyna then left the kitchen.

"Martyna!" I called out to her just before she exited, "thank you," I said. She turned to me, smiled, and then carried on upstairs.

Following her shower, Martyna arrived back in the kitchen and we worked as a team to prepare the breakfast. We talked normally and my fear of an uneasy atmosphere was unfounded. The girls arrived in the kitchen for breakfast at about 8:30 a.m. - Emily having got another ninety minutes of sleep!

Following breakfast and clearing away everything, Martyna said she had some paperwork to catch up on and would be in her room. The girls and I went into the garden and they helped me tidy up a few of the flower beds and clear away the dead branches from the three small trees we had. We managed to fill two large garden waste bags, ready for collection by the council for the following week.

Following a light lunch, we made our way over to the cemetery. Amy held on tightly to the picture that she had painted of her mum as we all walked towards Cheryl's grave. Emily and Amy went first, talking to their mum while Martyna and I again, sat on the nearby bench. Although I couldn't hear exactly what the girls were saying to Cheryl, it did seem like they were fully engaged in conversation. They appeared happy and I think it helped Amy so much with her recent spell of missing her mum.

"It's lovely to see the girls so comfortable talking their mum like this, George. I am sure it helps them cope much better with everything that they are going through," said Martyna.

"Yes, I'm sure it does. And I know I have thanked you before, but I really do appreciate your help in letting them talk to you about their mum as well."

"It's no problem at all. I'm glad they want to," Martyna replied, fixing her gaze on the girls. "And just so you know George, if ever you wanted to talk about your wife to me, I'm only too pleased to listen. It's a terrible thing for the girls to deal with, but it must be exactly the same for you. I can't imagine what you must be going through. I know you have Barbara and Derek, Luke, and Sally to talk to. But if you need someone else, I'm here for you," she continued, still fixed on the girls. I turned to my left to face Martyna.

"Thank you Martyna," I said gratefully. Martyna turned to her right to face me and flashed her wonderful smile at me, before returning to look at the girls.

After a good twenty minutes, the girls had finished talking to their mum, so they came over to the bench where Martyna and I were sitting.

"How did Mummy like your painting Amy?" I asked.

"I think she liked it a lot. And she liked that I painted it with her smiling."

"She did like it a lot, you did a really good painting Amy," added Emily, in a supportive, and now customary 'big sisterly' way.

"Did you tell Mummy about the garden this morning, and how well you both did in helping me tidy up?" I asked.

"Yes," said Emily. "Mum said she could see us and that it looked lovely when we had finished. I also told Mum about breaking the glass, but she was okay about it as it was an accident."

"Do you want to talk to Mummy, Martyna?" asked Amy.

"Yes, I will." Martyna got up from the bench and walked towards the grave. Amy and Emily sat either side of me on the bench.

"I hope Mummy tells her to stay with us," whispered Amy. I smiled at her and then pulled them both close to me for a cuddle. A few minutes passed and Martyna returned to the bench.

"Okay girls, shall we have a look at the flowers and give your dad some time on his own with you mum?" Martyna asked Emily and Amy. I looked at Martyna and thanked her. As the girls left and wandered off with Martyna in tow, I got up from the bench and headed over to Cheryl's grave.

"Hi Sweetheart. We've all been missing you a lot. I know the girls have had some difficult times recently, particularly Amy. But Emily too in her own way, even though she has tried to be brave and help Amy as much as she possibly could. I couldn't be prouder of them both as I'm sure you are too. I hope you liked Amy's painting. I think it captured you beautifully, especially the lovely big smile. The girls both have your smile so in a way, I still see yours every day."

I placed the red roses I was carrying into the vase replacing the old dying ones and sat down next to Cheryl's headstone.

"I had an exciting week last week. As you probably know, I had sex with Jana. I won't lie to you, it was good, great in fact. But it doesn't come close to what we had. I hope you understand why it happened. I'm only a man, with all the faults that come with that. I shouldn't have let it go that far with Jana, especially as I had, well-, you know, had sex with Fiona as well. God, I sound like a sex addict! And yes, I also have strong feelings for Martyna. I think I have a difficult conversation coming up with her tonight. I don't know what to do about any of it. I know you would want me to be happy and to get on with my life and meet someone new and build a new life for the girls. But it is awfully hard. It's hard trying to do the right thing for the girls. I don't want them to get close to people in my relationships only for the relationship to end and then the girls feel abandoned again. Not that you abandoned us! But you saw how Emily reacted to Martyna's date. Both of them have grown fond of Martyna. They are already worried about her not being here anymore, of losing her. How can I start a new relationship with anyone, knowing that if the relationship fails, it could be devastating to Emily and Amy? And how can I ask anyone to take on the responsibility of two young children? It's complicated sweetheart, and I don't have the answers."

I looked up from my sitting position and saw Martyna and the girls busily chatting and walking in and out of the graves. They seemed extremely happy together.

"I'm going to see Luke tomorrow, after work for a drink, you know in our local. Hopefully, he can give me some advice. Jen told me that he still feels guilty about what happened as he was the one that told you I had met Jen, the night before your accident. I'll try to put his mind at ease about that. And speaking of Jen - she told me all about you and her. I'm so sorry sweetheart, sorry that you couldn't tell me yourself. I'm sorry that you didn't feel secure enough in our relationship to unburden yourself by telling me this secret. It would have made no difference at all to us, how I felt about you and how I still feel about you. I blame myself. I'm sorry for whatever it was I said or did, that made you not trust me with this. But I want you to know that Jen told me it was a beautiful, loving, gentle experience for her and one she would always treasure. I know how she feels sweetheart because that's how I feel about what we had too." I stood up and looked down at Cheryl's headstone deep in thought.

"Miss you so much darling," I said smiling and a tear started to fall from my right eye. "Love you always and can't wait to see you again one day." As always when I visited Cheryl, I kissed my fingers and touched her headstone with them, lingering just a little longer this time. I looked up and saw Martyna and the girls coming towards me and quickly wiped the tear from my face.

The girls said their goodbyes to Cheryl and we made our way back to the car park. Emily and Amy walked ahead of Martyna and I, and although it was only a short walk back to the car, the silence made it seem longer.

"Are you okay George?" a concerned Martyna finally whispered as we approached the car. She could tell I was deep in thought and I think wanted to let me know that she was there for me.

"Yes, I'm fine. Thanks for asking," I replied.

We arrived back home and everyone was feeling a little tired. Amy asked if we could all watch a Disney film, which was met with squeals of delight by Emily and I have to say, Martyna seemed quite enthusiastic too! It was decided by a vote of three to one (me being the one!) that we would watch Pete's Dragon! It was the film version, not the cartoon and although the girls had seen it before, they seemed to like the film because I think they somehow identified with the little orphan Pete. We all sat on the sofa, the girls in the middle of Martyna and me.

"I will have to start making the dinner soon, but you guys can continue watching, okay?" I said before the film started.

"Daddy, I don't want you to miss the film. And I don't want you to have to make dinner for us," said Amy. "And even though we love your roast dinners, can we have Pizza instead?" I looked at Amy in surprise! Then I looked at Emily and Martyna in turn. They all appeared very eager for me to agree about forgetting 'making' dinner and ordering pizza instead!

"Ok then," I finally agreed after leaving an appropriate amount of suspense time!

Once the film had finished and the pizzas had arrived, we all sat around the kitchen table and enjoyed our meal. The conversation was flowing and Amy was asking all sorts of questions about dragons! Everyone appeared in a happy mood.

"By the way girls, I talked to Nanny yesterday and she was wondering if you wanted to spend next weekend with her and Grandad at their house. She said she could pick you up from school on Friday, and I could come and pick you up on Sunday. What do you think?"

"Yeah!" came the excited reply from both Emily and Amy.

"I'll let her know during the week. Martyna, can you let the girls' teachers know that their grandmother will be picking them up on Friday?"

"No problem, George," Martyna replied.

"Thanks. Oh, and Barbara said that if you would like to come with me on the Sunday to pick them up and stay for 'Sunday tea', you are more than welcome."

"Erm, let's see about that as I'm not sure what I'm doing," Martyna replied and after checking that the girls were not looking, whispered to me 'Let's talk later.' I acknowledged Martyna with a nod of my head in agreement.

"And one last thing," I said. "I am meeting Luke tomorrow after work for a chat as I haven't seen him for some time, so I won't be in for dinner tomorrow."

"That's alright Dad, we can cope without you," came a cheeky response from Emily!

"Oh, can you!" I replied and we all laughed.

"Daddy, I have something for Ben. As we have so many cuddly toys now, I thought I could give Ben my turtle, can you take it tomorrow to give to Luke?" said Amy. The cuddly turtle was a present I had brought back from 'Sea World' in Florida while on a business trip to the catering facility in Orlando.

"That's extremely sweet and kind of you Amy. I'm sure little Ben will love it."

"Yes, and he can also have my dolphin," added Emily.

"Thank you, girls," I replied and immediately felt an overwhelming sense of pride of my two girls.

After clearing away dinner, the clock ticked around fast and before I knew it, I was tucking the girls into bed and wishing them a good night's sleep. As I made my way downstairs, I could feel a churning in my stomach. What on earth was I going to say to Martyna? I entered the kitchen and saw Martyna sitting at the kitchen table, deep in thought. As she noticed me, she looked up and smiled.

"All done?" she said.

"Yes, all done. I think they will sleep well tonight, especially with a tummy full of pizza!" Martyna laughed. "Do you want a glass of wine? Red or white?"

"I'll have a 'white' please," answered Martyna. I opened a bottle of South African Chardonnay and poured two glasses, placing them down on the kitchen table. I took the chair opposite Martyna and after a quick 'chink' of the glasses, a cheers and a sip of the crisp, fruity wine, I placed my glass down on the table and looked at Martyna.

"So, here we are," I said just wondering what to say and how to begin this conversation.

"Yes, here we are," came Martyna's response.

"I'm not sure what you heard this morning when I was talking to Emily, so it means I'm really not sure where to start this conversation."

"I just want to say George, that I wasn't deliberately listening in on your conversation with Emily. I couldn't sleep last night either and when I came downstairs this morning, I heard Emily talking to you about my date last night, and the sadness in her voice about the possibility of me leaving, was upsetting for me. It somehow compelled me to continue listening. I'm sorry for that."

"No need to apologise Martyna. Yes, Emily is worried that you might leave us. I think you know exactly how the girls feel about you. As Emily said, you will never be Cheryl, but they think of you as their mum. They look up to you, they are so happy in your company and you have brought them comfort at a time when they are feeling all sorts of mixed emotions. It's a comfort, that unfortunately I can't give them. And maybe that's because I'm too close to the situation we find ourselves in. I sometimes think that they see me as a constant reminder that their mum isn't here anymore. They have memories of us as a family, all of us together. They feel something, someone is missing. When they are with you, it's different. Because we didn't know you until after Cheryl was gone, there is no reminder for the girls about their mum when you are with them. They relax with you. You make them feel safe and secure; in some respect you make them forget the tragedy in their life. You bring the best out of them."

"George, I'm not leaving. Well not leaving anytime soon."

"That's good to hear, thanks," I replied and smiled back at Martyna.

"It makes me happy that the girls feel that way about me. I love them dearly; but I would never want them to think of me as a replacement for their mum. I'm glad Emily and Amy know that. And you are too hard on yourself George. You give them so much comfort and reassurance. I think their only anxiety is the fear that you might also not be there for them one day and not through any fault of yours, but an accident, like their mother's. They love you unconditionally. You make them laugh, you're interested in what they do, what they have to say. You treat them well, you read to them, you instil in them the importance of good manners and good behaviours. You love them. Please don't ever feel you are not doing a great job as a parent, because you are."

"Thank you Martyna," I softly replied.

"But George, I heard more than that this morning. I heard you say that I deserve happiness, and that I will one day find someone to share my life with."

"Yes, I did say that. And I meant it. I just wanted Emily to understand that you have your own life to live, a life that will not include us and we have no right to prevent that in anyway. We should all be happy for you and just enjoy the time that we do have with you."

"You said to Emily that we 'can't stop situations from developing just because we want things to stay the same.' Our situation is developing George, and I get the impression you fear that and therefore, want things to remain the same?" replied Martyna. I took a sip of wine and placed it back down on the table.

"You know why, Martyna. You know I can't risk the girls' happiness."

"But if the girls fear me leaving anyway, does it really matter if I meet someone like Jack, fall in love with him, get married and have a wonderful life-, or, fall in love with you?" I looked up from my glass at Martyna, her green eyes piercing into mine.

"Martyna-,"

"Emily knows how I feel, she told you she has noticed the way I look at you. She also told you she has noticed how you look at me. She knows, George."

"She's become very mature over the last few months, that one," I said with a smile.

"She asked you if happiness was enough of a reason to get married. You replied by saying it needed other things, like love, compatibility and physical attraction."

"I know, and I truly believe that."

"You said that most importantly, these feelings needed to be felt by both people. Emily asked you if you felt these things for me-, and you didn't answer."

"I-,"

"It's okay George,"

"No, it's not okay. But the reason I didn't answer is because I didn't want to build any expectation with Emily that could potentially be false."

"I understand George. And I'm not pushing you for an answer right now. In fact, one of the reasons I entered the kitchen this morning when I did was to prevent Emily from pushing you further for an answer. But I want you to know that the 'other person' does feel that way-, about you." Martyna again smiled at me before lifting her glass and taking a large gulp of wine. I think it took a lot of courage for her to say these things and the wine was a justifiable reward for getting the words out.

"What about Jack and Zak, and Mack, Crack and Flack, and all these other blind dates that your friend keeps setting up for you?" I said. We both let out a comical sigh.

"You don't need to worry about that," Martyna said and stood up from her chair. "I'm going to have a shower and then I'm going to bed George. All I'm asking is that you think about us. Think about the possibility, think about your feelings and then maybe we can talk some more. Good night George, sleep well." Martyna, turned and left the kitchen.

I got up from my chair and poured myself another glass of wine, taking it through to the lounge and sat on the sofa. Now what? Last week in South Africa, I said to myself that I needed to do some serious thinking when I got back home. Well, I certainly did now! Jana was out of the picture but Fiona was still very much in my mind. And of course, the lovely Martyna. It was undoubtedly time for me to start making some decisions about my life, my future and most importantly the girls future. Any decision I made would have to made with the girls' best interests at heart. Even if that meant sacrificing my own happiness. But I would wait to see what advice I would get from Luke first. And should I seek advice from elsewhere too? Maybe Barbara? Maybe Derek? No not Derek! Sarah? Tanja? Even Nigel! No, but maybe Jennifer? Yes, Jennifer would understand my situation the most. Maybe she would be the only person to give me sound advice. I finished my wine and went to bed early.

29

I arrived at the office on Monday morning and was immediately met by Sarah as I exited the elevator.

"Morning George. So glad you're back, it was totally boring last week. To be honest, I almost asked for some time off!"

"Morning Sarah, good to see you," I replied. "Well, if you were bored last week, I can guarantee you won't be this week. We have a lot to do and I'm counting on your support." I walked past her and she followed on behind until we had reached my office. Although Sarah's skirts appeared to have grown a few inches in length, her tight fitting, low cut tops that revealed her ample breasts, were still very much in evidence and still very much admired by me!

"Coffee George?" asked Sarah as I entered my office.

"Yes, thank you Sarah. Listen, I'm going to need this morning to gather my thoughts about last week, and I also have a half hour introduction meeting with the new girl, Melanie. So, can you look at my schedule for this afternoon and block an hour's meeting for us, so I can go over what we need to do?"

"No problem, George. I'm on it," replied Sarah as she made her way over to the coffee station.

I sat down at my desk, pulled out my laptop, inserted it into its docking station and waited for it to spring into life. I then got this strange feeling that I was being watched! I looked up to see Frank standing in my doorway.

"Hi Frank, come in," I said.

"Morning George. Time for a quick chat?"

"A very 'quick' chat Frank, I have a lot of work to do." Frank entered my office closing the door behind him and sat down across the desk from me.

"So how was it?"

"How was what?" I replied pretending not to know what he was talking about. Frank let out a long disappointing sigh.

"You know what I'm talking about. The trip last week, how was it?"

"Just fucking with you Frank, that's all," I said with a big smile on my face. "Yes, it went very well. I think we have a fantastic opportunity in both cities. Different set ups in terms of either 'JV' or full purchase, but all extremely positive. But I need to put a proposal together this week and present it to the board next week in Frankfurt. Therefore, I'm going to need Sarah's support. Is that okay?"

"Sure, there's not much going on right now, so she's yours for however long you need her," replied Frank. There was a knock on my door and Sarah entered with two coffees.

"I thought you might like one too Frank?" she said placing the cups down on my desk. "Anything else I can help you with George?" she said leaning over my desk and exposing the top half of her breasts.

"Not right now, thank you Sarah."

"Well let me know if you do need anything. Oh, and I've set our meeting for 3 p.m. Is that okay with you?"

"Perfect, thank you again."

"My pleasure George," Sarah replied exiting my office and shutting the door behind her.

"She definitely wants you George, you do know that don't you?" said Frank.

"No. She does want something, but I don't think it is me. Anyway, as I said, I have a lot to get on with, so…" I said trying to indicate to Frank that our chat was over.

"How was Nigel, snivelling little prick that he is?"

"Funny you should ask that really."

"Why? Did he fuck up? Did Victor call him back early? Don't tell me you two got into a 'bitching' session with each other?" Frank said excitedly.

"Well, he did 'fuck up' and we did have a long, loud but very honest conversation with each other in the hotel bar one night. However, he made amends for his 'mistake' and took to heart my comments. By the end of the trip, he became a particularly useful resource for us. A better person, a changed man, if you like! We got on really well." There was silence and Frank sat there opened mouthed in shock. The silence didn't last too long.

"Fuck off!" was Frank's response. I couldn't help myself and laughed out loud. "You're telling me that you, you," Frank repeated to emphasise the point, "and Nigel, got on! What - like 'friends'," and he used his two index fingers to reiterate the word friends.

"Well, sort of. I know how it sounds and God knows, if you had told me that it would happen before I had left for Addis, I would have asked you to stop smoking the weed and lay off the 'shisha.'"

"But, but, but he's a total arsehole! A git, a twat, a fucking dick, a complete fucking idiot!" I lost it and had to laugh again. Frank getting upset must be one of the funniest things to see in the whole word! This normally calm, articulate guy, precise in his choice of words, being reduced to a foul mouthed, fumbling lunatic who could give Mrs Hansen lessons! Absolutely priceless and something any comedy writer would pay thousands to witness.

"Stop Frank, please," I said through my tears of laughter, "you're killing me."

"And you think it's funny!" Frank continued.

"Listen," I said through my laughter. "He is a changed man, well, at least he was last week. But let's say that he remains this changed person. It could work to your advantage. It might be that he thinks more clearly now and not just about himself, do you see what I'm saying?" Frank looked away and thought for a few seconds before returning his gaze back to me.

"Ah! You mean-,"

"Yes, it might be a good thing to have a 'changed' Nigel!"

"Thanks George. Keep me posted eh!" said a smiling Frank as he got up from his chair, picked up his coffee cup and headed for the door. "And George," he said turning just before leaving my office, "are you sure it's not you that has been smoking something?" I smiled and he left.

The next couple of hours went by quickly as I drafted out a structure for the two deals in readiness for my meeting with Sarah later in the afternoon. At 10:30 a.m. Sarah walked into my office.

"Melanie is here for her introduction meeting; shall I send her in?"

"Yes, thanks Sarah."

"I'll organise the coffees for you George."

"Thanks again Sarah, you know me too well!"

"Not quite well enough, but I'm working on it!" she quickly replied with a sexy wink of her eye! "Oh, and by the way, Melanie has already had an accident this morning, be gentle with her."

"I always am - accident? What accident?" I said looking up from my desk.

"I'll let her explain," said Sarah as she went to get Melanie.

As Mel walked into my office, I could see this huge bandage on her right-hand index and middle fingers. It looked like something out of an old cartoon, to emphasis the enormity of an injury and exacerbate the feeling of pain.

"Good morning George, sorry I can't shake your hand," said Mel as she approached my desk.

"Please come in, take a seat. What have you done there?" I replied. Mel sat down and Sarah followed her in and placed two coffees on my desk.

"A bit of a stupid thing really. My mum bought me a small cactus plant as a sort of present for my first day. You know, to put on my desk. Well, I had it in my handbag and forgot it was there. So, when I arrived this morning and Gavin showed me to my desk, I just instinctively reached into my handbag for my notebook and pen, and - well, stabbed the hell out of my fingers. The blood was everywhere! Looked like a scene from the 'Texas Chainsaw Massacre.' And well, I did unfortunately let out a chorus of swearing, which I have apologised for."

"I never heard a thing," I said.

"It was when you had your door shut and was talking to Tanja on the phone," added Sarah.

"And it was only the quick thinking of Sarah here, that saved me from getting blood all over my clothes," Mel continued. I looked up at Sarah, and she nodded in agreement.

"What was the obscenity, if you don't mind me asking?" I enquired.

"Erm, well, it was kind of-" stuttered Mel.

"What the fuck was that! Jesus Christ! Bollocks-, shit!" Mel's sentence was eloquently completed by Sarah, in perfect adaptation of the incident. We all laughed out loud.

Sarah left me and Mel to our meeting and luckily, Mel had no other 'incidents' for the rest of the day. I liked Mel. I liked her attitude; I liked the way that nothing fazed her and I liked her honest approach. I was glad she had joined the team and had a great feeling that she would become an asset for the company.

My meeting with Sarah in the afternoon also went very well. I gave her an outline of the proposals and asked her to 'put the meat' to the bones that I had prepared, leaving out the numbers as these would be completed next week when I meet up with Jana and Heinz. Sarah understood the requirements and liked the fact that she had some 'license' to prepare the offers in her own style. She again thanked me for giving her an opportunity to prove to others her capabilities and for the trust I had placed in her. I was only too pleased to help and again had a great feeling about her future career with the company. She was very bright, talented and could turn her hand to anything. You just needed to look beneath the surface to reveal her vast depth of skills, knowledge, and intelligence. Sarah was a fantastic girl and someday soon, someone was going to take her seriously in both her professional and personal life. And she would be thoroughly deserving of that opportunity.

I left the office just before 5 p.m. drove home and parked the car. I popped my head in to say hello to the girls and Martyna and picked up the cuddly turtle and dolphin for little Ben that had been kindly donated by Emily and Amy, before making my way to 'Mulligans' to meet with Luke. Everyone seemed happy and I could smell the sausage and bean casserole that Martyna had made for dinner. Martyna promised to save me some for when I later returned from the pub. I was running a little late so assumed Luke would already be there. As I entered Mulligans, I immediately saw Luke standing at the bar talking to Samantha.

"Hey Luke," I said as I walked up to the bar.

"Hello mate," came Luke's warm reply and we embraced in our typical manly hug.

"Hi George," said Samantha, "Usual?"

"Hi Samantha, yes please," I replied.

"If you want to take a seat, I'll bring it over, we're not busy at the moment," Samantha continued, pointing to our usual table by the window.

"Thanks Samantha," I said as Luke picked up his two thirds full pint of Stella and we made our way over to the table and sat down.

"So how are you mate?" said Luke.

"Yeah, good. But I have some things I would like to talk to you about."

"Sounds ominous! You okay?"

"Yeah, but before any of that, the girls wanted me to give you this for Ben," I replied smiling and handed Luke a bag containing the turtle and dolphin. After peeking inside the bag, my smile had transmitted to Luke's face.

"That's great. The girls wanted Ben to have these?" he said.

"Yeah. They said that they have far too many and little Ben would probably play more with them than they do! They are growing up fast! Especially Emily. She seems to have matured in the last few months. I know it sounds strange to say that of a girl who's not even nine yet!"

"Ben will love these. Give the girls a big kiss from their Uncle Luke and tell them I said thanks." Samantha then arrived with my drink.

"There you go George. Do you want to open a tab?"

"Yeah, that would be good Samantha, thanks. And take one for yourself."

"Thanks George. I haven't seen you in here for a while. How have you been?" asked Samantha. It was a question that, when most people are asked it, an instant response of 'yeah, fine' almost automatically rolls off the tongue. Even if you have the troubles of the world on your shoulders, that 'yeah, fine' or 'yeah, good' seems to be the default response because you either don't want to talk about your problems, or you are a little embarrassed by them. The trick, however, is to make sure there is no 'noticeable' pause between the question being asked and the response that you give. If there is, it inevitably arouses suspicion of the authenticity of the 'default' response, from the person asking the question or anyone close enough to hear the question! Unfortunately, I had paused a little longer than I should have done.

"Yeah, fine," I replied. Samantha looked at me with concern written all over her face, before turning to Luke.

"Okay guys, I'll leave you to it. If we are not busy, I'll come over later and take your next order okay? Enjoy," Samantha said and returned to the bar.

"You alright mate?" asked Luke.

"Yeah, yes-, I'm fine. But I do want to talk to you about a few things. You're my best mate, have been for twenty odd years. You know me better than anyone. You know my past, my present and I'm hoping you can help me with my future!"

"Fucking hell mate, that sounds serious. You sure you got the right bloke?" Luke replied smiling. I smiled too.

"How's Sally and Ben?" I said trying to lighten the conversation a little bit.

"They're great. Sally is happy with her work, and because her mum is looking after Ben during the day, we don't have to worry about him. And Ben loves his grandma, so all is good. We could have got a nanny like Martyna, well not live in, but a nanny. But it works great with Sal's mum. So, all good! But listen, I get the impression you didn't come here to talk about me and Sally and Ben. What's up mate?"

"Well, I have come to talk to you about 'you' as well, but I'll come to that later," I said before taking a few mouthfuls of Stella. "I'm not really sure where to start! Last Christmas, the second one without Cheryl, I was dreading because of how the year before turned out-,"

"Yeah, I know it was tough, the first one without Cheryl, but I thought you told me that last Christmas was really good? The girls had a great time, no tears and even Barbara and Derek seemed to have a good time?" jumped in Luke.

"Yes, that's right. But I think it was in no small way because of Martyna. We got on well, she helped me so much and it again, felt like a proper family Christmas. I suppose at that time, I started to have some feelings towards her even though she had only been with us for four months. But nothing happened and we continued our 'employer/employee' relationship.

"Right," said Luke, wondering where this was going.

"And then a couple of months ago, I met this girl on a plane to Frankfurt, Fiona. She was a young lady about to start a new life in Frankfurt for an investment banking company-, your line of work. Anyway, you know me, I've told you many times that I hate having to sit next to anyone on a plane and God forbid that someone wants to start a conversation with me. But after about thirty seconds after take-off, she grabbed my leg!"

"What? Just grabbed your leg?"

"Yeah. But let me explain. She was an extremely nervous flyer and there was a slight bit of turbulence and she just, well, just grabbed my leg out of pure fright!"

"You sure it was just your leg?" asked Luke smirking like a naughty schoolboy. I smiled back at him.

"Yes, it was just my leg. Anyway, we struck up a conversation and it turned out she was staying at the same hotel as me, so we had a drink in the evening at the hotel bar."

"Go on," said Luke, his interest and expectation growing.

"Nothing happened, we had a few drinks, well-, actually Fiona had 'quite' a few drinks and I ended up having to put her to bed in her hotel room."

"In 'her' room?"

"Yeah."

"And?"

"And what?"

"And what happened?" answered Luke, slightly frustrated.

"Nothing, as I said, nothing happened. We met at breakfast the next morning, she was a bit embarrassed and we swapped contact details, said we'd keep in touch. That's it!"

"What was she like?" asked Luke.

"Late twenties, blonde hair, slim, very pretty face, large reading glasses, you know 'librarian' style, great breasts." The great breasts comment pricked Luke's interest!

"Nothing happened then?" pressed Luke.

"Well not that time," I replied.

"So, there was another time?"

"Yes. I had to go back a few weeks later and Fiona had asked if she could meet me for dinner. I agreed. I thought why not, she was a lovely girl, we hit it off and I thought it would be a nice evening. And it was."

"Does that mean what I think it means?"

"Well knowing how you mind works, yes, it does!"

"Great! Good for you. Is that the first time-, since, you know, Cheryl?"

"Yeah. So, as you can imagine, I was a bit nervous. But it was great and we both had a fantastic time, so much so, we repeated the performance again in the morning!"

"Lucky bastard! So, what's the problem, she's being demanding? Wants to see you all the time; must be difficult her being in Frankfurt and you in London," continued Luke.

"No. Quite the opposite! Fiona would really like to have a proper relationship with me, as I suppose I would with her. But I explained my situation up front and told her I could not commit to a relationship. She understood and has placed no pressures on me at all. She's a terrific person, fun, lovely and any man would be proud to call her his girlfriend."

"So, what's the problem?"

"Well, there's this other girl, Jana. A young German colleague from Frankfurt. The last couple of times I had been to Frankfurt, she'd been flirting with me. Wearing short skirts, flashing her legs, which, by the way, are gorgeous. You know what, she would call me of an evening and tell me she was sitting in her apartment in her underwear or just stepped out of the shower, naked!" Luke looked at me in astonishment.

"She sounds interesting!"

"Yeah, well, you don't know the half of it. So, the night before I'm supposed to go on last week's business trip to Addis Ababa and Johannesburg with some colleagues, including Jana, she invites me to dinner in Frankfurt. She meets me at the airport but instead of going out for dinner, she takes me back to her place and cooks me dinner."

"Nothing wrong with that," replied Luke.

"No. Except, she goes into the lounge to fix some after dinner drinks while I offer to clear up the kitchen. And when I go into the lounge, she's sitting there in her underwear!"

"Fucking hell!"

"Yeah, fucking hell indeed! We ended up in her bedroom and I'm not even going to begin to describe the night I had with her. All I'll say is, whatever kinky fantasies you might have tucked away in the back of your mind, try multiplying it by one hundred and you'll get some idea of what I'm talking about." Again, Luke looked on flabbergasted and it appeared as if he was thinking about his fantasies and then trying to take it up a notch or two!

"Bloody hell! And this was the night before you went on the business trip with her?"

"Yes. We even carried it on for a few nights during the trip. But each time was different from the first night. Much gentler and much more like 'love making' rather than the frantic sex of the first night."

"So, what you going to do about Jana?"

"Well, that's already taken care of. I had a long chat with her the night before we came back from the trip and she understands that there is no future for us. She is young, wild and wants things in life that I can't give her. Especially having two children to look after."

"Wow, sounds like you had a great time last week."

"Yeah, it was a little awkward at the airport in Johannesburg before we went our separate ways, they were flying back to Frankfurt, while I was on the BA flight to London, but it was okay. And then, you never guess who I met in the BA lounge?"

"No, who?"

"Jennifer Parks!"

"You didn't fuck her in the toilets, did you?" Luke eagerly enquired.

"Luke!" I replied in some amazement.

"Sorry mate, talking about Jana has got my mind all over the place."

"Of course, I didn't 'fuck her' in the toilets. It was great to see her and we sat next to each other on the flight home. She'd been in Jo'burg for a photo-shoot and it was so nice to catch up with her."

"Yeah, it must have been nice. You two go back a long way."

"We do. However, Jen told me a few things on the flight that I never knew before. One of the things she told me was that you still feel responsible for Cheryl. That you think it was your fault for bringing up the coffee I had shared with Jen, the night before Cheryl died." Luke averted his gaze from me and looked down at his pint glass.

"She told you I met her a few months ago, right?" he said solemnly.

"Yeah," I said. "Luke, it's not your fault. Please don't blame yourself. Cheryl died because she was in the wrong place at the wrong time. That's all. Nobody is to blame. The night before - Cheryl and I arguing about Jen, none of that is relevant. I too, blamed myself for a long time. I thought I should not have let Cheryl go to bed that night without us resolving the argument. I didn't and the next day she was gone. But it could have happened even if I did. Nobody is to blame for Cheryl's death, believe me." Luke looked up from his pint at me.

"But if I hadn't been so stupid and mentioned Jen, things would have been so different. I knew from our university days that Cheryl hated Jen and wanted you to stay away from her. I should have just kept my mouth shut. If I had, I'm sure Cheryl would still be here today," Luke replied, his eyes beginning to glaze over.

"Hey mate. That's just not true. And besides, Cheryl didn't hate Jen and didn't want me seeing or talking to her because she thought I would stray. There was another reason." Luke looked at me quizzically.

"What was the reason?" I drank the rest of my pint and looked over to Samantha at the bar. She saw me looking and I indicated to her that I wanted another round. She acknowledged me and again, I turned to Luke.

"On the flight home from Jo'burg, Jen told me the real reason that Cheryl didn't want me to see or talk to her. You see, Jen and Cheryl knew each other before I even knew Cheryl. In fact, they were best friends when I had my brief fling with Jen. And when Jen and I split up, Cheryl sort of comforted Jen."

"Girls do that all the time. If one of them gets dumped by a bloke, they always rally round and take care of each other."

"Yeah, I know. But this was a bit more than just 'taking care' or each other."

"What do you mean George?" I hesitated for a few seconds, wondering if I should really tell Luke.

"They had an affair. A lesbian affair," I said somewhat muted. Luke just stared at me. Samantha arrived with our drinks and removed the empty glasses. She had observed Luke and I just staring at each other and decided not to comment before returning to the bar.

"You mean…" Luke finally replied. I nodded my head.

"Cheryl didn't want me to find out and although Jen promised her, she wouldn't say anything to me, Cheryl didn't believe her. That's why she made me promise not to ever see or talk to Jen.

"So how did Jen tell you something like that? I mean, it's not the sort of thing you just casually slip into a conversation!"

"Jen said that you had told her about Cheryl's accident and when I pressed her on if she knew why Cheryl disliked her so much, she told me. She thought I already knew; that Cheryl must have told me by now. It was a complete shock."

"I bet it fucking was. Jesus George, how do feel about all that?"

"A bit upset actually. Not about Cheryl and Jen and their relationship, but why Cheryl thought she couldn't confide in me. Why she couldn't tell me about it. I would have understood and it would have made no difference to us. Certainly not from my side. And it still makes no difference to how I feel about Cheryl today. But I must have done something or said something terrible for her not to be able to trust me enough to tell me about it. It makes me feel so bad."

"Mate, you can't beat yourself up about this. Cheryl knew you thought she was so perfect, and she was, is! So maybe she just didn't want to shatter your illusions about her."

"But that's my point. It wouldn't have done. I would still have thought she was perfect - perfect in every way. Perfect for me." Luke let out big sigh.

"I wonder if Sal knows?" he said.

"I don't know and to be honest, I'm not sure it's the sort of thing you should be asking her about."

"No, maybe you're right."

"Anyway, we are getting slightly off the point here."

"What do you mean?" asked Luke.

"The point was, is, that you can't blame yourself for what happened. You must promise me Luke, that you stop thinking this way. It wasn't your fault, okay?" Luke smiled at me and nodded his head in agreement. We both took a large mouthful of our freshly presented pints of Stella.

"So where are we with this Fiona, and this Jana sort then?" asked Luke.

"I'm coming back to that one."

"Fuck me George, a lot has happened to you over the last few months, I can't keep up."

"Well wait till you hear the next bit!" I said and took another gulp of beer. "So, when I got home on Saturday, Martyna and the girls met me at the airport, which was great, really nice actually. I was so pleased to see the girls and they had painted 'welcome home Daddy' posters. Really sweet. So, I was in an extremely good mood. But then I remembered that Martyna had told me she was going on a blind date that night. She'd been out on one a few months ago and I was fine about it. It didn't lead to anything anyway, some guy called 'Zak' or something. Anyway, since the first blind date, Martyna and I had had a conversation."

"A conversation? About what?"

"About us. About our feelings towards each other. It was pretty obvious that we had both grown very fond of each other."

"Wow, I bet that was a difficult conversation?"

"Just a bit, yeah. But we talked about it and I told her that because the girls had grown so close to her, which is true, they really have, that I couldn't take the risk of us becoming anything more than employer and employee."

"Why?" asked Luke.

"Well, because if things didn't work out, it would have been awkward in the house and maybe Martyna would have to leave and that would have been bad for the girls," I replied looking at Luke in a way as if to say, 'isn't that obvious?'

"Oh, I see."

"Anyway, this new blind date bothered me. It bothered me a lot to the extent that I was a little bit sarcastic towards her as she left the house that night."

"A little bit?"

"A lot actually. In fact, I was a bit of a shit." I sighed heavily.

"Jealous?"

"Yeah. You see Luke, I think my feelings towards Martyna are more than just being fond of someone. She's fantastic with Emily and Amy. She's gorgeous, has a fantastic sense of humour, intelligent, kind, gentle. She has wonderful body and…"

"You haven't, you know?"

"No, we haven't! You're not really listening, are you?"

"Yes, I am George, but with all the sex you've been getting lately, I just thought you might have forgotten to mention it or something. Sorry mate." I looked at Luke and a smile came over my face as I shook my head in amazement.

"Apology accepted," I said slowly, before continuing. "The thing is, I just don't know what to do. On the one hand there is this beautiful English girl, who I am compatible with both sexually and socially, and I really enjoy her company, who would love to have a serious relationship with me; but unfortunately, she lives in Frankfurt and has no experience of children, let alone my two children. And then, on the other hand there is this equally beautiful Polish girl who I am compatible with socially - don't know yet if we are sexually!" I said to reiterate the point to Luke that Martyna and I had not been intimate. "And I equally enjoy her company, who knows my two children almost as well as I do and also has strong feelings for me; but is my employee and if things didn't work out, it would have a devastating effect on Emily and Amy if she had to leave."

"Does either one, know about the other?" asked Luke. At last, an intelligent question I thought!

"Well, Fiona knows I have a live-in nanny and that's about it. As for Martyna, I haven't told her about sleeping with Fiona."

"Good. And neither of them knows about Jana, I take it?"

"Correct."

"Good, good," mused Luke.

"What are you thinking Luke?" I asked.

"Look George, I know you are an honest lad, sincere and all that. But for now, at least, I think you should keep it that way. Don't tell Martyna about Fiona and don't tell Fiona about Martyna. Oh, and tell neither of them about that little nympho, Jana!"

"What are you saying?" I again enquired.

"If I am understanding this situation correctly, you are in two minds what to do, right?"

"Yes."

"The first option is, keep Martyna as your live-in nanny, looking after the girls and pursue a relationship with Fiona. Positives: the girls continue to have Martyna, someone they have grown fond of who is excellent with them, trustworthy and reliable and you get to have a relationship with someone who you are compatible with, both socially and 'sexually' and because she lives in a different country, the relationship would not be too demanding."

"Ok, and the negatives?"

"The negatives are that Martyna might find someone on a blind date or whatever and leave anyway. This might cause a problem for the girls. And, even if you have Fiona, because you have strong feelings for Martyna, seeing her every day, living in the same house, it's going to drive you crazy, especially if she does find someone else."

"Ok, next option," I said pushing Luke along.

"Option two: Take a chance on Martyna and don't worry about the consequences of things not working out. After all, she might leave anyway! You would need to talk to the girls and it might be a difficult transition, but it could work out very well. You then tell Fiona that you can't continue to see her even as a friend…"

"Why not as a friend?" I interrupted.

"Because you've already had sexual relations with her. If you continue to see her as a friend, she will crop in conversations with Martyna and that could prove awkward."

"I see, but maybe I should be upfront with Martyna in the first place, you know, tell her I slept with Fiona. After all it would have been before Martyna and I get together, right?"

"And how do you think Martyna would feel when you say 'oh, I'm in Frankfurt this week and I'm going to have dinner with my friend Fiona, you know, the girl I slept with before we got together!"

"Yeah, that wouldn't be good I guess," I replied in agreement with Luke.

"Positives: You and the girls have someone in your lives that you already know, someone that you have all grown fond of over time. Negatives: If it doesn't work out, the girls could get hurt. Also, this Fiona girl seems fantastic, so there must be a negative there somewhere in giving her up."

"Ok, so I have two options."

"No. There is a third option." said Luke.

"A third option. What?"

"You do nothing!" I looked at Luke a little confused.

"So how does that one work?" I asked.

"Well, you continue seeing Fiona on a casual basis, get your, you know, sexual needs taken care of, and you continue to have Martyna as your nanny for the sake of the girls. However, you can't continue to have any thoughts of having a full relationship with Martyna anymore. They must be banished from your mind. You said Fiona isn't putting any pressure on you, so maybe this option works, well, at least in the short term. If Martyna does start seeing someone, it wouldn't matter to you anymore and if she eventually leaves, you find a new nanny. Simple as that!"

"Sounds simple Luke, but believe me, it's far from it!"

"Why?"

"I can't just turn my feelings off, like a tap. It doesn't work that way. I don't work that way!"

"Well then, I'm sorry to have to say this to you and please don't take offence, you know I love you mate, but you need to quit your whining and make your fucking mind up," Luke said nodding his head to emphasise the point.

"You're right mate, thanks."

"Anytime. But listen, in all seriousness, I'm no 'agony aunt' and no expert in relationships or anything like that. Maybe you need to talk to somebody else. A woman. Sal?"

"Do you think that talking to Sal would be appropriate?"

"I'm not sure. What about Barbara? I know she is Cheryl's mum, but you've often told me that you see Barbara just like your own mum. Maybe she can help?"

"Maybe," I replied reluctantly. "It could be a bit awkward, although she has pressed me on my relationship with Martyna in the past. Even 'double teamed' with Derek at Christmas to get information from both Martyna and I, about our relationship."

"Well?"

"I'm not sure. After meeting Jen at the airport last week, we said we would keep in touch. Maybe I should talk to her about it. What do you think?"

"Could work. She's distant enough to be impartial, knows about your situation and of course will give you a female perspective. Why not?"

"Thanks Luke, thanks again for all your help. Listen, just to change the subject, Barbara has asked to have the girls next weekend, so I was wondering if you and Sally wanted to do something on Saturday night? Maybe a meal, club, something?"

"And who are you going to bring with you; Fiona or Martyna?" Luke replied smiling into his beer glass. We laughed and the tensions of the conversation we had just had, eased.

I left Mulligans about 8:30 p.m. and was home ten minutes later. I entered the house, took off my shoes and went to the kitchen. Martyna was drinking tea and flipping through a magazine.

"Hi George. Did you have a nice time?"

"Hey Martyna. Yes thanks. The girls okay?"

"Yes, they're fine. Would you like some dinner? I saved you some of the sausage and bean casserole."

"Erm-, it sounds lovely and I'm sure It will taste fantastic, but I don't feel very hungry. Sorry."

"No worries George."

"I'm going to get changed and put my head in the girls' room, to check on them. Might have an early night if that's okay?"

"Of course, George," Martyna said with her usual infectious smile.

"Thanks, Martyna, good night," I replied and went upstairs. After changing and looking in on the girls, I laid down on my bed and shut my eyes. Even after a good discussion with Luke, clarity still evaded me. There was still a lot to think about.

30

The week went quickly and it was soon Friday afternoon. This was partly due to the pressure of getting the proposals ready for the board and partly because I just completely submerged myself in my work, trying to blot out any thoughts about my private life. I wasn't always successful with this approach though!

Sarah was a Godsend and stayed late on a few evenings with me to get everything finished in time. She prepared everything, gave great input into the structure and design of the proposals and we made a fantastic team. I was extremely thankful for her help and once again saw new talents in her ever-growing armoury of capabilities. Even though Sarah was still quite flirty with me, I think she sensed that I had other things on my mind and therefore, wasn't quite her usual playful self. She appeared genuinely concerned and, on several occasions, asked if I was alright or wanted to talk about anything. I declined of course, but I was grateful for her concern. And who knows, maybe I should have talked to Sarah about my dilemma. Maybe she could have helped me figure out my feelings and my fears, brought some sort of clarity and led me to a decision.

It didn't help either that I got a phone call from Fiona mid-week. I declined to answer it and instead let my phone run onto voice message.

"Hi George, Fiona here. I hope you got back okay from your trip last week, and of course had a great time. I'm doing fine here in Frankfurt and as you know, I'm in my apartment now. Was wondering when you are next over? Maybe I could make you dinner? Okay - let me know George and hope to see you soon. Take great care," was the message that she left in her usual cheery way. I sent her a text message, apologising and telling her I would call by the end of the week. It was now the end of the week!

Things had also been a little difficult at home with Martyna. Although we both acted as normally as we could around the girls, once they were in bed of an evening, we tended to keep ourselves occupied doing things in separate rooms. If I were in the kitchen, Martyna would be in the lounge and vice versa. It was probably a blessing that I had to stay late in the office a few evenings with Sarah working on the proposal. And although Martyna never pushed me, I got the sense that she was waiting for me to talk to her some more about my feelings. After all, she had told me of her feelings for me, which had taken great courage and yet, I had not reciprocated either one way or the other.

It must be awful for her and I knew the next conversation with Martyna could not wait much longer. However, I was still no closer to a decision and decided to call Jennifer to see if she was available for a drink tonight. As previously arranged, Barbara was picking the girls up from school today to take them back to her house for the weekend. Therefore, Martyna and I had already agreed that dinner would only be something simple tonight, possibly a takeaway. I called Jen.

"Hi George, this is a nice surprise. How are you?" answered Jen.

"Hi Jen, yeah I'm good. How are you?"

"Yeah, good too. I've had a busy week putting together my shoot from Johannesburg so I'm looking forward to the weekend. I bet you are too?"

"Yeah. Erm, Jen I know it is short notice, but I was wondering if you are free for a drink tonight?" There was a short silent pause before Jen answered.

"I was wondering when you would make this call to me. Is it about Cheryl?"

"No. Like I said on the flight home last week, I'm really okay with Cheryl and you. There's nothing to worry about on that subject," I replied sorrowfully.

"Okay, then what's going on George, what's up?" Jen said slightly concerned.

"I have some things, personal things that I would really like your advice on. A woman's advice and I can't think of anyone better for that advice, than you."

"You're beginning to scare me George. I'm no 'Guru' that is going to give you all the answers to life's questions."

"Don't be scared Jen, I'm not expecting you to have all the answers-, just most of them." Jen laughed.

"Look, I have to move something around but yes George, I can meet you later for a few hours if you want to. I am supposed to be meeting someone about another photo shoot in the Marriott Hotel at the airport. He's an old friend, just flown in from LA. I can put him off for a few hours. Can you get to the hotel?"

"Yeah, sure, it's just around the corner from my office," I replied.

"There is a bar in the foyer, could meet me in there about 7 p.m. that okay for you?"

"That's great Jen, I really appreciate it. Thanks so much."

"My pleasure George, I'm only too glad to help. See you later," she said and hung up.

I made a call to Martyna and made up a story that I was working late. Although I did feel a little guilty about the lie, I thought it was best not to share the actual details of my meeting with Jen. I knew she would be home alone as the girls weren't there, so I asked Martyna if she wanted to wait for dinner and I would bring in a takeaway. She was happy with this and asked if we could have fish and chips. Well, it was Friday after all!

I then thought I should call Fiona. I wasn't feeling good about the way I was treating this lovely girl. Fiona had not put any pressure on me at all. She wanted more for us but was happy with just my friendship and we really did get on well with each other. And we knew each other intimately. As I reflected on this, the images of her body and our love making came flooding into my mind and gave me a calm, comforting feeling. I called her.

"Hi Fiona, it's George. Sorry I couldn't get back to you earlier. How are you?"

"Hey George, lovely to hear from you. Don't worry, I'm sure you've been up to your eyes in it this week. You must be so tired and looking forward to the weekend," Fiona said. I sensed her genuine concern for my wellbeing.

"Yeah, it's been a long week. So, how are you? How's your week been?"

"Yeah, not too bad. I have been given my own list of corporate clients now, after shadowing this guy for a few weeks, so yeah, I'm happy. Frankfurt is good, lots going on, and as my apartment is so close to the city centre, I can just literally stagger home after a night out." My mind wandered to the first night Fiona and I met when she had a few too many drinks and was quite drunk.

"Be careful," I said, but before I could continue Fiona had already replied.

"I'm joking George," she said laughing down the phone. "I've just absolutely ruined my reputation with you after our first night, haven't I?"

"No, of course not. I also know the sensible Fiona, the one that charmed Pat and Meryl Brunswick!"

"So, when are you coming over next, do you have any plans?"

"Actually, I will be over next week. Arriving Wednesday morning, and leaving Thursday evening. I have to finalise my proposals and present them to the board."

"Great! Do you fancy meeting up? I would love to cook you a meal, dinner, try out my new Jamie Oliver book 'Cooking for One' which my mum got me when I moved in."

"That was thoughtful of her," I said sarcastically.

"Yeah, I know. That's what I thought! Wasn't sure if she was hinting that I didn't have any 'friends' or whether she thought I was too ugly to get a man!"

"Well, I can certainly tell you, without any hesitation, that you should try to get some friends," I replied.

"What-, does that mean you think I'm too ugly to-"

"Just joking," I quickly interrupted and we both laughed. "Seriously though, I would love to have dinner with you Fiona," and in that split second, I had decided that I needed to talk to Fiona and tell her one way or the other about what I was going to do. Even if at that precise moment, I had no idea what that was! It gave me a deadline, a specific date for me to stop 'pussy footing' around and to decide. It felt good, liberating almost.

"Fantastic! Thanks George. I have a car now, so I can pick you up from the hotel. You can bring an overnight bag with you if you want?" Fiona said probingly. That's when the brief feeling of liberation I had just experienced, ceased! Fiona asking me to stay the night with her felt very real. If I were to choose to make a go of things with Fiona, I would very much look forward to spending nights like these with this wonderful girl. If I choose to end it with Fiona and commit to Martyna, would I regret no longer having the intimacy with Fiona, an intimacy that we both enjoyed and thought was amazing.

"We'll see," I said. "Look Fiona, I'm sorry to cut this short, but I still have some work to do, so can I call you on Monday to confirm everything?"

"Yes, no worries George. I shall look forward to it. And to next Wednesday. Have a great weekend with the girls and talk to you soon. Take care George."

"You too Fiona, have a lovely weekend," I replied and we hung up. So now I have a deadline, I thought to myself.

Sarah and I finished up the proposals and I thanked her for all her hard work and effort. She really had done a splendid job and I was so proud of her. She too, was quite rightly proud of herself and it felt like a breakthrough moment for her. However, she obviously knew something was still troubling me and gave it one more shot of asking if I was alright. I thanked her for her concern, but I just said everything was okay.

Sarah left the office at six-ish and wished me a good weekend. As it was Friday, I was the only one left which suited me as it gave a me some time to collect my thoughts before meeting with Jennifer. The next fifty minutes flew by and before I knew it, I was in the car and heading for the Marriott Hotel car park.

I entered the foyer of the hotel just before 7 p.m. and immediately spotted Jennifer sitting at the bar. She saw me and waved me over.

"Hi Jen," I said as I sat down next to her. "Thanks for this, I really appreciate it. Thanks."

"No need to thank me George. But I have to say, seeing you twice in a week, people will start to talk!" she said, smiling.

"Would you like a drink?"

"Gin and tonic would be great. Shall we make ourselves comfortable over there?" Jen replied pointing to a secluded table in the lounge area. Jen made her way over to the table, while I stayed at the bar and collected our drinks. As I was driving, I just had a sparkling mineral water.

"There you go my dear, one G and T," I said placing the drink down on the table in front of her, before sitting down opposite her.

"You not drinking?" Jen enquired. "Driving?"

"Yeah, I'm driving. Cheers!" I said, lifting my glass and 'chinking' Jen's gin and tonic. We both took a sip of our drinks.

"So, what do you want to talk to me about George? If it's not about Cheryl, then what?"

It took me about twenty minutes to fill Jen 'in' on what had been happening to me recently. She listened intently and just let me ramble on until I was finished. When I had, my hope was that Jen would be able to make some sense of my predicament.

"So, what's your problem George?" she said. This wasn't really the reaction I was expecting from Jen!

"Well, I...I...," I stuttered despondently. "I don't know what to do. I have strong feelings for both women. However, I see difficulties in pursuing a relationship with either of them. I just don't know which way to turn. I don't want to hurt either of them and I need to consider Emily and Amy in all of this. I'm just - it's just so difficult." Jen picked up her drink, took a sip and placed it back down again. She then looked at me with her big hazel eyes, perfectly framed by her dark rimmed Gucci spectacles.

"How was your relationship with Jana?" replied Jen. I looked at her a little confused.

"What's Jana got to do with this?"

"How was your relationship with me, all those years ago?" I was still confused.

"What-"

"And although I assume your relationship with Cheryl was great, how do you think 'she' felt about it, now knowing what you do about the 'connection' between Cheryl and me?"

"I don't understand. What are you saying?"

"You're not very experienced George, are you? You may come across as a confident, self-assured, knowledgeable sort of 'bloke', but all said and done, you've not had many relationships, have you?"

"No, I suppose not. But what's your point?"

"I've had many relationships over the last ten years George. Some men, some women. But the one thing I can safely tell you about each one of them, is that none of them were 'easy', there's always difficulties."

"Sorry Jen, I don't know where you are going with this."

"Your brief relationship with this Jana girl, it had its difficulties, right? Our relationship back then, we had difficulties too. And although you may have thought your relationship with Cheryl was perfect, do you not think Cheryl would have found it difficult, especially keeping her secret about me?" I looked away from Jen and thought for a minute.

"But this is different," I finally replied.

"No George, it's not! I don't see what your problem is. In fact, I would say you don't have a problem at all. You just need to decide what you want. You're using the girls as an excuse and, although I hate to say it, I think you are still holding onto Cheryl and putting her so high up on this pedestal of perfection, that nobody even comes close to. Cheryl wasn't perfect, she was no saint just like you and I and most of the bloody population aren't." Jen sympathetically smiled at me before continuing. "Cheryl was great, kind, loving and you had a wonderful relationship, never forget that. But nobody is perfect and no relationship comes along without its difficulties. I'm not saying that you shouldn't be wary of problems and of course, you must consider the effects of your decisions on the girls. But you shouldn't shy away from life and relationships because there might be a few difficulties along the way. George-, George are you listening to me?" I was just staring at Jen, hardly moving at all and in deep thought.

"Yes-, I'm listening," I quietly said.

"I think the real problem here is that you are a man!"

"I'm sorry," I said, snapping out of my transfixed state.

"You had great sex with Fiona. You get on very well with her. She's pretty, funny, intelligent. Martyna's the same, but you haven't

420

been 'intimate' with her. The question is: are you willing to risk what you already know about Fiona including the amazing sex, for Martyna? Or do you stick with what you know and forever wonder what things would have been like with Martyna?"

"Hmm," I mused, still in deep thought.

"And because you're a man, you want to have the proverbial 'cake' and be able to eat every bit of it! Unfortunately, in this situation, you can't, you just can't."

"I like cake," I said and smiled at Jennifer. She smiled back at me.

"Look George, it might seem like I'm having a go at you. I'm not believe me. You just need to make up your mind, and yes carefully consider the girls and of course Fiona, Martyna and you! Never forget about you in all of this! But I don't think either scenario is bad. And whatever you decide; if it doesn't work out, well then, that's just life. You should know that better than anyone."

"Thanks Jen. Thanks for being honest with me. I really appreciate it. Should have come to you a long time ago with all my other problems. Have you ever considered a job in the UN?" I said.

"Shut up George," an embarrassed Jen replied. "But seriously, make a decision and go with it whole heartedly. They both sound amazing women. And if it doesn't work out, remember you can always come and cry on my shoulder, never forget that George. Although we haven't been close since, well, since we were close, we've now found each other again and I would like us to keep in contact, remain friends." I leant across the table and with my right hand, I gently took hold of Jen's left hand and lightly squeezed it.

We spent the rest of the evening reminiscing about old times and it felt so natural to have Jennifer back in my life. Although I had a tinge of guilt that Cheryl would be looking down on us in horror, it also crossed my mind that she would indeed by smiling and happy knowing that her secret was out and it had made no difference to anything. The time raced round to 8:30 p.m. and as I was in mid-sentence, I saw Jen looking over my shoulder at something or someone who must have just entered the lounge. I stopped talking and looked behind me in the direction that Jen had been looking. Standing by the bar was a slightly 'tubby' man dressed in a white, loose fitting suit wearing a white panama hat.

"Is that the guy you are meeting?" I asked as I returned to look at Jen.

"Yes. You don't recognise him, do you?"

"Should I?"

"Take another look," whispered Jen. I again turned to look at the man in white. It took a few seconds, but slowly the face recognition kicked in.

"That's not Ben - Ben Wesley, is it?"

"Yep!" came Jen's instant reply.

"Fuck off, no way, that's not Ben," I said in disbelief.

"It is, come on, let's go and say hello," replied Jen and she grabbed my hand and led me over to him.

"Hello gorgeous," Ben said as Jen walked up to him and he gave her a kiss on both cheeks. "And who's this beef cake you have with you?" This took me completely by surprise! Not only did Ben look vastly different to how I remembered him, but his voice was also different. Much different. Very camp!

"Hi Ben. Come now, surely you remember George, George Hart?" said Jen, introducing me to Ben.

"Hello Ben, good to see you, mate," I said extending my hand and firmly shaking his. Ben looked at me in absolute horror.

"George - George Hart!" Ben said slowly, before turning to Jennifer and saying in a very manly, butch voice, "So darling, how have you been, alright love?" Jen looked confused.

"It's okay Ben, no need for the pretence," I said reassuringly. It was an extremely uncomfortable moment for Ben. I, on the other hand was enjoying it immensely! Here was this guy standing in front of me, a tough guy, who had bullied me at school for many years, reduced to a total wreck because of his newfound sexuality. The thing is, I didn't care at all about his sexuality! I was more interested in how he was going to deal with the bullying issue.

"So, you guys kept in touch," I said turning to Jen.

"Yes, when Ben went to LA to work for a fashion magazine, he looked me up as he knew I continued my photography career."

"So, you work for a fashion magazine in LA?" I asked Ben.

"Yes-, funny how things turn out really, isn't it," Ben cautiously replied.

"Certainly is! So, you're going to be putting some work Jen's way, are you?"

"Well, that's the plan," and Ben's voice again became softer and more feminine. "She doesn't really do fashion shoots, but I know how good she is, so I'm sure she can do a great job for the magazine."

"If you guys will excuse me for a minute, I just need to use the ladies room," Jen said as she made her exit. Ben and I were left staring at each other before Ben finally broke the silence.

"Look George, I'm sorry about, you know, the bullying when we were kids, I was confused." I said nothing but nodded my head in acknowledgment. "I bet you're a little surprised I'm gay?"

"Yes, I am a bit surprised, but we are what we are. There's no shame in it and it doesn't make you a bad person." Ben smiled at me. "However, bullying - that does make you a bad person!" I continued. Ben's smile disappeared and a sort of nervousness took hold of him.

"I-, I said I'm sorry-,"

"Don't worry Ben, I'm not going to give you a hard time about what happened when we were kids. It's in the past and I suppose we all do things we regret when we're that age. Relax, everything is cool!" Ben's smile returned.

"Do you still see that great big guy from Birmingham, what was his name, Lee?"

"You mean Luke. Yeah, he's still my best friend and we see each other a lot."

"I bet he's going to get a real kick out of this when you tell him about me?" I looked at Ben and smiled.

"Yeah, I'm sure he will. You know, he has a son called Ben! So, when did… you know, when did you realise you were…?"

"Gay? I think I always knew. Even when I let everyone in the whole school know that Jennifer was my 'girl', I knew she wasn't. My dad was a hard man, he wouldn't and still doesn't today, understand about me and 'people like me', as he puts it. I think that's why I left for the States, start a new life, new beginning."

"Do you speak to your dad?"

"No. We haven't talked for years. I think he prefers it that way. Do you know, I think he tells his friends that I am some sort of hot shot lawyer to the stars in Hollywood! Can you believe that?"

"It's a shame. You don't deserve that."

"It's ironic really, you lost your dad when you were young didn't you?"

"Yes."

"And I think I even gave you shit about that at school. I'm so sorry George, I was such an arsehole. And here's me, with a dad that makes up stories about his son because he is too embarrassed to tell his friends the truth about me."

"You two boys getting along?" said Jen as she re-joined us.

"Yeah," I said.

"Yeah," said Ben and again we politely smiled at each other.

"Right, well I'm sure you guys have a lot to talk about, so I'm going to leave you to it," I said looking at my watch.

"Won't you join us for a drink?" asked Ben.

"Unfortunately, not. But have fun and maybe next time you are in town, we can all get together for dinner, how does that sound?"

"Wonderful!" replied Ben.

"I'll walk you out," Jen said and after a brisk handshake with Ben, Jen and I walked to the hotel entrance, arm in arm.

"So, you're a fashion photographer as well?" I asked Jen as we strolled to the hotel entrance.

"No, not really. But as I mentioned, Ben looked me up a few years ago and we met, funnily enough, here at the Marriott. It was a bit of a shock when I first saw him, his voice, his style of clothing, but we got on. Since then, he's asked me to do a couple of 'themed' shoots for weddings and 'prom' night, that sort of thing, and I think his editor loved what I did. He now wants me to think about a swimwear 'shoot' in the British Virgin Islands. It's not really my thing, but hey, the money is excellent!"

"I'll do it! Lots of hot girls in bikinis, Caribbean sunshine, yeah, tell Ben I'm interested," I jokingly said before pausing briefly. "It is hot girls I take it and not fellas in 'G' Strings?" I continued with a look of apprehension on my face, which quite rightly earned me a gentle slap on the arm from Jen!

"Thanks again Jen, for everything. You are wise beyond your years. Thanks for helping me see more clearly."

"No thanks needed. Keep in touch handsome," she said before her plump, red lips touched mine and we very tenderly kissed each other.

I felt a certain degree of calm while driving home and although I wasn't any nearer to deciding, the discussion I had just had with Jennifer made me realise that I had nothing to fear. And it was fear that was causing my anxiety about everything. Fear of making the wrong decision. Fear of affecting Emily and Amy. And fear of losing either Fiona or Martyna.

I parked the car outside the house and then made the short walk to the local fish and chips shop. After purchasing two cod and chips, I strolled home and entered the house, walking into the kitchen. As I passed the lounge, I heard Martyna call out to me.

"I'm in here."

"Okay, no worries," I replied. I turned the oven on low and placed the two portions of cod and chips inside to keep warm. At that point, Martyna appeared in the doorway. Again, only wearing tight fitting white leggings and a dark grey, loose fitting vest top. She looked fantastic!

"Did you get your work finished?" she asked. I quickly remembered I had earlier told Martyna that I was working late.

"Erm, yeah, yes all done. Just a few bits to finalise on Monday, but nothing major."

"What are you doing?"

"I'm sorry?" I said in surprise as if Martyna was still talking about my evening and somehow knew I was lying, and instead of working, had been talking about my feelings for her and of course Fiona, to Jennifer, who she had met at the airport last week!

"With the oven?"

"Oh, that. I need to get out of these clothes, so just keeping the food warm. Won't be long," I replied and walked past Martyna to the stairs.

"I'll warm some plates," Martyna said and smiled at me as we passed each other.

Although everything seemed normal, there was still an underlying, almost uneasy atmosphere between Martyna and I. So, armed with my newly instilled calmness about the situation, following my conversation with Jennifer tonight, I thought I should say something to Martyna. Having changed into beach shorts and a vest top, I returned to the kitchen. Martyna had set two plates on the kitchen table along with cutlery.

"What would you like to drink?" she asked me.

"I fancy a beer!" was my reply and Martyna duly went to the fridge and pulled out two bottles of beer, 'popped off' the metal caps and placed them on the table. While she was doing that, I retrieved our 'supper' from the oven and plated our meals. We sat down opposite each other, raised, and clinked our bottles of beer, and said cheers!

"Tuck in before it gets cold," I said. Martyna looked at me, smiled and picked up her cutlery, ready to attack the fish and chips.

"I am surprised you like this sort of thing," I said. "I think most non 'Brits' think we are mad, craving for this greasy, fattening British institution."

"I love it. And if I don't have it too often, it doesn't affect my figure," Martyna replied. I couldn't agree more. I had often worked with girls who were so scared of putting on weight that they would never indulge in eating things like takeaways and were constantly on diets, even though they looked painfully thin. 'Everything in moderation' was my philosophy and with regular exercise, I don't think you can go far wrong!

We chatted generally during our meal and it did feel more like the times before we had had our discussion last week. Even so, I thought I needed to say something, so after finishing our food and placing the plates and cutlery in the dishwasher, I suggested we take another beer and sit in the lounge. Martyna agreed. We both sat at either end of the sofa.

"Thanks for dinner George. It was nice. I enjoyed it," said Martyna.

"My pleasure, I know it was only fish and chips, but delicious all the same!"

"Yes."

"Oh, Emily and Amy called me earlier, to let me know they had arrived safely at Barbara's. They told me they had already called you as well."

"Yes. When I dropped them off at school in the morning, I asked them to let me know when they arrived at their grandmother's. I'm sure Barbara would have let me know anyway," Martyna responded and in that instant, due to the formality of the conversation, it felt as if the uneasy atmosphere had returned and once again there was the distinct feeling that an 'elephant' was in the room! A short period of silence ensued. In the end the silence was broken as we both said each other's name at the same time.

"You go," I said.

"No, it's okay, you can talk," Martyna replied. I paused and let out a sigh.

"I know you have been waiting for me to talk to you about 'our' situation and about-, what you told me last week regarding your feelings for me. I guess you are waiting to hear what my response would have been to Emily when she asked me if I feel love for you, compatibility, and physical attraction. I'm sorry it has taken so long. The answer of course, is a 'simple' yes. Yes, I do love you, I do think we are good together and God knows, I am physically attracted to you. But that's where the 'simple' ends and the complicated begins. There are other considerations. Big considerations. Emily and Amy. So, for now, I can't tell you what that means for us. I just need some more time. I'm sorry."

"I can give you time-," Martyna softly replied.

"Before you say anything else. I need to tell you something," I said interrupting Martyna. Although it was against the advice from Luke, I felt a need, a strong desire, almost a compulsion to let Martyna know about Fiona. Martyna looked at me, concerned with what I was about to say to her.

"What George, what is it?"

"A few months back I met someone. I met her, Fiona, on a plane to Frankfurt. We got chatting and coincidently, we were staying at the

428

same hotel. We had a drink together and got on very well." Martyna broke eye contact with me and looked at the floor.

"Go on," she quietly said.

"When I went back a few weeks later, we met up for dinner. One thing led to another and we ended up, well you know." Martyna was still looking at the floor.

"This was when?"

"March. It was after you had been on your first blind date. I didn't think we were going to be, well, in this situation, seriously discussing our feelings for each other."

"I understand that George. Do you have feelings for her? Is she part of the reason you need more time?" Martyna said continuing to look down at the floor.

"Fiona knows about my circumstances, about Cheryl, and Emily and Amy. And therefore, I have always been up front about not wanting anything serious with her. I admit, I do have strong feelings about her and she would really like for us to have a proper relationship."

"Are you seeing her next week when you go to Frankfurt?" Martyna said, finally looking back at me. I nodded my head. Again, she returned to staring at the floor.

"I just need to talk to her, that's all. You seem a little upset with me? I thought you weren't that interested in us. You were going on a blind date, and have been on another since then too-,"

"You don't need to explain George, I do understand. It does, upset me somehow, but I can't blame you in any way. We weren't, are still not together, so there is no reason for me to be upset. But I am a little."

"I'm sorry Martyna. But I wanted to tell you about Fiona. I think you should know. She is a lovely girl, and I would like to keep in touch with her, as a friend. Even if we - you and I, don't manage to get together, that's all Fiona and I will ever be-, just friends."

"I think I'm going to bed now, George. Thanks for telling me about Fiona." Martyna stood up from the sofa. From my sitting position, I lunged my hand forward, grabbing hold of Martyna's hand. She looked at me and smiled. I looked back at her, deep into her beautiful green eyes.

"I am sorry Martyna," I said. Martyna let go of my hand and left the room. I could hear her walking up the stairs and as I sat there on the sofa a feeling of anger came over me. Not anger towards Martyna, but towards me, for not heeding Luke's advice about telling Martyna that I had slept with Fiona. I had really fucked things up and it was one of those moments when you wished you could turn the clock back and do things differently. Unfortunately-, I couldn't, nobody ever can! I drank my beer and went to bed.

31

Without Emily and Amy around, Martyna and I both got up quite late on the Saturday morning. As I entered the kitchen at about 10:30 a.m. I saw Martyna sitting at the kitchen table deep in thought. Without appearing to break her concentration and without looking up at me, Martyna spoke.

"Coffee is freshly brewed. I haven't fixed anything for breakfast as I'm not hungry. I'm going to go and have a shower." She got up from the chair and started to make her way out of the kitchen.

"Martyna," I called to her and she stopped in her tracks, with her back to me. "Martyna," I called again and she slowly turned around to face me. I smiled at her, but before I could say anything, Martyna had again turned and continued her way out of the kitchen and disappeared up the stairs.

I made myself a coffee and sat on the same chair that Martyna had sat on. I could smell her, even though she was no longer in the room. Thoughts began to enter my mind. Luke was right, I should not have told Martyna about Fiona. That was a big mistake. Too late now though, and anyway, perhaps it was a good thing that Martyna knew. At least now, I had nothing to hide from her. Except Jana of course! But Jana was never in the picture really. Granted, she was a lot of fun, and we had some wonderful nights of varying degrees of sexual encounters. But we both knew it wasn't the 'real' thing, a long-term relationship, no, just a bit of fun. So, no need for Martyna to know about Jana. And what I had said to Martyna last night about Fiona, about her being only a 'friend', well-, was that really the truth? Did I still have strong feelings for Fiona? After all, If I had now 'blown' my chances with Martyna, why would I want to give up Fiona? I could continue to see her and see how things developed. So why should I tell Fiona that it's over when I see her on Wednesday-, why? I mean, the way Martyna is now acting, it's now very unlikely that we will be together. So why should I give up on a chance of a wonderful relationship with Fiona?

All these thoughts kept going around in my mind, until it hurt so much, that I needed to think about something else. That something else happened to be tonight, as my phone rang and I looked down at it to see Luke's name.

"Hello mate," I said as I answered the call.

"Hey George, just thought I would ring to confirm the arrangements for tonight," replied Luke.

"Ok," I replied.

"So, I've booked a table at 'The Ivy' in Covent Garden for 8 p.m. You know where it is, don't you? We've been there before, and then I thought about going on to a club. All good for you?" Although I hadn't been out with Luke and Sally for a while and was genuinely looking forward to it, my enthusiasm at that precise moment, was diminishing with every passing second.

"Yeah," I slowly replied, in some sort of trance.

"You okay George? You sound a bit, strange. Everything alright?" asked a concerned Luke. I thought for a second and then snapped out of my daze before replying.

"Yeah-, yeah everything's good. I'll talk to you later tonight, but no, everything is okay."

"Alright, well, if you are sure? Sal and I have to drop Ben off with Sal's mum so we thought we would meet you at the restaurant, that okay?"

"Sure, no problem."

"Well, I'll let you get on mate, I know it takes you while to get ready to go out," Luke said jokingly. I didn't rise to the bait as I would usually have done, engaging back and forth with Luke, with witty one-liners and 'piss taking' comments as were the norm when Luke and I light-heartedly assassinated each other's characters in a typical best friends' way. Instead, I just finished the conversation.

"Ok Luke, see you at later at 'The Ivy', take care," and I ended the call.

I finished my coffee and went upstairs. As I walked past Martyna's room, her door was open and I saw her standing by her dresser, looking into the mirror. She had obviously just stepped out of the shower as she had a towel wrapped around her middle and one on her head in the shape of a turban. She looked beautiful.

"Martyna," I called to her.

"Hi George," she casually replied without looking away from the mirror. "What can I do for you?"

"I just wanted to remind you that I am going out tonight with Luke and Sally. I did tell you in the week, but just in case you forgot, it's tonight," I said sombrely.

"It's okay, I remembered George. In fact, I'm going out tonight too." Martyna looked at me and although it couldn't have been, it felt like this was the first time that Martyna had ever looked at me and not smiled.

"Ok, well, have a nice time," I said and carried on along the landing to my bedroom. I shut the door behind me and sat down on my bed. This was very strange. I wasn't sure why Martyna appeared so upset with me. I thought I had done the right thing in telling her about Fiona. I thought it would be better to tell her up front, be honest with her. After all, it wasn't like I had cheated on Martyna. We weren't a 'couple', already in a relationship. We were-, nothing! Nothing at all when I slept with Fiona. Nor when I slept with Jana too! Martyna was going on blind dates and we had decided not to get involved! So why was Martyna behaving so distant towards me? The thought then struck me about tonight! Where was she going? Was she going out with her friends? Or was she meeting this 'Jack' bloke again? Is she trying to make me jealous? If she was, it was beginning to work! I got up from the bed and took a shower.

When I returned downstairs, Martyna was in the kitchen busy looking through her handbag.

"Coffee?" I asked as I entered the kitchen.

"No thanks, I'm on my way out," Martyna instantly replied.

"Going somewhere nice?"

"Just clothes shopping. I want something nice for tonight. I'll be back about six-ish, enjoy your day George." Martyna, pulled her keys from her bag and walked out of the kitchen, towards the front door and left. A deathly silence fell over the house and as I looked around the kitchen, it felt eerie and cold. No children's laughter, no smells and the hustle and bustle of breakfast - and no smiling Martyna!

I decided to keep myself busy for the day, completing the jobs that I had been meaning to get around to, but had somehow kept putting off. I hoped it would take my mind off Martyna and for long periods during the day, it did. But every now and then my thoughts would turn to her and to the questions about why she was upset with me. Unfortunately, I was not able to find the answers.

Martyna was good to her word and returned home just before six. After saying a quick 'hello' to me, she disappeared into her bedroom, presumably to get ready for her night out. Her mood had obviously not changed much during the afternoon. I decided to get myself ready and try to put Martyna to the back of my mind.

I left around 7:30 p.m. and headed for the tube station. Martyna was still getting ready for her night out.

"Martyna," I called out from the foot of the stairs.

"Yes," I heard Martyna reply.

"I'm leaving now. I'll see you later. Have a nice time."

"Yes, I will. I Don't know if I will be back tonight, so don't be surprised if I'm not." Still staring at the top of the empty stairwell, I felt a bit disappointed in Martyna's response.

"Ok, well, please be careful and again, have a nice time. See you later," I replied. "Or maybe not," I added quietly to myself.

I arrived at the restaurant in Covent Garden and the hostess informed me that the rest of my party had already arrived. As I followed her, I noticed not two, but three people sitting at the table.

"Here he is," said Luke and he got up from the table to give me a hug. "How are you mate, okay?"

"Yeah-, good," I replied before looking at Luke and Sally in turn, a little disappointedly.

"Hi George, good to see you," said Sally. I made my way around to her and bent down to give her a kiss on the cheek.

"Hi Sal, good to see you too!"

"This is Rebecca, a friend from work. Rebecca was at a loose end tonight, so I invited her to join us, hope that was okay?" Sally continued. I looked at this nice looking, albeit quite nervous, girl sitting next to Sally.

"Pleased to meet you, Rebecca, I'm George," I said extending my hand and giving Rebecca a warm smile.

"Nice to meet you too, George," Rebecca replied with an equally warm smile. Rebecca had long black wavy hair, blue eyes, and my original opinion of 'nice looking' changed very quickly to 'extremely attractive'. Although she was sitting down, I estimated her to be about five foot eight and if I were to take a guess at her figure, it would be 36-24-38. She had a 'fuller' figure than I was used to (when comparing to Cheryl, Jennifer, Fiona, Jana and Martyna – that makes me sound like I have a harem of women at my disposal!), and although I wasn't instantly attracted to her, she looked wonderful. I sat down next to Luke, opposite Rebecca.

"Sorry I'm a bit late, I think there was a delay on the tube," I said trying to engage in conversation.

"No worries mate. We have only just arrived anyway. We haven't even ordered the drinks yet," replied Luke. At that moment, the waiter came over and took our drinks order. As we all looked at the menus we'd been given, Sally tried to instigate a conversation to draw Rebecca and me into talking to each other.

"George is a Sales Director for a global in-flight catering company. He gets to travel all over the world," Sally said to Rebecca.

"That's wonderful, you must have so many lovely experiences of the places you have visited," Rebecca said looking at me. And of all the wonderful experiences that I have witnessed around the world, the one that came immediately to my mind was Alfred fucking Edna, 'doggy' style in the stores in the Addis Ababa facility!

"Yes, I have had some memorable experiences," I replied smiling. "But it's not as glamourous as Sally makes out. I do travel quite a bit, but I generally see an airport, a catering facility, a hotel and if I'm lucky, a local restaurant. After all, I'm not there on holiday!"

"Still, I bet it's nice to meet new people and experience different cultures?" Rebecca responded.

"Yes, it is," I said. "And tell me Rebecca, what do you do?"

"I work in the Customer Service department where Sally works. I started there as a part time shop assistant when I was sixteen. Was never really interested in school and therefore, didn't do well with exams. But since then, I've been to college, completed two NVQ's at level five and I'm now doing an 'Open University' Business degree. You have to close your ears to this bit Sally," Rebecca said, looking briefly at Sally before returning to me and cupping her hands around her mouth. "I don't really see my future at the department store!" she whispered and Sally smiled.

"I'm very proud of Rebecca," Sally said. "I have seen her progress over the last five years and I have actively encouraged her to gain qualifications and now, try to get this business degree. She's bright, intelligent, focussed, extremely reliable and is great with people."

"Thanks Sally, do you want to have a go at writing my CV?" Rebecca replied and we all smiled.

We ordered our meals and to be honest, the evening went well, even though I had been set up by Luke and Sally on a blind date! Rebecca was a genuinely nice girl and we got on very well. Conversation didn't dry up and flowed freely between us and I think we both felt very contented in each other's company. Before our desserts arrived, the girls announced that they needed to use the bathroom and duly departed, leaving Luke and I alone at the table.

"Before you say anything, it was Sally's idea!" said Luke as soon as Sally and Rebecca were out of earshot.

"That was a bit sneaky of you both. Especially as I only told you last week about my situation with Fiona and Martyna."

"I know mate, I'm really sorry. But I haven't told Sally about that and then she came to me with this idea about Rebecca and you, and, well-, what could I say? I just had to go along with it. Really sorry mate."

"You couldn't have called me and warned me about it?"

"Look George, I've known you a long time and if it's one thing I've known about you right off the bat, is that your face doesn't lie. If I had of warned you about tonight, Sal would have known as soon as you walked in. It would have been written all over you face. Then I would have been in deep shit with Sal! As it was, the surprise on your face was priceless and I think you handled it very well," Luke said with a sort of smirk on his face.

"Thanks mate," I sarcastically replied.

"So, what do you think of Rebecca, nice?"

"Look mate, she's very nice, great company, easy to talk to and generally a lovely looking girl-,"

"I can feel a 'but' coming along anytime soon," interrupted Luke.

"But, you know what I'm going through right now and somebody else is just not on the radar at the moment, maybe never!"

"So, what's the latest then, with Fiona and Martyna?"

"Well, I met with Jennifer last night."

"Jennifer!"

"Yes. I told you last week I might talk to her. As much as I appreciated talking to you and the advice you gave me, I felt I did need to get a female perspective. So, I called Jen and we met for drink after work yesterday."

"How was she? She okay?"

"Yeah, she's great. She was meeting someone about some work opportunity later so I only had a few hours with her, but I'll come back to that in a minute. Anyway, I explained my situation and quite frankly, she had a go at me!"

"What? Why?" was Luke's startled response.

"Not in a nasty way. She just made me realise that I didn't really have any problems, I was just fearful of making the wrong decision. She told me that to choose between being with Fiona or Martyna, neither choice would be a bad decision. Neither would be wrong. For me or the girls. I just had to make up my mind."

"Wow! As simple as that. Funny how a woman can see through all the crap! Mind you, I also told you that you needed to make your fucking mind up!"

"Yeah, but she also told me that she felt deep down that I didn't want to give up either of them, and I suppose she was right. But that can't happen, I need to decide."

"So, have you decided?"

"Well, after speaking to Jen, I felt much calmer about things and although I hadn't made my mind up, I thought I should be honest with Martyna about Fiona and sleeping with her…"

"Oh mate, you didn't tell her, did you?" Luke replied in the hope that I had not told Martyna about Fiona.

"Yep! I did. Last night when I got in, Martyna and I had a fish and chip supper and after that we had a discussion, and I told her about Fiona."

"Fuck! How did that go then - not good I take it?"

"No, not good. Not good at all. I explained that at the time, I didn't think anything would develop between us and that she was going on blind dates, so I didn't think I was doing anything wrong. She agreed with me! But she has taken it badly and has basically ignored me since. You know, kept out of my way. Short, sharp, to the point sentences. Only talked to me when I have asked her a question, that sort of thing."

"Oh, shit. Look, I did warn you to keep that bit of information away from Martyna. I knew she wouldn't be happy with that, just had a feeling. You didn't mention Jana as well did you?"

"No! Nothing about Jana. But Jana is not in the picture now. But I have to say, you were right Luke. Maybe I shouldn't have told Martyna about Fiona. But if I was going to be with her, I didn't want there to be any secrets about Fiona. But now it looks as though Martyna and I don't have a future, so maybe I should look at Fiona. Build a relationship with her. She's perfect too." Before Luke could reply, I spied the girls returning from the Ladies and whispered 'the girls are back' to him.

"So, have you missed us," said Sally as she sat back down at the table.

"I always miss you my princess," said Luke in a sincere, yet slightly sickly way.

We finished dessert and Luke had suggested that we go to a club not far from the restaurant for a 'bit of a boogie' as he put it, and some cocktails. Sally was the first to resoundly support Luke's idea. Rebecca and I looked at each other and with a shrug of our shoulders and with a pinch of reluctance, agreed to Luke's suggestion.

It was a short walk from the restaurant to the club and as in the days when Luke, Sally, Cheryl, and I used to go out as a foursome, the girls walked together, leaving Luke and I with an opportunity to continue our earlier conversation.

"So, what does it mean for you and Martyna, or even you and Fiona?" asked Luke.

"I'm in Frankfurt next week and I've agreed to meet with Fiona. In fact, she's cooking me dinner at her new apartment."

"That sounds nice. So, you going to tell her how you feel?"

"That was the plan, yeah."

"And how do you feel? I mean, to be honest, I'm not sure what you want. Is it Fiona or Martyna?"

"If you would have asked me that yesterday, I would have said Martyna. Now, I just don't know. The way Martyna is acting is very strange. We weren't a 'couple' when I slept with Fiona. We weren't in a relationship and she was going out on dates! Therefore, I don't understand why she is so upset with me."

"She might just need a few days to let things sink in. You never know, by tomorrow morning, things could be back to normal," Luke said trying to provide me with some sort of comfort.

"Maybe," I replied.

"But you still need to make a decision George. And if you are seeing Fiona next week, I think you need to make it by then."

"True. But the conversation I am going to have with Fiona, might just turn out to be vastly different to the one I thought I was going to have. If Martyna is no longer interested in me, then I would be mad to give up on Fiona. Just really confusing!"

"Try not to worry about it tonight, and just enjoy yourself. You never know, Rebecca might be 'the one' you are looking for," said Luke, trying to cheer me up. However, when I heard Luke say 'the one' it instantly reminded me of Cheryl and did nothing to lift my spirits. It only served as a reminder that Cheryl was no longer here with me, on this night out, enjoying herself with me and our friends. I decided not to say anything to Luke as I wasn't sure if he had forgiven himself yet and released the guilt he felt about Cheryl's accident.

We arrived at the club and because it was still relatively early, we walked straight in. The fact that we were two smartly dressed guys, accompanied by two attractive women also helped! Once inside we made our way to the bar and ordered cocktails. The girls secured a vacant table, while Luke and I waited for the drinks. It was quite a small club, but had a sizeable dance floor in the middle, which was surrounded by high, single leg, steel bar tables. There was also a mezzanine floor that overlooked the dance area which had normal lounge tables and chairs and seemed a little quieter. As we waited for the drinks, Luke noticed Sal in the distance signalling to him that they the girls were going upstairs to the mezzanine area.

"Have you thought about what I said to you regarding Cheryl?" I tentatively asked Luke. He looked at me and we locked eye contact for a few seconds before he let out a sigh.

"It's extremely hard George. Although I am thankful to you for bringing up the subject last week, and I do accept what you were saying, I think there will always be some part of me that thinks Cheryl's accident could have been avoided. Whether or not it was me that could have made it avoidable, I haven't quite come to terms with yet."

"Luke…" I began to reply.

"It's okay George. Really, I feel much better after our discussion, but it will take some more time. Baby steps. But thanks again."

441

The drinks arrived and I decided not to push this conversation any further, well at least not tonight anyway! We made our way up the stairs and found the girls sitting at a table overlooking the dance area.

"Two Cosmopolitans for you lovely ladies," said Luke placing the drinks down on the table. I was holding mine and Luke's drinks - a Caipirinha for me and Manhattan for Luke - and placed them down on the table.

"Thanks Luke," said Rebecca.

"No, not me, George bought the cocktails," replied Luke.

"Thanks George," said Sally. Rebecca looked at me, raised her glass and mouthed 'thank you' to me. I nodded my head in acknowledgement.

"Cheers everyone," I said, lifting my glass and we all 'chinked' our glasses. The evening moved along very nicely and Rebecca and I got on extremely well, talking about many different subjects. She was easy to talk to and I hoped that she also felt in good company. However, the conversation moved to dancing and was immediately picked up by Sally and Luke.

"Good idea Rebecca. Let's go to the dance floor," said Sally.

"No, I didn't mean, well not unless you want to, George?" Rebecca replied a little apologetically to me. Although Luke was quite a big guy, he was surprising nimble on the dance floor. In fact, when he was a kid in Birmingham, he had entered dancing competitions and done quite well, winning a few. I on the other hand, had never been particularly good at dancing. Not much rhythm and the coordination between my arms and legs, essential for any good dancer, was severely lacking on my part. Cheryl had often jokingly likened my dancing to a cross between a baby learning to walk and Mr. Bean! Hence the term 'Baby Bean' was born and she would always say to me when we were out at a club, 'Come on Baby Bean, time for a dance.'

"Erm, well, you see, dancing. Not one of my strengths-" Luke, being my best friend, knew that I was somewhat reluctant to hit the dance floor and 'throw a few shapes down' so did his best to deflect the conversation.

"Let's have another drink first, it looks quite crowded down there," he said.

"Come on Luke," said Sally, who by now had drunk sufficient alcohol to be marginally worse for wear, "let's leave these two alone and dance. I want to dance with my husband!" Luke looked at me, rolled his eyes, smiled, and took Sally by the hand. He led her away from the table, down the stairs to the dance floor.

"Sorry George. I didn't know that me bringing up the subject of dance, would have that effect. I take it you're not really in to dancing right?" asked Rebecca.

"Well, it's not that 'I'm not into it' it's more that I am not particularly good at it. In fact, 'terrible' would be a much better word to describe my dancing prowess!" I replied smiling. Rebecca smiled back.

"I'm sorry George. I should never have told you about it." The 'it' that Rebecca was referring to, was the fact that Rebecca takes dance lessons at a 'Salsa Dance School' and was telling me about it when Sally overheard our conversation.

"No need for apologies Rebecca. But do you know what, maybe you could give me the name and address of this dance school. I think I need to learn a few moves!" We both laughed and once again, it felt amazingly comfortable being in Rebecca's company. We continued to chat and look down on Luke and Sally having a wonderful time on the dance floor with each other. They looked fantastic together and I was happy for them.

It was at this point that I suddenly felt a presence by the side of the table and looked up.

"Hello George. Having a nice time?" said Martyna. It took me completely by surprise.

"Hi-, Martyna," I managed to stutter out. Martyna then turned to Rebecca and extended her hand in greeting.

"Hello. I'm Martyna, George's live-in nanny. Nice to meet you," Martyna said to Rebecca.

"Hi, I'm Rebecca. Nice to meet you too," Rebecca replied reciprocating the hand offering as the two ladies shook hands. Martyna then returned to me.

"Well, have a nice evening George and don't wait up for me," she said before turning and walking away from the table.

"Martyna! Martyna!" I called out after her, but she continued to walk away. "Sorry Rebecca, but will you excuse me for a minute?" I said and got up from my chair. I hurriedly followed Martyna until I managed to catch up with her as she was about to descend the stairs.

"What is it George?" she said as she turned to face me.

"What's wrong Martyna? Why are you so upset with me?" Martyna looked into my eyes, her own eyes moist with sadness.

"I'm not upset with you."

"Then why are you acting like this? Who are you upset with?" I replied. There was a slight pause.

"You have company George. Genuinely nice company," Martyna said regrettably, looking over my shoulder back at Rebecca. "Have a lovely evening."

"Rebecca? Rebecca?" I said twice in a state of panic. "Wait, no, you, you don't understand, Martyna-," but before I could get any words out of my mouth that actually made a coherent sentence, Martyna had turned and hastily descended the stairs before disappearing into the crowded dance floor. It felt as though my feet were stuck to the floor. I couldn't move! I felt like I was about to throw up, and not because of the alcohol! Then I remembered Rebecca. I let out a big sigh, regained some composure, turned, and walked back to the table where Rebecca was sitting.

"Everything okay George?" Rebecca asked, smiling at me.

"What? Erm, sorry, yes, all good. Sorry about that."

"No problem. Martyna seems very nice. Sally did tell me about your two daughters and that you are a widower."

"Did she," I said slowly nodding my head. "Yes, I have two lovely daughters and Martyna is my - our - live in nanny. And yes, Martyna is very nice," I replied, trying to avoid the 'widower' part of Rebecca's previous comment. At that moment Sally and Luke sat down, having exhausted themselves on the dance floor.

"Come on guys, don't you want to join us?" Sally asked looking at Rebecca and me.

"I'm done," replied Luke, puffing out his cheeks. "If you still want more, why don't you take Rebecca to the floor!" Luke continued in a gameshow host way, particularly as his words had a distinctly poetic resonance. Rebecca looked at me as if to ask permission!

"Go for it," was my instant response. The girls duly departed, leaving Luke and I alone at the table.

"What's up mate, you look like you've seen a ghost?" asked Luke.

"Martyna's here," I replied.

"What? Where?" Luke said looking around the immediate area.

"Not right now, but she was here a few minutes ago. She came up to the table, said hello, shook hands with Rebecca and wished me a nice evening!"

"And?"

"And turned around and left."

"That was it? Nothing else?"

"I excused myself from Rebecca and went after her. Caught up with her over there by the stairs," I said pointing at the stairs.

"What happened?"

"I asked why she was so upset with me and why she was behaving so strangely. She said she wasn't upset with me and again wished me a good night before quickly running down the stairs."

"Well, that's good isn't it? I mean, she said she wasn't upset with you, she was polite to Rebecca and wished you a good evening! What's wrong? Am I missing something?" Luke pressed.

"Yes. Yes, you are. Her eyes were full of tears. And if she didn't blame me, who did she blame. Because it's not Fiona's fault either. Fiona is not to blame. So, I don't get it!"

"I think you are 'over thinking' this situation mate-,"

"And she didn't give me a chance to explain about Rebecca either. I think Martyna thought I had lied to her about going out with you and Sally and instead had a hot date with Rebecca!"

"Oh fuck! Mate, I'm sorry. I didn't think-,"

"It's okay Luke, it's not your fault. But I think she feels I have betrayed her all over again!" The realisation that Martyna must have thought I had lied and that Rebecca was a date that I had arranged sunk in exceedingly quickly. After all, there was no sign of Luke and Sally when Martyna had approached Rebecca and I at the table. What else could she think! I needed to talk to Martyna and the sooner the better. I took out my phone and dialled Martyna's number. It was ringing, which was a good sign. Unfortunately, it wasn't being picked up. I tried two more times without success.

"I need to find her," I said to Luke. "I'm going to look around. I'll be back shortly."

I Left Luke at the table and headed down the stairs to the dance area. It was tough making my way around as the club had become considerably busier since we had first arrived. I checked everywhere without any success and concluded that Martyna had either already left or was in the Ladies. I waited outside the toilets for a good ten minutes to see if she would emerge. Unfortunately, she didn't so I headed back up the stairs to re-join Luke. When I arrived Sally and Rebecca were also sitting at the table.

"Where have you been George?" asked Sally.

"Erm, just to the Men's room, you know."

"Oh! Hey, guess who I saw dancing?"

"Who?" I eagerly replied.

"Martyna. It looked like she was having a great time. She was with some tall handsome guy. She didn't see us, and I didn't want to interrupt, they seemed quite 'close' if you know what I mean." Unfortunately, I knew exactly what Sally meant and I must have appeared very disheartened. "You alright George?" Sally continued.

"Let's get another drink, George," Luke said, quickly realising that a tense and potentially awkward situation was developing, and he ushered me away from the table to the upstairs bar.

"Thanks mate," I said as we stood at the bar waiting to be served.

"Don't mention it. I feel I'm to blame for this situation. If I had only told Sally about everything, she wouldn't have brought along Rebecca tonight and none of this shit would have happened."

"Once again Luke, don't blame yourself. It's not your fault. It just seems like-, like Martyna and I are not destined to be together. I just have to face it, stop thinking about it, get on with my life."

"You can talk to Martyna tomorrow morning before you get the girls and sort all this shit out. There's plenty to play for yet!" Luke said in an encouraging fashion, trying to fill me with hope. He put his arm around my shoulders before releasing me and giving me a gentle slap on the back. I didn't tell Luke that there was every possibility that I would not see Martyna tomorrow morning as she might not be back tonight! That thought, which had been growing since Martyna had first mentioned it before I left the house that evening, was beginning to alarm me.

We took the drinks back to the table and as much as Luke tried to move the conversation along and include me as much as possible,

I'm afraid my heart was just not in it. The girls had also noticed my mood and if I stayed any longer, it would have completely ruined, what up until that point, had been a perfectly delightful evening. I made my excuses about not feeling to good, apologised to all three of them got up to leave the club. However, before I did leave, I turned back towards Rebecca.

"Rebecca, I wanted to just say that I've had a fantastic night in your company. You are a lovely lady and I wanted to thank you. I have really enjoyed talking to you. You are funny, bright, remarkably interesting and I wish I could have been better company for you. I'm so sorry. Take care and maybe see you again sometime."

Sally looked at Luke, Luke looked at Sally. They both then looked back at me. I smiled, said goodbye, and made my way to the exit.

"What's going on Luke?" asked Sally as she appeared to instantly sober up.

"I've no idea," Luke pretended not to know. I think he didn't want to get into everything with Sally in front of Rebecca and, to somewhat protect Rebecca's feelings, he decided to wait until he was on his own with Sally before filling her in on the situation.

I made my way out of the club and walked to the nearest underground station which was Leicester Square. After changing trains at Green Park, I found myself some thirty minutes later, stepping out at Dollis Hill station, only a two-minute walk away from home. It was approaching 1:10 a.m. and the street was quiet apart from the noise from my own footsteps. When I arrived at my front door, I somehow hesitated before putting the key in the lock. Three thoughts raced through my head almost simultaneously. Firstly, would Martyna be in? Secondly, if she was in, was she in bed or still up? And lastly, was Martyna still out? The last thought triggered a fourth thought in my head. Would she be coming back tonight?

I entered the key in the lock, quietly opened the door and closed it behind me. The light timers had done their jobs and I could see light coming from the lounge. I took my shoes off and my jacket and made my way along the hallway to the lounge door. I stopped short of entering and hesitated. If Martyna was sitting in the lounge, what was I going to say? I had had the whole journey home to think about this scenario and yet, here I was standing outside the lounge, without a clue of what to say!

I walked into the lounge. It was empty. I felt a short-lived kind of relief. However, I knew I had to go into the kitchen next. Again, light radiated from the bottom of the closed kitchen door. No time for hesitation, I thought to myself. I opened the door and went in. Again, empty. If Martyna was home, then she would have to be in her room. I turned from the kitchen and slowly made my way upstairs, trying ever so hard not to make a sound and praying that the stairs didn't creak as they normally did when anyone went up them. Of course, they did! I finally made it to the top and peered around the corner to the right-hand side of the landing.

Martyna's room was the first door on the right, so I had to walk past it to get to my room. There was no noise coming from her room. The door was shut and no light could be seen at the foot of the door. I had no idea if she was in there or not. As I walked past the door, I briefly paused and wondered if I should slowly open her door to see if she was in there. I looked at her door, shook my head and carried on to my room, closing my door behind me. I guess I would have to wait until tomorrow morning to find out.

32

I awoke with a startle and immediately reached for my phone to see what the time was. It was 10:27 a.m. I lay still for a moment, listening for any movement in the house. There was nothing, no noise at all, in fact the silence was deafening!

After showering and dressing, I made my way to the top of the stairwell, passing by Martyna's room. Her door was shut, as it was last night and once again, the thought passed through my mind that maybe I should open her door and see if she was there. I didn't and carried on downstairs. I looked into the lounge, Martyna wasn't there, so I approached the kitchen door. I felt apprehensive. Was she there or had she not yet returned from the previous night? I opened the door and walked in. No sign of Martyna. The kitchen looked the same as when I had left the evening before.

I made myself a coffee and sat at the table. I checked my phone, no messages, and no missed calls. I decided I needed to look in Martyna's room. I had to be sure if she was in the house or not. I placed my coffee cup down on the table and made my way back upstairs, arriving outside Martyna's room and lightly knocked on the door.

"Martyna," I said softly. "Martyna," I repeated. There was no answer. I turned the handle and opened the door, slowly at first, but then opening it all the way. The room was empty and her bed looked like it had not been slept in. I closed the door and headed back to the kitchen. I picked up my cell phone from the kitchen table and called Martyna's number.

"Sorry, I am unable to take your call right now, but please leave a message and I'll get back to you. Thanks," was the usual recorded message that I heard as my call was diverted to her voicemail. "Hi, was just checking to see if you were okay? Give me a call when you can, thanks," I said into the phone after waiting for the beep. As I ended my voice message, I also decided to send a quick text message as well.

The time seemed to go very slowly as I pottered around the empty, quiet house. However, at 12:45 p.m. I heard my cell phone buzz, indicating I had received a text message. I eagerly picked up my phone and felt a sense of relief that it was Martyna texting me. I opened the message.

"Hi George. I'm okay. Will be back later. Will not be going with you to collect the girls." It was a concise message. At least I knew she was okay - well at least amongst the land of the living! I decided to make myself a sandwich before heading off to Barbara and Derek's to pick up the girls. As we were staying for tea I knew I wouldn't need much for lunch.

I left the house mid-afternoon and thirty minutes later I pulled into the drive at Barbara and Derek's house. The girls must have seen me arrive, because as soon as I stepped out of the car, the front door opened and Emily and Amy came running towards me.

"Hey girls," I said as I swept them both up in my arms for a group hug.

"Hi Dad," said Emily. "We missed you. But we've had great fun with nanny and grandad. We've even been in the pool!"

"Oh really! Not too cold I hope?"

"No, Grandad has put a heater in the pool so it was nice and warm," added Amy.

"A heater in the pool?" I said looking at Derek who had joined Barbara at the door.

"Yes, that's right," Derek said with a smile. "How are you George?" he continued and gave me a hug.

"I'm good Derek. And great to see you guys." I then turned to Barbara and gave her a hug and a kiss on the cheek.

"No Martyna?" Barbara enquired. "I did say she was more than welcome."

"Yes, I know. Unfortunately, she had a few things to do today, so was unable to make it," I replied hoping that I sounded convincing.

"Well, come in George," Barbara said and I just knew that she thought that there was more to my answer than I was letting on.

Once inside the girls led me through the house to the rear garden where it looked like they had all been prior to my arrival. I sat down on the rattan sofa, which was on the patio overlooking the sparkling pool. It did look amazingly inviting and it wasn't long before Amy asked if she could go back in the pool. Both Emily and Amy were good swimmers and Cheryl and I had always taken them to the local pool from an early age. They were just like fish, so at ease with the water.

"Can we go back in Nanny? Please?" said Amy.

"Of course, darling," replied Barbara. "I'll get you some fresh towels for when you come out. Coffee George?"

"Yes, please Barbara, that sounds good."

"Derek, keep an eye on the girls; George, maybe you can help me with the coffee?" I instantly got the feeling that Barbara wanted to talk to me away from the girls about something.

"Sure," I replied and followed Barbara to the kitchen.

"I'll just go and get the towels for the girls, perhaps you can make a start on the coffee," Barbara said as she disappeared out of the kitchen and up the stairs. By the time she had retuned and delivered the towels to Derek by the pool, the coffee was almost ready to be poured.

"So, you going to tell me George or do you want me to guess?" was Barbara's opening line.

"What do you mean?" I replied trying to delay the inevitable.

"George, I know you have only been here a few minutes, but I'm a woman. And I know something's on your mind. So, are you going to tell me?"

"Women's intuition eh!" I said smiling at her.

"Is it about Martyna?" Barbara pressed. I let out a sigh and looked at Barbara before pausing and returning to pouring out the coffees. "George, I'm not prying. Maybe I can help. I am a woman after all, older, yes, but still a woman," she continued.

"Honestly, it's nothing to worry about. I'm fine. But thanks for asking and I'm grateful for your concern."

"So, it is about Martyna?" I finished pouring the coffees and again looked at Barbara.

"I'm not going to go into detail with you, but yes, it is about Martyna. A lot has happened over the last few months. We've become closer."

"How close? Are you sleeping together?"

"Oh God no! No we are not sleeping together. We talked about our feelings and decided we should not get involved that way as it could jeopardise the girls, especially if things didn't work out between us."

"Very wise. So, what's the problem? Have you had a change of heart?"

"Yes, I think we both have and maybe things could work. We had another talk about things last Sunday and Martyna told me her feelings had grown stronger and deeper for me. However, in between our two conversations, I met a girl, Fiona, on a flight to Frankfurt. She is lovely, charming and on the second occasion that I met her in Frankfurt, well… one thing led to another and we, we slept together. She knows all about my situation with the girls and I told her that I wasn't looking for a relationship. She understands and although she would like to pursue a relationship, she has not made any demands on me."

"How do you feel about this girl - Fiona?"

"I'm not going to lie to you Barbara, I have strong feelings for her and although she lives in Frankfurt, things could just work out between us."

"But what about your feelings for Martyna?"

"Yeah, Martyna. I decided that I needed to choose between the two of them. But before I did, I wanted Martyna to know about Fiona - about me sleeping with her. I thought this was the right thing to do. After all it happened after Martyna and I agreed that we could not be together. She had also been out on a blind date since our initial conversation, so it wasn't like we were 'together', a couple or anything."

"Don't tell me. She took it badly, right?" was Barbara's response. I nodded my head.

"And now I don't know what to do. I would have chosen Martyna. However, since I told her on Friday about Fiona, she hasn't spoken to me, really. And to make matters worse, Sally and Luke set me up on a blind date last night with one of Sally's colleagues. We all went for a meal and then on to a club. As Sally and Luke were on the dance floor, leaving me and this girl together, who should just happen to stroll by, yes, Martyna. She must have thought that I had lied about going out with Luke and Sally, and just went out on a date instead!"

"Oh, George," Barbara said and gave me motherly hug.

"She didn't come home last night either. And from what Sally said, she was with a guy that sounds like her last blind date."

"Have you heard from her at all?"

"Yes, she texted me to say she was okay and would be home later. That's why she is not here, she wasn't back when I left the house."

"So, what now?"

"Well, I'm in Frankfurt this coming week for one night, Wednesday, and have arranged to meet Fiona. I was going to tell her that we could only ever be friends. But now, if I don't have any chance with Martyna, I'm starting to think that maybe I should try to make a go of things with Fiona."

"Is that the right thing to do?" asked Barbara. I paused for a second, pondering the situation.

"No, you're right Barbara, the right thing to do is to not be with anyone. I should just be concentrating on Emily and Amy. And I'm sorry Barbara, it must be so difficult for you to hear me talk about women other than Cheryl. I'm so sorry." Barbara placed her hands either side of my shoulders.

"I not saying 'be with nobody' or 'be with Martyna' or 'be with Fiona!' I don't know what the right thing is for you George. Only you can decide that and I'm positive you will always give Emily and Amy the highest priority in whatever you decide. But what I do know, is that you can count on the full support of Derek and I in whatever decision you make. Yes, it's hard for me as Cheryl's mother to hear you speak about your feelings for other women. But Cheryl's gone. She's not coming back and I'm sure she would have wanted you to find happiness, a new life, a new woman. Remember the past, never forget the happiness - but always embrace the future." Tears were rolling down Barbara's face and we again hugged.

We returned to the garden with the coffees and watched the girls having a wonderful time in the pool. The afternoon went quite quickly. Derek fell asleep as usual and it wasn't long before Barbara was busy in the kitchen preparing sandwiches and all sorts of food for our Sunday Tea spread. The girls only asked once about why Martyna had not joined me in picking them up and as I had done with Barbara when I had first arrived, I explained she had some things to do of her own, preventing her from coming. I think I was more successful and convincing with the girls that I had been with Barbara!

Following tea, and after packing up the girls' things, we said our goodbyes, gave our hugs and kisses to Derek and Barbara, and I strapped the girls safely in the back of the car. Just before I was about to pull away, my cell phone buzzed and I looked at it to see a text message from Martyna.

"Home now. Drive safely," was the brief message. At least Martyna was back! What her mood was going to be like was difficult to tell from the short message.

The girls duly fell asleep on the short journey home but awoke as we approached the house just after 7:30 p.m. I grabbed the girls' bags from the boot and we entered the house. Martyna was standing at the end of the hallway and upon seeing her, the girls ran over to her, as excitedly as they had done when I arrived at Barbara and Derek's earlier. Martyna knelt and gave them a group hug.

"I've missed you guys so much," she said with genuine affection. "Have you had a great time at Nanny and Grandad's?"

"We've had a lovely time, especially in the pool," said Amy. "And we've missed you and Daddy so much too!" she continued. Martyna looked up at me and smiled. It was the first time I had seen her smile in the last forty-eight hours!

"Next time Martyna, can you come with us to Nanny's house and bring your swimming costume. The pool is heated now, so you won't get cold," said Emily. Martyna turned to Emily and smiled.

"We'll see," she quietly replied.

"Right, girls! Upstairs for a shower please. School in the morning!" I said. The girls took their coats and shoes off and went upstairs to start their showers. "I'll be up in minute," I called after them, before turning to Martyna who had now stood back up. "Are you okay?"

"Yes George, I'm fine," she replied, again smiling at me with her naturally deep pink lips. "I have some things to do, so I will be in my room." Martyna turned and also went up the stairs leaving me alone in the hallway and alone in my thoughts.

I emptied the girls dirty laundry into the laundry basket in the utility room and quickly called Barbara to let her know we had arrived safely. After a five minute chat, mainly about the items the girls had left behind, I said goodnight to Barbara and made my way upstairs. Emily had already finished her shower and was dressed for bed. Amy wasn't that far behind her.

"Can I choose a book for our story Dad?" Emily asked.

"Of course, you can sweetheart," I replied. "What are we going to have tonight?"

"I think we should read 'Fing' because it is really funny and I like the way you do the voices of Mr and Mrs Meek and their terrible daughter, Myrtle. And you look like you need cheering up Dad. Are you okay?" My little daughter asking me if I'm okay, took me by surprise. But if she could sense how I felt about Martyna, it was little wonder she would notice when I was sad.

"I'm fine sweetheart, but thanks for asking. And 'Fing' is an excellent choice. Grab the book and I'll meet you on my bed in a couple of minutes. I'm just going to check on Amy." Emily smiled at me and went to get the book.

I entered my bedroom with a freshly showered Amy in her pyjamas, who immediately dived onto the bed where Emily was already lying, with the book in hand.

"Ok you two, make a space in the middle," I said as I climbed onto the bed. The girls snuggled up to me as I opened the book.

"Do you think Martyna might like to listen to the story Daddy?" asked Amy.

"I think she is quite busy in her room," I stuttered.

"Shall I go and ask her," continued Amy.

"Probably best not to disturb her," I replied. Before I could finish my sentence, Amy had slid off the bed and I could hear her knocking on Martyna's door.

"Hello Amy," I heard Martyna say as she opened her door.

"Would you like to listen to the story? It's called 'Fing' and is very funny. I'm sure you would like it," said Amy.

"That sounds like an incredibly good story Amy and I would love to come and listen to it with you. But unfortunately, I can't tonight. But enjoy your story with Daddy and Emily and maybe you can tell me about it in the morning. Goodnight Amy, sleep well." Amy reappeared in my room and jumped up on the bed next to me, resuming her 'snuggled in' position.

"Martyna said no. I think she is a bit busy," she said. With that, I began to read the book about a naughty, rude, obnoxious young girl whose meek and mild parents gave her everything she ever asked for, and more besides, who one day asks them for the ultimate thing - a 'Fing'.

I read for about half an hour and we followed that with a brief cuddle, before I took the girls to bed. I kissed them and wished them a good night and then headed downstairs. Once again, as I had done last night and this morning, I hesitated outside Martyna's room. And once again, carried on downstairs without knocking on her door. I went into the kitchen and opened the fridge, pulled out a bottle of beer and sat at the kitchen table. I popped the cap and took a long swig of the bottle. My cell phone buzzed and I pulled it from my pocket. A message from Fiona.

"Hey George. Hope you had a nice weekend? Looking forward to seeing you on Wednesday. Just thought! Is there anything you don't like to eat? Let me know. Take care, x."

It brought a smile to my face and for the first time since Friday, I felt a little happier. But that feeling didn't last long. I started to reflect on the conversation I had with Barbara earlier. Maybe the 'right thing to do' was exactly what I had said to her. Be with nobody, at least for now. Focus on the girls and tell Fiona on Wednesday, that as much as I feel close to her, the relationship can't go anywhere. Besides, Fiona already knew this, so it wouldn't be a surprise for her. We could just be friends. Yes, that was the right thing to do. As for Martyna, I would apologise to her, hope that our relationship would return to normal, by that, I mean employer / employee, and she would continue to be the girls live in nanny. It would be a tall order, given the feelings that we both had for each other.

I took another long swig of beer and as I put the bottle down on the table, Martyna appeared in the kitchen doorway.

"Hi Martyna," I said. "Do you want a beer?"

"No thanks George. I just wanted to give you this," she said walking slowly towards me and placing a sealed envelope on the table. I looked down at the envelope, which was addressed to me, before looking up again at her.

"What's this?" I said. Martyna paused and let out a sigh.

"It's my letter of resignation. I'll give you time to find someone else, but I think we both know the current situation is not tenable."

"Is this what you really want?" I replied, still looking into her eyes. Martyna sat down opposite me.

"I was wrong George. My reaction to you telling me about this girl in Frankfurt was wrong. You were right! We weren't together, we had decided that it was best for the girls if we kept our relationship on a professional level. I had been on a blind date, so there was no reason for me to react the way I did. I'm sorry George."

"Martyna, you have nothing to be sorry about. I should be the one apologising."

"But my resignation is not really about that. It's about my feelings for you. I told you last weekend about how I felt about you. Unfortunately, you haven't told me how you feel. And when I saw you with that girl last night…"

"Martyna, let me explain…"

"No George, please let me talk," Martyna said raising her hand and closing her eyes. It was obviously extremely difficult for her and she needed to get these words out. She opened her eyes again and looked at me. "It became very clear to me that we have no future together. I tell you how I feel, you say nothing. And yet, you go out on a date-,"

"Martyna, please let me explain-,"

"No need for explanations George," Martyna said, again cutting me off. "I think deep down you are not over your loss yet. And that is quite understandable George. You must have been through hell these last two years, so I don't blame you at all. You see your wife every day in Emily and Amy, a constant reminder of what could have been. And I know you struggle with that. But you are a great father George, and the girls are lucky to have someone like you. But I don't think you are ready yet to commit yourself to someone new - me, and that's a real shame."

"I did tell you I had strong feelings for you," I said.

"George, I love you! I want to be with you, I want us to be together, a family with Emily and Amy, a loving future. Can you tell me the same?" Martyna said in hope that I would reciprocate with equally meaningful words. The words didn't come from my mouth. As I looked past Martyna, I suddenly noticed that Emily was standing in the doorway. I rushed over to her and scooped her up in my arms.

"Hey, sweetheart, what are you doing out of bed?"

"What's going on Dad?" was Emily's upset response.

"Nothing sweetheart. Martyna and I are just having a chat. Nothing to worry about."

"Are you leaving us Martyna?" Emily soberly asked. Both Emily and I had fixed our gaze on Martyna, awaiting her reply.

"It's late Emily, you have school in the morning. Your dad and I have some things to talk about. Please don't worry. See you in the morning," Martyna replied in a comforting manner.

I carried Emily back up to her bed and tucked her in. I could tell that a lot was going through her mind and it wasn't unexpected when her questions started.

"I heard Martyna say she loves you Dad. Do you love her?" I looked at Emily and smiled at her.

"Martyna and I need to talk about a few things. It gets a bit complicated when you are an adult - feelings and stuff like that."

"Please don't let Martyna leave?" I laid down on Emily's bed and cuddled her. "Mummy left without saying goodbye to me. And now Martyna is leaving too. It's not fair." Tears formed around Emily's eyes and I could feel my own eyes welling up.

"Mummy never meant to leave without saying goodbye to you or any of us. Mummy would never do that if she had a choice. But unfortunately she never had a choice. And anyway, she never left us, because she is always with us in our hearts. And whenever we are sad or need help, all we have to do is think of Mummy and remember the happiness we had with her - her love, her smell, her lovely hair."

"And her smile and cuddles," added Emily through her tears.

I stayed with Emily for half an hour and she finally fell asleep in my arms. I gently manoeuvred myself off her bed and slowly walked down the stairs to the kitchen. Martyna was still sitting at the kitchen table.

"Is Emily okay?" Martyna asked.

"Not really. She's such a brave girl - they both are really. She asked me not to let you leave." This visibly upset Martyna and she placed her hands over her eyes. "She said that it was unfair that her mum never said goodbye and now, you were leaving too." Martyna reached for the box of tissues that were on the table and pulled out a couple. She patted her eyes and blew her nose, which by now was starting to stream.

"I'm sorry George. I can't do this," she said and got up from her chair. "I'll see you in the morning," she continued and made her way out of the kitchen, up the stairs and into her room. Once again, and as it had done on numerous occasions over the weekend, the house fell silent. I picked up my beer bottle, went into the lounge and sat on the sofa and thought what a fucking mess all this was! My life was perfect less than two years ago, perfect! I had a loving, beautiful wife, the mother of my two adorable girls, a good job, a nice house, friends, and a bright future ahead of me. Everything ticking along superbly. Then, one morning, a guy has a heart attack while driving along on the opposite carriageway of the A1, and wham! My life turns to shit!

That's not strictly true. Yes, the gaping hole that Cheryl's death created in my life was immediately evident. But I still had my house, my job, friends and most importantly, I had my girls, Emily, and Amy. I still had my adorable children to love, to look after, protect, comfort, and do everything I could to ensure their future happiness. I still had a purpose. And it was only right, that this purpose should be at the sacrifice of my own wants and needs. At least until they were adults, capable of looking after themselves. So, regardless of my feelings for Martyna or indeed Fiona for that matter, they needed to be suppressed, so I could fulfil my 'purpose' and do the right thing for my children. And one of those things was to persuade Martyna to stay. Convince her that regardless of our feelings for each other, we could make this work in a professional way. And if in time, she left because she met someone and wanted to start a life with that person, then that was okay. But it would be futile to just leave because we were incapable of having a professional relationship. Yes, for the sake of Emily and Amy, I needed to get Martyna to stay.

33

Breakfast the next morning was a little awkward. Amy was her customary self as she had no idea of the situation between Martyna and me. Emily was a little quieter than usual and Martyna and I did our best to act as if everything was normal.

"When are you away this week Dad?" asked Emily as we all sat around the kitchen table.

"Well, I fly out Wednesday morning, stay for one night in Frankfurt and then I'll fly home on Thursday evening. I should be back to say goodnight to you guys," I replied as cheerfully as I could. Emily got up from her chair, placed her empty cereal bowl and spoon in the dishwasher and exited the kitchen without saying another word. Martyna and I looked at each other, both saddened by what we had just witnessed.

"Is Emily okay Daddy?" asked Amy.

"Er, yes. I think she is just, um-, tired from your exciting weekend at Nanny and Grandad's house. Don't worry, she'll be fine. Unfortunately, I must leave too. Have a lovely day at school sweetheart and I'll see you later for dinner," I said getting up from my chair, and kissing Amy on her forehead.

"You have a lovely day too," a smiling Amy replied.

"I'll, see you later, Martyna," I said nervously.

"Yes…yes George, I'll see you later. Gammon okay with you for dinner later?" she replied trying to act as close to the old 'Martyna' as she could. I nodded, again smiled at Amy, and exited the kitchen. I noticed Emily sitting in the lounge. I went in and knelt in front of her.

"Don't worry sweetheart. I'll talk to Martyna and see if we can sort something out."

"Promise me you will try to make her stay Dad, please?"

"I'll do my very best darling, my very best."

I left the house and went to work feeling more upset than I had felt in a long time. It was one thing for me to be upset about the choices I had made. But it stung like hell, knowing that Emily was hurt because of my actions. Because I didn't have the courage to tell Martyna how I really felt about her. Because I let her believe I was on a date on Saturday night instead of making her hear the truth. And because maybe Jennifer was right all along. Maybe I did fear giving up either Fiona or Martyna for the sake of the other one. Maybe I did just want them both! It was on the drive to work that I decided that I would talk to Martyna this evening and get her to stay but purely in a professional relationship. I would then tell Fiona on Wednesday that we would only be friends and I would stop thinking about my own needs and wants. Instead, I would dedicate the next ten years of my life to Emily and Amy, to ensure their happiness. It was clear to me that this is what needed to be done.

As I entered my office, I suddenly realised that I had not responded to Fiona's text message about my likes and dislikes regarding the meal she was going to cook on Wednesday. I sat at my desk, unpacked my laptop, and placed it in its docking station, turned it on and then pulled out my phone. I re-read Fiona's message and then replied.

"Hi Fiona, sorry for not replying sooner. I'm happy with anything for dinner. Please don't go to too much trouble. Looking forward to seeing you Wednesday, George." I felt a strange sensation as I pressed the send button about the last comment in the text message. 'Looking forward to seeing you Wednesday' – as much as I was, it would also likely be a sad and uncomfortable evening, given I would be telling Fiona that we could only ever be friends. However, it needed to be done and I was hoping that Fiona would be understanding about everything, as indeed she had been from the moment, I had met her. Thinking about Fiona brought a smile to my face and my mind started wandering again. The question just popped right back in there! 'So, remind me again, why can't you carry on with Fiona?' a little inner voice said to me. 'Because you need to focus on the girls,' came the almost instant reply. It was like having two 'little George's' one sitting on each shoulder. One saying one thing and the other saying something else. Almost a 'Good versus Evil' an 'Angel versus the Devil.'

"If Martyna is not interested and is going to leave anyway, you would be mad to give up Fiona. She's kind, beautiful, undemanding, great body, sexually stimulating; you could just carry on with her and see how things develop," said the 'Devil' George.

"Amy and Emily must come first. You will only lose sight of their needs if you are distracted by a woman, any woman," was the 'Angel' George's response.

"How much distraction would Fiona be? She lives in Frankfurt for Christ's sake! It's not like you will be spending every day with her is it? Keep her keen and tell her 'you'll see how the relationship develops' of course, no promises!" again came back the response from 'Devil' George.

"That would not be fair to Fiona. You know you will always put Emily and Amy first. It would not be right to 'string along' Fiona and disappointing her every time you had to choose between her and the girls. You know the girls would win every, single time!" retorted the 'Angel' George. "Do the right thing George, do the right thing."

I placed my hands to me eyes and let out a long sigh. There was a knock on my door and as I looked up, I saw Sarah standing there. As ever, Sarah looked gorgeous, reverting to her customary dress code. A tiny, short, black skirt, a white sleeveless, low cut blouse, and tan coloured high heels. Even though all these thoughts about Martyna and Fiona were going through my mind, I couldn't help but think what she looked like underneath the few garments of clothing she was wearing!

"You okay George?" she asked, continuing her concern for me from the previous week.

"Yes, yes I'm fine. Busy weekend, that's all," I replied smiling at her.

"Coffee?" she asked.

"Yes, thanks Sarah. By the way, please can you set up a call with Heinz and Jana today, just to finalise a few things on the proposals for the board. I would like you to join me for that call. If there are any changes required, I would like you to get that done today if possible. As you know, I fly to Frankfurt Wednesday morning, so we really only have two days to complete everything and I want to take tomorrow to just review the whole proposal."

"I'm on it, George. I will look at your calendar and set up the call. And, thanks again George - you know, for believing in me and treating me more like a colleague than just some - well, this," replied Sarah, pointing to her body. "I'll get your coffee," she said and turned to leave. I smiled at her. Partly because yes, I was thinking about her body and partly because of the way she pointed at her body just like Jana had done! But more so I was thinking about how far Sarah had come since I had that chat with her at the Christmas party. She was confident now, not just in her looks anymore, but in her abilities as well. She was learning every day, never refused to take on additional duties and what's more, completed those duties with accuracy, imagination, and style. Sarah contributed, wasn't afraid to share her ideas and was earning the trust and respect of both Frank and Hilary. I was so pleased for her and proud of her for finally taking control of her own destiny.

It was this last thought that resonated with me. 'Taking control of your own destiny!' Was that something I was doing right now? Was focussing 'only' on the girls without even considering my own needs a recipe for disaster? I mean, if I weren't particularly happy, would that 'rub off' on the girls? Emily had already developed a sense of my moods and I'm sure it wouldn't be long before Amy followed suit. Would me supressing my own wants and needs, be harmful to my relationship with the girls? And anyway, surely it would be a good thing for the girls if I were to have a relationship with someone that could lead to a normal family life with them! Stop it George! Stop it! I was going around in circles. I needed to concentrate on my work and decided to push my personal thoughts away for the time being.

The rest of the day went quickly and the call with Heinz, Jana and Tanja and Nigel, went very well. I wasn't expecting the latter to be on the call, and Nigel appeared to be continuing his new, or was it old, persona? Once again, he was incredibly supportive of the work that Heinz and Jana had subsequently completed since returning from the trip and was in total agreement of my proposal approach for the board. Tanja called me for a 'one on one' following the call with everyone as she was again, pleasantly surprised by Nigel's conduct.

Just before leaving work my phone rang. I looked at the display and saw Luke's name.

"Hey Luke, how are you?" I said, answering the call.

"Hello mate. I'm good. More to the point, how are you? I didn't want to call yesterday as I knew things might be difficult, but what happened?"

"Well, Martyna stayed out all night. She wasn't back by the time I left to get the girls from Barbara's but was home when I got back."

"Did you manage to talk to her?"

"Once the girls were in bed, Martyna handed me her letter of resignation."

"Shit! What did she say?"

"She just said the situation was not tenable for her."

"But did she say why?" pressed Luke.

"She said it was nothing to do with me telling her about Fiona. It was because of the feelings she has for me. She told me she loves me and wanted to make a life with me and the girls. If I didn't feel the same, then she said it would be unbearable for her to live in the same house as me, you know, to just carry on as if nothing was different."

"But you do, I mean you do have feelings for her, right? Do you love her George?" Luke pressed. I paused. Luke was the first person to directly ask me that question.

"I," again I paused. "I suppose I do love her, yes, I do. But I didn't tell Martyna that. Somehow, I couldn't. I think I was scared to. I feared admitting my feelings for her."

"If you love her George, why can't you tell her?"

"Maybe I'm not ready for a new relationship. Martyna said she thinks I'm not completely over Cheryl yet, which could be true. It might be because I'm scared of failing with Martyna and the effect that would have on Emily and Amy."

"George, you will never be completely over Cheryl. She was your wife, your soul mate. She is the mother of your two children. Don't be too hard on yourself mate, Cheryl will always be with you. But if there is one person that understands, it's Martyna. She knew about your situation long before she fell in love with you. And although you can't start any relationship knowing if it will work out, you can't 'not' start one because you're thinking it won't!" replied Luke. I have to say, I was a little surprised by Luke's words of wisdom!

"It's too late now anyway. Especially after she saw me with Rebecca on Saturday night. Martyna thought I had lied about going out with you and Sally and instead just went out on a date!"

"Didn't you explain to her that you had no idea about Rebecca? It was all Sally's doing?"

"I tried, but Martyna didn't let me. She wasn't interested in any explanations. It's done mate. And I'm sure it's better this way. I'll tell Fiona that we can only be friends when I see her on Wednesday and I'll start a new search for a replacement nanny on the weekend. The girls will soon get used to someone else."

"They might get used to someone else George, but they love Martyna - as much as you do. Don't throw that away."

"Why are you doing this Luke? Why are you so invested in my happiness?" I said rather annoyed. Again, there was few seconds pause. "Well?" I pushed Luke for an answer.

"Because you are my friend George. I love you like the brother I never had. And as much as you always thought that it was me looking out for you when we were growing up, it was always the other way round. It was you that made me work hard at school. It was you that said we should go to university. It was you that gave me confidence. Yeah, I was bigger than you and I cracked a few 'skulls', but you did far more for me than I ever did for you. I would be a binman or a shelf stacker in Sainsburys if it weren't for you. And even though you said I'm not, I still feel responsible for Cheryl not being here. I'm damned if I'm going to let you lose Martyna as well. She loves you and you love her. So, what's the problem?"

"I can't do this Luke, I'll talk to you later," I said and ended the call. Almost immediately, my phone rang again. It was Luke. I rejected the call. I'm not sure of the reason why I was so upset with Luke. Was I in denial and I knew deep down he was right? Was it because he still felt responsible for Cheryl's death even though I had told him it wasn't his fault? Or was I just embarrassed by my lack of courage with Martyna and the fact that Luke had been the one to point it out to me? More than likely, it was a combination of all three, plus countless other reasons that were swirling around my head.

The journey home was not a pleasant one. I felt like the convicted felon taking a slow walk to the electric chair. As I pulled up outside the house and turned the engine off, I sat back in my seat for a few seconds and gave myself a pep talk. 'It will be fine George, act normal, the girls will be okay and will forget about Martyna in time. You need to concentrate on them and not yourself. Family and work, that's what you need to do. Tell Martyna you understand the situation and will start the search for her replacement on the weekend. Yes, that's what you need to do,' I told myself.

I put the key in the front door and entered the house. I could hear the girls and Martyna talking in the kitchen. It all sounded very normal, just like it had always been. I took off my shoes and went into the kitchen.

"Hey girls," I said as I entered. The girls were sitting at the kitchen table colouring in pictures of horses.

"Hello Daddy," said Amy. "We've made an apple pie for dessert!"

"Wow! That sounds amazing. Can't wait to try that," I replied. Emily didn't look up and continued colouring in.

"Hi Emily," I said. She stopped colouring and looked at me.

"Hi Dad," she said without emotion and then continued colouring in. I looked across at Martyna who shook her head sorrowfully.

"Well, I'll just go and get changed," I said.

"Yes, dinner will be in about ten minutes," said Martyna. "Okay girls, we need to start tidying away the colouring things so we can lay the table for dinner," she continued.

"Okay Martyna," said Amy, nothing came from Emily. I left to go upstairs as the girls started to clear away their papers and pens.

When I returned to the kitchen, Martyna had already plated up the food. The girls were sitting down and I took my usual seat at the head of the table. Martyna brought over the girls' plates before returning to the work top and bringing over two more plates for me and her.

"Thank you Martyna. This looks great." It did! Roast gammon, mustard mash, peas, carrots, and broccoli.

"Thank you Martyna," said Amy. Again, nothing from Emily. I looked at Emily. She looked at me, holding my stare for a few seconds before turning to Martyna.

"Thank you Martyna," Emily said. We all started to eat.

"So, what have you guys done at school today?" I asked trying to relieve the tension and act as normally as possible. Amy was straight in with a reply.

"Well, today Miss Raven told us about the great fire of London and how it started in Pudding Lane by the King's baker Thomas Farriner on the 2nd of September 1666!" I was impressed that Amy had remembered these facts and figures.

"That must have been interesting," I enthusiastically replied.

"Yes, it was and tomorrow, we have to paint pictures of what we think it must have been like. Miss Raven said she will show us what the buildings were like back then and then it's up to us to use our imagination," Amy continued, seemingly quite excited about the prospect of painting a picture.

"Well, I hope I can see your picture when it's finished. I'm sure you will do a great job on that. And what about you Emily, what did you do today?"

"Not much," was Emily's short reply.

"Em, what's wrong with you?" asked Amy.

"Nothing," Emily snapped back. Although I understood exactly why Emily was upset, I did feel a little disappointed that she was taking it out on Amy.

"Please don't talk to you sister like that Emily," I said. Amy looked at me; Emily didn't. There followed a few seconds of silence before Emily finally apologised.

"Sorry for snapping at you Amy," she said, still looking down at her food. I looked at Martyna, but she returned the same sorrowful look she had done before I went to change my clothes.

"Okay you two, after dinner, I would like to talk to you both."

"What about?" asked Amy.

"He's going to tell us that Martyna is leaving us now! Just like when Mummy left us. It's not fair," Emily shouted. She got up from the table and ran out of the kitchen, up the stairs and into her room. Martyna was about to get up and follow her.

"Please sit down Martyna and finish your meal. You too sweetheart," I said to Amy. "Let's just finish our meal, eh?" Amy looked at me worriedly, so I smiled back at her reassuringly. I stood up, removed Emily's plate from the table and placed it on the work surface. I reached for another plate in the cupboard and covered her meal with it. I sat back down and again smiled at Amy.

"It's okay sweetheart. We'll talk after dinner. I think it's best to give Emily some time right now. But please don't worry darling, everything will be alright." Amy looked directly at Martyna.

"Are you leaving us too?" she asked Martyna in a small, vulnerable voice. Martyna's eyes started to 'well up' as she looked back at Amy.

"Not for a while," Martyna softly replied. Amy looked down at her dinner and began to eat without saying anything back to Martyna.

We finished eating with the minimum amount of conversation. It was an extremely tense atmosphere. Although the smell of the apple pie was very inviting, nobody wanted dessert, so Martyna and I cleared away the dirty dishes and tidied up the kitchen while Amy continued her 'colouring in' on the kitchen table. No words were spoken. Once everything was done, I turned to Amy.

"Okay Amy, do you want to come with me and we'll go and talk to Emily?" I said.

"Yes. Can I take this picture to give to her?" Amy replied, holding up a beautifully coloured in picture of a tan coloured horse. Even though she must have been as upset as Emily was, she still wanted to do something nice for her sister.

"Of course, sweetheart. It's a lovely picture and I'm sure Emily will be thrilled with it," I said, trying to keep my own emotions in check. I scooped Amy up in my arms as she clung onto her picture, before turning to Martyna.

"Thanks, Martyna-, for dinner. And sorry for, well, you know - I'm sorry."

I made my way upstairs with Amy and we stood outside Emily's room. I knocked gently on her door before slowly opening it and we both walked in. Emily was lying on her bed, hands behind her head, staring at the ceiling.

"Hey sweetheart," I said and sat down on her bed, next to her.

"I've done this picture for you Em, look," Amy said holding out the horse picture. Emily looked at the picture and smiled at her sister.

"Thank you, Amy, it's lovely and my favourite colour horse too!" Emily got up from her bed and gave Amy a big cuddle. As I watched them embrace, I smiled and intuitively knew that I was doing the right thing. My focus had to be on the girls for the foreseeable future. If that meant giving up on Fiona and Martyna wanting to leave, so be it. It would again be like in the days and months that followed Cheryl's death, just the three of us, together as a family.

"Girls, come and sit down on the bed," I said. Emily and Amy duly obliged and sat down at the top end of the Emily's bed.

"What's going on Daddy? Why is Martyna leaving?" asked Amy.

"Martyna loves Dad, and Dad doesn't love Martyna, that's why she wants to leave us, isn't it?" jumped in Emily before I could answer Amy.

"You two will always be my priority, you do know that don't you? I love you both so much and will always do my best to keep you safe and happy. When Mummy died it was extremely hard for all of us and I tried my best to be both 'Mummy and Daddy' and take on all the things that Mummy used to do for all of us. But I couldn't do it. I'm so sorry that I failed you guys. I needed some help and that's how we found Martyna. We've all grown very fond of Martyna and I know she loves you two very much-,"

"She also loves you Dad, she loves you!" again Emily interrupted. I smiled at her.

"Maybe she does, but…"

"We love Martyna too. She's not our mummy but we do love her. Why don't you love Martyna Daddy?" came the interruption, this time from Amy.

"I'm so pleased that you both feel that way about Martyna. And you're right, she will never take the place of your mum. Nobody will ever do that. But sometimes, when two people get close to each other and start a relationship, it doesn't always mean that they stay together. After a while, they realise that maybe they don't like the same things or get annoyed about little things the other one does. What they thought was going to last forever, in fact is over quite quickly."

"But I think you do love Martyna. Just tell us if you love her?" again asked Emily, more insistently this time. These were tough questions coming from my two young daughters! What do they know about love anyway, I thought to myself? But then I realised just how much they did know about love. They know and feel the love I have for them, the love they had from Cheryl and the love they receive from their grandparents. And as it seems, just as importantly, the love they feel from Martyna! And they give that love right back by the bucket-load by the way they act, talk, cuddle, kiss, and care for those around them. So, although the girls might not know about the intimate side of a relationship and the love felt during the physical act of 'love making', they certainly did know what love is and experienced it every day.

"What I'm trying to explain, very badly, is that I can't risk having a relationship with anybody where you two become close to that person too, only for it to fail and cause you upset. We've only known Martyna for, well, nearly a year now, and you are both quite upset already about the fact that she could leave us. Imagine what it would be like if you had known Martyna for a few years and, well let's just say she was not just your nanny, but more like you mum, and then she decided to leave. I can't control Martyna's feelings, but I can control mine. And if Martyna feels that it is for the best that she moves on with her life elsewhere, then we must respect that and wish her well, even though we will all miss her. But I will promise you both that I will talk to Martyna and try to convince her to stay."

"The only way she will stay is if you tell her you love her," a sad Emily said. "And I don't agree with you Dad. We don't want Martyna to take the place of mum. But she makes us happy and I'm sure she makes you happy too. And I think we could all be happy together."

We all laid down on Emily's bed and had a cuddle, without talking and stayed there for a while. I think each of us had our own thoughts running through our heads that we just needed to think about on our own. I know I certainly did.

"Emily, I saved your dinner sweetheart. Do you want me to heat it up for you? You must be hungry?" I said, breaking the silence.

"I'm not really hungry Dad," Emily replied. "But thanks for saving it for me, I really like roast gammon." I smiled.

"What about some apple pie? And ice cream? Or custard?" I replied.

"Yes please," said Amy rather excitedly.

"That sounds yummy," said Emily.

We made our way back downstairs to the kitchen and saw a rather sad-looking Martyna staring into space sitting at the kitchen table.

"We would love to try some of your wonderful apple pie Martyna," I said smiling at her. The girls made their way over to

475

Martyna and both gave her a warm, loving cuddle. Martyna was physically moved by this affectionate gesture from the girls and looked up at me, again with tears in her eyes.

"Sit down George and I will get the pie," she said trying to hold back the tears.

"No, stay there, I'll get the pie," I softly replied and set about making the custard.

Dessert seemed a lot more relaxed than dinner had been and following it, the girls went upstairs for their showers. An early night was needed. After reading to the girls and putting them to bed, I made my way back to the kitchen. Martyna was once again sitting at the kitchen table.

"How are they?" she asked.

"A bit upset still, a bit confused, a bit angry, I don't know really. How are you?" I replied.

"The same as them. George, you do understand that I can't stay here, don't you? I love the girls and I love being with them. And I love you too. But you not feeling the same way about me, means that I just can't stay here. I'm so sorry."

"I never said 'I don't' feel the same way about you. Okay, I never said 'I do' feel the same way about you either. I'm scared Martyna. Scared of the future and of letting my feelings show. Scared of getting too close to anyone. Scared of getting hurt again. I told you the other night that Emily compared you leaving us, like her mum leaving. Well, the girls weren't the only ones Cheryl left. The pain I felt and still do about Cheryl 'leaving' is something I never want to feel again. And I do not want the girls to go through that again. You know that I don't mean somebody dying, I just mean somebody leaving, not being in their lives anymore. I was incredibly lucky with Cheryl. We knew we would be together for the rest of our lives. What we didn't know is that one of our lives would be so short. Statistics say that I won't be that lucky if I try again. It's not that 'I don't' love you."

"I understand George. I don't agree with not taking chances for fear of failure, but I do understand and especially about you wanting to protect the girls. My parents always told me that nothing worthwhile ever comes without sacrifice and working hard. I think you are worthwhile George Hart; the girls are worthwhile and I would sacrifice anything to be with you. And I'm sure we would both work hard to make our relationship work. But I don't have a crystal ball, a magical view of the future and I can't tell you that we will always be together. I had hoped we would, but there are never any guarantees in life, something I don't really need to tell you. You already know that." Martyna stood up and walked towards me. "I have some things I need to do, so I will be in my room. Good night George," she said, taking my left hand in her right hand and gently squeezing it, before leaving the kitchen and going upstairs to her room.

I made a cup of tea, took it into the lounge and sat on the sofa. Although a lot of things were racing through my mind, only one question kept popping up again and again. 'Are you being a fool, George Hart?' Why would you not want to grasp with both hands the opportunity of having a relationship with this gorgeous woman, who your wonderful daughters adore and who loves you? Why? Why George? Of course, the answer was because if our relationship fails, the girls will be hurt far more than they are hurting right now at the prospect of Martyna leaving. That's why George. That's why you can't get involved with Martyna and why you can't get involved with anyone. You need to concentrate on Emily and Amy and nothing else!

But what if it would be good for the girls to have Martyna not just as a nanny, but as a step mum? It might be a difficult transition for them, and it could cause conflict. After all, Martyna only really had jurisdiction over the girls when I wasn't around. That would change if Martyna was more than just the nanny!

For the next thirty minutes I batted backwards and forwards arguments for and against being brave and taking a chance on happiness with Martyna. Alas, there were no final outcomes other than it was probably best all round to just stick to the plan. I would tell Fiona on Wednesday night that we can only be friends and I would start the search for a replacement for Martyna at the weekend. I finished my tea and went to bed.

34

The next day once again went all too quickly and I didn't get a chance to talk much to Martyna. I did briefly tell her that we all really wanted her to stay, but if she had made her mind up, I would start looking for a replacement at the weekend. This appeared to upset her a bit and I again found myself alone in the lounge that evening.

I left before the girls and Martyna were awake the next morning as I had an early flight to catch to Frankfurt and I decided to drive to the airport myself instead of running the risk of the taxi turning up late. I nearly missed the flight as events unfolded that appeared to be determined to keep from getting on-board the aircraft.

Firstly, there had been a car collision, nothing too serious, a 'bump' between two cars, not far from the house. Unfortunately, the two drivers involved, a male and a female, seemed intent on delaying everyone around them by blocking the road and taking forever to exchange insurance details. They then proceeded to ask everyone in the long line of traffic that had built up at either end of their cars, for eye-witness statements. The whole thing took about twenty-five minutes which made getting to the airport in time to catch the flight a little harder. But as soon as I had got through the accident and of course, dropped my window to mutter 'inconsiderate arseholes' as I passed the two protagonists of the collision, I thought I should be okay.

However, I didn't account for every traffic light that I subsequently passed to be red! This just added to my frustration!

When I arrived at the short-term car park at Terminal Two, it took forever to find a parking space. I thought it would be relatively empty at that time in the morning. No such fucking luck! Yes, I was getting increasingly frustrated. After finally finding somewhere to park, I raced into the terminal to the departure area and security. I stopped in my tracks! The queue was long. Extremely long! I looked at my watch and saw that I had five minutes until boarding. And if the gate was the usual one, it was a ten-minute walk once I had passed through security. Looking at the queue I guessed it would take twenty to thirty minutes to get through. At this rate, I would miss the flight! 'Where the fuck had all these people come from at this time in the morning!' was my initial thought.

No time for complaining. I started asking people in front of me if I could go ahead of them as I was late for my flight. Most of them were surprisingly obliging and let me through. However, there were the odd comments like 'Oi you, we've all got flights to catch you know' and 'Wait your turn mate, you impatient prick.' Some just simply called out 'wanker' which if I'm not mistaken were mostly voiced from females!

I finally made it to the front, placed my hand luggage, laptop and all my metal objects into the provided grey bins, on the conveyer and proceeded to the x-ray machine. I got the nod from the security guy to walk through and, of course, the machine beeped! 'Fuck! I just don't need this,' I thought to myself.

"Step this way sir," said the security guy. I walked to the side of the machine and waited…and waited… and waited some more.

"Actually, I'm in a bit of a hurry," I said.

"Okay sir, just waiting for my colleague to take care of you, won't be long," was the security guy's very polite response. Another few minutes passed.

"I'm going to miss my flight," I said rather annoyed to the security guy.

"He's here now sir, don't panic. Or have you got something to hide?" he replied again very politely and smiled at me as if to say if you carry on moaning we'll conduct a full body search and it'll be 'touch your toes time!'

With the search finally over (I had left a pound coin in my jacket pocket! - fucking idiot!) and having collected my things, I ran towards the gate. As I was running, I could hear announcements that my gate was closing and thought I had missed it. However, as I reached the gate, the 'gate agent' greeted me with a smile.

"Just made it sir," she said.

"Thanks," I said, panting heavily and in a slightly sweaty state.

As I sat down in my seat, I felt a sense of relief and started to relax. It crossed my mind that this was some sort of punishment for not making time the previous evening to have a proper conversation with Martyna. I really should have talked to her last night and although it would probably have made no difference to her decision to leave, I at least would have upheld my promise to Emily and Amy that I would do all I could to convince Martyna to stay. I decided that I would try one more time on Friday night. It would have to be Friday as I was back late on Thursday evening and if Martyna's recent habits were anything to go by, she would have gone to bed by the time I got home. Yes - I would talk to her again on Friday!

The flight was uneventful and I wasn't bothered by loud-mouthed Americans or beautiful ladies touching my legs, or anyone for that matter! After landing, I made a quick call to Tanja before making my way out of the airport. I waited outside for my pick-up, which was going to be Tanja. However, to my surprise Jana's car pulled up in front of me. She dropped the passenger window, leant across the passenger seat, and looked up at me with her beautiful, big green eyes.

481

"Hi George, jump in," she said.

"Hi Jana. Where's Tanja?" I replied getting into the passenger seat.

"She had to take a call right after you called her, so she asked me to pick you up. That's okay, isn't it?"

"Sure, no problem," I said. Once again Jana was wearing a short skirt, exposing those lovely long legs of hers and my mind drifted back to few weeks ago and our nights of intimacy. Jana must have caught me looking at her legs.

"Yes, I still think about our nights together too," she said smiling. I looked at her and smiled back.

"So how are you Jana?" I asked.

"Yeah, not too bad George. Heinz and I have worked hard on the numbers and I've seen the draft of your proposal, looks good," she replied.

"I'll ask you again, how are you Jana?" I said.

"George, I'm fine. Miss you, but I understand and now I'm focussing on my career. Mind you, there is a new guy at work, my age, quite good looking, a bit of a twat, but has potential," she replied and once again turned and smiled at me.

"That's great," I said smiling back at her. We continued to chat openly for the rest of the short journey. It was wonderful to see her and although we knew much more about each other, both physically and mentally than the last time I came to Frankfurt, there were no embarrassments or awkward silences. It was great and we both felt extremely comfortable in each other's company.

When we arrived, Jana and I went up to Tanja's office. Heinz was already there and he and Tanja were chatting in German.

"George, come in," said Tanja and she got up from behind her desk, walked towards me and gave me the customary hug and a kiss on the cheek. "How are you?"

"Hi Tanja, yeah, I'm good thanks, you?" I replied.

"Yes, very well, still slightly 'confused' about Nigel, but apart from that, I'm good. And how are my girls?" I paused slightly and I think this gave Tanja a minor cause for concern.

"They're okay," I replied. Tanja looked at me quizzically.

"Let's talk later," she said.

"Mr. Hart, good to see you," said Heinz standing up from his chair and shaking my hand.

"Herr Mayer, always a pleasure," I responded. "How are you?"

"I'm good George, glad that Jana and I have completed the numbers and glad that you're here to present it," Heinz replied smiling. Although Heinz was excellent at what he did, he always struggled when doing a presentation. And it was particularly noticeable when the presentation was 'internal', to colleagues. I got the impression he thought because people knew him, he should be confident and have interesting things to say. That just seemed to heap a load more expectation on his shoulders and invariably, his presentations suffered because of it. So, presenting to the board, was quite daunting for him.

"No worries, Heinz," I said. Tanja had arranged for refreshments and we all chatted for a few minutes while we drank our coffee.

"So, what is the agenda for the next two days?" I asked Tanja.

"Well, you guys need to work together and insert all the numbers in the relevant places of the presentation. Oh, and decide who's doing what when you present to the board. I don't just want George to do it all," replied Tanja, looking at Heinz and Jana. "After all, it was a team we sent down there and the team will present to the board," she continued. Jana and Heinz looked at each other with a certain amount of apprehension.

"Speaking of the team," I said "Where is Nigel? He should be involved in this."

"Glad you mentioned Nigel, George. So, are you going to finally tell me what black magic, voodoo spell or hypnosis you put him under when you were in Africa to make him a different person?" asked Tanja. I looked at Jana and then Heinz who were just as intrigued, before returning to Tanja.

"We just talked, that's it."

"You do know he's been asking me how he can support the sales effort more and how he wants to 'educate' the catering facility General Managers so that they become more customer focused," Tanja said, surprisingly.

"That's good, isn't it?" I hesitantly replied.

"Yes, of course it's good. But I want to know how you turned this conniving, nasty, manipulating, total fucking twat into, well, Mother Teresa? The CEO of Ethiopian Airlines called Victor last week and heaped nothing but praise on Nigel, you guys as well, but Nigel? Come on, really?"

"We talked and he had an epiphany. That's all I can say really," I said smiling at Tanja. The more I smiled, the more she got wound up.

"Do you have something on him, George? A picture of him in a compromising position? A file? Maybe evidence of misconduct?" Tanja pressed.

"Nothing at all. But let's just see how he goes. Maybe he will revert to type, who knows? But for now, let's just enjoy working with him, okay?"

"Alright George, have it your way," Tanja said finally smiling at me. Anyway, getting back to your original question, Nigel has some meetings this morning that unfortunately he can't get out of, but he will join you this afternoon and share with you some things he learned from Lars that could help with the presentation, whatever that means. He also said he would like to take you all out for dinner tonight. 'Get the gang back together' I think was the phrase he used."

"I, er, unfortunately I already have a dinner date tonight. Sorry," I said.

"Can't you break it?" enquired Tanja.

"Not really, erm, it's an old friend who I haven't seen for a while, I promised I would go out for dinner," I stutteringly replied. Jana looked directly at me with disbelieving eyes.

"Well, you can tell Nigel yourself this afternoon. Now, I have a meeting to run to, but I will join you about 4:30 p.m. and maybe we can have a run through of the presentation. We present to the board at 11 a.m. tomorrow morning. The meeting should last two hours and the board has arranged lunch for us, so please don't go arranging any lunch dates for tomorrow George," said Tanja a little sarcastically.

"Understood," I said, saluting Tanja in a joking fashion.

Heinz, Jana, and I left Tanja's office and headed to one of the numerous meeting rooms that were available to set up our laptops and start work on finalising the presentation. As we left Tanja's office, Heinz darted into the nearest male toilet, leaving Jana and I alone.

"You're meeting that woman, aren't you?" She said to me somewhat annoyed.

"What?" I said trying to buy some time.

"The one you met before, the one you met on the flight. You're meeting her, aren't you?"

"Erm, yes. I am meeting her, Fiona. But it's not what you think."

"Oh really," came the cynical response from Jana.

"Jana! It's 'really not' what you think. We're just friends and although I told Tanja that she was an 'old' friend, that isn't strictly true, I'm not having a relationship with her and we are just friends, okay?" Jana paused for a second as if to gather her thoughts.

"Sorry George. Not sure why I was getting upset about it anyway. Nothing to do with me. We're all good, you and me, all good," Jana said and smiled at me. "Mind you, if you think I'm going to dinner with Nigel and Heinz on my own, you must be mad! You have to help me get out of it - deal?"

"Deal," I said and smiled back at her. Before Heinz had re-joined us in the meeting room, I told Jana that she should say that she had a call from her parents who were 'unexpectedly' in town tonight and wanted to see her for dinner, to get her out of dinner with Nigel. She thought it was a good plan and I said I would back her up with the story.

We worked efficiently for the rest of the morning and by the time Nigel had joined us after lunch, the presentation was pretty much finished. Heinz, Jana, and I had run through it so we knew who was presenting which parts. As Heinz and Jana were a little nervous, I volunteered to take most of the presentation on my shoulders, which they were grateful for. When Nigel entered the room, he made a direct line for me.

"George, great to see you. Sorry I couldn't be here this morning, but I had some things to attend to. How are you?" he said with great enthusiasm and friendliness.

"I'm great Nigel, you?"

"Never better actually!" he replied and as we shook hands, he leaned into me and whispered, "maybe we can have a quick chat later?" I nodded my head in agreement. "Heinz, Jana, good to see you guys. You know George, these two have been working really hard on the numbers and from what I've seen of your presentation, I think we can safely say the board will be impressed with the work you guys did down there," Nigel continued.

"The work 'we' did?" I said to Nigel. "You contributed too, Nigel."

"Yes, but I was only a support. You guys did the work. However, I need to share some things with you and although I'm sure your presentation is wonderful, we might need to change a few things."

"That sounds a little mysterious!" said Heinz.

"Unfortunately, yes, it is!" replied Nigel. We all sat down around the table and Nigel began to explain.

"Firstly, Addis Ababa. According to Lars Schuller, Victor is looking at more than just a Management Contract. The way he sees things, is that if we supply 'know how' and therefore attract more international business to the facility, then we should benefit more than just a flat management fee," said Nigel.

"I understand that Nigel, but Ethiopian Airlines is Government owned and I'm quite sure that they will not agree to relinquishing shares in the company," I replied.

"Correct," said Nigel. "But I think we have an opportunity to maybe include in our proposal some provisions for 'profit sharing' in addition to the 'flat' management fees on any new customers that we bring to the party."

"Ah! I see what you mean. We write into the agreement that we take a certain percentage of any profitability from increased sales from new customers. Good point," I said.

"Yes, I've had a quick look at the numbers that Heinz and Jana produced and I think there's enough in the forecast projections to make it worth our while and still please Aman and his board of directors. What do you think Heinz?" asked Nigel. Heinz thought about it for a few seconds and slowly started nodding his head in agreement.

"Yes Nigel, I believe you're right. We can definitely make a case that would be beneficial to both parties. The projected five year numbers support that. I'll make some adjustments to the presentation," said Heinz. I must admit, Nigel's idea was excellent and this was just the beginning!

"Thanks Heinz," said Nigel. "As for Jo'burg, I found out that Gert Schneider knows Victor from way back, and Lars too! Now knowing how Lars operates I think he will have been trying to convince Victor that we can get this business at a cheap price. To be honest, I think Gert actually expects us to go back with a 'low ball' offer and for this to be a long drawn-out affair."

"You're right Nigel, I had a chat with Gert in his office before we left Jo'burg. He told me he does know our board members. And he also told me that he would not sell his business on the cheap. In fact, he even knows some of the tactics that could be used to pressure him into selling at a knock down price. I personally don't think it will work, he's too shrewd and knows how to get things done down there. Therefore, my proposal is a fair offer based on the numbers," I replied.

"Speaking of the numbers, Jana and I managed to track down my niggling suspicion that something wasn't quite right with them," said Heinz. "There appears to be a 'missing' amount of about €50,000 at today's exchange rate. It took a while to find, but it's definitely missing. It could just be an error, however, everything else is so precise, that in my opinion, it's been taken out of the business," added Heinz. We all looked at him despondently,

"Okay, we need to let the board know about that, but I don't think it makes any difference to the proposal. If we get this deal done, we need to investigate and make sure it doesn't happen again," I said. "Anyway Nigel, what's your point about the Gert, Victor and Lars triangle?"

"The point is that your proposal is a 'fair proposal' and in any other circumstances, I think the board would accept it."

"But," I said tentatively.

"But, I think we need to exceed Gert's expectation, a few 'extras' if you like. It wouldn't cost a lot and I think in the end would save a lot of time and the additional cost of a long, drawn out process."

"Do you have something in mind?" I asked. Nigel looked at me and smiled.

"Yes George, I do! Now remember these are only ideas; firstly, we offer Gert a five per cent signing bonus if the deal is done before September this year. Now, I know that it is only three months away, but it is possible. Secondly, we need to add a 'non-compete' clause to prevent Gert from starting up another company in competition to us and using his contacts to lure our business away."

"That is already in my proposal," I said.

"Yes George, I know. But I think we need to extend it to five years and include his current senior management team. We can't run the risk of all the current team resigning on day one and then 'fucking off' to a new catering company that just so happens to be secretly owned by Gert!" I nodded my head in agreement. "Lastly, Gert will know that we will want some of our 'own' people on the senior management team down there, so I suggest that he is involved in the selection process, if he wants to. This will accomplish two things. Firstly, it will allow him and whoever we want to run the show down there, to build a relationship, which is important because although Gert will be out of the business, his contacts could prove useful to us. It would do no harm to utilise this situation. And secondly, I believe that Gert would be happier to let his business go if he were involved in the selection process of his successor."

"What do you mean Nigel?" asked Jana. Nigel thought for a moment.

"We all saw how Gert was with his senior team down there. A bit arrogant, non-caring, almost distant…"

"A bit like you are…, was…" I quickly corrected myself. Nigel smiled.

"Yes, a bit like I was. But I believe that deep down he cares for his people. If we can get Gert on our side, he can be influential in keeping the senior team in check. Obviously, we might want to make some changes, but again, we can't have everyone leaving as soon as we take over."

"I have to say Nigel, I like what you've had to say. What do you think Heinz, Jana?" I asked.

"I agree with Nigel. I think we should take his points on board and adjust the proposals accordingly," said Heinz.

"Yes. Sounds good Nigel. Really good," answered Jana.

We amended the proposal and when Tanja joined us later in the afternoon, we had a dummy run which now included the points raised earlier by Nigel. It went really well! Tanja was impressed by the changes and appeared to be warming to Nigel. As we were about to pack up for the day, Nigel called me to one side.

"Hey George. I just wanted to thank you again for our 'chat' in Addis. I'm trying hard to be the sort of person I was and to make a difference, a positive difference."

"I think you are Nigel. Your thoughts and vision about the proposals impressed me. The board will know that this was a complete team effort, including yourself. And no need to thank me."

"And I have made some headway with my wife too!"

"Congratulations, that's good news."

"Yes, early days and we are taking it one step at a time, but at least she has stopped the divorce procedure, for now anyway. Thanks again George."

"I'm really pleased for you," I said smiling at him.

"And on a different note. How would you feel about heading up the sales for the region, assuming we are successful in Addis and Jo'burg?" This took me by surprise, even though the thought had crossed my mind.

"Are you serious?" I asked.

"Yes. I've talked to Tanja and she hates the thought of not having you in her team but understands that this would be a fantastic opportunity for you. Of course, we would also appoint an operational Vice President for the region."

"Speaking of that, I know that Frank Stanley is very keen on being considered for such a role," I said. Nigel smiled.

"Frank may or may not get the position. But whereas in the past it would have been down to what was best for me, it will now be down to the best person for the job. Frank's in with a shout, as is the next man, or woman! Think about the Sales position, George."

"I will. Thanks Nigel."

"By the way, as you and Jana can't make dinner. I'm taking Heinz to a little casino I know, I'm on a lucky streak!"

"Don't lose your shirt, or Heinz's come to think of it!" We both laughed and walked out of the room.

Jana gave me a lift back to my hotel and although we were both a little quiet in the car, she seemed okay. As we pulled up outside the hotel entrance, she stopped the car and turned to me.

"George, I know we are 'not' having a relationship and I know you are seeing this 'friend' of yours tonight, but if you fancy a fuck, I could come by your hotel room later?" I was a little taken aback by Jana's words and openly chuckled. I looked at her and smiled, shaking my head in disbelief.

"Jana - look you know I can't do this. You are a wonderful girl and deserve much better than me. You need someone in your life that you can grow with, that you can develop a meaningful and loving relationship with."

"I know George, and I will. I just thought that maybe that could happen after tonight?"

"I'll see you tomorrow Jana," I said and proceeded to get out of her car.

"Can't blame a girl for trying," she said smiling at me. "I'll pick you up at 9 a.m. okay?" Jana continued. I leant back into the passenger seat.

"Drive carefully, and thanks Jana, thanks for everything."

After checking-in, I made my way to the room. I looked at my watch and saw that it was 6:20 p.m. Fiona had texted me earlier in the day to say she would pick me up at 7 p.m. and I had in turn confirmed this via a return text message. As I unpacked my clothes for tonight's date with Fiona, I wondered if I should call home. It would be great to talk to Emily and Amy, but I knew that it would be Martyna answering the phone. I had already told her that I would be seeing Fiona, so I guess she wouldn't be in a particularly good mood with me. I decided not to call.

35

After showering and getting dressed, I made my way down to the reception and then outside to wait for Fiona. I had my rucksack with me that contained a bottle of red and a bottle of white wine, which I had purchased at the company employee shop. As I waited, I looked at my phone and noticed I had a new text message. It was from Martyna! I opened the message and although the name appeared as Martyna, it was in fact from Emily and Amy.

"Hi Dad, hope you are having a nice time and can't wait to see you tomorrow (if we are still awake when you get back!) Love you, Emily & Amy. xx" I should have called them. None of this mess is their fault and I shouldn't let my anxiety about talking to Martyna affect my relationship with Emily and Amy.

I was about to call when Fiona arrived driving a little Opel Corsa. She waved at me as she pulled up, smiling, and looking ever so sweet in her big librarian glasses. I waved back before getting into the passenger seat. My call to the girls would have to wait.

"Hi George, great to see you," she said as she leant over to me and kissed me on the cheek.

"Great to see you too," I replied and in that moment, it hit me that it was going to be an extremely difficult evening. I still had feelings for this lovely girl, but I knew that I had to tell her once and for all that we could not develop a relationship beyond that of friendship.

"I hope you haven't been waiting too long, the traffic was a little bit worse than I thought it would be."

"No, not long at all. Right on time. So how have you been? I bet you're glad to finally get out of this hotel and into your own place?"

"Absolutely! When you stay in a hotel for a few days, it's quite nice, you don't have to worry about cleaning and washing up and ironing. But after a while, you just get so bored and you want your home comforts. You even look forward to the ironing!"

"Well, I wouldn't go that far," I replied pulling a face of contempt. "But I'm glad you've settled in. What are the neighbours like? It's an apartment, right?"

"Yes, it's an apartment. There are only two apartments per floor and there are three floors. I've met the guy opposite, Alex, good looking, quite muscular and genuinely nice. I've only ever said hello to the two couples on the ground floor and as for the top floor, I've never seen anyone from up there. I don't hear them either, which is wonderful."

"So, you like the guy opposite, do you?" I said sensing that this could be an opportunity for me to slip into the distance and allowing Fiona to move on. Fiona looked at me and smiled, before returning her eyes to the road in front.

"What's the matter George, you're not jealous, are you?"

"Me! No, not at all. I think it's good that you have someone next door who's, how did you say, good looking, muscular, almost 'Chippendale-esque.' You go for it, girl," I said trying to genuinely sound enthusiastic for Fiona. However, for some stupid reason, I did feel a hint of jealousy, which I was hoping Fiona wouldn't pick up on. Once again, she looked at me and smiled, before looking back at the road ahead.

"There's more chance you would get lucky with him than me," she said continuing to smile.

"What?" I replied somewhat confused.

"He's gay. He has a boyfriend called Hector."

"I see," I said letting out a sigh of relief.

"So, you were a little bit jealous then?"

"No, not at all," I said regaining my nonchalant posture.

"I see you have your overnight bag with you," Fiona said, pointing at my rucksack.

"Oh this! No, unfortunately it only contains two bottles of wine. One red, one white. I wasn't sure what you were cooking so bought one of each." Fiona smiled again.

"Just kidding George, relax," she replied. "How are the girls? I bet they miss you so much when you are away? It must have been difficult for them when you were in Africa? And I suppose, difficult for you too?" I hesitated slightly, as I had done before in Tanja's office earlier on in the day, but this time, I don't think Fiona made anything of my hesitation.

"The girls are fine. And yes, it is difficult when I'm travelling. But they have Martyna to look after them. And she is wonderful with them. They all get on so well, I sometimes feel like an outsider," I replied and gave a little smile.

"Martyna? Your live-in child minder?"

"Yes."

"It must be a weight off your mind knowing you have someone so nice, looking after Emily and Amy. I can't imagine how difficult it must be entrusting someone with your children. She must be a special lady. And I know from what you have told me, how special Emily and Amy are. I would really like to meet your girls one day." I looked across at Fiona and smiled, nodding my head.

We arrived at Fiona's new place in Sachsenhausen, south of the river Main, and parked the car in the underground car park space that came with the apartment. It was a short walk to her building entrance and we chatted candidly as we had always done. We were both amazingly at ease in each other's company and for the first time in a while, my thoughts were not immediately formed around my situation with Martyna. We entered the foyer of the building and climbed the impressive stairway to the first floor.

"This is me," Fiona said as we reached a large, heavy wooden front door with 2A prominently displayed in the middle of it. She opened the door and Fiona invited me in. It was a large apartment, two big bedrooms, the master had an ensuite, a main bathroom, large kitchen diner decked out with modern, white satin touch cupboards and grey marble worksurfaces and a large lounge that included a small balcony that had a view of the city.

"Very nice!" I said after being given the guided tour by Fiona.

"It's home - for now anyway."

"Is the furniture yours, or did the place come furnished?"

"No, it was all here apart from the beds, I bought those new. Didn't like the thought of sleeping on someone else's bed and mattress - gives me the shivers!"

"What about when you stay in a hotel?"

"Yeah, I know it is irrational, but I guess the mindset is that a hotel is very temporary and this -" she said gesturing to the apartment with her hands, "well, this is more permanent." I smiled at her.

"Really good to see you Fiona," I said. "Now, what fine culinary delights have you created for us?"

"I don't want you to get your hopes up too much. I'm not the best of cooks in this world. However, I thought I would have a go at preparing lamb shanks with a rosemary, red wine jus accompanied by a horseradish mash and veg."

"That sounds wonderful! Can't wait to get stuck in," I replied in eager anticipation of a fantastic meal.

"Wait! You didn't let me finish. I said, I 'thought' I would have a go at the lamb shanks, etc, etc. But I 'chickened out' and have ordered pizza instead. What was I thinking! I could never prepare a meal like that. I'm really sorry George, forgive me?" I looked at Fiona and just started to laugh. After an initial look of horror, she joined in the laughter.

"You have absolutely no need to apologise Fiona. Takeaway pizza is perfect. Bloody marvellous! And a bottle of both red and white wine will accompany it beautifully!" I said.

We sat in the lounge and made a start on the white wine while we waited for the pizza to arrive. When it did, Fiona grabbed the pizza, chicken wings and garlic bread from its packaging and laid it out on the dining table in the kitchen diner, before calling out to me that it was ready. I made my way into the kitchen and was greeted by a slightly sad looking Fiona.

"I am really sorry George, you know, about the whole cooking thing. I'm a crap cook, always have been. Never been confident about it."

"Hey Fiona, please stop apologising. This looks great and do you know what, I can't think of anything more I would like right now than a piece of that meat feast pizza. And I can't think of anyone I would rather be eating it with, than you. So, cheer up, sit down and let's eat!" I said and gave her a quick hug. Fiona responded by placing her arms around my neck, prolonging the hug, before finally letting me go and sitting down.

The food was outstanding for a takeaway, and it wasn't long before we had eaten everything.

"I'm thoroughly stuffed!" I said after finishing the last piece of garlic bread and leaning back in my chair, putting my hands behind my head.

"Me too!" came an equally exhausted reply from Fiona. "Go and take a seat in the lounge and I will be through in a minute when I've cleared this away."

"How about I do it, and you can get us another drink?" I replied. And then I suddenly remembered the last time I was in a girl's apartment in Frankfurt, following dinner and offering to clear up while the host fixes drinks! Yes, Jana's place. The thought raced through my mind that I would return to the lounge and find Fiona sitting on the sofa in her underwear! I have to say, it was not an unpleasant thought!

"No, don't be silly, you go and relax, I'll be in shortly," Fiona said, getting up from her seat and starting to clear the plates from the table. "There's scotch, brandy, vodka and spiced rum in the side cabinet. Or if you want to open the red wine, I'm okay with that," she continued. I looked up at her from my seat and the image of her in her underwear that had previously been at the forefront of my mind, faded. Not because it wasn't an exciting thought, after all, she was incredibly beautiful. No, it was because this was not Jana. This was a woman who was every bit as stunning, sexy, and intelligent as Jana. But was also warm hearted, homely (even if she couldn't cook!), caring and gentle. Fiona was someone who would never just 'strip' down to her underwear and feel comfortable about doing so! No, Fiona was quite different to Jana. Someone who was looking for a permanent relationship, a woman who had vulnerabilities, but still possessed amazing poise and self-confidence (again, except with cooking!). The thought again passed my mind why I would not want to pursue the opportunity of being happy with this woman? She was almost perfect! Beautiful, intelligent, loving, engaging personality, family oriented and a thoroughly wonderful woman. Most men in the world would give their right arm to be in a relationship with someone like Fiona. So, what was really stopping me?

What was preventing me from saying 'you know what, me and this girl could be really happy together?' Was it the girls? Would Emily and Amy not get on with Fiona? No, I couldn't see that being a problem. Was it because of my fear of relationship failure and the effect on Emily and Amy? The very same excuse I have been using to avoid getting involved with Martyna? No, it wasn't either of these two reasons. It then hit me like a bolt of lightning! It was much simpler than that. It was of course-, Martyna! As much as Fiona would be perfect for me, and me probably perfect for her, it was Martyna I really wanted to be with.

"Let me help you Fiona," I said and I picked up the remaining plates from the table. We cleared everything away and went into the lounge. Fiona opened the red wine and poured two glasses, handing me one and we sat next to each other on the sofa.

"Good wine George," she said after taking a sip of the Cabernet Sauvignon.

"Yes, I like it too. I hope you don't mind only drinking the wine, but I must give an important presentation tomorrow to the board about the expansion into Africa. Can't wake up pissed tomorrow morning!" I said with a snicker.

"No, that won't do. So how is it going? Do you think the board will accept your proposals?"

"I think we have a good chance that they will. Obviously, this is only the first step and once we have agreed what we want to offer, the hard part will be negotiating with the other relevant parties. But yeah, I'm quite confident about tomorrow."

"That's great George. Does this mean you might be spending more time in Addis and Jo'burg?" I hesitated for a second and my mind slipped back to the earlier conversation with Nigel.

"Maybe," I replied, not willing to share my thoughts with Fiona just yet as I hadn't really thought too much about what Nigel had said.

"I think it would be great for you and the girls if you get an opportunity to go and work down there, especially Jo'burg. Obviously, it's one of the most dangerous cities in the world. However, it would be a wonderful experience for you all down there. And if you keep your eyes open, stay away from certain situations and places, you'll be fine and have a great time," Fiona replied. I looked to my left at Fiona, somewhat puzzled by her response.

"How do you know? I mean, how do you know so much about living in Jo'burg?" I asked.

"Oh! Well, my dad is South African. Before my mum and dad split up, we lived in Jo'burg. Well first we were in Cape Town, but then moved to Jo'burg. I was there from about the age of six until I was eighteen I suppose. That's when my parents split up and Mum wanted to come back to Germany. Dad moved to England and I sort of stayed with him for a while, as I got a finance job in London. Sorry George, I never really told you any of this before, did I?"

"No," I said a little shocked. "But that's okay. So, what was it like growing up in Johannesburg?"

"It was great. Me and Tom had a wonderful time…"

"Tom?" I interrupted.

"Yes, Tom, my older brother. Sorry George, I've never mentioned Tom either, have I. Tom's two years older than me and is a pilot working for Virgin Atlantic. I don't get to see him as often as I would like, because he's always flying around the world, you know. But when we do get together, it's really nice. He's married to Stephanie and they have a little girl, two years old, called Grace."

"Wait a minute! So, you have a brother who's a pilot for Virgin, is married and has a little girl?"

"Erm, yes," Fiona said almost apologetically.

"So, you are an aunty? Wow! That's great. For some reason, I just assumed you were like me, an only child. But I'm really pleased for you. That sounds stupid, I know, but when you are an only child, it kind of hits home when you hear people talk about their siblings. As you had never mentioned Tom before, I took it you were just like me. Now I'm a bit jealous," I said smiling and in a joking sort of way.

"Sorry George, I didn't mean to make you feel that way," replied a concerned Fiona.

"I'm joking!" I said. "I really am pleased that you have a brother. Especially a brother you get on with. It must be great."

"Yes, it is, but still a little insensitive of me. Sorry George."

"You have to stop apologising Fiona," I said leaning towards her and placing my hand on top of hers. We looked at each other and smiled. "So, tell me what your childhood was like growing up in Johannesburg?"

"It was great! We lived in a gated community, so security was extremely good. Once you drove inside the gates, you would never know you were in a gated community. It was massive! We had a 'residents' club house, serving meals and drinks, a couple of tennis courts, play parks for the kids, basketball court and a lake in the middle. The security cars drove around the estate regularly, but to be honest I never really noticed them. Our house had a swimming pool, four bedrooms, a guest annex, and a maid's quarters. We didn't have a live-in maid like most of the families on the estate, but we did have a lady come in once a day during the week to do the cleaning and washing and things like that. We also had a gardener and once a week a guy would come in and clean the pool! I suppose I was quite 'privileged' really."

"Wow. What did you dad do for a living, you must have been rich!" I said. Fiona started to laugh.

"No, we weren't rich by western standards. But my dad was quite high up in a mining company and because of the cost of living, we could afford so much more. And that's what I mean about you and your family. If you went down there to work, you and the girls would have more financial resources to have a wonderful time. Especially if you get offered an 'ex pat' package. It's basically an outdoor life for the kids down there. Sports, swimming, horse riding, safari - the weather is brilliant! Does take a bit of getting used to though, having your traditional Christmas dinner wearing shorts and T Shirts, outside on the patio, in the sunshine! And then going for a dip in the pool in the afternoon to cool off."

"Sounds fantastic. Where do I sign up!" I said enthusiastically. "But what about the crime?"

"George, I'm not going to lie to you. It can be extremely dangerous there. But as with most cities in the world, even London, there are places you just don't go to, avoiding trouble. The same applies for Jo'burg. You must be more careful, be more aware of your surroundings and the people around you. If you take precautions and stay vigilant, you stay safe!"

"Thanks Fiona, I mean, for the insight. I didn't tell you this earlier when you asked, but yes, there could be a possibility of me moving down there with the family. Nothing concrete yet and I've only just found out about it today. However, maybe I could pick your brains if things develop further, about life down there."

"I'll come down with you and show you if you like," Fiona said as quick as a flash, giving me a suggestive wink. We again both smiled at each other and took sips of our wine.

"So, how's your job going?" I asked.

"It's going well, I have my own client base now and I'm starting to make headway with them. It takes a while to build up the trust element of the relationship, but I'm getting there. And the work is quite exciting, especially when you manage to pull off a deal worth a few million."

"And your colleagues? How are they treating you?"

"Difficult to say really. The girls are a little bit 'off-ish' with me at times, if you know what I mean. This is going to sound terribly arrogant and egotistical, but I get the impression that they are envious of how I look," Fiona said, again apologetically.

"You're right," I said. "It does sound arrogant and egotistical," I jokingly added to which Fiona smiled acknowledging the joke, but still slapping my thigh as a reprimand! We laughed. "No, seriously, you could be right. I mean you are amazing, truly, I mean it - and this can be threatening to some people."

"But George, I've been nothing but nice to these girls. I mean, I always make the coffees, I always pitch in and help them with their customers, I ask them for advice - even when I know the answer, just to try and make them feel superior. I even try to do the 'girly' bit by asking about the guys in the office and any gossip going around. But they just tend to push me out and stick to their own clique. It's a little frustrating, but to be honest, I don't really give a shit about them," Fiona replied, her last sentence tinged with a touch of anger.

"So, what did they say?"

"What did who say?"

"The girls - about the gossip and guys in the office?"

"George, you're not jealous again are you? Like when I told you about Alex, my neighbour?" she smiled.

"A bit," I said half-jokingly. It was only half-jokingly as well, because for some stupid reason, I once again felt a little apprehensive of what Fiona would tell me about the guys in her office. I mean, any guy in his right mind, would want to be in a loving relationship with this girl. Therefore, I'm sure Fiona would have been 'noticed' by the guys in the office, from the moment she first walked in. Fiona smiled back at me.

"Well, where do I start!" she said, still smiling and looking a little smug with herself.

"Oh no," I said with a sigh of dejection, still playing along with being jealous. "So, I'm not your 'Superman' anymore?" Once again, we both laughed.

"There are five guys in the office, two are gay, one is married, one's a 'twat' and the other," she paused.

"The other?" I enquired.

"The other asked me out on a date."

"Really? Interesting. How did it go?"

"Did I say I went?"

"Did you?"

"Yes. But you shouldn't just assume," Fiona said, a little embarrassed.

"So, what happened?" I asked eager to find out. And at that precise moment I was genuinely interested in how she got on. Not in the slightest bit jealous, but curious in a way how I would have imagined that a brother would be talking to his sister about her going on a date. "So?" I again asked. Fiona sighed and looked at me.

"George, this is difficult for me."

"Why?" Again, there was a pause as Fiona took another sip of her wine. She looked a little upset.

"Hey Fiona, it's okay," I said tenderly, putting my arm around her shoulder. "I'm just messing with you. You don't have to tell me anything. I'm really sorry Fiona." We hugged for a moment and I could feel this gorgeous woman's body against mine. It felt wonderful, warm, genuine, and loving. We let go and looked into each other's eyes.

"You don't need to apologise George. It's difficult for me because-, because you know how I feel about you. I know we cannot be together, but it doesn't stop me feeling the way I do about you. And going on a date, well, it feels like I've cheated on you," she said looking down at the floor in embarrassment.

"Hey, don't be silly," I replied. "I'm really happy for you. We had a wonderful time together Fiona and I will always treasure that night. And I feel so much for you, who wouldn't? You are almost perfect for me. But it could never work for us, you living here in Frankfurt and me being in London, possibly Johannesburg. And of course, there is Emily and Amy. You owe me nothing Fiona, and therefore, I am genuinely happy that you decided to go on the date."

"Thank you, George," she replied and we embraced again.

"So how did it go?" I finally said. We again let go of each other and I got another reprimanding slap on the arm from Fiona for asking. We again smiled at each other.

"It was okay I suppose. He was nice, we got on. A bit boring and the conversation dried up a few times. But that tends to happen on first dates, doesn't it?" she said looking at me for reassurance. It's funny because I had never really experienced that! Maybe it's because of my years of experience in a sales job, where you must always make conversation with the customers, even when they are as boring as hell! You always push the conversation along, ask questions, make them feel important. That was the game. And having been with Cheryl for so long, first dates were kind of new to me. But with Fiona, Jana, Martyna, Jen, Sarah, Tanja, Sam and just about any woman, or man for that matter, I met, I could always hold the conversation, never allowing it to dry up.

"Yes, that can happen," I said agreeing.

"When I said it felt like I had cheated on you, I didn't mean that I slept with him."

"Hey Fiona. You're a grown woman. A beautiful woman. And in the few months that I have known you, I feel so lucky that you chose my leg to grab on that flight to Frankfurt."

"Stop it George," Fiona said, again smiling and administering another slap on my thigh.

"It's true! I'm so glad that we met and although we cannot be anything more than friends, my hope is that we can be good friends. Almost like another brother for you, and a first sister for me. You are amazing and if my two girls grow up to be someone as loving, intelligent and caring as you, I think I would have done a good job as a father."

Fiona looked lovingly into my eyes, and we kissed.

"Do you fancy staying the night, for old times' sake?" she softly whispered to me. I smiled back at her.

36

It was about 8:55 a.m. when I saw Jana's car pull up outside the hotel. I had already checked-out and was waiting for her just inside the foyer. I picked up my bag and rucksack and made my way out to meet her. The previous night's events had in a way, forced me to decide about my future and I wanted to make sure I started acting on that decision as soon as possible. And that meant talking to Martyna!

"Late night George?" Jana said as I sat down in the passenger seat.

"Yeah, something like that," I replied and shut the door. Jana continued to look at me for a few seconds before finally, putting the car into gear and driving off.

"So, how was your evening with your 'old friend' George? Was it filled with stories of years gone by and reminiscing about old acquaintances? Or did you just end up having copious amounts of sex?"

"Jana!"

"All right George. Sorry! I'm only joking. A bit sensitive this morning, are we?"

"I didn't get much sleep last night, that's all, okay. Now, what's the plan for this morning?"

"Well, we are all set up in the board room and we can use the room as soon as we get there. The board will join us at 11 a.m. so we have time to run through everything and make any last-minute changes."

"Good. Let's hope we don't have to make any changes," I said looking down at where I thought would be Jana's lovely legs. "Where have your legs gone?"

"What?"

"Your legs-, where are they?" I said referring to the fact that for the first time ever, Jana was not wearing a short skirt, but trousers! Jana smiled at me.

"You sound disappointed George. Are you?"

"Well yes, I am actually! What's happened to your fucking legs?" I asked again.

"I decided that I would look totally professional today. A suit and long sleeve blouse, not see through, not so you can see my bra, no. Just very professional." I looked at her and started laughing. I'm not sure why, it just made me laugh!

"Something funny?" she asked.

"No, not really. It's just I would have bet my last pound that you would have worn a short skirt today."

"Well, you'd be 'broke' then, wouldn't you," she snapped back at me.

"I guess I would. But seriously, why the trousers?"

"I know that you and probably all the men in the room today would prefer to see my legs. And I would normally prefer that you saw them. After all, they get me noticed and as I've told you before, if it helps me to progress my career, I have no problem with it. That feminist shit is not for me! However…"

"Ah, we're getting to the real reason now," I said with bated breath.

"However," Jana started her sentence again, "I was having breakfast this morning and managed to knock a whole cup of hot coffee over myself. Burnt my legs, inner thighs and everything! Really painful. It has left red blotches on my legs, so I couldn't wear a short skirt."

"Jesus! Are you alright? Should you go the hospital?" I said rather concerned about her well-being and a little bit embarrassed about previously teasing her.

"No, it's okay. I put some cream on and bandaged my legs. I was wondering though, if you wouldn't mind taking the bandages off later and applying some more cream for me?" Jana replied in a seductive way, before turning to me and licking her lips! For a split second, the thought of being in between Jana's legs gripped me like a pregnant woman squeezing the expectant father's hand, when about to give birth!

"Keep your eyes on the road you," I said smiling back at her. She returned to watching the road and a big smile ran across her face.

"Are you sure you're okay though?" I asked sincerely. "I mean, Heinz and I can handle things if you need to get your…, looked at, you know, your…, well, your…"

"My what George? My vagina?"

"Well, yes, and of course your legs."

"Stop worrying George. It's not that bad. And anyway, there's only one person I want looking at my vagina," and again Jana turned to me and licked her lips. I smiled and shook my head in wonderment. Jana's flirting was so over the top that it was comical and what's more, she knew it too! But it was great fun and it made me feel happy that we had reached such a wonderful understanding with each other.

We arrived at the office and after parking the car we made our way to the boardroom. Tanja, Heinz, and Nigel were already there waiting for us.

"Morning George," said Tanja and she gave her usual hug and kiss on the cheek. "Don't forget, I want to have a chat with you before you go today, okay?"

"Morning Tanja. Yes, I think we have time this afternoon. Morning Nigel, Heinz," I continued.

"Good morning George. How was your evening with your friend?" asked Nigel. I thought for a moment, thinking back to last evening.

"It was very nice," I replied. "And how did you two guys get on? Win? Lose?"

"With Nigel's help, I actually won last night!" said an excited Heinz. "Not a lot. But left the casino with more than I went in! Amazing!"

"Wow! Good for you. But what do you mean 'with Nigel's' help?"

"I just gave Heinz a few tips about playing the percentages, nothing really. However, it seemed to work though," Nigel said.

"And you Nigel? How did you get on?"

"Yeah, had some luck. Won about €200. Not a bad night. But we didn't stay out late. I wanted to get home, spend some time with my wife. Had a lovely evening," Nigel said with a satisfied smile on his face.

"Okay - when you guys have finished your personal meeting, we have some work to do people. I suggest, we just get straight to it and you three run through the entire presentation for Nigel and me, is that okay?" said Tanja pointing at myself, Heinz and Jana.

"Sounds good boss," I said and Jana set up the presentation on her laptop, ready to be projected on the big screen.

The presentation lasted about fifty minutes, with me taking the lion's share of it. The change-overs between myself, Heinz and Jana were smooth and it must have gone well as far as Tanja and Nigel were concerned, because there were no interruptions from them.

"Very good! Incredibly good indeed. You've done a great job and I think Victor, Lars and Cristina will be pleased with your proposals. Although, we need to be prepared for their questions, one of which I know from Cristina will be centred around the investment return, especially for Jo'burg. Heinz, the numbers seem a little 'light' and that missing money will cause concern," said Tanja.

"The numbers are what we consider to be realistic, taking into account when we can actually attain new business through winning contracts and the risks of losing any current contracts," Heinz replied. "As for the 'missing' money, it could be a clerical error, but I somehow think it is not. That particular issue will need investigating."

"Heinz is right," I added. "We have taken a 'conservative' approach to the ROI and tried to be as pragmatic as possible. But nobody has a crystal ball, we can't determine exactly what will happen in the future." As soon as I said these words, my mind drifted to Martyna, who had used the 'crystal ball' phrase when speaking about a potential future for us. I quickly pushed that thought aside and got my head back to business.

"Ok. Nigel, any thoughts?" Tanja said turning to Nigel.

"Well, I agree with you Tanja, the proposal is excellent. And you are right that we need to think about the potential questions that the board will have. Lars will be his usual 'bulldozer' self and will be aggressive in attacking the numbers, you know, 'why haven't we considered German knowhow and reduced operating costs by thirty per cent', that sort of thing. So, I think we need to anticipate that by explaining some of the reasons behind the numbers. Heinz - are you comfortable doing that?" said Nigel. Heinz looked a little apprehensive.

"I'll do it," both Jana and I said at the same time. We looked at each other.

"Jana can do it," I said in a reassuring way to the group. I then looked back at Jana and gave her a nod of endorsement. She smiled at me and mouthed 'thanks' in acknowledgment of my confidence in her.

"That's good. As for the other questions that might come up, I think we, as a team, have the ability to handle it and to give the board enough faith to get these proposals approved by the Executive Committee," said Nigel.

"Thanks Nigel. For all your support and contribution to this project. It's been a pleasure working with you on this and I think I speak on behalf of both Heinz and Jana when I say that we have all enjoyed the time we have spent with you," I said.

"Stop it George, you'll make me blush. But no, it is me that must thank you all. I know I have been a bit of a dick in the past and treated some of you, well let's just say badly. The trip to Addis and Jo'burg and in particular a late night in the bar at the Radisson Blu Hotel, made me realise what a…"

"Twat!" interrupted Tanja, before immediately putting her hand to her mouth in embarrassment at saying it out loud. Nigel looked at her and smiled.

"Well, I was going to say 'mess' I have made of things. But yes 'twat' would also be appropriate. The point is, all of you had every right to be cautious of me and to be suspicious of my motives. But I hope that your opinion is changing and will continue to change as we work closer with each other in the future." I walked over to Nigel and shook his hand.

"Thanks again Nigel," I said. Even Tanja gave him a quick hug and there was a real sense that the five people in the room had cemented a real, long lasting bond.

The presentation to Victor, Lars and Cristina went very well. We all presented confidently and although Heinz and Jana were visibly relieved when we had finished, you could also tell how proud they were of their performance. The Q&A session that followed the presentation was more about clarification of some of the points rather than objection or disagreement of the proposals and the team manged to field these with ease. Even Lars came up to me afterwards and congratulated me on the efforts of the team. It was agreed that the board would take the proposals to the Executive Committee and although nothing was ever guaranteed, there was a sense that the approval would be a formality.

Following lunch with the board, Victor pulled me to one side.

"Well done George. The whole team has done a fantastic job."

"Thanks Victor. I think we had a good team and I include Nigel in that."

"Yes - Nigel. We've all noticed a change in Nigel. Tanja tells me you had something to do with that, right?"

"No, not really. We had a chat, a 'clear the air' conversation over a few glasses of bourbon. That's all."

"You're too modest George. However, whatever you did, it certainly has helped. Not only Nigel, but everyone. A better Nigel makes for a better company. So, thank you," said Victor. We smiled at each other and shook hands.

My flight back wasn't until early evening which meant all being well, I should be home by around 8 p.m. Hopefully, the girls would still be awake and I could say good night to them. Victor had asked Jana to make a few minor changes to the presentation so that they could present it to the Executive Committee. I had plenty of time so I offered to help Jana to make the adjustments, which she gratefully accepted. As we sat in her office making the changes that Victor wanted, Tanja walked in.

"Hey George, don't forget I would like to talk to you before you go back. What time are you leaving?" Tanja said.

"My flight's at 6:45 p.m. so I'll probably need to be at the airport about 5:30 p.m. something like that."

"I can take you to the airport," Jana said.

"Thanks Jana, much appreciated," I replied.

"Let's meet in my office about 4:30 p.m. okay with you?" continued Tanja.

"No problem, I'll see you then." As Tanja left the office, Jana looked at me.

"Thanks for your support today George. Thanks for showing your confidence in me. It helped me a lot to understand what I need to do to progress with the company. Short skirts and low-cut tops will only get me so far!"

"No worries Jana. You did an excellent job today under difficult circumstances."

"Difficult circumstances?"

"Well, your, you know, your, well it must have been quite painful standing and sitting for that matter…"

"Oh, you mean my vagina?" she said smiling at me. "You can say the word George. Or if you want, we can say it in German." With that Jana yelled out 'meine schöne muschi' which roughly translated means 'my beautiful pussy!' As luck would have it, a colleague was walking past Jana's open office door at the time. He tuned to his left, looked in on us, paused for a second, again looked straight ahead and walked off without saying a word! Just another day at the office, I thought to myself.

"Erm, yeah," I replied looking slightly embarrassed.

"Well, the offer still holds if you want to get a later flight and help me with administering the cream?"

"You don't stop you, do you?" I said laughing. Jana looked a little sad.

"It's so unfair George. I know we can't be together, but I just have this thing about you. You make me want you, without you even realising that you're doing it! It's like you've cast a spell on me and I am completely defenceless against your powers. I've had a few relationships George and I've never felt like this before. You can't even call what we had 'a relationship' really! It's like three, one-night stands! But whatever it is, I just can't get you out of my mind. I know what you're going to say and I totally agree with you. However, you have to understand that it's going to take me some time to get over you. And I'm going to flirt with you like crazy until you give in," she said as her previously saddened face, turned into a smile. It was my turn to look a little sad.

"Thank you, Jana. For everything. Your work, professional approach, your short skirts, low cut tops-, your legs and come to think of it, your whole body! Thank you for your kindness and the wonderful, intimate experiences that we have shared, some of which I have never experienced before. But most importantly, thank you for being you. If my circumstances were different, if our lives were more compatible, I think we could have made each other incredibly happy. Although it's not meant to be, I would like to think that we will always be close friends and believe me when I say, I'll always be there for you. The banter we have and your sense of humour is priceless to me. From the moment I met you and the 'spider in the shower' conversation on the phone that night, I knew you were someone I wanted to know. And I never want to stop knowing you. Is that enough for you?"

"I suppose it will have to be," Jana sighed and we embraced in a tight hug.

We completed the changes to the presentation, continuing our 'banter' with each other. She was teasing me about my 'old friend' and I was doing the same to her about this new guy she had mentioned. Funnily enough, it was this guy that had passed by her door when she shouted out about her beautiful pussy! We laughed a lot and the time soon slipped around to 4:30 p.m.

"Ok Jana, I have to go and see Tanja now. Are you sure you can give me a lift to the airport?"

"The airport, my apartment, take your pick?" she said playfully.

"I'll meet you back here," I said and as I left Jana's office, I had a lovely, warm feeling about our relationship.

Although Tanja's door was open, she hadn't seen me approach, so I knocked on the door. Tanja looked up from her laptop.

"Ah, come in George. Take a seat, I'll be with you in a minute. Just need to finish this email," she said and continued typing away. I went in and sat down in the chair the other side of her desk.

"I can come back if you would prefer?" I said.

"No, no. There," she said clicking her mouse and sending the email. "Right-, so George," she continued, looking at me. "What's up?" This took me bit by surprise, although in some ways I was expecting Tanja to quiz me, especially about the girls.

"Nothing really, everything's okay," I replied, trying to pass off everything as being normal.

"George. I've known you for ten years. Your face doesn't lie! Something's not right. Now I know I'm not your mum, and before you say any satirical remark about me being old enough, I caution you that I am still your boss!" she said smiling. "But seriously, I get worried when I see you like this. Although I just made the 'boss' comment, you know that we are more than just that. If I can help, I would like to. Is it the girls?"

"In some ways, yes. At least they are a large part of the puzzle that I need to solve. But I intend to do that by the end of the weekend. So please don't worry Tanja. And if I haven't solved it by the weekend, I will definitely come and talk to you. And thanks for your support."

"Are the girls okay though?"

"They're strong and robust, and so grown up for their age that I sometimes forget that they are only coming up for nine and seven! However, they are also vulnerable, scared and I sometimes wonder if I can cope with looking after them - protecting them. They have been through so much in their short lives, that I'm worried about fucking things up further for them. Making the wrong decisions…"

"But you have-, what's her name, Martyna to help you now. I thought she was doing really well with the girls?"

"She is-, and that's part of the problem. I won't go into details with you just yet Tanja, but Martyna is also part of the puzzle that needs solving. It's complicated!"

"You clearly seem uncertain about things. I want you to know George, that I'm here for you. Call me day or night. If you just want me to listen, I'll listen. If you want advice, I'll advise you. You can count on me George," Tanja said giving me a reassuring look.

"Thank you, Tanja. You've helped me so much over the years, I feel it should be my turn to help you," I said. I then let out a sigh and continued in a more positive way. "But I'm determined that things will be settled by the weekend and so let's get back to positive thinking. I think the day has gone very well and I think we have a great chance to get this Africa expansion on the road!"

"Yes, I agree. But that brings me to something else I need to talk to you about. Nigel came to see me last week and floated the idea of you heading up the Sales department for 'Sub Sahara' should this project get off the ground. After a little deliberation and I have to say some particularly good persuasive argument from Nigel, I agreed with him that it was a fantastic opportunity for both you-, and the girls. It would mean living in Johannesburg, obviously an 'ex pat' package and probably on a two or three year contract. Nigel asked me if he could be the one to float the idea with you and I agreed. He told me this afternoon that he had a word with you yesterday."

"He did, you're right."

"And how do you feel about that George? Is it something you would be interested in?"

"Erm, I would need to think about it. Particularly about Emily and Amy. A foreign country, quite a dangerous country, and I know this sounds really stupid, but my first thought was the girls would miss visiting their mum's grave." I paused for second, looking down at my shoes, knowing that it would not just be the girls that would miss that.

"George, it's a big decision and nobody is expecting an answer just yet. Christ, we don't even know if the Executive Committee will approve the proposal and then there's the negotiations to get through. So, there's no rush. Think about it and we can talk some more when you are ready."

"Thanks Tanja. And I really appreciate you thinking of me. I know it would be a wonderful opportunity. So, let me think about it."

"Actually, it was Nigel's idea and although I originally thought that he just wanted you out of the picture here in Europe, I realised that he just thought you were the perfect person for the job. And he is right!" There was a slight pause before Tanja continued. "I have to stop thinking of him as such a fucking twat!" We both laughed out loud.

"I will make sure I thank him," I said.

I said my goodbyes to Tanja and headed back to Jana's office. It was just after 5 p.m. and Jana was busy packing away her laptop.

"All finished?" I said as I entered her office.

"Yeah, all done. I sent a copy of the final presentation to Victor's PA, copying you, Heinz, Nigel, and Tanja. She said she will distribute it to the board."

"Great job Jana, thanks again for all your hard work."

"My pleasure George. It's been good working with you. I hope this is just the start though. Do you think we will be involved in the negotiations? If it gets that far?"

"I'm not sure. But hopefully, yes! Are you still alright to give me a lift?"

"Depends - airport or apartment?"

"Airport-, please," I said smiling at her. She smiled back.

"I told you, I shall keep trying!"

Jana dropped me at the airport and I have to say it was a strange feeling saying goodbye to her. Although we both understood that we were just friends, it was kind of difficult to shake off the fact that we knew each other intimately and had passionately enjoyed each other's bodies. Our hug was long, and we did kiss each other on the lips as we said our final goodbye. I stood outside the terminal and waved as she drove off and a small part of me did feel a little sad.

Upon entering the terminal, I immediately looked up at the large departures board in the main concourse and noticed that my flight had been delayed! Not really what I wanted to see. This meant that I would probably not be back in time to see the girls and wish them a goodnight. I thought I should call them and of course Martyna to let her know I would be late. I rushed through security and once I was through, I found a quiet corner in which to make my call.

"Hello George," Martyna said as she answered my call.

"Hi Martyna. How are you?" I replied somewhat uneasily.

"I'm okay George. You?"

"Yes, look erm, I've been delayed, probably about an hour, so it means I'll not be in until about 9 p.m. I'll grab something to eat here at the airport, so don't worry about fixing dinner for me."

"Are you sure? It's no trouble for me to leave you something. I will probably be in bed by the time you get here, but I can leave something for you to warm up?"

"Thanks, Martyna, but please don't worry. I'll grab something here. And sorry for being late."

"That's not your fault George so no need to apologise. Do you want to speak to the girls?"

"Yes, that would be great, thanks," I replied.

"Hi Daddy, when are you coming home?" asked an excited Amy.

"Hi sweetheart. Unfortunately, my flight has been delayed so I won't be back now in time to see you before you go to bed. But I'll absolutely be there for breakfast with you guys tomorrow morning, okay?"

"That's a bit disappointing. I was hoping to see you tonight."

"I'm really sorry darling, but I can't control the flight."

"I know. Not to worry."

"So, how have you been? Has school been good?"

"Yes, we've been continuing to learn about the Great Fire of London and Miss Raven said that we should all ask our parents to take us to Pudding Lane to see where it all started. Can we go Daddy?"

"I think we can arrange that Amy. We'll make a day of it, have lunch somewhere and maybe do some shopping too."

"Thanks Daddy. Martyna has been a bit quiet, but we have done our best to cheer her up and try to make her laugh. I hope you can talk to her soon?" This brought a lump to my throat. I knew I needed to end this situation for the sake of the girls' future happiness.

"I'm sure Martyna really appreciates your concern and attempts to cheer her up. But are you okay?" I said.

"Yeah, we are fine. Do you want to talk to Emily?"

"Yes, that would be great. Have a lovely evening darling and again, sorry I can't be there to tuck you into bed tonight. Love you."

"Love you too. Hang on," and she was gone.

"Hi Dad," said Emily.

"Hey Emster, how are you?"

"I'm okay. Wish you were here though. Martyna seems very down. Amy and I have done our best, but it's just not working."

"Okay sweetheart, Amy told me how you've been trying to cheer up Martyna. I'm sure deep down she really appreciates it. As you probably heard, my flight is delayed, so I will talk to Martyna tomorrow evening when I get back from work. I'll try to convince her to stay, I promise sweetheart."

"I know Dad. I have to go. I'll see you tomorrow. Love you," Emily said despondently. Again, I felt awful.

"Love you too sweetheart. I'll see you tomorrow." I thought that the call would end, but to my surprise, Martyna came back on the line.

"Hi George. Are you sure you don't want me to leave you something to eat? It really is no bother?"

"Thanks again Martyna, but no it's okay. Listen, can we have a chat tomorrow evening, once the girls are in bed. I think there are some things we need to clear up and…"

"Yes George. That will be fine. There are some things I need to tell you too. Have a safe flight and I'll see you tomorrow morning. Take care," and Martyna hung up.

I slumped back in my seat and let out a huge sigh. The events of the last forty-eight hours and this call with the girls made it truly clear in my mind what was the right thing to do!

37

I got into the house just after 9:15 p.m. and all was quiet. After taking off my shoes, I emptied my dirty laundry into the laundry basket and proceeded upstairs to change out of my work clothes. Martyna's door was shut as I passed by it and the house was incredibly quiet. I looked in on the girls and they were both sound asleep. After not getting much sleep the previous night, I decided I would go straight to bed.

I got up early, showered and got dressed. I popped my head in the girls to say good morning and they were already awake. I gave them a quick kiss and cuddle and asked them what they would like for breakfast.

"Can I have some toast please Daddy?" asked Amy. "And can I have strawberry jam on it?"

"Of course, sweetheart. What about you Emily?"

"Yes, I'll have the same please," she replied. "Dad, did you talk to Martyna last night?" she continued.

"No. As my flight was delayed, I didn't get back very early so Martyna had already gone to bed. But when I talked to her on the phone yesterday from the airport, I asked her if we could talk later tonight. So, don't worry sweetheart, we'll try and sort something out later, okay?" Emily smiled at me and I left the girls to get dressed into their school clothes.

I entered the kitchen and made a fresh pot of coffee, before sliding four slices of bread into the toaster. I got out two mugs and four glasses and laid the table including cutlery, butter, and the jam that Amy had requested. As I stood by the counter waiting for the coffee to percolate, I heard someone coming down the stairs. I looked over to the doorway to see Martyna entering the kitchen.

"Good morning George. How are you?" she said and smiled at me. A good start I immediately thought to myself!

"Morning Martyna. I'm good," I said a little hesitantly. "Coffee is almost done and I've put on some toast for the girls. Do you want some too?"

"That would be nice. Is there anything I can do?" she replied.

"No, no, take a seat," I said and moved to the fridge to get the milk and juice, placing them both on the kitchen table. As I returned to the counter for the coffee, which by now had completed percolating, Martyna picked up the juice and began pouring it for the girls.

"How was your trip?" she asked. I was a little stunned as I immediately thought Martyna was really asking 'how was Fiona?' However, I quickly pushed this thought aside.

"Yeah, good. Look, Martyna I know I asked you on the phone yesterday, but is it okay that we talk tonight?"

"Yes George. I have a few things I need to tell you too. So, maybe we can sit down together when the girls are in bed."

"Thanks, Martyna," I said and a nervous smile developed across my face.

"Morning Martyna," said Amy as she entered the kitchen and sat down at the table.

"Good morning Amy. Did you sleep okay?" Martyna replied in her usual warm and friendly way.

"Not bad, but I'm glad it's Friday! And I'm glad Daddy is back," she said looking up at me from her seat and smiling at me.

"And I'm so very glad to be back too!" I said placing my hand on the top of her head.

"Morning Martyna," said Emily, as she too entered the kitchen and sat at the table.

"Good morning Emily. And how did you sleep?" again Martyna enquired.

"Okay I suppose," Emily said looking down at the empty plate in front of her. She then looked up at Martyna. "And you? Did you sleep well?" Martyna smiled and I'm sure the same thought went through her mind as had gone through mine! Emily had grown up a lot in the last few months and it was like having another adult sitting at the table with us.

"Not too well," Martyna replied softly but still maintained her warm smile.

"Right, here you go girls," I said bringing over a plate of toast. "Now who wants a second piece? Tell me now and I can put the bread on to toast while we eat this lot."

"I'll have another piece, please," said Emily.

"Can I have a 'half' please Daddy?" said Amy.

"Me too please!" chipped in Martyna.

"A 'half' eh! I suppose we can manage that for you two," I said, and as I smiled first at Amy and then Martyna, I felt a connection with her that had been missing for a while. She was smiling back at me, but it wasn't just her mouth. It felt like her eyes were also smiling at me as they had done before. The feeling took me by surprise and I tried to hide it by turning away from her to the counter to re-load the toaster with bread. In that split second, it was as if a dam had broken because as soon as I had my back to the girls and Martyna, conversation just burst into life as they all started talking about school, homework, Harry Styles and just about everything else! It was somehow like things used to be. The tension that had been lurking in the background for the previous week or so, just seemed to dissipate and it was lovely to hear laughter again around the kitchen table. I even took a little longer to make the toast than I needed for fear of spoiling the flow of the dialogue that had been built up!

After saying my goodbyes to the girls and Martyna, I made my way into the office. It was about 8:15 a.m. by the time I arrived at my desk. Although I didn't see Sarah, I noticed her PC was on so I assumed that she was already in. I unpacked my laptop, inserted in the docking station, and turned it on.

"Coffee George?" came the call from my open door and as I looked up, I saw Sarah standing there.

"Morning Sarah. Yes, that would be great. How are you?"

"I'm good. Looking forward to the weekend of course, but yeah, I've had a good week. How did it go in Frankfurt?"

"Very well. And thanks again for all your hard work. Your presentation was fantastic. So much so, that following the meeting with the board, they wanted me to make only a few changes to it, so they could use it to present to the Executive Committee! That's how good it was. Well done." Sarah smiled at me.

"Thanks for that George. I mean, you didn't have to tell me that, but I'm awfully glad you did. And it was a team effort, it wasn't all me!" she said as she turned and left my office to get the coffee.

Even before my laptop had fired up, I heard a knock on the door.

"Morning George. Time for a quick chat?" said Frank who was now standing in my doorway.

"Morning Frank. Yes, come in and take a seat. Just need to get the laptop going and I'll be right with you," I replied. Frank came in and sat down at my desk, opposite me.

"Well, I guess you know what I'm going to ask?" he said.

"Of course, Frank. You want to know what the flight was like?"

"Very funny."

"No? What the hotel was like?" Frank looked at me and tilted his head to one side as if to say, 'stop fucking about.'

"You know very well! So, what happened? How did it go?"

"Oh! How did the meeting with the board go? Well…" I began to say as Sarah entered my office with two cups of coffee.

"I saw you come in Frank, so I made you one too," she said with a pleasant smile. Frank looked at her in amazement and said thank you.

"Thanks Sarah. I need to talk to Frank now, but I would also like to give you a full debrief about Frankfurt, as I think the success of the meeting had a lot to do with the work you put in with the presentation," I said.

"Thanks George. I'll look at your diary and put a half hour slot in for us, ok?" she replied.

"Perfect. Thanks." Sarah left my office and closed the door behind her.

"So, it was a success then, from what you just said to Sarah," asked Frank.

"Yes Frank, I think it was a success. The board loved the proposals for both Addis and Jo'burg and will take them to the Executive Committee for approval. And the format of the proposals is mainly due to the hard work put in by Sarah. Just remember that when 'appraisal' time comes around!" I said reminding Frank to include this work that Sarah had done for me. "If it gets approved, which we don't see any problem with, the next step would be to formalise the proposals and initiate talks with the relevant parties."

"Wonderful! And how was our friend, Nigel?"

"He was good. In fact, he was extremely good. Encouraging, gave good, thoughtful input and stepped in when required to reiterate and support our reasons behind the proposals. I have to say he was excellent."

"That's all good George, but what does that mean? Does he have someone in mind for a position down there?" asked Frank. I paused for a moment as I thought about the offer Nigel and Tanja had given me to work in the new structure for Sub Sahara.

"Look Frank-, nothing has been decided about that yet. We are still far away from agreeing anything."

"I understand that, but surely some thought must have been given to possible candidates?"

"All I can tell you is I did get the opportunity to mention your name to Nigel…"

"Great!" shouted Frank in a triumphant manner, pumping his fist in the air as if he had just scored a goal in the World Cup Final!

"No, let me finish Frank. I mentioned your name to Nigel, but Nigel is a different man these days. I get on well with him and in the past that would mean I may have had some influence. But the change in him means it works both ways."

"What do you mean George?"

"He's not about 'influence' and 'what's best for him' anymore. He told me that the person that would be given the opportunity in the new set up, would be the person that is best suited to the job. Whether that be you, Daniel Mulzer, or anyone else in the organisation, male or female! Whoever gets the position, will have earned it! Through hard work, dedication, knowledge, and experience. It won't be because of friendship or influence. Do you understand Frank?" I said. Frank paused and looked thoughtfully for few seconds.

"Yes George, I get it. Daniel Mulzer is going to get the position, isn't he?"

"Frank! You're not listening," I replied somewhat frustrated. "It doesn't mean Daniel will get the position! It means, what I have just said; whoever is the best person for the job, will get it! Do you understand now?" Frank looked at me a little puzzled.

"So it really will be based on skills set, experience and knowledge?"

"Yes. Each interested party will be given the opportunity to apply and will be given a fair chance at stating their case. As per any other appointment in the company. I know you may feel sceptical about Nigel being able to do something like that, given his previous track record. However, believe me, he's changed and you stand as good a chance as anyone in filling the position. Just be cool, wait to see what happens, wait for the opportunity and, well, don't blow it!"

Frank was in deep thought as he left my office and I could tell that he was already planning out his 'speech' to convince the selection committee, which incidentally, would include Nigel, of his suitability for the position. I did feel a bit sorry for him. Here I was, already being offered a role down there in Africa and being asked to think about it. And there was Frank, desperate for a position and not even at the interview stage! However, I had bigger worries on my mind than Frank's future and therefore, soon dismissed all thoughts about his and indeed, my own future career prospects.

The rest of the morning went quickly and without any further interruptions from Frank. Mel (the new girl) asked me if I had a few minutes to spare, to go over some ideas she was working on with Gavin about approaching a new low-cost airline for their business at Stansted airport. I was only too pleased to say yes and spend the time with her as after two short weeks, Mel was displaying the sort of aptitude and creativity I felt she had from the moment I saw her step out of the lift at her interview. As comical as it was that day, she displayed determination and a sense of resilience and courage, that I knew would hold her in good stead for the sales role that she currently held, and a promising future career.

After lunch, I completed a debrief about Frankfurt with Sarah. She was most interested and seemed to take in every detail that I shared with her. She even made some notes about the type of questions that were asked by the executive board and I could tell that she would use this knowledge in any future presentations that she was involved in. Once again, I realised how far Sarah had blossomed into a valuable member of the team over the last few months. Don't get me wrong, she was still wearing short skirts, low cut tops and always playing the 'sexual inuendo' game with me, which I didn't mind in the slightest! But she was also much more involved in her work, more conscious of her abilities and infinitely more confident about how she could add value. She even asked about potential opportunities for her in the new Sub Sahara organisation! Now that would be quite interesting, I thought!

As I was about to leave the office to go home, I received two text messages. The first was from Fiona; 'Just wanted to thank you for Wednesday night and to wish you good luck tonight. Call me if you need anything. Take care George, x' read the message. I smiled and immediately thought of my little 'librarian' with her flowing blonde hair, blue eyes, and big glasses. I looked at the second message. It was from Luke; 'Hey mate. Feeling a bit bad about our last conversation. Can you meet me in Mulligans after work for a chat? 5:30 p.m. okay?' I also had been feeling bad about the way my conversation with Luke had ended on Monday. Luke was my best friend, a person I had grown up with and shared many of my best and worst experiences in life with. I wasn't very gracious during our last phone call and although I wanted to talk to Martyna tonight, I felt I owed it to Luke to see him and put things right between us. Besides, I could still talk to Martyna after seeing Luke. However, I needed to call Martyna to let her know. I called the house.

"Hello," came a voice that I didn't instantly recognise.

"Hi, erm, who is this?" I enquired with a mild hint of alarm.

"Are you one of these pervert calls, wanting to know what I'm wearing and all that? Just 'fuck off' and go away," and the call was ended. I looked at my phone to make sure I had dialled the correct number. Yes, I had! What was going on? I called again.

"Hello," once again was the response. And then it hit me! The voice-, I recognised it.

"Is that Sally?" I gingerly asked.

"George! Sorry, was that just you on the phone," came a slightly embarrassed response from Sally.

"Yes, it was. What are you doing answering the phone in my house? Where's Martyna?"

"Sorry George, I was passing and as the girls hadn't seen Ben for a while, I stopped by. And then Martyna got a call from one of her friends about some emergency that she wanted Martyna to help with. So, I told her that I would stay and look after the kids and let you know. I was just about to when you rang here."

"So Martyna's not there?"

"No. She said she would be back later though. Anyway, no worries, I'm here and Martyna had already made dinner, so I will take care of everything."

"You know that Luke has asked me to meet him in the pub, don't you?" I asked.

"Yes. Don't worry, I'll hang on here until you've finished with Luke or Martyna comes back. It's no problem George. Don't worry about anything."

"Thanks Sal, I really appreciate it. Good job you were passing by. I'm just leaving work now, so I'll drop the car off outside the house and then walk down to Mulligans. Are the girls okay?"

"Yes, they're fine George and I think Ben loves being the centre of attention with his two older 'sisters', you know how he is?" replied Sally. It's funny, although Emily and Amy were not Ben's sisters, ever since Ben was born, the girls always treated him like a little brother and although he was only three, you could tell there was a special, almost familial relationship between the three of them.

"Are you sure you don't mind?"

"Not at all George. Luke told me about the call you guys had and I think it's important you talk to each other," Sally replied.

"Yeah, I think you're right. Okay, thanks Sally, I'll see you later. Take care and tell the girls I'll be back to tuck them into bed. Bye," I said and ended the call.

My first thought was that I hoped Martyna and of course her friend was alright. Maybe it was a child-minding emergency? Maybe one of the kids that her friend was looking after was ill or something? Either way, I was glad Sally was there to look after the girls, and equally as glad that she takes no shit from potential perverts on the phone! Good girl, that Sally!

I then texted Luke to tell him I'd be at the pub to meet him. I did feel bad about Luke. After all, he was only trying to help me and give me advice. And I never really knew how much he believed I had helped him in the past, how much he thought he owed me. He didn't owe me anything! He was my mate, my brother in arms - my best friend.

Finally, I quickly replied to Fiona reiterating that the only 'thanks' for Wednesday night, would definitely be coming from me to her! She really was a wonderful person and I was so pleased to have her in my life.

38

After arriving at home and parking the car, I decided to just pop inside to make sure everything was okay with Sally and the girls. As I put my key in the lock and opened the door, the playful noises coming from Emily, Amy and Ben from the lounge gave me great comfort. Sally must have heard me opening the front door and was stood in the hallway.

"Hi George," she said and walked towards me giving me a hug and kiss on the cheek.

"Hi Sal. I know I said I would just dump the car and go to meet Luke, but I just wanted to make sure everything was alright."

"As you can hear," she said placing her hand to her ear, "the three of them are having a wonderful time." I smiled as I listened to the commotion going on in the next room!

"Has Martyna been in touch?"

"No, erm, but I'm sure everything is fine. And don't worry George, I'll be here until you get back. Go and have a chat with Luke and take your time. I'm just about to serve up dinner and hopefully bring an end to that racquet," Sally said, smiling as she did so. "Oh, and sorry about the phone call, I didn't realise it was you. My 'alter ego' came out and suddenly my protective side kicked in. Sorry about calling you, well, you know."

"No worries Sal. Listen, thanks again for looking after the girls. I'll see you later, have fun," I replied and turned to walk back out of the house.

"You too," she called out to me.

I made the short walk to Mulligans and my mind turned to Luke. A feeling of guilt swept over me about Luke. I knew he was struggling with Cheryl's accident and he was only trying to give me advice about the situation I currently found myself in. Yet, all I did was get annoyed, put the phone down on him and refused to take his next call. Some friend I was! As I walked, my mind drifted back to when we were younger and still at school. We both made it through the school football trials together and were so good that we played our first game for the school for the year seven team and we were only in year five!

"I'm a bit scared. The other lads look so big," I remembered saying to Luke just before kick off in that first game.

"You're a much better player than me George. Paul bloody Gascoigne you! And if anyone tries a 'Vinny Jones' on you, I'll kick their fucking 'ead in," was the comforting 'Brummie' response from Luke. We won three-nil and I managed to score two! That was just one of many examples over the years where Luke had looked out for me, made sure I was okay, had my back. When we were around fourteen, we were walking back from a party one night. It was quite late and as we walked across a large, grassy roundabout, four lads came running towards us in the opposite direction and were about to jump us.

"If you can handle one of them, George, I've got the other three," Luke said to me just as they approached. And that's what happened. Although Luke did have to help me 'finish off' my one once he had dealt with the other three. He was fearless and always so protective of me. His upbringing in Birmingham on an extremely tough, rough estate had a lot do with it. It was one of the reasons his parents moved away from the area as soon as they got the opportunity to do so. They feared he would grow into the gang culture that surrounded the estate and ruin his life.

When my mum died, he was the first person I told. I called him first when I found her lifeless body on her bed. He immediately shot round to my house and sat with me while we waited for the ambulance to arrive. He was the first person I called when both Emily and Amy were born as I was when Ben was born. He was the first person I called that fateful day back in August 2016 after the police had informed me of Cheryl's accident. I know, it should have been Barbara and Derek I called, but I didn't, it was Luke first. Luke has always been there to support me, defend me and care about me. And I have always been there for him too! But on Monday during our phone call, I was a complete and utter 'shit' to him. He didn't deserve my annoyance and irritation. He was doing what he had always done. Helping me in my time of need.

As I approached the pub door, I hesitated slightly before going in. I wasn't sure why I hesitated. I knew Luke would forgive me as soon as I had apologised and told him what an arse I had been. And I knew that we would have a great evening over a few beers and by the time I would go home, our relationship would be as strong as ever.

I stepped into the pub and immediately saw Luke standing at the bar with his back to me and being served by Samantha. I walked towards him and as I did Samantha, noticed me, and waved, giving me a big smile. This prompted Luke to turn around.

"Hello mate," he said and gave me a big hug.

"Hey Luke, sorry I'm a bit late. I popped into the house to say hello to Sally. She's got her hands full with those three you know," I replied laughing.

"It's great to see you George and listen, I'm really sorry about the call we had on Monday. I was only…"

"Stop Luke," I said holding up my hand. "You have absolutely nothing to apologise for. I am the one that owes you an apology. An apology for being a complete fucking twat! I'm so sorry mate," I said and started feel a little emotional.

"Come here, you big gay!" Luke said and again he hugged me. After releasing his grip, he turned back to face Samantha.

"Hi George, you okay?" she said.

"Yes, thanks Sam. You?" Samantha smiled at me and let out a small sigh.

"Yes, I'm okay too," she replied before moving on to serve the next customer. Luke turned back around again to face me and was holding two drinks in his hands. A pint of Stella in his right hand, and, and a Gin and Tonic in his left hand! I looked at him slightly confused.

"Well, I hope mine's the pint?" I said cheerily.

"Yep!" came Luke's quick response. Again, I looked at him with the same confusion as before.

"And the G&T?" I asked. Luke looked past me and over my shoulder in the direction of our usual table by the front window of the pub. I turned to follow his gaze and as I did so, I stopped in my tracks. Martyna was sitting at the table!

"George, I know you might think I am interfering and I know that's probably why you got upset with me on Monday. However, I am your best mate and I couldn't let all this 'stuff' that's going on continue without at least giving you both the opportunity to really talk to each other. I feel terrible about Saturday night and Rebecca, which I have now totally explained to Martyna. She knows the whole story with that. And I feel terrible about the advice I have given you in the past! I'm no fucking 'agony aunt' and have no place giving you advice about anything. But I do think you feel something quite deep for this young lady and I know she does for you. I couldn't live with myself if I didn't at least try to provide you with some sort of opportunity to, well at least talk about everything. Do you remember when we were kids? We were fearless! Nothing stood in our way. And I think it is fear that is holding you back with Martyna. It was you that told me all those years ago in that Uni bar to go and speak to Sally. I was scared shitless, but you gave me the encouragement to talk to her." It was ironic that I had only just been thinking about how fearless Luke was as a kid. I didn't realise he thought I was too!

"I knew how good you were with the ladies, I just thought you talking to Sally would give me an opportunity with Cheryl. And it did!"

"Well, I'm returning the favour mate. So, take these drinks, go and sit down over there and talk to this lovely woman to see if there is any possibility that you two can be together."

I again looked over at Martyna and as I did, she waved in acknowledgement. I smiled, before turning back to face Luke. A plethora of emotions were running through my mind all at once. I was angry with Luke for doing this behind my back, and yet so happy that he had because it was great to see Martyna sitting at 'our' table. I understood Luke's motives and once again, this big guy was only looking out for my best interests. He was once again being my best friend and doing what best friends do! However, would it make any difference? I had already made up my mind about my immediate future. This could be disastrous! No. I had promised the girls I would talk to Martyna about staying and that was what I needed to do. But how?

"What am I supposed to say to her Luke?"

"George, you always know what to say. You always find the right words. Look mate, I'm not saying you and Martyna will end up together. But you at least owe it to yourselves and to Emily and Amy, to talk about things and, see where it goes." Luke was still holding the drinks. "Take these, mate," he continued, "I'm going to go now and help Sally with the kids. I'll see you later. And take your time, we love looking after the girls!" he said with a genuine smile on his face.

I took the drinks from Luke and watched him leave the pub, waving to Martyna as he left. I turned to face Martyna sitting at the table and slowly walked over to her. She once again looked fantastic! She was only wearing blue jeans and a white sleeveless top, but as I have mentioned before, Martyna looked fantastic in anything.

"Can I sit down?" I asked cautiously.

"Of course, George. Don't be silly," Martyna replied in her usual friendly manner. I sat down opposite her and placed the drinks on the table.

"Cheers!" I said and lifted my glass. Martyna picked up her drink and we chinked glasses before I took a long swig of my beer.

"I didn't know anything about this George, honestly. Sally dropped by with Ben and said that Luke would like to talk to me in the pub. She said she had called you to let you know what was happening and that she would stay with the children. I didn't know you were going to be here," said Martyna.

"I'm really sorry Martyna. I think we have been the victims of a set-up here!"

"Do you think so!" she replied mockingly.

"I didn't know anything about it either. I got a text from Luke to say meet him here for a drink. So, I called home to let you know and then Sally answers the phone, thinks I'm some sort of pervert and hangs up on me!" Martyna nearly spat her drink out as she chuckled to herself. "So, I called her back and she gives me some cock and bull story about you being called to an emergency by one of your child minder friends, and as she just 'happened to be passing' she volunteered to look after the kids. Total bullshit! Sneaky fuckers, the pair of them!" Again, Martyna laughed.

"I didn't really suspect anything, so agreed to meet Luke. I know how much he means to you and now, I know how much you mean to him. I suppose it shows they care a lot about you."

"Yes, I suppose it does. But listen, if you want to go back to the house and have dinner and then after the girls are in bed, we can have a talk about things, like we were going to anyway, I'm fine with that?"

"No George. I quite like it here and I think it's quite nice to be away from the house. What do you think? Shall we stay here?"

"I'm good. At least let me buy you dinner?"

"That would be lovely."

"So, what now? I mean, I'm not sure where to start."

"Well let me then. Firstly, Luke told me about Saturday night and Rebecca being one of Sally's work colleagues. I apologise George. I did think something was, well let's just say, I got things wrong and I'm sorry. I should have let you explain." I smiled at Martyna and she reciprocated with her warm, vivacious smile.

"I'm sorry too. I should have made more of an effort to explain things to you."

"I didn't really give you much chance did I," she said slightly embarrassed. "And in case you were wondering George, I stayed at Abi's place on Saturday night."

"Abi?"

"My child minder friend. She was with me on Saturday along with a few others."

"Including Jack?" I enquired solemnly.

"Yes, including Jack. But nothing happened, I promise you," Martyna said sincerely. I nodded my head in appreciation of her sharing that information with me. There followed a slight awkward silence.

"How were the girls today?" I asked finally breaking the silence. Martyna thought for a moment before answering.

"Amy was her usual self, happy, talkative, engaging, just lovely really. She told me she couldn't wait for you to get home to tell you that we all needed to go to 'Pudding Lane' at the weekend to take a picture of her there so she could show Miss Raven on Monday." I smiled as I invariably did when I thought about the girls.

"And Emily?" I asked. Martyna let out a sigh.

"Emily is hurting. She puts on a brave face, but I think she feels let down by…"

"I know. I've let her down badly and I have not been the father I want to or intended to be."

"George, you didn't let me finish. I think she feels let down by her own reaction to me leaving."

"So, you are leaving?"

"We'll come back to that later. But I think Emily has grown up so much over the last few months that she feels she shouldn't be upset about something like this. However, she is! And it is totally understandable. I have tried to comfort her and let her know that her feelings are normal and that things will always happen in life that are unexpected, a surprise, both good and bad. But currently, Emily can only see the 'bad' and I can't blame her for that. Losing your mum must be a terrible thing at her age." I looked up at Martyna and I think she could sense my sadness. "George, I didn't mean that it is in anyway less terrible for you." I again nodded my head in acknowledgement. I had previously told Martyna some time ago that my parents were dead and the age I was when they died. However, I hadn't fully explained that mum had taken her own life. And hearing Martyna talk about how Emily must feel about not having her mum around, reminded me of my own feelings when both my parents died. After all, I wasn't that much older than Emily when I lost my dad. I also think Martyna was referring to the fact that the impact of losing Cheryl was just as hard for me.

"So, you think she blames herself for feeling upset about it?" I asked.

"Yes. However, I do think she still feels that we, me, and you, have not maybe given ourselves a chance and therefore that also makes her unhappy. But predominantly I think she feels embarrassed about everything. You know, she apologised to me today, for putting too much pressure on me. She said I had the right to live my own life and be happy. And if that meant not being with her, Amy, and you, then she will accept that. It brought a tear to my eye and we had a lovely cuddle," Martyna said trying to keep her emotions in check.

"She's far too old for her age," I said smiling. "And wise!" We both laughed again.

"Do you want something to eat?" said Samantha. I looked up a little startled and saw her standing by the table. I looked at Martyna, who nodded.

"Don't worry about the menus. It's Friday, so it has to be fish and chips, alright with you Martyna?" I asked. Again, Martyna nodded in agreement and her beautiful smile returned to her face.

"Two fish and chips coming up. Do you want a refill?" Samantha asked looking at our half empty drinks.

"Thanks Sam, that'll be great," I replied as she returned to the bar to process our order.

"Two Fridays in a row! I'll be getting flabby George," said Martyna. The image of Martyna's perfectly toned stomach and pierced naval sprang to my mind. I couldn't imagine one ounce of fat on Martyna's gorgeous body!

"Getting back to you Martyna, have you decided if you are staying or going?" I tentatively asked. Martyna stared at me for a few seconds before downing the remaining amount of her gin and tonic.

"I think we have something, you and I. Something that has not yet fully matured, but given the right conditions, love and attention, could grow into something quite beautiful and special. I'm not sure if you 'feel' that too?" I paused for a second before answering.

"I think we have grown fond of each other over the time that you have been with us. I think the girls love you very much and obviously do not want you to leave."

"And you George?"

"Of course, I don't want you to leave," I replied looking deeply into her stunning green eyes. Samantha returned to our table carrying our drinks.

"I'll put this on a tab with the two meals, if that's alright with you George?" she said placing the drinks down on the table. "Won't be too long for the food."

"Thanks Sam, I really appreciate that," I replied. Samantha walked away and again, Martyna and I were alone. I say alone, the pub was getting quite full by now, but although there was the usual hubbub of people's conversations, due to the tenseness of our situation, it seemed to just fade into the background.

Martyna picked up her drink and downed it in one. It took me by surprise!

"I'm going to tell you some things," she said. I guessed the downing of her Gin & Tonic was a necessary 'courage booster' for what she was about to say.

"Ok," I gently said.

"I liked you from the first moment I met you. You looked so sweet, sitting in between Barbara and Sally when I came for the first interview. It looked like you were being guarded by two 'rottweilers', fiercely protective of their master. But I didn't know you and certainly didn't love you. But the first day I started, that morning at your house when I arrived with that big heavy box of CD's, something changed. You were kind and thoughtful. You made me feel at ease straight away. You looked handsome in your suit and tie. You smelled wonderful," Martyna said, looking away from me as if replaying that morning in her mind.

"I also thought…"

"No-, please George, let me continue," she interrupted. "And as the days and weeks went by and I got to know you better, I saw how you were with Emily and Amy. How loving, open, and honest with them you were. How you comforted them, read them stories at bedtime, played with them; all these things you did for them. I also saw how they responded to you. The love and care they have for you. I've worked for quite a few families George and I have never seen this before. Not even in my own family. And always in the background was the fact that you had lost your wife and the girls had lost their mother. You all seemed to embrace that loss and it was never a subject that was brushed under the carpet. I was amazed!

"Martyna-,"

"I haven't finished yet George. As the weeks passed, I started to have strong feelings for you. Then you invited me to spend Christmas with you and you gave me the bracelet and earrings. I just felt so much closer to you. Especially being invited to Barbara and Derek's on Boxing day."

"I had similar feelings especially when I saw you sitting on my bed on Christmas morning in your pyjamas!" I said and then instantly realised that maybe it wasn't an appropriate comment. Martyna looked at me a little startled at first, before smiling. "Sorry, I just thought you looked wonderful," I continued, slightly embarrassed.

"When I told you about my last employer groping me, you were so kind and understanding. An experience that had previously made me feel cheap and dirty, you somehow liberated me from it. I have never told anyone about that incident, only you."

"The guy was a fucking idiot and you were in no way to blame. He should have been charged with assault," I said a little angry at the thought of her previous employer's actions. "You didn't deserve that sort of behaviour." Martyna nodded.

"Thank you, George. But that's all in the past. I knew after that evening when I told you about it, that I was falling in love with you. But I thought I couldn't allow this to happen. Like you, I was terrified that my feelings would compromise my job and relationship with Emily and Amy. So, I tried to suppress them; went on that horrible blind date with Zak."

"I was a little jealous, you looked stunning that night," I said rather blushingly.

"I did get that impression George. And when I came back from the date and had such a wonderful evening with you, well it just confirmed everything I already knew. And when I kissed you on the cheek, I really wanted to kiss you on the lips and for you to take me to bed." I looked at Martyna a little amazed at this admission from her.

"I thought it was just the alcohol and pushed away any thought that you might be interested in me. But I have to say, the next day, at the park, when we played football with the girls, and you fell on me…"

"It wasn't a red card George," Martyna jokingly interrupted. I smiled.

"It so was a red card," I replied also smiling. "But the point is in that moment on the grass with you on top of me, I felt something between us. And I'm not just talking about your right thigh wedged between my legs! I hadn't had that feeling since, well Cheryl and it was wonderful."

"I deliberately fell on you. I'm sorry. It was a cheap stunt and although I told you that morning not to read anything into the kiss on the cheek from the night before, that was because I was slightly embarrassed. However, I wanted to know what it felt like to be on top of you," Martyna said.

"And, what did it feel like to be on top of me?" I enquired. Martyna sighed.

"Not that great actually!" she said before laughing. "I'm joking, it was wonderful too, George! I knew then that I wanted to be with you. But then we had that conversation where I told you how I felt and you, well you told me you had some feelings for me, but we couldn't pursue anything because of the girls."

"That's right Martyna and to be honest, I don't think things have changed much. The girls must come first."

"I agreed with you then and tried to subdue my feelings for you. When I went on that date with Jack; before I left, I really wanted you to tell me not to go, to stay in and spend the evening with you. But you didn't."

"I know. I was such an idiot. I hated the thought of you going out on that blind date. From the moment you told me on the phone when I was in Jo'burg, I couldn't stop thinking about it. I'm so sorry for the way I treated you that night. I didn't know what to do, what to say to you. I was scared I suppose."

"Scared of what?" Martyna replied. I paused for a moment.

"Scared of letting you know my true feelings for you, I suppose," I finally replied.

"I was scared too George. However, the next evening, following me hearing your conversation with Emily that morning, I told you exactly how I felt about you. I told you to take your time and think it over. You never came back to me George."

"I know. I should have said something to you. I'm sorry. I just needed some time."

"I understood that. But then you told me that you had slept with this Fiona girl. I have already apologised for jumping to conclusions about that and I do realise that it happened after we agreed we had no future. But it happened while you were thinking about us. It made me realise that it could happen again. That's when I decided that I couldn't stay in the same house and have the feelings that I have for you, if you couldn't commit to me in the same way," Martyna said sadly.

"So, you want to leave?" I asked. Martyna leant forward and grabbed my hands in hers.

"I want to have a relationship with you. I would like to try to see if we can make it work. Take it slowly; consider Emily and Amy every step of the way. Maintain our mutual respect and develop our bond. Grow our feelings and love for each other by spending quality time together, not as employer / employee, but as trusted, loving partners. I want to share my life with you and Emily and Amy. It is frightening because we don't know what the future holds, nobody does! But these are the things I want and all I'm asking is - do you want them too?" came back Martyna's emotional response.

"I…"

"Don't be afraid George. I know how happy your life was with Cheryl and I know you think that you can't be that lucky again. All I'm asking is that you give us a chance and don't miss out on future happiness because of the past,"

"You're right. I fear losing again, and the pain that it brings. Not just to me, but the girls as well. And whether that be through a breakdown in the relationship or, as with Cheryl, being taken away unexpectedly, I'm not sure I can put myself or the girls through that again."

"I understand George, but I hope you know that I have no intention of hurting you or Emily and Amy. Do you remember what you said to me when I told you about my first blind date with Zak?"

"Sort of," I replied a little dismissively.

"You told me that life is unpredictable, full of surprises, some great and memorable and some tragic and terrible! You said to make the most of every opportunity to find happiness and to not let anything get in the way of that and to not fear making mistakes; to chase your dreams for happiness and to respect the past but look to the future."

"Pretty profound stuff eh!" I said regrettably and letting out a long sigh.

"You should listen to your own words George. I don't know what will happen in the future! But I want to try to be with you and Emily and Amy. This is what I want. My only question to you, is - do you?" Martyna pleaded, still holding my hands. I paused and looked down at our hands clasped together on the table, before returning to look into Martyna's moist looking eyes.

"I want to try too," I said and leant forward. We kissed each other, holding the embrace for a good few seconds, before finally easing apart, while still holding hands. A broad smile ran across our faces and we both felt an instant feeling of relief. Martyna looked gorgeous, happier than I've ever seen her before and for the first time I actually believed that we could have a future together. That somehow, all the pieces of the puzzle would fall into place to reveal a picture of a happy and contented family. A father and his two beautiful daughters and his wonderful new partner, possibly future wife. A future that could include more children, a brother or sister or both for Emily and Amy. A future of comfort, joyfulness and without fear and trepidation. As I was thinking all this, I still had a smile on my face. However, my smile faded in an instant and my fear returned. This was immediately recognised by Martyna.

"What's the matter George? Are you okay?" Martyna caringly enquired. I paused for a moment, again looking down at our hands, still joined, before once again looking up at her.

"Before we commit fully to this, us, I mean, a relationship, there is something I need to tell you."

"What George, what is it?" Martyna anxiously asked.

"Something happened earlier this week in Frankfurt. It could have an influence on us-, and therefore, I think you should know about it up front before, we go any further."

"What happened George? Is it Fiona?" Martyna said softly with a hint of fear in her voice as to what I was about to tell her.

"I don't want there to be any secrets between us Martyna. Therefore, it's only right you should know. I need you to know what happened in Frankfurt. I-"

------------ TO BE CONTINUED! ------------

AUTHOR BIOGRAPHY

Phil Dinnage was born in London but moved to Crawley, near Gatwick Airport, with his parents and three older brothers when he was only six months old. Growing up in a competitive sibling environment, sport, and in particular, football was always his first passion. However, at school, he also developed an interest in creative writing which centred on real life and both the comedy and tragedy that always seem to encompass it.

After nearly 40 years of working, with over 25 years in the In-Flight Catering industry, having travelled to many parts of the world, exploring different cultures, embracing two serious relationships and having five children, it is only now that Phil feels able to write about life, knowing that he has a broad range of experiences to inspire his writing.

So, if you like romance, comedy and adult themes (and some bad language!), then you'll hopefully love Phil's debut novel, Moving On.